"As she did in her superb short-story collection, *White Swan, Black Swan*, Sharp, a former dancer, dramatizes the romance, ambition, and obsessive eroticism of the dance world in her ravishing first novel, adeptly partnering real-life figures with fictional creations. Set in the early 1980s at the height of American ballet's frenzied popularity and the onset of the AIDS epidemic, it stars the genius dance master George Balanchine, now aging and haunted. As he dreams of creating one last epic work, a sumptuous *Sleeping Beauty*, two young dancers long for greatness. Adam, a sexual magnet for men and women, has left Balanchine's company for Baryshnikov's and become a star, but Sandra, fragile and elusive, continues to dance in Balanchine's corps. Opposites attract, but love is a liability in their competitive realm. Just as a dancer fuses with her roles, Sharp fully inhabits the troubled psyches and hard-driven bodies of her commanding yet maddening characters, describing with transporting detail everything from a costume's cut and sparkle to a tragic kiss. Sharp's bewitchingly sensual and trenchant tale embodies the sublime and the monstrous aspects of dance and explores our depthless capacity for exultation and suffering."

—*Booklist* (starred review)

"[An] unflinching, informed look at American ballet circa the 1970s and '80s. Anyone who has ever been serious about the arts will recognize its capriciousness. Sharp's description of Balanchine sliding in to watch class for a few minutes before choosing dancers for his company nails it. . . . The atmosphere is just right."

—*The Buffalo News*

*continued . . .*

ALSO BY ADRIENNE SHARP

*White Swan, Black Swan*

# The Sleeping Beauty

ADRIENNE SHARP

Originally published as *First Love*

*Riverhead Books*

*New York*

**THE BERKLEY PUBLISHING GROUP**
**Published by the Penguin Group**
**Penguin Group (USA) Inc.**
**375 Hudson Street, New York, New York 10014, USA**
Penguin Group (Canada), 90 Eglinton Avenue East, Suite 700, Toronto, Ontario M4P 2Y3, Canada
(a division of Pearson Penguin Canada Inc.)
Penguin Books Ltd., 80 Strand, London WC2R 0RL, England
Penguin Group Ireland, 25 St. Stephen's Green, Dublin 2, Ireland (a division of Penguin Books Ltd.)
Penguin Group (Australia), 250 Camberwell Road, Camberwell, Victoria 3124, Australia
(a division of Pearson Australia Group Pty. Ltd.)
Penguin Books India Pvt. Ltd., 11 Community Centre, Panchsheel Park, New Delhi—110 017, India
Penguin Group (NZ), cnr Airborne and Rosedale Roads, Albany, Auckland 1310, New Zealand
(a division of Pearson New Zealand Ltd.)
Penguin Books (South Africa) (Pty.) Ltd., 24 Sturdee Avenue, Rosebank, Johannesburg 2196,
South Africa

Penguin Books Ltd., Registered Offices: 80 Strand, London WC2R 0RL, England

THE SLEEPING BEAUTY

Previously published in hardcover as *First Love* by Riverhead Books: July 2005
First Riverhead trade paperback edition: July 2006
Riverhead trade paperback ISBN: 1-59448-198-9

The Library of Congress has catalogued the Riverhead hardcover edition as follows:

Sharp, Adrienne.
    First love / Adrienne Sharp.
      p.   cm.
    ISBN 1-57322-310-7
    1. Ballet dancers—Fiction.   2. New York (N.Y.)—Fiction.   3. New York City Ballet—Fiction.
4. Balanchine, George—Fiction.   I. Title.
PS3569.H3432F57      2005                                                    2005042794
813'.6—dc22

PRINTED IN THE UNITED STATES OF AMERICA

10   9   8   7   6   5   4   3   2   1

*For my sister, Debra—always true*

eorge Balanchine, as a student of the Imperial Theater Ballet School in St. Petersburg, danced a child's role in *Sleeping Beauty* in 1914 and fell instantly in love with that world of beauty and artifice, dancers and stagecraft. He had been up to that time a reluctant student at the school, but everything changed for him the evening he first performed in *Sleeping Beauty*. Dressed in a golden cupid costume, he was carried out onto the great stage of the Maryinsky Theater and set down on the lip of a golden cage. Balanchine, enraptured by the music, the sets, the costumes, the dancers, the theater itself, understood for the first time the culminating purpose of the dull exercises at the barre he was forced to endure every day. "I sat on the cage in indescribable ecstasy," he told Solomon Volkov in Volkov's book *Balanchine's Tchaikovsky*. "Thanks to *Sleeping Beauty,* I fell in love with ballet."

It was a ballet Balanchine long wanted to do for his own company in America, New York City Ballet, with choreography of his own, but he never saw this dream come to fruition. He felt that the New York State Theater stage was too small and the ballet too expensive. Balanchine did not want to do it "bargain basement." Yet, it was a project he thought about repeatedly. He entertained the idea of doing the ballet for Suzanne Farrell in the early 1960s, but abandoned the project after her departure from New York City Ballet. Balanchine's interest in the ballet was ignited again with the arrival of Gelsey Kirkland in the 1970s and yet again with Darci Kistler in 1980. But it was not to be. Balanchine's health was failing. In November 1982, he was admitted to Roosevelt Hospital, suffering from symptoms of what we know now to be Creutzfeldt-Jakob disease. Balanchine remained in the hospital until his death.

Eight years later, in 1991, NYCB finally performed its *Sleeping Beauty,* an abbreviated version of the Maryinsky's 1890 production and one staged by Balanchine's successor, Peter Martins. The ballet incorporated the only piece of choreography Balanchine ever created for his company from *Sleeping Beauty,* the Garland Dance for Act I.

# The Christening

*In which Aurora is born,*
*and at her christening her fate is decided*

She wore an outfit she'd selected herself especially for the occasion: textured mesh tights, a bathing suit, party shoes, and in her long hair, a large, artificial flower, a peony, plucked from her dead mother's hat. As they walked the hallways of Juilliard's third floor toward the big studio, Sandra held her father's hand. They were thinking she might take some kind of dance class, maybe tap, but the lady on the phone said she would have to come in to the school to audition. All around them were other girls and she hadn't known there would be other girls, a hundred girls wearing leotards and pink tights and ballet slippers, their hair braided and pinned, and immediately upon seeing them, Sandra wanted to go home. She tugged on her father's hand, but he ignored her. He was fascinated by what they'd stumbled into, this secret world within the world. He pushed her forward to have a number pinned to her bathing suit, filled out a form. They had to wait. Her name was called, *Sandra Ellis*. She was measured, told to point her foot, lift her leg. Two elderly Russian ladies examined her from all sides, conferring first in their own language and then speaking in heavily accented English to her father. She was gifted. She was beautiful. She was admitted to the school. There was no tap class. This was the School of American Ballet.

ADAM WANDERED THE loft, holding his mother's glove, the one with the fur cuff, and the big empty space of his house opened like cement acreage before him. He could just make out the murky image of himself, a dwarf, reflected in the polished concrete floors. The dwarf's arm flapped: the glove, which he was flipping as he walked. His parents weren't home, hadn't been home, would never be home, and it was dark, past his bed-time, the big windows sheets of blackness. On the sofa in the center of the loft, his godfather Randall sat reading aloud, and when Adam passed him, put out an arm. *Come here.* Adam crawled onto his lap and Randall let him turn the pages of the fairy-tale book until he found the story he wanted. A boy climbing a beanstalk, a briar-covered castle, a princess in a pump-kin coach, a wolf following a girl. This one. Randall began the story. Adam slid the fur part of his mother's glove along his chin. *Are they still at the theater?* Randall nodded and continued to read. Adam yawned. At the theater, his parents wore costumes and makeup, but they didn't speak, they danced to music. Randall turned the page. The wolf swallowed a granny whole. The theater was like that. It had opened its jaws and swallowed his parents.

WOMEN IN COSTUMES enveloped him, pushing past him toward the stage where the oiled canvas dropped. From the wing where he stood, little Georgi Balanchivadze could see beyond the proscenium to the darkened blue and gold facade of the Maryinsky's interior; he was inside a Fabergé egg, all beauty and artifice, an egg that held within it even the czar himself, Nicholas II, seated above the stage in the imperial box embellished with his royal insignia. On the stage, real water erupted from the cascading fountains, half-hidden behind the great stone arches and elaborate statuary of the castle, and within the hall itself stood pages and heralds, king and queen, the resplendent lords and ladies of the court, the draped cradle of the baby Aurora, the genies bearing gifts, and the six fairy godmothers, the Fairy Candide, the Fairy Fleur de farine, the Breadcrumb Fairy, the Fairy Violente, the Fairy Canari, the Lilac Fairy. Georgi, already dressed in his garland costume for the next scene, stood rigid, exhausted and euphoric, and gripped his small prop, a wooden stick glued round with cloth flowers. It was his first time in the theater, and the steps he had practiced over and over again in the school studios were now being executed to perfection on the czar's stage by the legends of the Imperial Ballet. The ballet he watched so intently was *Sleeping Beauty,* and as the Lilac Fairy waved her wand, she dusted with her golden magic the king, the queen, the stage, its players, and the little boy standing spellbound in the wings.

ACT I

# The Spell

*In which Aurora comes of age and falls victim to a spell*

*S*andra stood in the doorway of the studio, watching, as he made his way down the hall. Mr. B moved slowly, as if he were knee-deep in surf, and if there hadn't been so many pictures of famous dancers on the walls, she thought he probably would have put out a hand to steady himself. Around him she could hear the whispers, *It's Mr. B.* He hadn't been in the studios for weeks and suddenly there he was, wearing his western shirt and his plain pants and his Wallabies and his Indian bracelet. His heart had been fixed two years ago and he was supposed to be well, but they all knew that he wasn't, not fully. It was an older, frailer version of him that they now loved, Mr. B and yet not quite Mr. B, his shade, and therefore infinitely more precious. His old girls, his mermaids, the ones he knew well, stepped out of the eddies to embrace him, to kiss him, to hold his hand. *Mr. B, Mr. B.*

She wasn't one of them, and so she hung back. He didn't really know her. By the time she'd been taken into the company, he was too sick to work or to get to know his new girls. He didn't even know her name, Sandra Ellis. She was only eleven in 1972 when he choreographed the Stravinsky Festival that made stars of a whole generation of girls, and she was just fifteen when he did the Ravel Festival, and by the time she joined the corps de ballet he no longer taught company class. Because of his angina and his cataracts and his dizziness, he had made few ballets, and those only for the dancers he loved and had worked with many times before. But now it was 1981, and he would work and there would be another festival. Festivals always sold tickets and Mr. B had spent the past sixty years of his life thinking about how to sell tickets to the ballet. Back in February, he had held a press conference at the Russian Tea Room to announce a Tchaikovsky Festival for June, and it was now May and she was here, finally in the right place at the right time. There were not many ballets left in Mr. B, nor many muses, and she, along with every other girl in the company, wanted to be his last one.

She knew she wasn't a likely candidate. First of all, she was blond, and Mr. B was notorious in his preference for brunettes. He was always saying, "Now, dear, blond is fun and fine on the street, but not so good onstage." She'd started bleaching her hair as pale as Christmas tinsel when she was fifteen and her dad got sick again. And she was small, where Mr. B generally liked big— big, tall girls with long legs like horses and feet like elephant trunks—strong, but supple. Worst of all, she was old, already twenty, and Mr. B liked young—sixteen, seventeen, eighteen at most. But Mr. B had missed her teens. She'd spent them in the corps, where she knew she'd remain forever, until the day his gaze fell on her and he saw something he wanted to use. His gaze hadn't fallen on her yet.

But she, always, looked at him. She looked for him in the corridors, in the wings of the theater, and on the rare occasion when she'd been in the rehearsal studio with him, she could look at no one else. None of them could.

Watching Mr. B at work she often felt like a voyeur, because what happened inside him was so private. She loved the way he would tilt his head as he listened to the music the pianist played for a few measures, maybe more; and then he'd begin to move in his thick suede shoes, demonstrating the steps that came to him from somewhere. His eyes were black as an owl's while he listened for the message, lips pursed, eyebrows raised, and then the pupils would contract and he'd be here with her again, with all of them again, as they waited to be told what to do, what to dance. He was in two places, here and somewhere else, but she felt he didn't really belong here, he was here only to transmit what he'd drawn from that other place. It was like her father with his writing. There'd be nothing on the page, and then there would be this tale of Fort Sumter or Vicksburg or Appomattox and the words would be in a language she recognized, but they described a world of a hundred years ago that she had never seen nor had her father. Yet, it seemed as if he had once lived there. Her dad wore clothes, ate food, used buildings and streets and pens like everybody else, but he was not like anybody else, not at all. Nor was Mr. B.

When Mr. B disappeared down the corridor, most of the girls around her slipped off to the dressing room before the next round of rehearsals to smoke and drink Diet Cokes and talk about his appearance. But Sandra followed him. Her pointe shoes crunched her toes together painfully; without untying the ribbons, she slipped off the heels and scuffled down the hall, her wet hair unraveling into a long, long ponytail, her big bag full of shoes and warmers and Evian and Altoids heavy on her arm. She hadn't eaten lunch, and she was hungry and tired; but she forgot all that when she found Mr. B at the end of the floor, in a studio with Suzanne Farrell and Gordon Boelzner, the company's assistant conductor, the door shut.

Through the small window, Sandra could see Mr. B standing silently before Suzanne, his head bent, not looking at her, not needing to, holding her wrist lightly with his fingertips. Mr. B had been making ballets for Suzanne since she was seventeen and now she was thirty-five, and though her face had thickened and softened and was no longer entirely recognizable as the face in her early photographs, it was still a magnificent face, the figurehead of the company, the face Mr. B had loved to look at longer than any other. Abruptly, Mr. B raised his head, and for a moment Sandra thought he'd seen her, but he was simply gesturing with his chin for Gordon to play. And then he began to move with Suzanne, first stage right, then stage left, downstage, up, directing her softly with his hands, steering her through a long series of slow, delicate bourrées punctuated only occasionally by still, prayerful poses, which made Suzanne look like the statues of the Virgin at Sandra's grandmother's church in Vicksburg. Mr. B demonstrated these poses for her, of supplication, of offering, of benediction, of consummation, and when Suzanne assumed them, Sandra could see exactly what Mr. B must have intended, but had merely sketched. Suzanne knew him so well he could gesture with his finger and she would know what he wanted and how to give it to him, whereas Sandra could see nothing in that gesture but the vaguest outline, sometimes only the direction he wanted Suzanne to move in. And at this knowledge, Sandra felt the lip of a great hopelessness kiss at her. She watched with a combination of admiration and despair as Suzanne's long, elegant feet moved swiftly across the studio floor, her torso and arms calm up above, gently pressing back the air. Suzanne and Mr. B did all this without speaking, at times Mr. B's eyes half-closed, but Sandra could see through the glass that Suzanne's mouth was moving, though he never answered her. Sandra edged closer to the door and then she heard it; Suzanne was reciting the Ave Verum Corpus in Latin and Mr. B was pacing her movements to the words of the prayer, the words a heartbeat beneath the skin of the dance.

*Ave, Ave, Verum corpus.*
*Hail true body,*
*Born of the Virgin Mary,*
*Sacrificed with nails,*
*On the cross for us men,*
*Cleanse us by the blood and water*
*Streaming from thy pierced side,*
*Feed us with thy body broken,*
*Now and in mortis examine.*

This was the "Preghiera", the first movement of *Mozartiana*. That's what Mr. B did to his old ballets, the ones he felt he hadn't ever gotten right, made them over again and again until he was satisfied. He'd used this same Tchaikovsky music in 1933 for Tamara Toumanova and then he used it again in 1935 and again in 1945 and now he was using it once more for Suzanne.

At the end of it, the music ceased, and Mr. B had Suzanne walk off the stage in silence. Sandra turned from the door and went down the long corridor toward the dressing room, feeling as if the breath had been blown out of her, a lion had roared right in her face. She knew, just from the little she saw, that *Mozartiana* would be the highlight of the festival, that Mr. B was making a masterpiece, and that she wasn't going to be a part of it.

WHEN SHE WALKED out into Lincoln Center Plaza late that May afternoon, the buildings were glittering, all white sparkles and gold ornamentation, the big square boxes of State Theater, the Metropolitan Opera House, the Recital Hall, Juilliard, and in the center of them all, the circular fountain, an eruption of light-pelted water. She'd spent every day of the last ten years here, in one building or another, or a few blocks south at the Professional Children's School, or thirty blocks north on Central Park West, in the Eldorado, in the apartment she shared with her father. This was Balanchine's whole world, too. He'd spent the past thirty years living in various apartments in the West Sixties, working at the theater, approving costumes at Karinska's, eating at the Empire Hotel coffee shop across the street.

She had thrived in this world, on the predictability not only of the daily classes, but also the inexorable journey from one level to the next, from the pink tights and black leotards of the beginners in A Division to the graduating D class. She had expected the journey from corps de ballet to ballerina to be just as sure, but there were signs all along the way that certainty was not a defining principle in the world of ballet. Each year at the school, a few girls were invited not to return the following, having put on weight or gotten too long in the body or too short in the leg or having failed to master the increasingly difficult steps, until at some point, Sandra realized she was the only girl left of her original class. Mr. B didn't come to the studios much to see them, but they all knew him by sight. His name was constantly invoked. Their bodies were being trained to dance his ballets. His dancers rehearsed in their studios. And come *Nutcracker* time, the girls filled his theater in their shiny polichinelle costumes and their golden angel dresses complete with fabric wings and stand-up halo and their party dresses with the wide velvet sashes and the ruffled pantaloons. The orchestra's rehearsal space in the basement of the theater became the children's dressing room by Thanksgiving, with long tables laid with makeup and rolling racks at the perimeters of the room holding the costumes of taffeta and silk and felt. She could still recall exactly the excitement of being herded up the narrow stairway to the stage, standing there with the other girls waiting for her entrance for the party scene, the wings too small to hold them all, that space reserved for the company dancers and the various props—the barrels of artificial snow, Marie's bed, the enormous six-foot-tall skirt Mother Ginger would wear like a circus tent, beneath which the polichinelles would hide. The music sounded as if it were summoned up out of the air, as if it were the air, and when they rushed onto the stage with its tall painted backdrops of doors and windows and bookcases and tables, it was like entering a picture book, a weird two-dimensional world, magic its third dimension. Their bodies animated the scene, the energy from the audience bombarding their space and ricocheting back, the whole theater alive. One season, early on, when she was just ten, Mr. B himself had played Drosselmeyer, with the black cape and the black patch over one eye, whiskers spirit-gummed to his cheeks, a white wig stuck on his head, and his nose lengthened into a pointed hook. Sandra had been mesmerized by him; even when she was clapping hands with another girl and doing the small jig and choreographed do-si-do, she couldn't stop looking his way. When Drosselmeyer pulled the

Nutcracker doll from beneath his swirling cape and held it high above them, she and the other children jumped for it. *Give it to me!* But she was not looking at the doll with its scarlet soldier's uniform and its gold sword, nor was she jumping for it. She jumped for Balanchine. *Look at me. Look at me.*

She sat down on the granite ledge of the plaza's big fountain. The enormous framed posters that hung on the wall outside of New York City Ballet's State Theater advertised the spring season. She was one of eight corps girls featured in the ad, all of them costumed in chiffon dresses, artificial flowers and jewels studding their long hair. They always picked pretty girls for these posters, not necessarily the best dancers—corps girls, girls who could be spared to pose for a day-long shoot. Her hair had been curled and set by the stylist and it hung like a cluster of scrolls. She was positioned in front, her head turned to one side, almost in profile. She was often told she looked like a blond Tanaquil LeClercq, and in this photograph she could see it. By this age, though, LeClercq was already married to Balanchine, the entire season shaped around her talents, her beauty immortalized in a long series of roles, *Bourrée Fantasque, Metamorphoses, La Valse.* And thirty years later, in those same ballets, Sandra stood at the side of the stage, six days a week, sewn like a bead to a decorative frill, an accent, not the fleur-de-lis. When she first started in the corps she was exhausted all the time; during a ballet season, she never saw the light of day, except for the run to Lincoln Center in the morning and the dash across the plaza from the studio to the theater at six, where she danced in twice as many ballets as the principal dancers for a quarter of the applause—and a splinter of the satisfaction. Last season she'd begun to fantasize about what would happen if she simply broke rank and spilled out onto the stage, poured herself into a dance that belonged to someone else.

But tonight, by a fluke in the schedule, she wasn't dancing at all. Her best friend, Adam LaSalle, was dancing *Coppélia* with American Ballet Theatre at the Met; a big poster of him, hair carefully askew, bare-chested, half-costumed, hung across the plaza by the Met's box office. In a few minutes she would go over there to watch the performance from the wings. Adam had gone through the school with her and into the company, had been promoted to principal dancer and then suddenly last year, despite Mr. B's disapproval, had defected to Ballet Theatre, where he was cast in one after another of the leading classical roles in quick succession—Franz, Albrecht, Siegfried, Solor. Adam made a public triumph of each one, agonized over them all in private. He was a perfectionist, the son of two dancers, and he wanted to dance well—partly for their approval, partly to spite them.

Sandra hadn't seen him for a couple of months while he'd been off on tour—Ballet Theatre toured all the time—and she knew he was waiting for her there in the dressing room, wanting her there, but she hung back. What they did together the night before he left on tour was still too vivid, and it made her uneasy to think about it, covered her like a coat of fine grit she couldn't quite brush away. Adam's ferocious tongue, his hands, the soft skin of his scrotum, his movie-star jaw and nose and cheekbones, what he said to her as he groaned and had her wrap her legs around him—all these things about him, some familiar, some until that night unknown, kept her sitting there at the fountain while he prepared for his performance a hundred yards away.

Thirty minutes later, when Mr. B emerged from the Juilliard

building, she was still sitting there. She watched him from a distance, an old man walking slowly across the plaza to State Theater.

If she didn't know who he was, she'd never look at him twice.

*A*BT'S MAKEUP ARTIST was already with Adam in his dressing room at the Met when she arrived. He was holding a sponge to Adam's face and Adam had his eyes shut against it, against the swipe, swipe of the Pan-Cake that tinted his flesh orange-brown. He sat bare-chested and bare-legged on a metal folding chair before the dressing room mirror, wearing only his dance belt, while his beautiful face was transformed into an exaggeration of its beauty. This ritual, this transformation of the ordinary self into an exotic, pleasingly costumed attraction, was a necessary part of their art, fueled the vanity that helped propel them out onto the vast, intimidating stage. Adam's hair glistened a dirty blond, the color of his father's, but his eyes, when he opened them and saw her there, flashed a hot blue neon entirely his own. Sandra knew right away that he hadn't forgotten what they'd done and that he wasn't going to pretend it didn't happen, even though they never talked about it, not once, any of the nights he'd called her from his various hotel rooms in Tampa or Miami or Chicago or San Francisco or Los Angeles. Without moving his torso or head, Adam put out his hand for her to hold; when she took it, his fingers closed around hers immediately. His hand was warm and large, the size of it one of the reasons he partnered his ballerinas so well; in his hands lay security, balance, lift, and for her now, arousal. She was glad someone else was there, moving like a shadow about them, eclipsing their image in the mirror and then revealing it, each time Adam with a successively finished face, the reddened lips, the painted eyes, the blackened eyebrows. When the makeup artist paused for a moment to assess his work, and when Sandra pointed to one of Adam's brows, he moved in to lengthen it. "How's that, Mr. LaSalle?"

Mr. LaSalle.

She'd met Adam when they were both fifteen, in the tenth grade, in an English class at Professional Children's School, a class filled with child dancers and actors, musicians and models, all of whom longed to be somewhere else. That day she'd been slumped low in her chair, embarrassed, her hair falling over her face and catching on the brass buttons of an old Levi's jean jacket she always wore, reading her essay assignment aloud. She'd written about her father's breakdown in 1971 when she was ten, not his first breakdown, but the first one she remembered clearly, and how she went to visit him in the hospital in a locked ward. While she read, she saw Adam up in the front row turning around in his chair to look at her. She knew who he was, an arrogant jerk, the best dancer in the boys' class at SAB who hardly spoke to anybody. But that day he spoke to her. After class he waited for her by the door of the building and started asking her all kinds of questions about her family and where she learned to write like that. At first she didn't want to tell him anything, all of it was personal, but then she saw in his face something naked, and in that instant she stopped thinking of him as an arrogant asshole, and she told him she tore that essay right out of one of her notebooks. She'd kept a journal since the fifth grade. Eventually Adam would read them all. Her hair blew wildly while they stood there in the wind by a metal trash barrel, talking, until finally Adam gathered up her hair in his fist, winding it around and around his hand the way you'd reel in a kite, and asked her her name, and she told him, Sandra Ellis.

Adam stood, the makeup artist handed him his towel, and Adam draped it around his shoulders. He nodded his thanks, and the man said, "Good luck tonight, Mr. LaSalle," and withdrew. And then they were alone.

Adam reached for her then, immediately, put his hands to her neck and then to her hair, let his fingers run down the slippery length of it as if he were testing the water of her, took hold of the waist of her shirt and tugged on it to pull her closer. She wanted to be closer, but she also felt ridiculously, paralyzingly shy. "Sandra," he said. "Look at me." But she couldn't do it. He was so naked standing there in his dance belt, so close she could feel the heat of him. He was wearing nothing, she realized all at once, so she would see his body, so he could slay her with it. She didn't know where not to look, at his elaborately painted face, at his dark brown nipples, at the blond hair that ran down his abdomen, at the bare back of him reflected in the mirror, the long spine, the T-shaped axis of his dance belt that left exposed the beautiful planes of his ass. Her body had remained essentially what it was at fifteen, but Adam's had changed enormously over the past few years, had thickened and broadened and grown muscular as an athlete's, his shoulders big now and his legs almost bulky. A haphazard webwork of blue knobby veins pushed at the surfaces of his arms and calves and thighs. For reasons Sandra couldn't explain, she wanted to kneel down and suck at the skin of his stomach, but instead, when Adam bent to kiss her, she ducked her head and turned away. She could feel him standing there, behind her, looking at her, and then after a minute, he moved to the mirror, lit all around by big, frosted bulbs.

His face in the glass, when she finally turned to take it in, was grave; he stood there fingering the cross his godfather Randall had given him. It was small and valuable and old, encrusted with tiny mosaics, and she watched Adam put it around his neck. He wore it always when he performed, but it wasn't his only talisman. On the ledge, a set of small wax superhero figures—Superman, Batman, the Green Hornet—were arrayed in battle. Taped to the dressing room mirror was a black-and-white photo of his mother in costume for *Medea,* circa 1960; a telegram of one word, *Merde*; the long white feather he'd worn in his turban for his first *Bayadère*; and a new one, the Polaroid he'd taken of her when they went to Connecticut this past February. The sight of it made her flush. He must have carried it with him on tour, brought it back here to the Met to look at, this picture of her, with her hair falling all over her bare tits and her lips swollen like that.

They'd taken her dad's old 1961 Mercedes from the garage and drove out of the city just to drive. It was February, raining on the windshield, wipers going like mad. They'd played the radio, taking turns twirling the dial. Adam was leaving the next day for his tour, and she was sad; he knew it and was holding her hand, and eventually she curled up on the front seat, her head in his lap, her hair falling all over his legs. Occasionally, he'd drop a hand to her and stroke her hair, then her cheekbone, her neck, the neckline of her dress; terror at her own desire kept her motionless. They drove until it was dark, and she said nothing when Adam pulled off the Interstate and checked them into a one-story motel, the Flamingo. Once in the room they stood there awkwardly, but when they went to the end of the hall for ice, they found the indoor pool that saved them.

The lights were off because it was after eleven, but the heater was still on, and the water was warm. A plastic flamingo drank at the deep end, the bird reflected in the glass walls around them, and the whole room stank of chlorine. They got in wearing their clothes and swam silently, until Sandra's dress dragged behind her like a weight and she couldn't move anymore. They hung on together then by the flamingo at the deep end of the pool, in the dark, the air feeling colder than the water and chilling the parts of their bodies above it. She touched Adam's wet calves with her feet and they whispered at each other, their voices contained by the curve of cement. She saw a woman's high-heeled shoe beneath a chaise and pointed to it for him to see, but Adam didn't want to look at a shoe. Her dress sucked up to his skin as he held her against the pool wall, buoyed her up with his slick, chlorine-smelling body, and he kissed her, his hands pressed to her face as if to push her away. Strands of her hair stuck to his cheeks. It was a strange sensation, kissing in the deep water, his body buoying hers up. And then Adam pushed himself away from the wall and swam lap after lap, his shoulders and upper back moving just out of the water, and she watched him, waiting, knowing he would come back to her, that she didn't have to do anything but wait. And when he did come back, breathing hard, they started it again. This time his hands went under her dress, and then he was inside her, and he was alternately moaning or lowering his head to put his tongue in her mouth for her to suck, and when they came they were both shuddering; it was her first time, and when it was over, she couldn't move. Adam's body and his arms braced against the wall behind her were the only things keeping her from sinking to the bottom of the pool and drowning. He had to help her, finally, out of there, take her by the hand back to their room, and once they were there, they did it again, their wet clothes in a heap in the tub ten feet away, and when they were finished, Adam took out the camera they were supposed to be using to photograph nature.

They'd been best friends for years, Adam had even lived with her and her dad for weeks at a time, and she'd spent plenty of nights at his place, in his bed, Adam on the floor in a sleeping bag. They'd never done anything like this, some unspoken pact between them rendering their relations entirely platonic, except for that one time long ago, which they'd never talked about, which had come to feel like some weird dream. They were confidantes, best friends, that was all, even after Adam was promoted and his schedule began to depart radically from hers. And yet, clearly, somewhere during that time, Adam had quietly commenced a sexual life that didn't include her, because nothing they did together that night at the motel was new to him, she could tell. He'd never talked to her about girls in the company, at City Ballet or here at Ballet Theatre. She'd thought she'd known everything about him just as he knew everything about her, but she was wrong.

Outside the dressing room she heard the usual pandemonium, dancers heading toward the wings to warm up at the portable barres, to test out the stage, the shanks and boxes of new pointe shoes rapping against the flooring, the orchestra in its green room below the stage warming up. In here, Adam quietly put on his tights, the shirt, the leather vest, the leather ballet boots, the costume of Franz, the village flirt, whose infatuation with Dr. Coppélius's doll nearly destroys his engagement to Swanilda. Now and then, as he dressed, he turned to look at her as if he might say something, but it wasn't until he was finished that he came over to her and put his hands on his hips.

"What?" he said. "What is it? You're sorry about what we did? Tell me quick."

So it wasn't going to be like that other time. They were going to talk about it.

But in the speaker they could hear the orchestra begin the overture, first the horns, then the strings, then the drums.

$\mathscr{C}$OPPÉLIA WAS a confection, a village farce, full of mime scenes and folk-flavored dances, and in it Franz was not the usual prince, not noble or tragic or somber, but a boy—impulsive, unsophisticated, playful, and utterly charming. And in this ballet Adam was perfect, a perfect Franz. He was dancing tonight with Cynthia Gregory, one of the company's senior ballerinas, in a rare appearance in this ballet, and she speared the steps and tossed them off with a meticulous bravura. The stage was capacious and hot, a fertile medium for what they did upon it—she, six feet tall on pointe, almost too tall for him, almost conquering him, a majestic Swanilda, not a soubrette, and he, strutting himself across the square as he showed off for her, and to her chagrin, for the doll in the balcony window above them. ABT did a thousand of the old-fashioned three-act ballets, the nineteenth-century classics, an entirely different repertory from what she danced at City Ballet. But these big ballets were crowd pleasers. Like large meals, they made the audiences feel sated, and they filled the house. And the Met was a colossus of a theater.

Though the audience couldn't tell, Sandra could feel Adam

holding back, his performance a bit uncertain, and she knew it
was because of her. She'd upset him and now it was throwing
him off. All around her in the black wing were girls and boys in
rustic peasant costumes and headdresses, waiting for their entrance. Pacing among them all was Mikhail Baryshnikov, in
street clothes. He was directing Ballet Theatre now, had danced
with the company since he defected from the Kirov in the seventies. But last year he had suddenly come to City Ballet, to
learn *Apollo* and *Prodigal Son* and *Stars and Stripes* and then to
run out, back across the plaza, worried about the way his muscles were bulking up from the Balanchine repertoire. He had
caused some excitement in the company, though Mr. B was sure
never to act too excited about any one dancer, any male dancer,
anyway. But Mr. B had been too sick to do more than coach
Baryshnikov in ballets he had already made, too sick to make
anything new for him. And so Baryshnikov had come back
here, to *this* new thing, directing.

Sandra watched him watch Adam out there, Baryshnikov's
expression meditative, reserved. Was he disappointed in Adam?
She couldn't tell, tried for a moment longer to decode his face,
and then she pushed through the crowd of corps members, a
stranger among them in her jeans and her Property of New
York City Ballet T-shirt, until she was just visible, not to the audience, but to Adam, the blue and yellow stage lights shining on
her face. She wanted to let him see what she couldn't show him
back in the dressing room. Eventually Adam did look at her, and
when he did, she raised her chin and gave him a slow smile; she
could practically see something unfold within him in response.
His performance suddenly became expansive, enormous, and
she stood there without breathing as he mimed so beautifully

the section where he takes a butterfly from Swanilda and then, to her horror, kills it and pins it to his shirt like a brooch. At her reaction, his spread arms and astonished face said so clearly, *What's wrong?* that the audience laughed. When he laid Swanilda in the low backbends over his arm as they listened together to the ear of wheat, the audience sighed. Swanilda shook the wheat and heard no rattle, which meant Franz was not her true love. Adam took it from her to shake, then shrugged, and after Swanilda gave it to a friend to listen, she threw it on the ground and stamped her foot, breaking her engagement to Franz, who stalked off. The orchestra in the pit sent up a drum roll, and the dancers in the wings elbowed her out of the way to get onto the stage, where they broke into a folk dance, a czardas. By the end of the act, when Adam tries to climb a ladder to the balcony to see the doll and is chased off by Dr. Coppélius, Baryshnikov began to laugh. As Adam climbed the ladder again, he looked for her in her wing and gave her a wide grin. He was enjoying himself now.

At curtain, Adam and Cynthia shared an ovation and a paper throw, bits of the evening's programs torn into squares and hurled up at the stage by the fans where the pieces fell like confetti on his shoulders and feet and on Cynthia's upraised arms. The curtain call was an art in itself, both ritualized and improvised. A few stems wrapped in foil or cellophane and corseted with ribbons hit the stage and Adam went about gathering them up and presenting them to his ballerina, though most had notes for him, as they discovered later in the wings. They'd laugh about it, but now he made a courtly show and offered all the flowers to Cynthia. When she pulled an orange rose from its trappings and handed it to Adam, he bowed his head, then raised it to emit the smile that sent a rolling wave of shrieks across the orchestra to the balcony. Sandra was startled by the roar, with its hint of sexual hysteria, but the other dancers around her, some of them already drifting off to the dressing rooms, some standing there in the wings to watch the call, seemed unfazed. A few girls backstage were whooping it up, too, and Sandra felt just the weirdest touch of something at the sound of it. And then Adam looked at her. Did he think she'd made that noise? No. That wasn't why he was looking. He wanted to make sure that she was watching all this, that she saw.

## TWO

*A*dam needed her to come with him after, to his place; he'd had to insist on it back there in his dressing room and eventually he'd gotten her to agree, persuaded her to call her father and tell him she was staying over tonight, though Adam knew she worried about leaving her father alone for too long. But Adam had gotten what he wanted, and they were now ascending the freight elevator in his parents' building, a turn-of-the-century industrial warehouse in Hell's Kitchen, the neighborhood he'd grown up in and escaped, temporarily, with every sojourn to Lincoln Center. He felt charged from the evening—not yet exhausted as he knew he soon would be, taken over first by the ravenous hunger, then by the fatigue—but energized by the performance he'd given and by the knowledge that Sandra had witnessed it and the curtain call that followed. This adulation had begun like a ripple last year and had lapped at him all across the country while he toured these past months, the swell following him on his return to New York. This was his first paper throw at the Met, and he knew it was as much for

him as for Cynthia, whose reputation was already firmly estab-
lished. Sandra had seen it, as he'd wanted her to, and now it was
another thing they shared, along with all the other secrets they'd
shared over the past years. The walls of the elevator were draped
in gray moving blankets, and he watched her, leaning against
one, head down, her hands in the pockets of her jeans. He
moved closer to her, certain now that this diffidence was not re-
jection, and at his touch, she tipped her face up to his. He could
see there the same look she'd given him from the wings, and it
was a look that made him ache somewhere deep in his ribcage
and down in his balls. He was about to kiss her because he was
dying to feel her tongue against his, when he heard above them
the sound of his parents' voices, fighting it sounded like, at first
a blur and then the sounds sorting themselves out, becoming
clearer as they approached his floor. "Jesus Christ," he said to
Sandra, and she put out a hand to soothe him, but he turned and
slammed his body against the elevator grate, rattling it as they
rose upward. When they clattered to a stop, Adam saw his parents in the dark, cavernous dining area in the center of the loft,
the long banquet table between them like a sandbagged fence.
They were nearly naked, his father's hand raised and fisted, and
at the sound of the elevator grate drawing back, his dad lowered
his hand and turned toward them.

Frankie was a larger, older, more magnificent version of
Adam himself, broader everywhere, his hair a little longer and
therefore wilder, the blond now shot through with gray, and
Adam saw his dad's penis was thickened, swollen, behind his
boxers, as if he and his mom had just gotten out of bed, drawn
by some argument away from what they'd started. Adam
stepped in front of Sandra so she couldn't see this. They should
have gone to her place, like they usually did, but he'd wanted to

have her alone, away from her father, here with him, his. Now
he was paying for the impulse. At Adam's stare, his father turned
away and disappeared into the deep shadows of the loft, limping
slightly from the arthritis that had ended his career. There remained just his mother, Lucia, her hair still bound up in its signature ponytail on top of her head, like some 1962 Barbie in a
gauzy slip, her body so thin and tautly muscled that even at this
distance and in this little light, Adam could make out the articu-
lation of her arms and trunk. In the pictures of her, the ones
that he worshipped, her body was not so lacquered and hard, but
luminously strong, her hair a thick, black sheath that followed
her like a partner. Over the years, his father had scraped that
beauty from her, layer by layer. Adam made a sound now and
stepped toward her in the dark, but she turned away and went
back toward the bedroom. If Sandra weren't here, he'd have followed her.

As it was, he moved aside and let Sandra off the elevator,
slapped his palm against the metal button to send the thing
down. Not that Sandra had to be protected. She'd seen plenty
of what went on between his parents over the past five years.
There was a point when he'd practically lived with her and her
father to get away from it, had set up shop back in the little
maid's room off their kitchen. Even though the ceilings here
were eighteen feet high and the polished concrete floors rolled
on and on and on, unbroken save for a few walls at the perimeters of the loft that demarcated the bedrooms, it seemed there
was never enough space to comfortably house their family of
three. At first Adam went to his godfather, Randall, then more
and more often to Sandra, arriving distraught or enraged or de-
spairing or defiantly cool, and she'd open the door and take him
in, get the blankets and the pillow to put on the narrow bed in

the maid's room, sit with him while he shook or cried or paced. She was the only one at school who knew what happened at his house, and until he'd met her, he thought he was the only one with trouble at home. He'd made himself entirely vulnerable to her, which already frightened him, and now that they'd done together what they had with their bodies, he felt more vulnerable still. He'd felt this naked with no one but Randall, but he was certain of Randall's love, it was the one great certainty of his life. Sandra could be the second. Just her presence soothed him; her nature was essentially calm, all the emotion held in a pen deep inside her or released into those journals she'd written in compulsively since she was a little girl.

She came and stood next to him now, and when she took his hand—*she* took *his* hand—the big space suddenly seemed to him to breathe. It held hardly any furniture—the big table, a few sofas to the right—but a lot of art. Against the walls hung some of the big canvases Randall had collected in the sixties—a Rothko, a Rauschenberg, a Pollock, a Frankenthaler, a portrait of Randall done by his old friend from Yale, John O'Connor, when O'Connor was nobody and his work was worth nothing. The whole loft had once belonged to Randall, but he'd given it to Adam's parents as a gift, with the caveat that he could still house there the larger paintings in his collection. The left side of the loft was entirely bare. It was the area his mom used as a studio, all her props stacked against the walls. Mannequins, bird cages, long bolts of cloth, bamboo poles. As her body aged, she'd come to rely more and more on props. At forty-one, she was no longer dancing with Martha Graham, but as a solo artist, booking herself a series of gigs at colleges and smaller venues all across the United States and Europe. She wasn't home much anymore, nor was Adam, maybe not a bad thing for any of them.

Behind him, Sandra said his name softly, calling him back from the place he was going, and he felt her lean her head against his shoulder. He loved that, that she would do that. The light from the big windows, moonlight or streetlight, gave her hair and skin a phosphorescent gleam, and Adam reached for her. In the next instant, the loft began to shake, music plowing toward them from the set of enormous speakers, each one as tall as a man, stationed at the deep end of the loft. His father had gone down there and apparently had found one of the big reel-to-reels he wanted to listen to, now, 1 A.M., top decibel. Sandra held him back, and if it weren't for her hand on his arm he wouldn't have even realized he'd leaned forward, tensed, to do what? To charge down to the end of the loft and rip the tape off its reel, prop his father's body against the grand piano while he throttled him with the slippery brown plastic?

"Come on, Adam," Sandra said, pulling on him, leading him in the direction of his room, which stood like a white box at the opposite end of the space from his parents' room, a distance that had once frightened him, this dark endless maw dividing him from them. At one point Randall had built him window boxes and hung them on the outside walls, as if Adam lived in a little house within a house, and in the boxes Randall had planted flowers. The boxes hung empty now and had for years; but inside, the room remained the same red color he'd chosen when he was six. He hadn't bothered to change anything else, either. The World War I–era biplanes he'd once built with Randall still swayed on plastic wires from the ceiling, and the metal suit of armor, an exact replica of a twelfth-century set at the Metropolitan Museum of Art, still stood watch in the corner. His bed was a single, fitted with a Western stage-coach headboard Randall had found at a theatrical prop store when Adam was in the fifth grade. It was ridiculous that he still lived here, like this, at twenty, and he resolved in this instant that even if he traveled half the year now, he would get his own place. He'd moved out once before, when he was eighteen and still at NYCB, but within a few months, he'd blown all his money, couldn't make the rent, couldn't stand living in a dark studio apartment after having all this space, and so he'd moved back. He'd have to try it again, after his birthday, when he'd start getting the income from a trust Randall had set up for him. He'd have money enough then to buy himself some space and distance from his parents. His father had turned the music down, but still Adam could hear it, the *thunk* of the bass, the squawk of a violin, and whatever fabulous energy he'd had ten minutes earlier was gone, replaced by the familiar rage and confusion.

He turned to Sandra, who stood there biting her fingernails and looking at him, and he was sure she was wishing, as he now did, that they'd gone to her place, or, worse, that she'd gone to her place without him. He shucked off his jacket, his two-thousand-dollar leather jacket, a celebratory indulgence from last year to mark his escape from City Ballet, and threw it on the bed, where he had hoped he would already be lying with Sandra, doing what he'd thought about doing the whole time he was away. Instead they were standing here feeling awkward as hell. What a fucking mess. But he didn't want to talk about it, didn't want to think about it. "Look," he said to her, "would you just dance with me?" Obediently, she took off her own jacket, the same jean jacket she'd had since tenth grade, and put out her arms as if they were going to do the Virginia Reel. He laughed. "No, like this," he said, and he got behind her, put his hands to her waist, and began to talk her through the pas de deux from *Coppélia,* the grand wedding adagio that he'd fin-

ished two hours ago at the Met. As they moved, he felt his knotted emotions come unknotted and his temper pacified. The
brain, preoccupied with the musculoskeletal, lodged its energy
there, forgot about emotion. He carried her out of his room and
then back into it again, using the space of the loft when they
needed it for the larger, more expansive movements, drawing
her back within the walls of his bedroom for the smaller, more
intimate ones. She was so light compared to Cynthia, not even a
hundred pounds, nowhere near it, that he found he thrust her up
into the air almost too quickly, and when he brought her down
again and leaned her back against his torso in the exultant, swaying arabesque, he was surprised to feel how her body fit along
his perfectly. They had never danced together like this, never
fooled around like this in the studio, and now that they were, he
didn't know why they hadn't before. They just hadn't. In adagio
class at SAB he was always paired with taller girls because of his
own height, and once he joined the company he was quickly
promoted ahead of her, charged with partnering one after another of the principal girls.

And yet, Sandra had the strength, the beauty of any of them,
and what was more, in his arms, here in this stupid, half-
darkened loft, she gave off a startling vibrancy, electric even in
her hesitancy as she considered the unfamiliar steps. She had in-
credible aplomb for a girl who'd spent her career in the corps,
an attention-grabbing fearlessness he hadn't seen her exhibit before, and as she dove through the body of the dance with him,
he found himself astonished. What was giving her this charge?
He had watched her in the studios and on the stage for years and
still he didn't know she was capable of this.

When they finished the last of it, he turned her in his arms to
face him. They stood there in the doorway of his room, panting,

staring at each other. Her hair had spun itself into a nest of gold that gave her height and a peculiar beauty, and he watched as it slowly fell and settled along her shoulders. She was watching him, waiting for him, and he knew she would follow him, allow him anything. The power of that knowledge made him shake. He dropped to his knees and kissed her hand, turned it over and licked her palm, put his mouth to her wrist and sucked at it, right at the spot where it pulsed. He heard her emit a long, slow exhalation, and at the sound, he reached around behind her and shut the bedroom door. Without getting off his knees, he stripped her of her clothes, her ridiculous T-shirt, her jeans, and there she was, standing above him, standing in his room as she had a thousand times, but now, suddenly, unbelievably, almost naked, breathing hard, her ribs and chest heaving, from the effort of their dance or from embarrassment at what he'd just done. He recognized that he held her at a disadvantage—she was undressed, he was not—but he needed that advantage, needed every advantage. He knew too clearly how he felt about her, but her feelings for him were as yet unexpressed. She stood, looking down at him, waiting for him to do something, to lead her somewhere, her long hair so pale in this light it looked colorless, falling forward over her breasts and ribs. The hair between her legs rose in a narrow strip behind her cotton underwear, Hanes, little-girl underwear, the same underwear she'd been wearing for years. Jesus Christ. She still saw herself that way. He leaned forward now and put his mouth to her, to that cotton, used his tongue against it, and as he did so, he felt her shudder. No. She was pulling at him, pulling him away from her, and when he looked up, he saw her mouth pucker to one side in the way he recognized as her preamble to tears.

"What is it?" he asked her.

"Who else have you done this to?" she said.

He hated that she was thinking about this, hated it; so he answered her quickly with a lie and the truth. "Nobody else," he told her. "It was always with you," and he shook off her hands.

Because of the way he looked, women and men had made their bodies available to him too often, dancers from his dad's company, boys he'd met at parties here in the loft, girls from ABT, and he'd used them all, quietly, while he waited for Sandra to give him some kind of sign, while he waited for the resolve to confess his own feelings, always afraid that whatever they had between them would vanish like vapor at the act of penetration. He'd stopped waiting, stopped being afraid, the day he and Sandra took that drive. When she put her head down into his lap, he thought she would feel his hard-on, the longest-held hard-on in the history of the world; finally he had to stop the car, get her and her long hair and her beautiful shoulders and tits and legs out of his lap, out of the seat where she stretched oblivious to the fact that he was going to die. But he wasn't sure, once they got into their motel room, if he was ready to do this with her. So he stalled. They bought two Cokes and grabbed some ice from the machine, discovered then the indoor pool. If there hadn't been a pool at that motel, he'd have had to take a shower. But there was a pool and she got into it with him. Yet, the pool didn't cut his desire, didn't cool him as he expected it to; instead it combusted him, and finally, finally he was fucking her, in the cold and the wet, her dress so saturated with water it was like another person between them he had to wrestle, half-hidden in the dark, the big, bland eyes of the glass windows gazing on. And then, the next day, he'd had to leave her for eight unbearable weeks, and when he called her he was too afraid to ask her how she was feeling about what they did, afraid she'd have re-treated from him, afraid she'd be regretting it.

He was her first, this much he knew, and he knew also that what he was doing to her now was another first, well, almost a first, but he was doing it to her for real this time, not like that time five years ago, in his room when he hadn't known what he was doing, was operating by instinct, this insane desire to put his fingers and face in her privates. He had watched her all night at one of his parents' big parties, watched her helping serve drinks, wearing this low-cut dress with blue sequins his mother had given her, watching the way the dress lay on her body, the way the V of the neckline buckled away from her when she leaned forward. It seemed to him she smiled a strange smile when she turned to him and used a finger to push her hair behind one ear. He wanted to thrust his tongue into her ear. He was shaking. He thought he was going crazy. He needed to be committed somewhere, fast. By the end of a few hours of this, he thought he was going to have to run laps around the loft. When Sandra went to his bedroom to lie down, it wasn't five minutes before he followed her.

He'd stood in the doorway of his darkened room and he could tell by her breathing that she wasn't asleep, but that she was pretending to be and that he had to pretend she was, as well, in order to do what he wanted to do to her. He thought at the time he was sick for wanting to lift her dress, for wanting to lick and suck at her cotton underwear, for wanting to get his mouth inside her underwear, for wanting to kiss her, which he couldn't do because that was her face and she was supposed to be asleep. So he kept his face between her legs, intoxicated by the strange smell of her, by the taste of her, by the fact that she was letting him do this to her, letting him kiss her there. He thought he would die; his heart was lurching in his chest like a kicking foot. When he finally pulled aside one of the elasticized bands of her underpants and when he finally got his tongue right up the center of her parted flesh to this hard knot he couldn't leave alone, she made a noise that unnerved and electrified him. He knew this was why he had put his head between her legs in the first place. He didn't know where or how it ended for a girl, he only knew how it ended for him, in that messy and surprising way he'd discovered on his own, which he tried to keep from happening to him that night.

But he didn't get to see how it ended for her because she sat up suddenly and looked at him, as if he had awakened her, and then he started thinking maybe he really had. He didn't know what she was thinking. She said nothing, she did nothing, just looked at him, her mouth open and her hair tangled in the strap of her dress. It wasn't until later, with other girls, that he understood he had actually made her come, that despite his ignorance he had brought her to the very end of it all, and that she had sat up to look at him after, amazed and speechless. But back then he didn't know this, and back then he couldn't think of a single thing to say, a single possible explanation for what he was doing. So there was nothing for it but to take his hand out from under her dress, to hear her sigh as he did this, to back out of the room and pretend nothing had gone on, that he'd just come in and crawled on the bed like that to look for a coat or something. The minute he left, he felt like an idiot, but having walked out he felt he couldn't go back. Why had she sighed like that? He hated himself.

But tonight, he wasn't pretending he was looking for a fucking coat, and this time she wasn't asleep or pretending to be. He

knew now he wasn't a sick person and he knew now exactly
what he was doing, wanted to show her what he now knew, but
the smell of her and the taste of her were making an idiot of
him. This was now, not then, they were twenty, not fifteen, they
were in the doorway, not in a bed full of coats, but the two times
were all mixed up in his mind and in the dark of his bedroom.
Was she remembering too? He couldn't see her face, she made
no sound. Above him he could hear her hands scrabbling against
the closed door like headless creatures, and as he brought her off,
he held on to her, and then she got down onto her knees on the
floor beside him and clung to him, hung her arms around his
neck. *Adam.* He wrapped his clothed body around her and covered her, couldn't keep himself then from whispering her name,
from whispering, *I love you, I've always loved you,* and to his relief
and wonder, she said the words back.

In THE MORNING, Adam woke before her, the gray light
coming in from the windows faintly doubled by the glow of the
Christmas lights strung over them. For years he'd habitually
plugged in the decorations and used them as night-lights, and at
2 A.M., when he'd finally had enough of Sandra's body, he had
stumbled out of bed to put them on. Then he could sleep, holding her close to him. She was still right there, beneath his arm.
He could see only a little of her from this angle, her shoulder,
the line of her jaw, her hand cupped against the wall, this narrow
bed too small for them both. Her presence in his bed this morning amazed him, but the implications of it also frightened him
some; he was now responsible for her, in ways that extended far
beyond those required of him during their friendship. But he
was ready for it. It was what he wanted. He got out of bed qui-

etly and pulled on his jeans, found a belt to hold them up with, and went noiselessly out into the loft.

He was right; he had heard voices. Randall was here with Joe. The whole loft was shot with light, one long wall of it made up of windows, floor-to-ceiling things that rolled suddenly and unexpectedly into arches on top. From those windows Adam could see all the way to the Hudson, nothing but the low, flat tenements and warehouses of Hell's Kitchen laid out before him. It was gray today, late, not early, as he'd thought, but raining. That's why it was so dark. Soon it would be summer, with the fifteen-hour days and the thick heat and the absence of shadow. Joe and Randall sat at the table with his father, just where Frankie'd stood last night in the face-off with his mom, but this morning his mother was nowhere in sight, probably at one of her many yoga classes. For the rest of them, Monday meant a day off from the theater, from rehearsal, from class. But Lucia was afraid to rest, afraid the little she had left would get up and walk away from her if she sat down.

The three men were bent over something on the table, none of them aware of Adam yet. His dad's face was empty of the anger that had marked it last night. Adam watched him sip from a giant-sized plastic mug, filled, he knew, not with coffee, but with the Coke Frankie used to get through each day. Joe passed something that looked like a box down to his dad, Joe's dark ponytail flicking across his shoulder blades as he moved, the thing held back with the broad green rubber band from the *Times*. Adam rubbed his hands through his hair, which had been cut to fly in fifteen different directions when he moved on the stage and probably looked that way now. He had once loved Joe Alton, his Uncle Joe, who brought him snow globes from every city his company toured, who played Monopoly and Go Fish and Chutes and Ladders with him endlessly, when no one else could stand to or would. But when Adam was ten, Joe had had an affair with one of his dancers, a man with a gaunt face, his eyes set so deep in their sockets they made his face a skull, his hair mowed so short it stood up from his scalp like the crew cuts Adam wore as a toddler. And when Randall fled to Europe, to Cologne, to escape the spectacle of this, Adam suffered through the loneliest months of his life. The company, Joe's company, cracked apart without Randall's money, nearly went bankrupt. Eventually, Joe went to Cologne and brought Randall back, and though the two of them went on, Adam's feelings for Joe did not. Joe had become someone like his father, whose philandering strafed and mutilated the people around him, and the sight of Joe's hands and mouth and person had since then made Adam want to back away.

Adam went down the length of the loft to the stove for some coffee—there was always a pot going in their house—and he made enough noise there to be noticed eventually. He heard a chair scrape back, and when he turned he saw Randall coming toward him. Randall still moved like a yacht, prow forward on the water, even though he was not really well; his two bouts of pneumonia just after Christmas had stripped him of mass, left only the memory of what he once was. It pained Adam to see how Randall shifted his bones across the floor; in the gray light his skin seemed luminescent and thin, like the skin of a bubble. He had been for twenty years Joe's muse, once so big Joe had christened him his *moose,* and Joe had ridden him, his talent and his money and his beauty, as if Randall were his own personal packhorse. When Randall drew close enough, Adam embraced him and breathed him in. Randall still smelled like himself.

"So how did it go last night?" Randall asked.

"It went well," Adam said. "I got a paper throw." He ducked his head. Randall was just about the only person in the world he would tell something like this to. There was self-aggrandizement enough at his house to outlast the universe, but to Randall he could say anything, share anything, and never feel like an idiot or a braggart. Adam looked down, abashed enough by what he'd said anyway, and when he looked up again, Randall was smiling at him, looking almost like his old self.

"Beautiful boy," Randall said.

He had always been Randall's beautiful boy, from the day he was born. And yet, it had been a while since Randall had been able to see his boy dance. The week before Adam left on his tour, he'd slipped out of his last costume-fitting wearing his tunic for *Le Corsaire* under his coat and took a cab straight over to Randall and Joe's apartment on Park Avenue. It was only seven o'clock, but Randall was already in bed; he had propped himself up in the big four-poster to watch Adam dance at the foot of it the boy's variation from the ballet. It was the fifth big role he'd learned over the past season, a bravura piece that showcased the technique, this runaway technique he'd begun to possess all at once after years of painstaking training. When he turned nineteen, he'd gotten this surge of strength, his muscles bulking up as if he'd taken steroids, which he hadn't. He could suddenly do everything. Nothing was beyond him. It had been Randall, who'd danced with New York City Ballet in the fifties, who insisted Adam be given a ballet technique, who understood from his own career the beauty classical training gave a dancer of any stripe. It was Randall's training that had made him one of Joe's pillars, Frankie the other, and the two of them had helped make Joe's name as a choreographer. Joe Alton. That evening in his grifted costume, Adam had made the floors and furniture quake from the beats, the barrel turns, the scissored leaps, the grand turns ending on one knee. When Randall put his hands together and shouted his bravos, Adam gave him the full treatment—the elaborate series of bows he made every night at the curtain of the Met—head bent, hand to the heart, the sweep of the arm across the body from one side to the other, open chested, the gaze up to the balcony, the final posture with head lowered again. Modesty and pride.

From the table thirty feet away, Joe shouted, "Hey, Adam. C'mere. Take a look at the set for your dad's ballet." Randall smiled and jerked his chin to indicate Adam should go, and so Adam pushed himself away from the stove and ambled down toward the table to look at the maquette. The set was a sleek, emotionally vacant 1950s hotel room, the bed wide and long and low, covered with a maroon spread; in the large picture window stood a green car, big with curves and fins and a silver grille, the brown hills beyond it closer than they should be. It looked like California. His dad, at forty-five, was retiring this year from Joe's company, and this ballet was for him, a pièce d'occasion. He'd had his hip replaced last year, and after spending two seasons enraged by what he couldn't do, by the mobility he'd lost, after threatening to slit his wrists with a kitchen knife or to hang himself from the skylight, he'd accepted a teaching position at Juilliard and prepared to retire. He could no longer jump, had little extension, his range of motion had become so circumscribed, almost all he could do was pose, like one of Leonardo da Vinci's anatomical studies in Randall's books. Was this what lay ahead for Adam? The men in the books stared straight forward, their trunks and limbs overlaid with various lines that indicated what motion was possible for each. Leonardo had not seen classical ballet, had no idea what the art would come to demand of the body, what ruin it would leave of it.

"So what do you think of the set?" Joe asked. "Good enough for your father?"

Adam nodded noncommittally.

"Watch this," his dad said, leaning forward. "The hotel window opens up and I'll walk out onto a ramp as the set's retracted."

"That's an uneven surface," Joe said. "Do you think you can manage it?"

"I think so," his dad said, shoving himself away from the table, and they could all feel the irritation, which came off him like thunderous heat.

At that moment Adam heard the door to his room open and Sandra emerged, wearing one of his shirts over her jeans, and he loved seeing this, that she'd opened his bureau and put that on. He felt the muscles of his arms and chest and thighs fill with blood, a rush, a swelling, some atavistic response to the sight of her, to the sight of his mark on her. He'd never felt this before. With the other girls he'd been with in hotel rooms or dressing rooms or back bedrooms filled with coats or in some girl's rat hole of an apartment, the idea had been to get away immediately after, to pretend nothing had happened, to make no public proclamation of possession; whatever claim or interest they'd had in each other had been, for him, extinguished at climax. As Sandra approached him now, he rounded the table to meet her. She was his and they could all see it.

But no one was looking. His dad drank from his mug. Joe stared pensively at his maquette. Well, why should they stand at attention? Sandra had spent the night with him a hundred times. She was so much a part of their lives, her presence this morning was utterly unremarkable to everyone but him. And maybe to

Randall. Randall was looking at him now, at the way Adam had drawn himself up. Randall always knew everything. Back those many years ago, when Adam had confessed to him what he'd done to Sandra in his room, how she'd acted, sitting up like that and staring at him wordlessly, Randall had reared back in his chair, cigarette held up high, telling Adam that they were both way too young. They were just fifteen. And so Adam, already a little uneasy about what he'd done, and chastened by the way Sandra had written about it in her journal, *Adam put his fingers in my vagina. I don't know why he did that,* had listened to Randall.

But it was as if a light went on inside him anyway, something shining out of him that women and men could see, and Adam had found himself repeatedly propositioned. And at some point, he just let it happen, even if it wasn't entirely satisfying, wasn't exactly what he wanted, whom he wanted. He had left City Ballet still feeling for Sandra this desire, thinking leaving would probably cure it, but it didn't cure it, because now when he saw her it was always outside of the studio, at his house or hers, on the street or in restaurants, where he would think, *Why are we seeing each other? What is this? What are we to each other?* Yet he couldn't go a week without seeing her, made himself try sometimes, some kind of ritualistic practice of cool, but then he'd find himself at her door and she'd let him in, and she was the cool one, as cool as if she'd been packed in ice. He'd shamble into the living room where she was playing music with her father. He'd stand there and turn pages for them, his sight reading terrible, looking for her nod when it was time. How was it he could turn the head of every woman in the street on the way over, but she remained fixed on the black lines and notes on the pages in front of her?

It drove him crazy, and when he talked to Randall about her

again at Christmas a few months ago, he talked and talked, couldn't stop himself though he wanted to, Randall's face alternately serious and bemused as he listened, and *this* time Randall urged him to speak to Sandra, to let her know how he felt. Ballet girls were like sleeping princesses, Randall said, their sexuality lodged in some subterranean vault, unawakened. She was older now. Maybe she was ready. But if Adam was waiting for *her* to kiss *him,* he would wait for a hundred years. So finally Adam had kissed her, and now as Adam saw Randall looking from him to Sandra, Adam was sure Randall sensed that this had happened, that the cistern had been unlocked, the door flung open. Sandra had brushed her hair, which was very, very straight and very fine, and sometimes to make it fuller, she stood with her feet planted apart and bent forward from the waist, brushing the hair backward from the root to the tips and then she straightened and brushed it back and it was like watching water rush over a dam. She'd done that in his room with his brush this morning, while for some reason he stood out here. He shouldn't have gotten out of bed. He knew he was standing there looking slack-jawed in love with her, and as he struggled for a neutral expression, he saw Joe was gazing at him speculatively. Christ. But Joe was turning to his dad.

"Frankie," he said, "what would you think if we used Adam in the piece?"

His dad stopped with his mug halfway to his mouth. "What do you mean?"

"He could be the fantasy-you after you step through the hotel. Adam could meet you on the ramp. You're looking at your younger self, and he looks just like you at twenty." Joe looked at Adam. "What do you think?"

And Adam knew exactly what he thought, that Joe wanted to

use him to sell tickets. Now that Adam was getting all this press with Ballet Theatre, Joe wanted a piece of him, as he'd used his dad of Paul Taylor fame and Randall from City Ballet. Another beautiful boy to sell tickets. Well, Joe could get one of his own boys already on the payroll. Adam looked quickly at Randall, who was keeping his face blank, and yet he saw there something, and that something kept Adam from rejecting Joe out of hand.

"I don't know," Adam said slowly.

"Wait a minute," Frankie said. "Exactly what is this going to leave for me?"

"There's plenty of music left for you," Joe said quickly, without looking at him, his eyes on Adam.

"Ballet Theatre's set to go on tour soon," Adam said.

"When you're back then, in August."

"So now you're postponing the premiere?" his father said. "It'll run right up into my teaching gig at Juilliard."

Joe wasn't even looking at his dad, didn't care what he was feeling, didn't care what anyone was feeling, his attention like a flame on Adam, and Adam felt the way that attention made him flush, despite himself, and it was the first time he understood something of what held Randall to Joe. "What do you think?"

"Maybe," Adam said slowly. He looked at Sandra ducking her head—she was trying to dodge this scene—"Maybe. If Sandra can dance with me." The minute he said it he knew it was what he wanted, a chance to dance with her, to showcase her. Her talent was locked down there in that cistern, too, but he'd had a glimpse of it last night, and it was in a state, raging, ready to fling itself out.

Frankie put his mug down with a crack. "Fuck this," he said and stalked off. Adam watched the back of him disappear with a feeling of sick triumph that made him breathe hard, as if he were the one walking away. He looked at Randall, who lifted his chin at him. *It's all right*. Adam turned to Joe. Joe hadn't moved and he didn't move until he had Adam again. Then Joe looked at Sandra.

"We're booked at the Joyce," he said to her. "You won't have to dance in the street."

Joe wasn't going to get to him through Sandra.

"We'll think about it," Adam said, and he took Sandra's hand and led her to the elevator.

IN THE CAGE going down, Sandra said, "Adam. Where are you taking me?"

And he had to say, "I don't know."

The minute they hit the street, he smelled the garbage piled in plastic-sack mountains all around them, stinking and wet from the rain. His parents were proud to live in this part of the city, like cowboys, but Adam had watched once from his bedroom window as the police chased a man across one of the flat rooftops down below and shot him dead. That memory, along with the trash and the men in doorways with panes of cardboard half-concealing them, and the whole bleak, urban wasteland from Times Square to the Lincoln Tunnel, blew a big hole through Adam's heart. Being at Sandra's or Randall's was like being in a different world, but this morning they were here in his world, and he kept his hand on Sandra's arm, dragging her a few feet, thinking of the Cupcake Café, where they sometimes ate, and it was at this point that he realized he'd never put on a shirt and neither of them were wearing shoes. It was cold and wet and they were going to have to go back upstairs. Whatever he wanted to say to her, he'd have to say quickly. He stopped walking.

"Look, Sandra, I want you to do Joe's ballet with me."

She squinted at him through the light rain. "You know City Ballet goes to Saratoga in the summer."

City Ballet. Fuck City Ballet. She was chained to the place like a slave, and the company had done nothing for her but use her body in a lineup. Four years and she was still in the back row.

"Sandra, look." He stopped and ran his hands through his hair. "I just, I want you to have a chance to be out there, to be looked at, to get out of the corps for a change." Her face had turned tense and unhappy now, but he plowed on. "I've been thinking about it, Sandra. If you don't get out of the corps soon, in the next couple of years, it's going to all be over for you."

At this, she began to cry, standing there barefoot, her hair now damp from the weather, and though he held her elbow, he didn't look away or take back his words. She looked so small and thin, and through the open neckline of the shirt he could see her collarbone standing out. She was too thin, too small, definitely too small for Balanchine—he pretty much liked his ballerinas tall and dark-haired, with small heads, long legs, long feet. His taste was so specific, and his taste ruled, the company run on Balanchine's obsessions and predilections. It was one of the reasons Adam had left: Men were nothing there. In Balanchine's world, ballet was woman, and Adam had thought he would go out of his mind dressing up every night in the tights and the T-shirt or the jewel-encrusted tunic to function as the setting in which the ballerina, usually Suzanne Farrell, shone. In rehearsal, when Adam was partnering her, Balanchine would say over and over, *I don't want to see you, Adam, I don't want to see you.* Adam was supposed to be invisible, the unfortunately necessary support for Suzanne. And so many of Mr. B's dancers were made now in Suzanne's image—as if there were only one standard of perfection. Sandra was spitting in the wind there, working her ass off, dancing her heart out, and all that talent would never be realized. Balanchine was too old, too sick, too tired to see it.

Slowly, Sandra stopped crying and she hung her head, not even trying to shield herself from the rain which was coming down harder now and driving into them slantways. He stood in front of her to protect her from it. "Sandra," he said, "you know I'm not going to let that happen to you."

## THREE

*O*n the morning, he made himself his favorite breakfast—sweet tea and an English muffin buttered and piled high with caviar—and stood in his kitchen to eat it, looking out the paned window to the gray sky, over the brick and mortar of the next building. It had been a bad night, with vivid and troubling dreams; he felt weak and his limbs trembled slightly. There was something wrong with his brain. He had begun to have brief, pointed hallucinations that broke into the surface of his consciousness and then pulled out again leaving no hole. He would be walking across the apartment and there would suddenly be sky all around and a cathedral with its great steps, or a rock and a fire and the drapes of a blue-black backdrop, a face, sometimes a voice. He was convinced that, like Schumann, he was going mad. At the periphery of his vision, there were flashes of light like miniature fireworks, and in his ears a constant roaring, a racket and tintinnabulation that never ceased.

When he finished the muffin, he went out to the white living room. He had bought two adjacent apartments and knocked

down a wall to have this space, like a stage, or like the space beyond the stage, beyond the wings, where props were stacked and
ropes soared to the ceiling. He lived alone now, and in this place
he had put little. His last apartment, with Tanny, he had furnished as if it were a magnificent stage set—a French chandelier, a grand piano, a pendulum clock, a framed print of an
Audubon eagle, blue silk couches that looked as if they had
tumbled from a stagecoach. Polio had stolen from Tanny everything that had once enchanted her, including her own beautiful
dancing body, so he had made it his mission to provide her with
enchantment. Now, he served no interests but his own. Tanny
had been his fifth and last wife, from whom he had been divorced for a dozen years. He had been married to one woman
or another since he was eighteen years old, and now he was
tired, his solitude a relief.

He opened the ironing board and spread over it the shirt he
would wear today. He listened while he pushed the iron over the
cloth to the music in his head, *Mozartiana,* the music Tchaikovsky
had made in 1887 to show Russia the marvels of Mozart; it was
music he had worked with before, and to which he was now, in
his seventy-seventh year, prepared to do justice. He finished the
shirt and put it on. It was still warm and he buttoned it almost
to the top. He hated, always, to look at his scar, the white crease
that marked where his flesh had been parted for the bypass. In
that instant, his body became no longer a monument, but a storage facility, where the hands of man rearranged and repackaged
what God had given him. He had not felt the same about himself since, but he dressed the body and made it walk and he was
going to use it to make a Tchaikovsky Festival for the spring
season. He put on the scarf he wore like a cravat to obscure the
crepe-paper folds that had taken over his neck. On his wrist he

put the beaded bracelet his fourth wife, Maria Tallchief, had given him thirty years ago during their marriage, and he looked in the mirror: a young boy stood within it, black hair combed back, features vaguely oriental, dark kohl on his eyelids. A fiction. He was old.

It was 1981, and his hair was white, though still he wore it brushed back from his forehead as he had since he was twenty years old in Russia. His nose had lengthened imperially and his top teeth protruded in an overbite he closed his lips to conceal. He was no longer thin. He had put on weight, which he did not like, but his body liked it, and he could not lose it. It was the body of an ordinary man, not the body of a ballet dancer or ballet master, and this pained him. He stood for a moment in the still room and he raised his hand. In ten minutes he would be in a studio at Lincoln Center with a hundred and five dancers looking to him. He was George Balanchine.

OUTSIDE LAY THE West Sixties, his neighborhood for almost three decades now. He had practically worn a trail from his various apartments to Lincoln Center, the beating heart that had not let him down. The buildings rose up about him, some with the smooth sides of the modern age, others with the cornices and statuary of a hundred years ago. He had lived in older cities, in St. Petersburg, in Monte Carlo, in Paris, but he preferred New York, and the city had, in return, conferred her favor upon him, had built him a theater. Even Diaghilev had not had that, not in Paris or Monte Carlo, though he had ruled there like a god for years, gathering up talent in his palm and setting it down on the stages of borrowed theaters and opera houses. George had been twenty-one when he met Diaghilev for the first time to beg for a job for himself, his first wife, Tamara, and the girl who would be his next, Alexandra Danilova.

Diaghilev had sat on the chaise longue in the salon of his friend Misia Sert, wearing his black suit with the black silk lapels. His cheeks made jowls; deep pouches lay beneath his eyes. His skin was grayish, and as Tamara and Alexandra danced a piece of George's choreography, Diaghilev brought a large white handkerchief to his face again and again. He never smiled, but once he yawned, and George saw the long rows of his tiny white teeth, child's teeth, that lined his gums both top and bottom. But his eyes were not a child's eyes. George kept his face a blank, his feelings held inward, his habit from long ago. They were penniless, the three of them, having escaped starvation in Russia only to see their little European tour arranged by a Russian friend fall to pieces. A few months before, in Berlin, Tamara had sold her hair to pay the hotel bill. She danced now with the short shelf of it swaying lissomely above her bare neck and arms, and George forgot to watch Diaghilev for a time. When he looked back, he found Diaghilev's eyes on him, reflective, meditative, and George allowed himself to be studied. He wanted to be bought. And so he was.

He became the ballet master of the world's most famous dance troupe, the Ballets Russes, and for it he would create his first masterpiece, *Apollo,* and yet when Diaghilev died, the company had fallen like spears of wheat, loosened, dancers lost, ballets lost. There was no stopping the unraveling. Ballets were like butterflies. George had redone enough of his own to know this, had lost enough that he had forgotten and could not restage. They could film him all they wanted, mark up the scores, commit to memory the steps, but still the ballets would slip away, as

Diaghilev had, the diabetic coma slowly stealing his breath. His coffin had floated on a barge down the canals of Venice, the handles of the coffin burnished silver, the box itself black and gold. Balanchine got the news in London where he was filming a dance number for a movie. One of the other dancers had bought a paper, saw the headline, came running.

SERGE PAVLOVITCH EST MORT

*H*E TOOK A CAB to his church, the Cathedral of Our Lady of the Sign, at Park Avenue and Ninety-second Street. He did this sometimes, more often this year than any other, took a cab over to stand downstairs in the small chapel before going to the theater, the windows open to Park Avenue, the street quiet and green. He liked the quiet, the polished parquet of the chapel floor laid in a herringbone pattern—no stone floor here in America—on the lectern, thin gilded legs like a young girl's, behind the altar, a simple iconostasis. The blue lights and the red bulbs of the votives burned steadily, safer than candles, their color a compensation for the wire filament. A minute went by. Two minutes. Three. He waited.

Perhaps he should have gone to Suzi's church on West Seventy-first Street, to gaze at the statue of the Virgin standing quietly in her niche, arms at her side, palms forward and open, that posture the one he had used for *Mozartiana*. If he were in St. Petersburg, he would go to the Cathedral of Our Lady of Kazan, where his father's choral music was sung, the voices of two hundred boys rising in pianissimo toward the apex of the cathedral, where angels and saints flew on the painted and gilded ceilings and clung to the tops of the columns. The boys gave voice to those winged creatures. High above the worship-pers, clotting the walls, hung enormous icons in great gilt frames, their solemn faces tilted down toward earth or tipped up toward heaven. American angels bore their wings outstretched like hawks, as if God were a mouse to be caught. Russian angels folded their wings, as if they were ascending a swift elevator to heaven. Russian angels decorated Tchaikovsky's elaborate stone monument in the Alexander Nevsky Monastery, one reading a book, the other bearing a cross, already on its way to God. The last year of his life, Tchaikovsky had composed the requiem for his own funeral. Strange comfort, to invent the last moments one's body would spend in the comfort of other bodies before being abandoned to the ground. You had that one last hour among them.

He too would do the same. A requiem. His own to Tchaikovsky's piece. His hand placed in Tchaikovsky's.

There would be a parade of angels across the stage, their wings a story high, a procession of monks swinging incense at the end of long chains, weeping mourners, and at the tail of the progression, a boy holding a candle like the ones he himself had carried about the church every Easter and every Christmas. Wax, wick, no glass, no wire, light pinched out by two fingers, by a sigh, by a breath. His mother and auntie had cautioned him and Andrei and his sister Tamara to hold their candles upright during the service. They, like all the women, would bring their candles home from the evening service on Holy Thursday. To bear them, still lit, down the street and over the threshold of their door was a good omen; the women then carried the can-dles into each room of their St. Petersburg apartment, lighting the candles by the icons, blessing the house, protection against evil, that little flame a power against the dark. Back in the doorway again his mother permitted him to hold what was left of the candle as it burned down.

On the stage, he would have the boy blow it out.

BEFORE HE WENT to the studios, he stopped by Karinska's shop to check on the progress of the costumes for *Mozartiana*. Karinska had been making costumes for him since 1932 in Europe, here since 1939, when she had a single cutting table in a room at the old School of American Ballet on Madison Avenue. They had grown old together in America, and now she had row upon row of cutting tables in a loft on Sixty-third Street near Lincoln Center and he had row upon row of beautiful dancers on the stage at the New York State Theater. They were all so beautiful it no longer mattered so much who was cast for what. They could all now do anything, were capable of everything, unlike the girls of the thirties and forties and fifties, when he had struggled to work with their limited techniques, to work around what they could not do. The racks of costumes that clothed them were rolled up against the walls, and everywhere were bolts of cloth and mesh, ribbons and braids, laces, jewels, buttons, gold and silver threads. Costumes were constantly being made and remade, reworked and refurbished as the girls who once wore them vanished, only to be replaced and replaced and replaced. They were shades, a flicker, reduced to a photograph, as he soon would be.

Behind him a sewing machine roared down the length of a satin bodice. At a table to the side, a piece of mesh yardage glinted with bright colored jewels, the tall many-paned windows all around him letting in long strips of morning light. In a minute he would tell Karinska what he wanted for the requiem.

Karinska would know a Russian angel. But for now, *Mozartiana*. Beneath the row of windows stood a line of dressmakers' dummies, their costumes for the ballet already basted together upon them, the tunics and shirts and bodices, some already skirted with thick bales of tulle, some not yet finished. The names of his dancers were pinned to the shoulders of the dummies, and George paced by the thin paper tags marked Castelli, d'Amboise, Andersen, Farrell. He paused there, by Suzanne's mannequin, the mannequin of his last great muse. He had made ballet after ballet for her, but this would be the last of the many ballets he had given her.

He touched the basted costume and began to fuss with its details, giving the skirt first the shape of a bell, then tugging away at the underskirting so the tulle lay flat. He pleated a few inches of muslin to puff the sleeves, tied a bit of velvet ribbon at the bodice, repinned the neckline. One of the seamstresses, a pincushion spiky with pins on her shoulder, left her machine to stand quietly by his side as he experimented, offering him various fabrics and notions. He could not get it right. He had had black costumes for the ballet in 1933, and then half-black, half-white ones in 1935, and then white alone in 1945, but none of that was right, none of the steps exactly right. Now he would have the right steps, the right color. For the first time, he was dressing Suzi in black. It would be his last ballet, his black ballet. He let his hands roam over the materials. Black tulle, black satin, black marquisette, black organza.

## FOUR

Even though it was almost dark when Sandra got home, her father wasn't back from school yet. She had told him she would be home by supper. She put her bag down on the gilded marble table in the entrance hall and called out. The lights were on in the dining room, but the living room was dark beyond its double doors, as were the hallway and the kitchen. If her dad were here, every light would be on, twenty lights. He had used her grandmother's money to buy this big rambling apartment in the Eldorado in 1971, when they first moved to New York from Mississippi, and by now it was worth a fortune. It even had a little maid's room off the kitchen where Adam would sleep when he stayed over. Back when they were both in school, Adam had lived here for weeks at a time. Her father had just been released from the hospital, and for months he had shuffled around the apartment as if he had a hood over his head and gloves on his hands, seeing nothing, feeling nothing. When Adam moved in, her dad never said anything about it, and when Adam went back to his parents' house, her father didn't say anything about that either. If Sandra woke up in the middle of the night from a bad dream, sweating and stumbling around in her nightgown trying to walk it off, Adam would be the only one who knew. He'd hear her out there in the kitchen and he'd get up, try to cajole her back to her bed, sit with her, comb her hair. She'd started bleaching her hair winter white around then, and it was so brittle that as he combed, little bits of hair would break off and litter her shoulders and spine.

She always knew when her father was going to be sick again. He'd sleep late, slap around the apartment in his soft bedroom slippers, grade papers slowly at the dining room table. Some mornings he'd wash and dry his pajamas and put them back on again, while they were still warm, then sit at the table, smoking vacantly in the clean clothes, staring at nothing. He could smoke a whole pack, sitting there. When it got dark he'd put on his long black overcoat and walk up and down Central Park West. All the doormen knew him. He'd wear the coat with this Russian fur hat, also black, and up there on his head it looked like some kind of small mammal sitting on snow; his hair was so light it almost wasn't blond, but silver. When Sandra was younger, back when they still lived in Mississippi, her grandmother would send her out after her father when he'd been gone walking too long. On those nights too he was just walking, walking away from himself, some self he'd left behind on the last block or on the sunporch or in her bedroom, where one minute ago he'd sat with red checkers in hand, studying the board, while she waited and waited for him to make his move, the move it became increasingly clear he wasn't going to make. Finally he'd say, *Excuse me, Sandra,* and that was it. She'd stack up the pieces and fold up the board and wait for her grandmother's call. Her dad always seemed surprised to see her when she emerged from the darkness in her shorts and pink flip-flops with the big mod flowers on the straps to tug at his hand.

She always prayed that when she found him he wouldn't be doing anything too bizarre, and mostly he wasn't. Mostly he'd just be strolling, but occasionally she'd find him staring off into the street, watching the traffic lights change, as if that were a truly fascinating thing, or staring into the lit windows of somebody else's house or looking over a fence at a garden full of hydrangeas or mums, which they had plenty of back at their own house. Even in July, when her great-uncle Isaac was scolding her too frugal grandmother—"Baby, you've *got* to put on your air"—her father would be out pressing himself into the dark, wet heat. He was probably out taking a walk right now.

She had always been afraid of being like her father. She could see he never felt the same way waking two mornings in a row. She was safe only in the studio, because the studio was always the same—the barres, the exercises, the teachers. Mr. B was always there, every day, up until the last few years, anyway. The women he'd danced with at the Imperial Ballet and at the Ballets Russes, Alexandra Danilova, Antonina Tumkovsky, Felia Doubrovska, were there too, every day, taking their students through the barre, through the center, through the divisions, and if they were lucky, onto the stage, where they would dance the ballets those women had danced, or some remade version of them. The purpose, the progression, the culmination were all clear.

But for her father there was no such clear progression. He was appointed to the Naval Academy and then quit plebe year, taking with him his black overcoat and his shame, went to Ole Miss and made it almost all the way to his doctorate before eloping with her mother, the dark girl with the crooked nose

and the smart mouth. He won a big history prize for his dissertation when he finally finished it, but her mother died and he
burned all his writing, started writing again and then stopped
because he hated himself for being able to do it, started and
stopped, published a book and stopped, and each time he
stopped, he faltered.

This past season, winter season, it had happened to her, too,
that faltering. For the first time, she'd found herself chopping
through the barre at company class, each exercise endlessly rep-
etitious; at night she'd stand on the stage, numb, her *Nutcracker*
costume stuck on her, looking at the tape marks on the stage
floor and wanting the whole thing to be over. She'd be so tired
after each performance she'd have to take a cab uptown, hearing
her grandmother's voice in her head, *Take the bus*. She'd just sit
on her bed once she got home, wearing her pink terry-cloth
robe, looking at the ornate mahogany furniture her grandmother had bought for her in Vicksburg and shipped north for
them when they moved. She'd take a cigarette from one of her
father's packs and smoke it, waiting to see if Adam would call
her from his hotel in Miami or Chicago or wherever, picking
the odd paper snowflake, shiny with flame retardant, from her
hair. She felt like she'd die while she waited for Adam to call
her, but she didn't know exactly why, what exactly was bother-
ing her, whether it was how many more years she would be
condemned to dance Snow, one of forty girls skating about in
white, pompon wand bobbing in hand, pelted by paper
snowflakes dropped from the catwalks, or how many more
months it might be until her dad got sick again and left her in
the apartment alone or how many more weeks it would be before Adam would come home and what he would want when
he did.

At least she knew the answer to one of these now. They had stayed up for hours last night in Adam's room. Adam knew exactly what he was doing, and she didn't know anything. He was experienced and she was not. She was small and idiotic and he had to tell her everything, *Use your hands like this, don't be scared, I'm not going to hurt you, give me your mouth, let me know if it doesn't feel good, hold on to me.* He was both her old friend and this new Adam, absolutely naked in his desire for her, no backing away from it, no pretending that this was not what he meant. He wanted her and she yielded to him, wanting him to have whatever he wanted, and while he took it, they professed their love for each other again and again. It seemed they couldn't tire of it, some compulsion driving them to repeat the sentence, to speak it with amazement, with pleasure, with conviction.

But they had been quiet together this morning when they came back up to the loft, drenched with rain, and she had, at that moment, hated him. They undressed in his room without speaking. Adam put on his favorite comfort clothes, his old blue sweatpants and a black flannel shirt, and she put on some clothes he offered her, silently, another soft shirt and a pair of his old jeans from the ninth grade that were still way too big for her, a pair he had to loop one of his belts about, drawing it tight to knot it for her before the pants would stay up. Then they sat hidden in his room until Joe, Randall, and Frankie had gone, until she and Adam had the big place to themselves. Eventually, they played board games at the long dining room table. They did this all afternoon, playing first Stratego, then Monopoly, and finally a furiously paced double solitaire. She beat him at every game. She could do something better than he could. They had played together like this for years, for mindless amusement. It was familiar, and their argument floated free of them as they played. When it was time for her to leave, they kissed and kissed in the elevator, at the opened door of her cab, Adam's tongue and lips so soft, a softness that barely disguised their greediness, until she thought he might climb in and ride uptown with her.

She went down the dark back hallway past the chaos of her own room, with the green toile everywhere and the big, solid suite of mahogany furniture, and looked in her dad's bedroom, just to be sure he wasn't there. He wasn't. He had the smaller room with no view; her room, like the living room, looked out over Central Park. His bed was still made up, the coverlet with the pompon fringe smooth and untouched. Sandra went down the hall to her dad's study in back, but he wasn't there either, just his books and papers and photographs and old maps. He was supposed to be working on a book about the siege of Vicksburg in the summer of 1863, but Sandra suspected he hadn't written much of it yet. She wasn't sure if he had even started.

She sat down at his desk, amid the engravings of Vicksburg and the facsimiles of soldiers' letters and photographs of a hundred years ago in which Pemberton's men looked as alive and vivid as men walking the streets and hills of Vicksburg today. A framed photo of her parents, taken on their wedding day, 1961, sat on her father's desk, too. They'd eloped to the courthouse right across the street from her grandmother's house, and then her parents walked back across Jackson Street and announced what they'd done. Her mother's sister, Adele, snapped their picture with a Kodak camera. By the time Sandra was born six months later, both her parents had left school and moved into her grandmother's house, where, bankrolled by his new father-in-law, her dad spent all day on the sunporch, writing his dissertation. Then he went a week without sleeping, took twenty thousand dollars of her mother's inheritance, and bought a black

Mercedes sedan. Her mother had him committed. Two weeks later, while Sandra slept in a crib in the back bedroom, her mother was killed in that car, plowed it into a tree.

None of this could be foreseen in that wedding photograph. Her mother's face would always be for Sandra that face, but her dad's face had been so changed: too much electroshock therapy, too many drugs, too much time spent in self-loathing and solitude. For two decades her dad had been alone, repelling the women drawn to his beauty and his talent, repelling them when they came too close. Love was so frightening that her father preferred to live without it—or so powerful he could have no other. He wasn't handsome anymore, but still his face was arresting. Mr. B's face looked so serene in his old age. There was so little that was serene about her father.

She turned the picture of her parents facedown. And then she heard her dad open the front door. She listened for a minute to hear if he would come down the hall to his study. But he didn't. When she came out, she saw him sitting at the piano in the living room, alone, still wearing his coat and hat, playing Schumann. He smiled to see her. She came and sat next to him on the bench and watched his hands move. He had beautiful hands. He had the music set out and she read along while he played and she turned the pages for him. It was a piece Balanchine had used last in *Davidsbündlertänze,* one of a group of pieces to which Mr. B had set several couples, each pair moving in their own small world, not quite connecting to the other couples. It was a ballet full of grief and fear and madness and unrequited love. The end of love. A farewell to love. It was a hard ballet for Mr. B to make. Sandra had heard he'd walked out of rehearsal one day before he'd even started working, all eight principal dancers gathered there in the studio to learn a dance Mr. B couldn't find it in himself to do. Ten minutes later he came back, choreographed the whole thing. He was seventy-five years old and he was saying good-bye to the impulse that had driven him through life: the worship of a woman's beauty, the celebration and display of it. Her father had said good-bye to all that when he was twenty-six. Balanchine was on his second marriage at that age, and he would marry more women after that, but her father had had nothing more, no one more, his soul scraped black.

She leaned her head on her dad's shoulder and felt the movements of it as he played. What was he thinking about, his own madness, his own wife? Sandra was in his way, but she knew he wouldn't ask her to move. The notes seemed to vibrate in the air around them, palpable enough to reach for, skimming over the couches and tables and chairs and lamps, sticking to the draperies, beating against the windows.

$I$N THE WINGS of State Theater, Sandra lined up with the other girls for their entrance in *Vienna Waltzes,* one of the most beautiful creations in the company's repertoire—and she danced in its most beautiful section, the last, to waltzes from Richard Strauss's *Der Rosenkavalier.* When Mr. B discovered none of them could waltz, he made *Vienna Waltzes* for them as a lesson, and that lesson had become another masterpiece, an audience favorite. It was a company favorite, too, because it was so beautiful and because of the shoes. They didn't have to dance on pointe. For the Strauss they were outfitted in heeled dancing shoes, white satin ball gowns with layers of under ruffles, long white gloves, and jeweled wigs—all of them made brunette for the occasion, a stage full of dark-haired girls for Balanchine. And the boys were just as glamorously costumed, in tuxedos with tails, ruffled shirtfronts, and short white gloves. No flesh would touch as they danced.

The fetish of the glove, the dropped glove, the glove as keepsake was behavior Sandra had not been fully able to understand until yesterday. She had brought home the shirt she borrowed from Adam, had slept in it last night, had worn it to rehearsal and class today, had made up in it, and had only just taken it off. She wished she were dancing with Adam tonight as she had the other night, that he waited for her in the wings in his tuxedo, that it was his face that would look into hers, his gloved hands that would slide along her arms, hold her waist. His hands had been around her waist that night, against her upper back, at her elbows, between her thighs, as he stroked and prodded her into the series of lifts and turns and slow poses through which Swanilda and Franz unfold and consummate their love. Her hair had been loose and long and it had slid between them, catching in his fingers, sticking to his shirt buttons and to his arms. Her clothing, too, had made rough obstacles, her T-shirt bunching up in his hands as he supported her in pirouette, her pant legs crackling and whipping against his calves as her legs moved between his legs, slapping at his face when he raised her high above him. Their dance had been awkward and clumsy and addictive and exhilarating. She would move in front of him, commandeering the lead, and then he'd force her to relinquish it as he pushed her body off the ground and into the air or bent her over his arms or along his back. She had no choice but to relinquish the lead, relinquish everything. Adam owned her body, ruled it, made it do what he wanted it to. She had never danced with anyone so accomplished. But Adam would be sitting in the audience tonight, not dancing with her. It was his turn to watch her.

She stood there in the wings pulling on her gloves, careful not to touch her hands to her hips until the gloves were safely on. If they soiled the fabric with the oils from their skin, Madame Pourmel, the wardrobe mistress, got upset and they'd hear about it later. Certain objects were sacred at NYCB—costumes, props, even the pianos in the studios. The pianos were not ledges for ballet bags, and the costumes were for princesses, not for the oily fingers and hands of human girls.

The girls and boys from the fourth section, "Gold and Silver," took their calls, and then the stage emptied and darkened, and the trees were raised, which never happened without the hushed gasp of the audience. With each dance, the ballet grew progressively more elegant, until the forest clearing became, at last, a grand ballroom, the roots of the raised trees lit up like elaborately tangled chandeliers. The mirrors hung along the back of the stage reflected the crystal lights and Viennese society at the height of its luxury and sensuality. Behind her, her partner, a boy from the corps like her, readied himself, his hands at her waist. Mr. B stood with Suzanne in his wing, the first wing, downstage right, the spot from which he watched every ballet. Suzanne's gown, a white dress similar to Sandra's own, was made even more beautiful by the necklace, which hung, weblike and glinting; the worked bodice; and the headpiece, which always looked to Sandra like a jeweled spider. Mr. B had had the seamstress embroider a tiny silver rose on the underside of Suzanne's train for her to see each time she bent to lift her skirt.

And then the music surged from the pit and Sandra was out there in the hot wet air, her partner's hand on her back as they began the first of the waltzes, a slow walk about the stage, which was unusually glittery and romantic tonight. Because of his vision problems, Mr. B had been asking for the lights to be brighter and brighter, complaining he couldn't see, until they'd all begun to feel as if they were performing in a gymnasium. But not tonight. Sandra didn't have much experience with partnering—in the corps her main duties were spacing and synchronization—and because she was partnered rarely, she was still ridiculously afraid of falling or being dropped, and so she never stretched the movements to their fullest dimension. Dancing in the loft with Adam, she had let go of that fear; he had the strength and the experience that enabled her to let go. With him, nothing bad could happen. But letting go was addictive, and having done it once, she wanted to do it again. What was ordinarily a rote trek around the stage, carefully measured to avoid a collision with another couple, became tonight a few minutes' opportunity to seduce her partner—not the boy with his arm around her waist, but the one out there in the audience. She was aware of her bare neck and her bare breasts and her bare upper arms, and she wanted to display them all for Adam, let him look at what he wanted.

She could see other people looking from the wings: the stagehands who liked to watch this ballet, the corps members from the last movement or two, Mr. B. His head tilted, he watched them, wearing those strange glasses, the frames with one black lens and the other one clear, the glasses he'd worn off and on since his cataract operation. Even with one eye he saw things no one else could, could divine capabilities within a dancer she herself was unaware of. That night, it seemed to her his head was turned in her direction, that his one eye followed her around the stage.

And then they were off and Suzanne was left there alone, dancing almost by herself because her waltz is meant to be danced with a dream lover. She moved, and occasionally her partner joined her for a moment and vanished, and Suzanne alone in her beautiful dress was reflected a hundred times in the mirrors, as if Balanchine couldn't get enough of her. He had wanted her for his sixth wife. Her partner entered and exited. When Suzanne married a boy from the company in 1969, Mr. B was in Europe, and his grief was so terrible he didn't want to come back to the thing he loved even more than he loved her, his company. NYCB was nothing to him without her. But it wasn't he who left the company, it was she. Six years later she came back, and in every ballet Balanchine made for her before and since, he was her true partner; whatever boy was cast was shadowed by his ghost. She was always dancing with Balanchine, for Balanchine. On the stage now, she danced with him, for him, and her yearning after this dream, her efforts to make the dream palpable, were terrible and beautiful to watch.

THE STAGE DOOR at State Theater was not a very impressive thing. Behind a low concrete wall at Sixty-second Street and Columbus, a small stairwell led down to the door, behind it a tiny linoleum-block foyer and a guard with a buzzer at a metal desk. Adam met her at the top of the stairwell, wearing the black beret he'd bought on Ballet Theatre's European tour last year. Between that and the long dark coat, he looked entirely un-American, and the klatch of fans waiting at the stage door kept turning to stare at him uncertainly, with vague recognition. How was it she had been friends with Adam all this time and been immune to his beauty? That was Adam, that was just the way he looked, but now, suddenly, she was aware of how others looked at him. She ducked her head, and when she reached him, he got down on one knee and kissed the inside of her wrist, as he had the other night. He wanted her to remember that night.

The little crowd around the door was watching them now, and two young girls began to approach, thinking, probably, that Sandra was one of the ballerinas in the company, the blond Karin von Aroldingen. Who else could inspire such treatment? Sandra didn't turn her head, and her posture seemed to freeze them. How surprised they would be if she signed her name in their programs. *Sandra Ellis, who's that?* Then, when they discovered she was just a dancer from the corps, they'd consider their programs ruined. Even Sandra, as a little girl, had collected the autographs and signed pointe shoes of only the principal ballerinas.

"Sandra, you were shining out there," Adam said. "The old man must be blind." And he held a hand up over one eye, covering it like the dark lens of Mr. B's glasses.

She started to laugh despite herself, it seemed so disrespectful, and thought about telling him how Mr. B had seemed to look at her tonight, not just at the beginning of the ballet but later, too, during the big waltz. But she wasn't sure enough about it, so she said nothing, and Adam stood and offered her his arm. They walked together over to the Empire Hotel coffee shop, a company hangout of sorts—it was right across from the theater. Adam held the door open for her and as she walked in and headed for a table in the back, she could see everybody's eyes flicking swiftly to Adam behind her, then shifting to her, and then back to Adam. It was weird and embarrassing, this attention, even peripherally. It was as if a movie star had walked in behind her. And then she realized that to the crowd of dancers—and to the balletomanes and dance critics who came in here after a performance hoping to overhear dancers in conversation or to watch dancers eating dinner or whatever thing they came in here to do—Adam *was* a movie star, no longer just one of a roster of principal dancers at NYCB, but Adam LaSalle of American Ballet Theatre, the American Nureyev. He'd been making an enormous impression this past year at ABT and his reviews had been adulatory, tremendous. And what's more, he wasn't embarrassed by the attention, he was enjoying it, it was one of the perks of the stardom he'd chased. He was staring at her as they sat down, wanting her to acknowledge the stir—yet another weird dimension to their relationship, which had already gotten weird enough. He was famous, he was gorgeous, they'd been naked together, and now they were sitting in a public place, people were staring at him, and at her, wondering what she was to him.

Whatever she was, she was sure to be a disappointment to them, because unlike Adam, she preferred to be nondescript. As a child she had been so pretty that wherever she went she was stared at and petted. Old ladies would grab at her hair and stroke her face. By the time she entered her teens she'd already decided she was not going to put on makeup and tube tops like the other girls, and she knew she wouldn't put flowers and snoods in her hair for class, nor would she pin her leotards into a V in front or cut them low in the back, so low that Madame Danilova would say to the other girls, "Your mother buy and you cut. I even see your tights. You want me to see your tights?" She didn't want the attention the other girls seemed to solicit, the attention Adam craved.

She looked over the menu to avoid everybody's eyes; when Mr. B came in here he always ordered a sandwich of his own design, never off the menu—feta cheese and tomato or his own version of a club. Adam got coffee. She ordered a steak. This was the only time of day she was actually hungry and really had time to eat a meal. The rest of the day she was rushing from class to rehearsal to the theater. Eventually the others in the diner stopped staring at them, and Adam held out his hand for hers, even though they were surrounded not only by strangers, but also by colleagues—his former, her current—who would, of course, take note of the gesture. Their friendship had long been a subject of speculation. She gave Adam her hand and he sat there holding it, his thumb making slow circles on her palm. Around them she could hear bits of conversation—about Karin and how beautifully she'd danced tonight with her partner in the uniform of an officer, about the girl in "Gold and Silver" who lost her earring, which was rolled and kicked across the stage until finally somebody, with a brisk connection of heel to earring, shot it off to the wings—but she couldn't focus on it, she was lost, something warm at the base of her spine, and the whole time Adam was just looking at her and stroking her hand. And then the glass door up front by the cash register swung open, and Mr. B walked in with Suzanne.

He stood there a moment, looking around the room at the tables and the place got quiet for a second—*That's George Balanchine!*—and when Mr. B's gaze reached all the way toward the back where Sandra was seated, she started and jerked her hand away from Adam's. She watched as Mr. B took a table at the front with Suzanne, and Adam pivoted around in his seat to see what she was staring at. When he turned back to her he said, "What?"

She shrugged. She didn't really know why she'd pulled her hand away. She could feel her face flushing. Adam sat back and shoved a saltine cracker into his mouth, his eyes on her. She knew he was staring at her and yet she couldn't look at him. Her eyes were constantly drawn to Mr. B and Suzanne twenty feet away at the front table. Mr. B was still wearing the jacket and the silk cravat he'd worn to watch *Vienna Waltzes,* and Suzanne had wrapped about her shoulders the black floral shawl she wore all the time, and had let her hair down. Her hair was thin, flat, brown, not as long as Sandra's, just past her shoulders. Suzanne looked, at this distance, like a girl, and to Mr. B, looking at Suzanne from the far end of the telescope of his great age, she would always be a girl. He had discarded his wives one by one as they journeyed deep into their twenties, but now that he had passed his seventh decade, thirty-five was still youthful to him. Adam's coffee and Sandra's steak arrived, which she cut and ate, but she didn't know it. Mr. B leaned closer to Suzanne; Suzanne lifted her eyes to the waitress. His lips moved as Suzanne stirred her coffee, and he gestured at her with one hand. How could she not look at him? Suzanne put down her spoon, used a finger to hook her hair behind her ear. Then, finally, Suzanne turned her face to Mr. B and they sat, looking at each other quietly. Mr. B closed his lips over his teeth and raised his chin. And then Sandra couldn't see anymore because Adam stood up abruptly, blocking her view, threw down a fifty, and without a word strode from the restaurant, setting all the crockery and glasses and silverware on their table rattling before her.

She wanted to jump up and run out after him, but she also didn't want Mr. B to see her doing this. Or Suzanne. Or anybody. She put down her fork and waited a minute, a couple of minutes, but not too long because she didn't want the waitress to come back. By the time she made it outside, she couldn't see Adam. She walked a few feet in the direction of the Eldorado—she and Adam sometimes stayed over at her place when they were both performing—but Adam wasn't up ahead. And then she looked down Broadway and saw him striding toward a cab, his arm raised. Adam had gotten the door open when he heard her calling his name and he turned. He saw her, but he kept hold of the cab door, not getting in the cab, but not letting it go either. He would wait for her, though, she saw that.

"Why did you walk out of there?" she asked when she reached him. He turned his head. He wasn't going to answer, it was obvious why he'd walked out of there, it was obvious why she had pulled her hand from his. "Adam." She was afraid to try to touch him now, so she touched the door of the cab.

"It's not right, you know," he said without looking at her, "the way you all preserve yourselves for him. You're not his fucking harem."

"That's not fair."

"No? Is it fair that Farrell's husband can't be with her? Can't even be in the same city with her? That Balanchine pretends he doesn't exist and so does she?"

"That's a special case," she said. But maybe it wasn't. For years Balanchine had called Karin von Aroldingen's husband *your other half,* couldn't bring himself to say his name.

"No. It's not a special case. It's the same case for all the girls in the inner circle, all the ones he's chosen. Maybe for them there are compensations. But what about for the rest of you—the ones he doesn't know exist? Are you required to pretend as well?"

She looked down a minute, and as she did, she felt the cab door jerk away from beneath her hand. Adam had read her gesture as hesitation, and maybe he was right. In one gesture, he'd gotten in the cab and had shut the door behind him. The cab was already heading downtown, away from her. He was going back to Hell's Kitchen. Maybe. Or maybe he was going somewhere else. Where? He had a whole life she didn't know anything about. He knew everything about her, but there was so much she didn't know about him. The heat of the cab was still in her hands. She put them in her pockets. She was stupid, she hadn't said the right thing, she didn't know how to act, but she knew this: She should have been in that cab with him, not standing on the curb across from the empty plaza of Lincoln Center.

IN HELD AUDITORIUM at Barnard, her dad had no painted backdrop, no soft lighting, no costume, nothing interesting to look at, just a few dull props—his papers, his books, his gold-rimmed reading glasses. Yet the audience watched him as he fumbled up there on the low stage. Once he started his lecture, he'd be okay, but this part, just before he began, which for Sandra was the part spent hidden in the wings, was unbearable for him. And, therefore, for her. All around her, people held books in their laps for her father to sign, and practically every one of those people had asked her if the seat next to hers was taken. She had saved the seat for Adam, but she knew now he wasn't going to show. She had called and called him last night when she got home from the coffee shop, but there was no answer at the loft, and between rehearsals she had called him today, the receptionist at ABT taking three messages from Sandra before she was too embarrassed to call again. Adam didn't want to speak to her, she had ruined everything, he had probably gone off with some normal girl, she couldn't even blame him. She was miserable, and she kept fidgeting, crossing her legs and arms and then uncrossing them, and she couldn't keep herself from turning around to see if Adam might be sitting somewhere in the back. The auditorium was full. Her father had a following.

At last her dad put on his glasses and began to talk about the summer of 1863, about the bodies of the Federals that lay for days rotting and swelling in the Mississippi sun after two foiled assaults against the Vicksburg bluffs, the sight and stench of the men unbearable to the Confederates who had shot them down, until finally Pemberton sent a message to Grant: "In the name of humanity I have the honor to propose a cessation of hostilities for two hours and a half, that you may be enabled to remove your dead and dying men." In the weeks that followed, to escape the incessant Union shelling, Vicksburgians packed up their oriental carpets and their chairs and their feather beds and took up residence in hillside caves, laid out their suppers while the checkerboard city was punched with fire. Now and then as he spoke, her father squinted through his reading glasses or looked over them at the auditorium. She raised her chin at him. It was going well. He gave her a half-smile and looked back at his notes. All around her, Sandra could feel the audience falling into that place and time, gliding over the dark streets and the ravaged bluffs, breathing the smell of magnolia and mortar as it rose on a current, crawling into a dirt cave, led there by his voice, though it did not have the vowels and consonants of Vicksburg, but the sharpened twang of Memphis. When her father spoke, he forgot where he was, forgot he hated public speaking. He didn't mind lecturing at home. He'd basically educated her through recitation. The Gettysburg Address. *The Rape of the Lock.* The Psalms. She'd barely paid attention at Professional Children's, hadn't even graduated, having made it only partway through the eleventh grade. Even before she was taken into the company, she didn't have time to study for tests or pore over the pages of her algebra book—or any book. She took three ballet classes a day, ran over to PC between them, eating an apple and a sandwich on the way, wet tights sticking to her jeans. Nothing she learned over there was of any importance to her, to any girl in D Division, or to Mr. B.

Halfway through the lecture her dad lost his place, right in the middle of a sentence, and stood staring out toward the back of the room. At first she thought he was pausing for dramatic effect, but as the pause lengthened, embarrassingly, into a full-scale stop, it became clear something was wrong. He lifted one brow, as if something surprised him, but otherwise didn't move, and when he did eventually begin once again to speak, it was not about the summer of 1863. Because of her panic, it took her a while to understand he was talking about a different summer, the summer she was ten, the summer before they moved to New York. Her father had sat in the car in the wooden garage out back, garage doors shut, gunning the motor, until Grandmother sent Aunt Patsy out and called the fire department. Most of the rest of that August he spent in the hospital, and Sandra spent it hiding in the basement. She didn't like her bedroom anymore. Her grandmother had just bought her the new mahogany suite as a bribe to keep her in Vicksburg, and the pieces looked to Sandra like monster roaches. Her old bedroom furniture had been piled in the basement, in the corner, and Sandra would go down there to sit with it, the white bureau and headboard with the gold gilt flowers, the white vanity, everything all laid out as it had been upstairs. Except it was there, in the unfinished part of her grandmother's basement. She couldn't know then her father would come back, that her grandmother would concede upon his return that he could, after all, accept the post at Columbia, that the two of them would move to New York, that she would buy them an apartment and give them an allowance because her grandmother considered her father's salary a pittance. All she knew then was fear, and so she sought comfort. Sitting on her old bed, which had once been dressed in layers of white tulle and chiffon, Sandra would stare into her grandfather's basement office, by then abandoned—at the black dial phone on his metal desk, around which were arranged five gawky floor lamps with yellowing fabric shades. The long extension cords for the lamps disappeared into the dark perimeters of the office, headed for electrical outlets Sandra couldn't see. At the edges of the oriental carpet sat thronelike chairs, grouped in coteries. Behind the desk rose a wall of files; several feet before it was a partition with a glass pane in it, dividing this part of the basement from the furnace. From this spot, her grandfather had run his businesses—the properties, novelties, jukeboxes, taxi service, and occasional money lending that had made him a small fortune. On Sundays, before her grandfather died, the men had played poker down there, all of them in the shiny black suits of elderly Southern gentlemen.

But her father was not remembering her summer. He was remembering his own—the hospital ward with the gray vinyl sofas in the visiting room where she'd seen him once in his hospital pajamas, crying. Why was he thinking about this? She uncrossed her legs and put her feet flat on the floor, inched forward in her chair. She was going to have to make him look at her, she was going to have to say *Dad*. The audience coughed and shifted uneasily and she was just about to open her mouth when it seemed her father slowly became aware of all this, for he stopped talking and removed his glasses, polished them with the end of his tie, put them back on and looked straight into her anxious face. She mouthed it: *Dad*. He cleared his throat and turned back to the papers on the lectern. And he began again, reading in the sonorous, professorial voice that let her know that while his lips described the festering ooze the Mississippi had become as it fell in the June heat, his mind roamed widely else-where. At the end of it all, her father closed his books and notes and acknowledged the applause, and Sandra stayed in her seat still sweating while people flooded the podium, where her father signed his name over and over again in the flyleaves of the books he had authored. He never looked at her.

When the room emptied, Sandra waited, watched her father put his books and papers into his black leather satchel. Then he looked up, and he stood there a moment, his expression naked and bewildered, and Sandra felt a big wide belt buckle snap itself tightly across her chest. When he came and sat beside her, she saw his hands were trembling against the brass latch on his briefcase. She put out one of her hands and held his, and they listened together to the last of the noises from the hallway—footsteps, voices, the odd door. Her father cleared his throat.

"That summer," her father began, "I felt I had become some-thing really unspeakable."

She wanted to say something, but nothing came out, just a se-ries of dry clicks.

"When do you go to Saratoga?" he asked.

"July," she said. "Why?"

"Because I believe," her father said, "that I'm about to be-come unspeakable once again."

He lowered his head, and with her free hand she touched his face.

USUALLY HE SPOKE little about the work, but this after-noon Mr. B was in a garrulous mood. Forty of them had been called to the main rehearsal hall for a "new ballet," another bal-let for the Tchaikovsky Festival.

For this ballet, Mr. B explained, he was using the last movement of Tchaikovsky's Sixth Symphony, which he told them
was "the De Profundis, how we all end up." He described the
music for them in his high nasal voice: the blizzard of woodwinds, the burial hymn "Repose the Soul" that brought everyone in the Russian Orthodox church to their knees to weep
beside the open coffin, to the realization, as he put it, that, "This
man is dead." Then came the trombones and tubas, and as the
melody died down, the strings and woodwinds made the last
sounds—"everything stops, as if a man is going into the grave.
Going, going, gone. The end."

Mr. B explained that most of them were to be dressed in
hooded gowns, dark gowns of deep red, burgundy, black, with
golden sleeves, and that they would wear gold masks over their
faces. After them, in the middle of the movement, a dozen angels would appear, dressed in white, with enormous wings and
golden hair, perhaps holding lilies. Girls with garlands, their hair
down, would float out after the angels, and at the end of the
movement, a group of prostrate monks in black would make the
shape of a beating heart slowing to a stop. They were to be the
mourners, angels, and monks—a funeral procession. That wasn't
how it all ended up, finally, but that was what he told them that
day, and the girls began looking at one another. Ballet was not
supposed to be about death, but about a beauty so artificial and
so perfect it existed in a hemisphere apart from death.

Sandra stood there and listened to him speak, his white hair
blown back from his face heavy with age, and she felt very
young in her twenty-year-old body and very far away from him.
This was what she had been wanting for years, to be in a studio
with Mr. B when he was making a new ballet, but now, because
of her father, there was no pleasure in it. They had walked home

last night holding hands, and she had felt as if they were walking into a black wall that could not be avoided. Her father did not go to bed until very late; she got up once to look for him, but when she found him she could not speak a word. He was seated at the piano, smoking and talking, to no one, to himself, to her grandmother, to his mother, to her mother, arguing with them, pleading with them. She recognized the sounds. She stood outside the big living room doors that were slid partway shut, and listened. She stood there until he finished talking and got busy solely with his cigarettes, and then she went and lay on her bed in a cold sweat. And even though she happened to be standing now in a long shaft of light that fell from one of the high studio windows, she felt just as cold and panicked. She wrapped her arms across her body and held herself. And at just that moment, Mr. B turned toward her and said, "Angels will have golden hair and tall wings," and he demonstrated with his arms, not out, but up. He was staring at her, lit as she was, and she was not prepared for this, had not even been paying attention, and she drew in her breath, knowing he was seeing both her and the illuminated angel of his imagination. She couldn't think, all thought blasted out of her, couldn't move, not even to make herself stand straighter, as an angel might. His stare was penetrating.

"Take down your hair," he instructed her, and as all the other girls turned to look at her, she did, pulling out many blond hairpins and then, finally, a rubber band. Her hair fell in a thin sheet to her waist. She stood there holding the handful of pins as the company girls looked at her too, tried to figure out what he thought of her, their heads whipping from her to Mr. B and back again. "Russian angel," he said finally, satisfied, and then he turned to show them how they were to walk in two lines, organizing their columns to have them make a procession across the big open space, gesturing to the rehearsal pianist to begin playing. *Mozartiana* would open the festival and this ballet, *Adagio Lamentoso,* would close it.

They began to move, Sandra walking blindly, Mr. B at the head of them; he turned occasionally to make sure they were following him, demonstrating exactly what was to be done. He was working so quickly now, Sandra was afraid even to take a minute to put her hair back up, and she walked with the pins in her hand, trying not to make a conspicuous fist around them. The movement was only nine minutes long, and to most of it there was simply walking and posturing. In front of them, Mr. B said, Karin would grieve and mourn. She was one of Mr. B's favorite dancers. She could act. She knew how to use a stage. At the last bars, Mr. B paused. Here, he said, he would have boy, a beautiful small boy, stand on the darkened stage and blow out a single candle. They all knew at once: *That boy is Mr. B,* and a small, sick feeling of unease stirred past them. Mr. B was anticipating his own death, blowing out his own candle, the way the mourners did theirs at the end of the Russian Orthodox funeral service. Dead. Gone. Her father was sick and Mr. B was going to die and she would have nothing without them, her whole world would go dark.

aryshnikov was coaching him in *Don Quixote,* in the role of Basil, a new role for Baryshnikov, that of coach, and a new role for Adam, yet another one. Adam stood behind this small but fabulously made dancer to imitate the sharp turn of the head and the stylized arms of the Spanish-flavored dance. Adam was tall and he envied Misha's compact build, the tight, small poses he assumed, held, broke, with such staccato plasticity. The rehearsal was not going well, and not only because of the difficult steps. He wanted to be doing this, had followed Baryshnikov to ABT to be doing this, had watched Baryshnikov walk out on Mr. B and NYCB after trying the place out for just a season or two, and had thought, *I could do that. I could leave.* Baryshnikov made it seem easy. But it was not easy to be a Baryshnikov. Behind him Adam worked and at the same time he struggled to console himself: he would be taller and therefore nobler, his movements grander and more expansive. Eventually. Meanwhile, he struggled for the clean preparations and soft landings for which Kirov dancers were famous. He was tired, the demands of the past year, the long series of new roles he'd had to master stacked up behind him like teetering dominoes, and he still had a month of performances ahead of him at the Met for their New York season, the company's most important.

Today he wore two sets of warmers over his legs to keep his muscles heated and flexible during the short periods when he and Misha would stop and talk through the steps, stop and move, stop and move, difficult on the body, the periodic cooling and stiffening of the muscles, which were then called upon to spring fully into action. He shook out his legs, shifted his weight from one foot to the other as he watched Baryshnikov mark the next sequence. He was watching, but he wasn't concentrating. His mind was on Sandra and what had happened between them the other night. He bent forward and curled his back. It seemed like every part of him was aching. He'd spent every day the past year with the company's physical therapist, getting massage and ultrasound as his body made the adjustment from the kind of roles he did at City Ballet to those he danced here at Ballet Theatre. And the adjustment was not only physical—these roles called for a range of emotional expression, basically the acting that Balanchine had so abhorred. *Don't act. Don't project anything. Just dance, dear.* At Ballet Theatre, Baryshnikov was always asking him to emote—how do you feel here as you extend your arm, as you approach your Kitri, as you hoist your body in that circle about the stage—are you crushed, enamored, playful, confident, melancholic?

Playing all these different emotions this past year had prodded and poked at his own. At City Ballet he had been aloof, from other dancers and on the stage. He had been promoted almost immediately upon joining the company, and soon after that, things had begun to change for him: the other dancers stood back and let him take the center row in class, he was deferred to in the canteen, when he passed in the studio hallways there was a small silence and then behind him the conversation picked up. By the end of his first year he had begun to substitute for Peter Martins as Suzanne Farrell's partner, his own coolness considered a good match for Farrell's. Balanchine had liked the way they looked together, their bodies together yet not quite together, moving within the same quiet orbit, elegant and private. But here his connections with his ballerinas were visceral and direct—they flirted and kissed and laughed and anguished with each other and for each other—and because of it Adam had begun to want this kind of color in his own life: love, anguish, rage.

When he was upset or angry with his parents, dance was a place to dive away from them, but, he was discovering, dancing was no balm when it was Sandra who'd disturbed him. He forgot steps, couldn't focus, found his usual, impeccable balance mysteriously withheld from him. He'd done a shitty thing to her, not returning her calls, not showing up at her dad's reading. He had actually made it all the way uptown, but then he turned around and went home. He was ashamed of the impulse, but he wanted her to know, if just for twenty-four hours, what it felt like to have his affection withheld as she had withheld hers from him. At the Empire, it was as if he had vanished, her eyes fixed on the point in space behind him occupied by Balanchine. He'd stood it until he couldn't stand it any longer—it went on and on, what did she think would happen if she kept staring at Mr. B, that he would rise from his chair and anoint her? Or perhaps she knew nothing would happen at all, she wouldn't even be noticed, and that was why she could stare at him, unblinking as a detective, secure in her cover. She was one of a hundred girls vying for Balanchine's now wavering attention, arraying themselves before him like flowers. Finally, he had to get up from the table, at first just intending to go to the men's room, but as soon as he was on his feet he realized he needed to leave the restaurant entirely.

Outside, he had paced up and down, thinking surely Sandra would follow him, and then finally he started walking down Broadway, eventually raising his arm for a cab. He was so angry with her that he thought for a minute about going to the small studio apartment of this red-haired girl in ABT's corps or down to the East Village for the boy he'd been with on the European tour. But he ended up going home, to his stupid room that seemed even more kidlike than ever before and where he finally had to beat off like a fifteen-year-old in order to sleep. He'd had little sleep again last night, and today—today was a failure. He was like one of those bumbling men in the evening adult class, pathetic, uncoordinated, and boundlessly eager. Scratch the eager. Just pathetic and uncoordinated. He knew if he was going to survive this—this relationship, this day, this rehearsal—he'd have to set things right with Sandra.

Adam walked to the back barre to steal a drink from his water bottle, and through the double studio doors he could see the face of Alexander Godunov, like Baryshnikov another Russian defector, who would alternate with him in the role of Basil. If Adam couldn't master it, Godunov would do all the New York performances at the Met this spring. Well, fuck it. Let him. Adam was sick of this speeding train he was on.

"Is like this, Adam," Misha called, and he spun the series of eight pirouettes that Adam had not yet been able to spin, ending on one knee, head thrown back, as if by demonstrating it well enough and often enough, his own perfection would throw itself at Adam and stick there. The studio doors swung open and in strode Godunov, ready for *his* rehearsal, taking over the studio as if he owned it. Godunov, with his thousands-of-dollars-per-performance pay, wasn't half the dancer Adam was. His technique was spotty, his feet not quite refined, but he had the cachet of the Russian dancer, and because of this and his dramatic defection, the hours-long standoff at JFK, and the black leather pants and the big gold medallions worn on chains about his neck and his appearance on Johnny Carson and his movie-star girlfriend, he sold tickets; Baryshnikov put his name up on the casting list again and again. ABT was run on the star system, had always been run on the star system, the old director, the million-airess Miss Chase, running the place like some modern-day Diaghilev, stocking the company with big-name defectors and foreign guest artists, unlike New York City Ballet, where Balanchine and his ballets were the stars, no published casting in advance for his programs. No stars. No princes. That's why Adam had come here, to be a prince, to be a star, but there weren't enough spotlights to go around.

"Tomorrow, Adam," Misha said. "We work again tomorrow."

Adam nodded and dragged his bag out the door and down the hall toward the men's dressing room, all the dancers streaming around him, 2 P.M., changing studios for the next rehearsal, his big satchel heavy with shoes and tights and warmers and sweatshirts and bottles of water and pills—his favorites the Dexedrine he sometimes took at the end of a long day to help him get through the evening's performance, when adrenaline didn't seem like it was going to be enough. The studios were as large as the studios of NYCB, some even larger, but strung from the ceilings here were the long tubular hoses of the building's ventilation system, brightly painted. In one studio, the girls were rehearsing the mazurka from *Coppélia*; in another, the four girls for the pas de quartre in *Swan Lake* linked arms to run through the tight series of quick, sharp movements that had to be performed in exact synchronicity; in the last studio, Martine van Hamel was running through Kitri's variation, her short dark hair loose and tousled, graying rehearsal tutu pulled up over her leotard, open fan in her hand, which she turned this way and that coquettishly, looking in the mirror as she did so to assess the effect. All this he saw on his way to the dressing room, and when he reached it he sat down heavily on the long bench, put his head in his hands. In half an hour he was scheduled for a run-through of the *Don Q* pas de deux with Martine, but then he was free and he decided he'd take a cab up Broadway to Lincoln Center and find Sandra. He couldn't work until they were reconciled.

$\mathcal{B}$UT  WHEN  HE was dressed in his jeans and leather jacket and striding through the reception area toward the elevator, he found her waiting for him on one of the black couches by the desk, duffel beneath her legs, elbows on her knees, head forward, her long beautiful hair falling about her. He stopped: he couldn't believe she was here. She was still, as if she'd been here a long time and had moved through nervous worry and impatience and indecision and into this state of motionless grace. A few other dancers lounged near her, their legs slung over the arms and backs of the sofas, smoking cigarettes, dropping the ashes into their empty cans of Tab. She didn't even look up until he was right in front of her and actually spoke.

"Sandra. How long have you been here?" He put his bag down at his feet.

She looked up at him blankly and touched her tongue to her lips, then put her lips together. At the expression on her face, he took in a breath. She looked at her watch, but when she finally spoke to him, she didn't answer his question. "My dad's getting sick again," was what she said. And from that he knew he wasn't going to have a chance to tell her that she couldn't pull her hand away from his like that. He wasn't going to get to say it because she wore the face he dreaded and feared, the one she wore when her dad got sick the last time and she was making those nocturnal jaunts around her father's enormous apartment.

Adam would be back in the maid's room off the kitchen, and he'd hear her out there, stumbling around the dining room, going to the kitchen, getting into the refrigerator. He'd push back the dark and his dreams, force himself out of his narrow bed to go find her. Her father had gotten some idea of opening a bookstore that specialized in the War Between the States, and he'd stockpiled so many books in their apartment that Adam couldn't even get around, had trouble finding her. He had to search for her. Sometimes she'd still be standing there in the kitchen by the open refrigerator door, her face and gown lit. When he took her by the elbow, she'd turn toward him slowly, that drowned expression on her face, her long nightgown weighted and heavy, and he'd struggle with it and her. He was the only one who could save her. Her father was just out of the hospital and he was an entity unto himself, drifting speechless and unseeing through the apartment. Sandra could turn the oven on and crawl into it, he'd never know. Her aunt had gone back to Mississippi and there was no one, no one but Adam as witness.

Adam would grip her elbow and steer her back to her bedroom, to her bed, a mahogany peculiarity more fit for an English queen than a girl, where he'd sit next to her and brush her hair. He didn't know what else to do to soothe her, and his mom, when he was little, used to help him to sleep by drawing her fingers along his scalp from his forehead to the back of his neck. She'd sing to him, *Be quiet, little man, you've had a busy day, it's time to put your toy cars and trains away.* The song was in his head as he made long steady strokes down Sandra's back, the brush almost never catching in her fine hair, down to the waist of her nightgown, which he could feel was sometimes actually wet, as if she were drenched with fever. Eventually her eyes would close and she'd slump against him. At that point he could persuade her to lie down on the bed and he could leave, his arms twitching with fatigue, feeling overwhelmed and defeated and frightened by what he couldn't understand.

One night he'd heard the suck and buzz of the refrigerator too late, and by the time he found her she was already throwing up into the toilet, and the smell was appalling, in the room, on her. He cranked open the window and ran her a bath. It was the first time he saw her naked; even though he knew her body so well, there were still surprises, and he'd backed out of the room, embarrassed by her complete vulnerability. She looked thinner naked than she did in practice clothes, which offered no cover but somehow offered disguise. At those times, it was a relief to move back to his parents, but when he did he'd worry about her, wake in the night in his own room thinking he'd heard her somewhere out there in the dark, or worse, he'd wake to find himself coming, having dreamt about her, what he saw of her in the bathroom as he pulled off her gown. But this happened only in his dreams. By day he was wary of her, and though she eventually got well, as did her father, he couldn't forget the other self that he had seen. Maybe it was this more than anything else that had kept him from her all these years. And now here it was once more, that face, making a thick plaster cast over her own. *My dad's getting sick again.* Adam knelt down before her.

"How do you know?" he asked her.

"You're going off on tour and I'm going to be here all alone," she said.

"No," he said. "You can join me. After Saratoga."

She shook her head. "I can't leave my dad."

"You can't stop what happens to him." Worse than this, Adam actually thought her father was contagious. When he got sick, so did Sandra, but it wasn't going to happen this time.

He stood and picked up her bag and his own, put one over each shoulder and gave her his hand. He didn't want to talk about it here, where those other dancers were now staring at them openly. Drama in the reception area. He didn't want the whole company to know about his girlfriend and her sick father. They took the big freight elevator down together in silence, and when they got to the street and the blinding sunlight, he took her hand again. Before, he was helpless to do anything to save her, but now he could. He wanted her here with him at ABT, where he could protect her, promote her. He'd been a child, a pawn, a student, but now at this point in his career he was a force, somebody with power to wield. He was determined to talk to Joe tonight, to tell him he wanted to do his ballet with Sandra. If they danced together at the Joyce in August, he'd have ABT's management come and see her there, spare her the regular audition at which, he knew, she would balk. It had to happen easily, while City Ballet was on hiatus, a contract she didn't have to go out of her way to seek—and he'd convince her to accept.

They walked hand in hand up Broadway, and he felt her fingers curl through his, and that little motion killed him, as if she were putting her life in his hands, and he closed his fingers around hers.

$\mathcal{H}$E TOLD HER he'd come by her place later tonight, but first he had to see Randall. He left her at the Eldorado and took a cab back across town and down Park Avenue. Randall and Joe lived in an apartment that had once been Randall's mother's. The apartment was old and the rooms many and small, nothing particularly grand about it. Randall had let Joe bring in a decorator ten years ago when they got back from Cologne, because if Joe couldn't fuck with grandeur, he wanted to live with grandeur, and Randall's victory had left him feeling both magnanimous and guilty. In trucked the chandeliers and layers of raw silk drapes, the mirrors and busts, heavy doors pried from some monastery, thick sofas. Whatever they had in here before, 1960s Warhol chic, had been sold or rearranged or given to Adam's parents, and whatever had been left was put in one of the back bedrooms, which had become Randall's retreat. It held the old pine table from the kitchen, art books stacked high all over it, and their old bed, minus the headboard, covered with a simple white bedspread, its surface erupted with raised dots; the best chair from the old living room wore the disguise of a white sheet. Everything was white; the room looked like an operating theater.

Randall was not there—not in his *hole,* as Joe called it—

when Adam arrived, but in the living room with Joe and one of the new boys from Joe's company, Eric Gonzalez, who had out-fitted himself in a black T-shirt and a brown leather vest like some sixties rock star. Adam hadn't yet met Eric, but he'd heard Joe blab about him, about his boundless talent, his unique style. Unique? Within a minute of looking at him, Adam could see he was just a younger version of Joe. No wonder Joe loved him.

"Here's my superstar," Joe said to Adam, his hand on Eric's shoulder, and to Eric, "This is Adam LaSalle, currently of American Ballet Theatre."

There was a moment when the two shook hands where they measured each other, and Adam had a fleeting urge to arm wres-tle with Eric. Had Joe decided Eric would do the role Adam had waffled about? You couldn't hesitate for a minute in this world—if you did or if you looked wrong for the part in any way or if you were too tall or too small or you were injured, you were out and replaced in an instant. There was always somebody coming up behind you, ready to take on what you couldn't—or wouldn't.

"A pleasure," Eric said. "I'm a fan."

Adam nodded, wondering if he really was and what he really was, and it seemed to him Joe was slow to remove his hand from Eric's body. Adam turned to look at Randall, who was sitting across the room in a ridiculous paisley chaise, punched through with upholstery buttons and trimmed with dangling fringe balls, as if it had been created in some überfaggot's dream work-shop. But Randall's eyes were on Joe as Joe handled Eric. The whole time Joe talked to Adam about the roles Eric had done the past season and what he had planned for him the upcoming season, he had his hands on Eric's shoulders or at the back of his neck or around his body, half-caressing him, half-turning him like a gem for Adam to admire. Was this why Randall had been looking so bad lately?

Adam shoved his hands in his pockets and endured the next thirty minutes, determined to wait for Joe to bring up, as Adam knew he eventually would, this last ballet for his dad. Was it a necessary condition of the choreographer to speak incessantly of his work, of what he'd done and what he was going to do, as if what he'd done was so ephemeral it might dissolve like sugar in water, as if what he planned to invent had to be approached first with a phalanx of words? Or was it just Joe who needed to do this? Balanchine never had to, he walked into the room and went to work, but Balanchine was a world unto himself. Adam made fists inside his pockets. He wanted to do this dance, but he wasn't sure he could stand to be talked at this way by Joe for hours on end, to have Joe handle him as he pushed and prodded the dance onto his body. He'd managed to avoid touching Joe for years, but a lot of unavoidable physicality went into the choreographic process, plenty even in a regular rehearsal. Someone was always shoving at his port de bras or adjusting the tilt of his head or the angle of his lifted leg. His old teachers at SAB had stamped to count out the revolutions when he turned a series of pirouettes, had gotten down on their hands and knees to fix his feet. If Joe made a dance on him, he'd be touching him, talking to him, breathing on him, caressing him. Adam turned to Randall and gestured, palms up.

"Excuse us," Randall said, and Adam held on to Randall as they made their way down the back hall to the white room. Randall sat in the armchair, the sheet over it wrinkled and draped around him in a way that unnerved Adam, who sat in a straight-backed chair. The room was filled with Randall's art books, almost all of which held, Adam had found on previous occasions, Randall's odd, thin handwriting up and down the margins, and in this marginalia Randall would ponder the history, influences, and interpretations of the works. Just for fun. Sometimes he'd penciled an appreciation with an exclamation point, and Adam would scour the page opposite. Which work was it that so moved Randall? By Masaccio's *Annunciation* he'd written, *There is no better!* Randall had left City Ballet in the late fifties, left Balanchine and Tallchief, LeClercq, Adams, d'Amboise, Wilde, Kent, and Magellanes behind to study art at Yale. When he came back to New York with his degree, he'd planned to open a gallery; then he met Joe, and Randall put on his tights again, for a while anyway, and started signing checks. He'd do anything for the people he loved, no matter how they treated him. And it was this thought that made Adam say, "Fuck Joe."

Randall didn't respond.

Adam studied Randall's face as he tried to light a cigarette, his long delicate fingers, the long slant of his thighbones, the tall, once broad back now somehow reduced as if the whole package of him had been shrunk and in some mysterious way bound. The sheet that lapped at his shoulders and curled up about his elbows made Randall look almost like a swaddled baby. Randall had finally got his cigarette lit and he leaned back in the armchair to smoke it, looking at Adam.

"I met Joe when I was your age," he said to Adam. "Or just about. Impossible to know, that young, all the hills and valleys you'll face." He took a drag.

"Are you and Joe in a valley right now?" Adam asked.

Randall exhaled. He smiled. "You don't know everything about us, Adam."

Adam shook his head. He wasn't sure exactly what Randall meant, but he understood it had something to do with trying to put a fence around himself and Joe to keep Adam out. But it was too late for that fence, there had already been one intruder, maybe more.

Randall blew a small line of smoke his way. "What do you do when you're lonely and scared, Adam?"

Adam ducked his head. Randall knew what he did when he was lonely and scared. Adam had told him about those hotel rooms he'd lived in on tour that were made so dark by their blackout curtains they could have been catacombs. He had been so lonely within them he would fuck anyone, at first the girls he met in restaurants or bars or lobbies, the boys who would hit on him anywhere because he looked like a movie star, but then even a company boy and a few of the girls, which was a mistake because he had to see them again, every day; as revenge for having been used, they would discuss him, what he did to them, what they did to him. He had touched them, opened his mouth into theirs, inhaled their breath, came in their bodies and mouths and then walked away. They discussed the size of his dick, the taste of him, the sounds he emitted, his predilections and technique, until there was nothing left to talk about. So it was nothing. It all meant nothing. But still he wouldn't be forgiven for it, wasn't sure he himself could forgive it, dreaded Sandra finding out about it, dreaded the possibility that he might do it all again. He was afraid he couldn't face that loneliness another time, the touring this summer, the longer gig in the fall. He had to have Sandra with him. He had to do this dance with Sandra, would have to endure Joe.

When he looked up, he saw that Randall was looking at him, had been looking at him the whole time. "So what's going on?" Adam said. "Is Eric going to do that role in Dad's ballet?"

And Randall said, "Joe's already started on the choreography for you and Sandra."

"He's already started it?" Adam drew a breath. "How did he know I'd say yes?"

Randall lowered his cigarette. "Because I told him you would."

Adam scooted his chair forward until he could put his arms around Randall's neck. For a minute he thought he might sob, but Randall's hand on his shoulder forestalled him. All his life Randall had been making things happen for him. What would he do when Randall was gone?

WHEN SANDRA OPENED the door, Adam could see right away she'd taken one of her father's Valiums. Her eyes were blurred. She was wearing a big T-shirt and some thick woolen socks, and she slid each foot along the floor toward him, as if she weren't sure exactly where the floor was. Jesus. He'd have to check later and see how many pills her dad had left, get rid of some. The man filled his prescriptions, but wouldn't medicate himself, so his medicine chest bulged with stuff for Sandra to swallow. Adam wanted to tell her right away about his conversation with Randall, but he knew she wouldn't be able to handle it in this condition. He'd have to wait. The apartment was overheated; he could hear the hiss of the steam heat coming from the living room radiators that should have been turned off. It was already May, and outside the sky had turned dark and angry with heat, at times even rumbling with it.

"Where's your dad?" he asked her.

"Asleep."

"Are you cold?" When she shook her head, he went into the

living room and cranked the valve of the heater. She followed him and watched him do it, as if she didn't know what else to do. He straightened up. He could see her ribs through her thin T-shirt. She stood there watching him, not moving. On the dining room table she'd shoved aside some of her father's papers to set up their Scrabble game. "I already started," she said when she saw him looking, and he could tell that she had; there were words all over the board. If she'd done all that, maybe she wasn't as bad off as he thought.

"Have you eaten anything?" he asked, and when she said no, he went into the kitchen anyway, to put something on bread. He knew what she'd eat and what she'd be most likely to regret later and vomit up. He brought a chicken sandwich out to her and sat while she picked it apart with her fingers and put small pieces of it in her mouth. She could be like that, not do what you wanted her to. Give her a sandwich and she'd eat it her way. Come late for the Scrabble game, she'd start it without you. But since she was making at least a show of eating to please him, he tried to reciprocate by reorganizing the tiles she'd given him. He couldn't seem to find any combination of letters that made a word more than three points; after a while he stopped trying and looked up at her and she came and climbed onto his lap.

They kissed, but at the sluggish feel of her tongue, he drew back. He shouldn't have gone to Randall's. He should have come with her straight here and she never would have taken that pill. Or pills. He looked at her again sharply.

She had a beautiful and unusual face, the nose aquiline, her mother's nose, the curve of it exotic, paired as it was with her father's blue eyes and platinum hair. But her lips were her own, her mouth an orchid that had opened only for him. No one had kissed her before he had. He touched her face with one finger.

He had fallen in love with this face and with her immediately that day she read her essay aloud in English class. The rest of them had written bullshit, but she'd written about her father's nervous breakdown and the rubber pads the orderlies used for electroshock therapy. Adam had never heard anything like it before, and he kept turning around in his chair to stare at her as she read, though she kept her head bent studiously over her paper. At the time, he couldn't believe her courage, but later he understood it was just reckless despair. He'd found out soon enough that her father was getting sick once again. He had to wait for her after class at the door of the building to try to talk to her, but he'd been awkward with her up close. She was so beautiful. He hadn't realized that. She never wore any makeup or put flowers in her hair or wore chiffon skirts in class like the other girls at SAB always did, the other girls who had caught his eye in the hall or in partnering class. They stood by a metal trash barrel and she emptied the pockets of her jean jacket into it as they talked—little pieces of papers, gum wrapper, and lint drizzled into the can, and she gave them her attention. Her pale hair flew all around them in the wind, like delicate feelers, until finally he'd gathered it all up in his hand. He had to see her face. And once he was touching her, he didn't want to let go. She had stared at him, but she didn't pull away. He had the impulse to kiss her, would have kissed her, if he had known then how to kiss a girl.

"Let's go to bed," he told her now.

They walked together down the hall, past her father's bedroom door, light still shining beneath it—the man was afraid of the dark—and into her own bedroom clotted with green toile. The material was everywhere—over the windows, on the chair, in a rumple on the unmade bed, climbing the upholstered headboard, on the bench at the foot of the bed—and the pattern was absurd, these white-wigged couples from the 1700s dancing the minuet amidst background shrubbery. He had been in here a million times, but tonight it was different, tonight he was sleeping in her bed, no more maid's room. She was twenty; she was old enough. He watched her wander around picking up dirty clothes and dropping them into a bigger pile in the corner; like magnetic shavings, the soiled items clung to one another and trembled. Her room was a wreck, as usual. She unzipped her duffel; a booty of hard, ribbonless pointe shoes clunked to the floor.

"I forgot to sew these," she said.

"You'd better set the alarm," he told her.

She looked at him blankly for a minute. "And I never checked the schedule. I'd better call in." She picked up the phone and dialed and he sat down on the bed and watched her listen to the recorded message. Maybe she wouldn't have rehearsal until late afternoon. They could both skip company class and sleep in. He was already imagining it when she lowered the receiver and turned to stare at him.

"What is it?" he said.

She held out the receiver.

He stood and while he held it to his ear she dialed the number again, and he was standing there listening to Rosemary Dunleavy's plastic voice say, "Ellis, Kumery, Freedman, Fedorova, Balanchine. *Mozartiana.* Main." Balanchine was going to use her in *Mozartiana,* in something small, for just four girls. Wordlessly, Adam handed her the phone and she hung it up.

"I didn't think he knew who I was," she said, looking at him, but there was something, something in her eye that belied the statement. She knew he knew who she was.

So it had happened, somehow. Balanchine had noticed her. She'd been in the corps for four years and he'd finally noticed her. It was a good thing, it was a really good thing, but somehow, to his shame, he didn't feel so good about it. He hadn't even had a chance to tell her about the dance with Joe, and now it wouldn't matter to her, wouldn't mean anything next to this. Adam sat down on the edge of her bed. The coverlets and pillows smelled of the baby shampoo she still used and the perfume she had chosen for its distinct scent—not for Adam's nose, but for Balanchine's, though he didn't know it. The old man liked perfume. He was famous for it, buying perfumes for his ballerinas, matching the scent to the girl. He loved to get on the elevator and be able to tell who had been there before him, in whose wake he now stood. And now he had lifted his nostrils to the wind once again.

Adam had to say something. So he opened up his mouth and said, "That's really great, Sandra."

She started to talk to him then, something about Balanchine and *Mozartiana,* about Suzanne Farrell, some prayer or a statue, but he couldn't focus and he couldn't answer her. He sat there, his head in his hands, while she went on and on. Finally, just to stop her, he put his hand out and pulled her down onto the bed, rolled on top of her. He could feel the bones of her ribs and pelvis beneath him, and he felt the short, hard pulse of her breath. With his weight he had silenced her. He put his mouth to hers, concentrating, trying to bring this thing off, but he couldn't, he was exhausted, his body was not cooperating, his dick would not get hard, the way she felt beneath him was suddenly not right. He could hear the tick of her big metal alarm clock on the bedstand right by them. Outside the window came a crack of white, heat lightning, startling him, and as he gave up and rolled off of her, he felt her hand course across his back to soothe him.

I N THE MORNING he watched from the bed as she went through her dresser looking for just the right thing, the right combination of dancewear and lingerie. The girls would wear anything: spiderweb-patterned tights from Saks with the feet ripped off of them, lace-edged camisoles and Capezio dance trunks, zipper and Lycra tees from the Gap. She bent to rummage through her bureau drawers. He couldn't see her face. When she straightened up, she could see his, and she said, "What?"

He shrugged.

"What?" she asked again.

It must be all over his face, so he said it. "Just don't get too excited about one rehearsal, Sandra."

The remark was a mistake. Jesus, it was just one crappy remark, the miserable fear behind it utterly transparent, to him, anyway. He sat up to make it right, to take it back, but she'd begun throwing things at him—at first he thought it was the clothes, the leotards she held in her hands, but then he saw they were his own things coming at him—his pants, his T-shirt, his Jockeys, and she was shouting at him, something about how *he had everything and she had nothing,* as if he wanted her to have nothing, when in fact he wanted her to have everything. Each item he blocked with his hands came back at him again until he realized she wanted him to keep his clothes and get dressed, she wanted him out. He got out of bed and put on his pants, held on to the stuff she'd thrown at him as he made his way down the back hall and through the dining room to the front door.

She was still talking at him as he waited for the elevator, but by then he wouldn't look at her, just stood there with his head down and his jaw working, willing the elevator to come. He was happy for her, he was happy for her, he just couldn't say it.

When he arrived at the loft, his mother was wandering about her studio area in her footless tights and a ratty leotard, the elastic straps of it coiled and twisted, one of them knotted in an effort to shorten it, the loop standing up like a rabbit's ear. For a minute Adam saw her as he had as a child—her midnight hair wound up in a cone atop her head, her makeup a vicious series of slashes, her arms and legs pale against the stark fabric of her *Deep Song* costume. She had moved like a snake, first coiled, then rigidly erect, her hands the head, her feet and legs the sinuous tail. She'd frightened him in the audience at the theater, but what had frightened him then was her theatricality and her strength. What frightened him now was the opposite. She simply was not that good a dancer, had never been, though he couldn't see it back then. And he wished he couldn't see it now, but now that was all he could see—that and the relentless ambition that drove her forward but had been able to drive her only so far.

Adam dropped his keys on the long black table by the elevator and his mom looked his way at the sound.

"What are you doing here?" she called. "Don't you have rehearsal?"

He nodded. "I'm not going in today."

"Why not?" She walked toward him and he could see the sweat on her face and neck; she'd been working for a while, was at the end, not the beginning, of her session. "What's wrong?"

"Nothing." He looked down, could feel her looking keenly at him. So he offered up an explanation. "I just feel kind of messed up today." But that wasn't enough.

"What's going on?"

He shrugged.

"Are you sick?"

He shook his head. But he didn't want to tell her what it really was, didn't want her to know that his relationship, so new, already had a turbulence of its own. He'd always thought he could do better at this, be better than his father. But he was a prick, just like him, probably a bigger one. His dad had never deliberately chipped away at his mom's talent. He tried to shake off his mother's hands. But she didn't back away; instead, she moved closer, put a hand to his cheek.

"Look, Adam. No matter what happens, you have to be at that barre in the morning. You'll discover it's the only thing you can count on."

Had she spent the past thirty years looking for consolation at the barre? Adam had been doing that for what felt like too long already, and he was tired of it, tired of turning to dancing to make right what was not right in his life. He wanted his life to be right, he wanted to love Sandra and to have her love him, to be with him, and he wanted that to be steady in a way he could see nowhere around him, not with his parents or her father or Randall and Joe.

"What were you and Dad fighting about the other night?" he said suddenly.

His mom dropped her arms, looked away. He thought she wouldn't tell him, but then she said, "Your father wants to have another baby," and she gave a short laugh.

A baby? That was the last thing in the world Adam could

have imagined his parents had been fighting about. So his father wanted a baby. *Now* he was ready for a son. Standing there, Adam felt sick, totally erased, and in a minute he could imagine the whole thing, his parents bent over this new baby, his dad walking the floor with him the way Randall had once walked with Adam. Adam had had colic and he'd been told how he would lay his head on Randall's shoulder and vomit down his back as Randall paced with him, trying to help him find a position he could tolerate. He could see it all and his mother took his hand, he thought, to comfort him, to take the vision away, but instead she was saying to him, "Adam, are you and Sandra using protection?"

He winced at her question, the baldness and weirdness of it. They talked about a lot of things, but this he did not want to talk about with her.

"You don't want her to get pregnant, Adam."

"Jesus, Mom."

"Okay." She lifted her hand from his.

Adam turned and made the march across the loft to his room, his ridiculous room, the nursery, where he tore off his clothes and got into the shower. He stood in there for a long time, examining beneath the lather the ropy veins that ran so prominently through his arms, legs, hands, and feet, looking at his toenails, which were as mangled and discolored as any girl's who danced on pointe, relishing the sensation of the showerhead massage, letting it drive away his mother's question, her answer to *his* question. His mother would never have another baby, this he knew, but his father wouldn't need her, he could find anyone, any one of the girls he screwed if he wanted it enough. Adam put his head into the water. Another truth: he hadn't been using protection with Sandra. He'd had it pounded into him since he was thirteen years old to use a condom, always use a condom. So Adam had used rubbers with everyone, but not with Sandra. The first time he hadn't even known they were going to do it, they were just taking a drive like they'd done a hundred times before. And now he didn't want to use a rubber with her because he didn't want her thinking about what they were doing or the possible consequences. He was afraid if she thought about any of it she'd stop sleeping with him, and now that he had had her, there was no way he could go back to what it was like between them before. But he wasn't a child or an idiot; he knew it was possible they could make a baby and it was up to him to make sure that didn't happen.

When Adam was dry, he climbed into his bed and lay there naked, curled on one side. Above him the ceiling stretched far away and the light from the river filled the vast space between his body and the top of his room. His mother had gotten pregnant with him when she was twenty years old, and Randall had had to give the loft to his parents as a bribe to keep her from having an abortion.

r. B stood by the pianist for a moment, looking over the score, and then he came to the center of the studio where the dancers waited. He made a few jokes to the other girls about their boyfriends, and Sandra looked down, grateful he didn't know anything about her, or about Adam, or so she hoped. What did Mr. B know about these other girls? What could he see? Could he possibly know what she had done last night when Adam had rolled his body abruptly off of hers and sat on the edge of the bed, defeated? That she, emboldened by her Valium, had gotten out of bed and knelt in front of him to draw him back to her? And could Mr. B know what had happened between her and Adam this morning, the fight they'd had that sent Adam groping for his clothes and tumbling out the door? Could he know that her dad wasn't sleeping anymore, was becoming unspeakable? Whatever had happened, was happening, she couldn't think about it, had to shed it all now. She was here, and Adam and her father could not be in this room with her.

Sandra looked up. Mr. B sniffed and turned to the mirror. He had his women with him, wherever they all were the night before, whomever they were with. Now, they were his, and for once she was one of them, and for them he would create. Mr. B rolled up his sleeves and began to demonstrate with his hands what he wanted, or else half-danced the steps in his street clothes. She watched, shaking a little, as he worked with Nina Fedorova, a dancer with a beautiful line and extension that he deployed again and again in a series of deep arabesques. These girls were all older and he knew them and he worked with them first, and that was good because she was all nerves. Then he motioned Sandra forward and, holding one of her hands, had her do a développé to the side, moving on to the next girl, and the next, until he had all four of them with their right legs up there in one direction or another, and then he had them break the tableau and lunge into a low bow, a révérence. Mr. B worked quietly and the steps were not imposed upon them, but adapted, gently, as they slid into them, like dresses altered to fit their shapes.

Sandra felt him watching her as she danced. She was new to him and he was assessing her, but she was also different from the other three, not necessarily a good thing. She was smaller, for one thing, and Balanchine usually liked height. She was small-boned and thin, which was good, but she also had a certain skittish fragility; he liked strength. When she paused at one point to fuss with her thin woolen tights, he waited patiently: he understood how a dancer must feel just right in order to attack a series of steps, to expose herself even to herself, most of all to herself, and to him. The dance was beautiful, the ballet's "Menuet," where the four of them moved past, under, over, and around one another, sometimes doing the same steps, sometimes doing small solo phrases filled with movements Mr. B felt they did particularly well and wanted to showcase. Suzanne would be entering the stage just after them, and she would step into her own perfume, each of them a note in her fragrance. Mr. B had them turn, then jump toward one another, and then run to new positions on the floor. "No, let me see, please. Feet are dead. I want feet alive." They ran harder, faster, feet in front of their bodies, the other girls reaching their places before she did. Sandra cut her eyes to Mr. B to see if he'd noticed. He had. She bit her lip.

Then Mr. B turned to her and had her bourrée in a straight line from upstage center all the way to downstage center, a place she'd almost never been in her whole career, where he had her render a high kicking jump, followed by another kick, a larger one, and then a quick twist into a révérence. "Tha-a-t's right!" The other three began to watch her more closely as the hour went on. Mr. B continued to work with her, giving her more, stringing out her variation, and Sandra felt a weird excitement, an exhilaration tamped down so carefully it gave her body an explosive energy, and anything Mr. B asked for she could do. A wire connected her to him and she could feel his pleasure run across it, and she didn't want to stop, to feel it cut. At the end of it all, he said, "Good, good."

He took a step back and she and Mr. B looked at each other. "Sa-a-ndra," he said, rolling her strange American name across his Russian tongue. "Like Suza-anne. Good."

WHEN SHE LEFT the studio, she found a small crowd of dancers standing outside the door who had watched their rehearsal while waiting to get in for their own. A few of them looked at her the way the girls had inside, appraising her, and she looked down. She wanted to talk to somebody about what had gone on in there, but whom could she tell? She had no girl-friends in the company; the friends she'd made from the school had dropped out years ago. And when she got older there were the problems with her father and she didn't want anyone to know about that. So she'd kept to herself. The place was so competitive anyway, it was difficult for real friendship to flour-ish. Even as little girls they had all been so quiet in the dressing rooms, focusing on the class ahead of them, the business to be done. The teachers had floated, supreme and aloof, through the halls and studios, the girls' frantic competition for their atten-tion reaching an apex at Christmastime with their feverish gift-giving. Danilova was pelted with presents—perfume, note cards, scarves. She wore a scarf, always, tucked into the waistband of her chiffon teaching skirt, and it was a coup for the girl who had given it should Madame wear it. Sandra had spent hours in Bloomingdale's one year picking out a scarf, which Danilova had never worn. She had been, at fifteen, as lonely as the other girls, half of whom boarded with families that had daughters in the school or in the company, ballet families, but not their fam-ilies. These girls were hungry for love and attention. Sandra with her dead mother and her sick father was just like them, but there were no teachers at the school who could become her mother. There was the wonderful Mrs. Finn at the desk, with her glasses and her cropped hair, but to her, Sandra was one of a hundred daughters, two hundred daughters. And there was no one, certainly not Mr. B and definitely not Mr. Kirstein, who lumbered occasionally out of his office and down the halls, to act as a father.

And what would she say, anyway, about working with Mr. B today, if she had someone to say it to? That it had been great?

That it had been wonderful? She understood why Mr. B always said, "I don't like words. I don't trust words." She didn't trust them either, unless they were silent ones, written in her journals. Those were the only true words because they were written just for her. She was the only one who ever read them, except for Adam. He wanted to see the journal she'd torn her essay from, and once he read what was in there, he couldn't stop. He got into the whole stash of her spiral notebooks and read her life. He knew her the way no one knew her. And he was the only person she could talk to, now, who would understand this. He had worked with Mr. B, had been in a room with him, knew what it was like to be in the room with him when he was making a ballet. But after this morning, she wasn't sure Adam would want to hear about it.

He had watched her fumbling around trying to get her stuff together, trying to find her prettiest leotard, and after a while, he had said wryly, "Don't get too excited about one rehearsal, Sandra, one ballet, okay? Mr. B's put a lot of girls into one ballet and then never used them again." She'd turned to stare at him, leotard in her hand. Like she didn't know that, like she hadn't been at City Ballet long enough to know that, to know how capriciously fortune and doom were decided. Even her entry into the company had been decided that way. Balanchine had arrived in the doorway of the studio one day, unannounced, to watch class for ten minutes. Arms folded, he had surveyed the room, and days later his decision trickled down—this girl and this and this. Why? He liked the look of this one's arms and neck, that one's arch of the foot. Who knew? It was an accident, an act of God—this one chosen, that one left behind, his decisions autocratic, impossible to challenge, and utterly demoralizing. The teachers said work on this and this and this, but this and this and this didn't seem to matter. Even they didn't know. If they pushed a talented student at him, he balked. *I know the few I am waiting for.* And so they all waited for his decisions, jostling uneasily against one another.

She knew all about waiting, better than Adam, who had never had to wait for anything he wanted. He'd always had everything while she'd had nothing. That much she'd said to him, that and a few other things, until he was pulling on his pants, pulling his shirt on as he flew down the hall. She went after him, stood at the door to watch him wait for the elevator, his head down and his jaw thrust forward. He wouldn't look at her, wiping at his eyes with the back of his hand. Had she caused this? Did she have the ability to do this? He'd always played at being so impervious to her; he'd always decided what time they'd spend together, when that time was up. Whatever she felt, whatever she wanted, she was used to concealing because it didn't matter. Adam would do what he wanted, even if that meant leaving City Ballet, leaving her. But he had cried this morning because of her.

He was rehearsing at the Met this afternoon, she knew that much, and she had time enough now to go across the plaza and catch him there, tell him she was sorry. It wasn't his fault if their positions at City Ballet had been so inequitable, if he'd had roles and she hadn't, if crowds gathered at the studio door to watch him, had gathered at the door since he was a boy at SAB, all the mothers transfixed. He was gifted. He was beautiful. He had been chosen. He had as little to do with it as she had to do with what had happened to her, with what was happening to her now.

THE MET WAS, without a doubt, grander than State Theater, the foyer hung with Chagalls, the house lit with low-hanging chandeliers that ascended to the ceilings on retractable cords at the start of a performance to clear the sight lines. She had never danced on this stage. She knew only her own, and the Juilliard stage where the SAB workshops for the graduating students were run every spring, where all the parents and talent scouts and company directors filled the seats to spot new talent and hire it. This stage, for this rehearsal, baldly lit and hung with the scenery for *Don Quixote,* looked enormous, unassailable, much more intimidating than it had looked the other night when she had watched *Coppélia* from the wings. The opera performed here, the big visiting European dance companies. Nureyev and Fonteyn from the Royal Ballet had danced here. Makarova from the Kirov and Bruhn from the Royal Danish. Carla Fracci from La Scala. Baryshnikov. The Bolshoi defector Alexander Godunov. It took enormous personalities to fill this space, and Adam had had to learn this past year to fill it, and at the same time how to fill out the roles in all these new and unfamiliar ballets. He had danced *Swan Lake* with City Ballet, but Mr. B's *Swan Lake,* a truncated one-act thing, bore little resemblance to the full-length, three-act-plus apotheosis Ballet Theatre did here on this stage. Even the *Don Quixote* that the company rehearsed now was a different beast from Mr. B's own, his vehicle for Suzanne and himself a literary rendering of the novel with the great dreamer and his Dulcinea. In Ballet Theatre's version, Quixote was a footnote, an old fool stumbling about, comic relief, the real business of the evening the romance played out between Basil and Kitri.

Sandra stood at the back of the theater and looked down its long aisles. Dancers were scattered here and there in the seats, more of them seated at the sides of the stage or on the proscenium, a few of them standing, bulky warmers pulled up over their legs and making incongruous the tulle and satin of their skirts and vests. Alexander Godunov stood in the center of all this, half-marking, half-dancing the boy's variation of the famous *Don Quixote* pas de deux, tended to by Mikhail Baryshnikov, who watched him intently, intervening here and there to suggest, to demonstrate, to admonish. Sandra had thought she would be watching him coach Adam today; she scanned first the stage and then the seats, but Adam wasn't there, wasn't anywhere.

She went back out onto the plaza, blinking, the sun bright, so bright she practically walked into the freestanding poster advertising ABT's spring season. The poster was mounted in a metal frame that stood perpendicular to the big glass doors of the theater and its row of box office windows. Adam's image soared two people high: hair tousled, expression both imperious and intense, torso bare, muscles of his arms and chest cut and articulated. She didn't know when the photo had been taken, didn't really know all that much about what Adam had plunged into when he left City Ballet last year for this company, where he was all alone, without the dancers, coaches, teachers he had known all his life. And ABT was using him, maybe overusing him, making the most of him, nobody there to say *Slow down,* even undressing him, turning him into beefcake to sell tickets. Mr. B would never allow a photograph like this.

And then, from around the other side of the glass and metal display, she heard two girls talking and they were, she realized after a moment, studying the poster opposite and discussing its subject. *Who's he doing this week?* one of them said, and the other answered, *Some lucky little girl. Or boy.* They laughed. Sandra edged closer to the poster to hear better, but the two girls were walking away. They could be talking about anyone. It could be anyone's photograph on the other side of this stand—Baryshnikov, Godunov, Patrick Bissell. But it wasn't; she rounded it, stood where the girls had stood. It was Adam again, exactly on the one side as he appeared on the other. What did Adam do here across the plaza that she didn't know about, that he hadn't shared with her, that he'd done in private?

She knew Adam didn't do well when he was on his own. She knew him. Two years ago, when he was eighteen, he had moved into his own apartment for a few months, a minuscule studio in Midtown, and he was always after her to come stay with him there. When she finally visited him, she saw he had nothing—a mattress on the floor, clothes thrown all around, no food in the fridge, just cartons and wrappers and garbage and drug paraphernalia on the counters, in the sink. Vials of stuff he'd swiped from his parents crowded the bathroom—tranquilizers and muscle relaxants and painkillers. She didn't say anything about it and neither did he. They sat cross-legged on his bed on top of the pillows, their backs against the wall, and watched the TV on the chair, sitcom after sitcom. Anytime she looked over at Adam, she found him looking at her, an odd, intense expression on his face, which she understood later as panic. Finally he got up and rolled a joint, which he smoked until it was a tiny pinch of paper between his fingers. He didn't want her to go, ended up coming back with her to stay in the maid's room, where he remained until the end of the month when he broke his lease, sold his mattress, loaded his laundry baskets of clothes into a cab, and headed back to Hell's Kitchen. That was Adam. Anything was possible.

She had seen the boys at the stage door after *Coppélia,* the boys waiting for Adam, the girls waiting in the wings to look at him as he left the stage. That was just here in New York. What about the last two months, when Adam was away on tour? He had called her from his hotel rooms, and they'd gone down the line of what had happened on their respective stages, who'd given a magnificent performance and who'd been a disaster, how they had done and how they were feeling, and he was there, she could put out her arm and feel him. She hadn't even thought to wonder if there was someone else in the room with him or if he would, after they hung up the phone, go out to find someone, anyone. But it had been a long tour.

She walked away from the poster. Whatever he had done, whatever he was doing, she had to know. She'd call the loft, find out where he was, find out if the gossip was true.

THEY AGREED TO meet where they always did, under the big clock in Grand Central Terminal. Adam had started taking these trips in ninth grade, riding the commuter trains by himself out to Connecticut, getting off at Wilton or Weston or Stamford, and then taking another train back into the city. The brown seats, the conductors' rhythmic chants as they made their way down the aisles calling out the stops, the motion of the train itself calmed him, he told her, and by the time he got home, he didn't care anymore about what had bothered him. The ride exhausted it, rocked it out of him. She started joining him on these trips in tenth grade. But once they were out of school and in the company, there was no time, no afternoon or evening to waste, not that way, not during a season. But they were doing it now, both of them needing to do it; she'd called him at home and he was there and he'd said yes, though they couldn't ride for long before they both had to be back at the theater. He was performing tonight. He couldn't call in sick for that.

He was waiting for her, pacing, holding a brown paper bag,

which she knew contained oranges. That was always their treat. He had bought them in the subway before he came up to the station, and she knew just where he'd bought them, at the stall with all the newspapers and cigarettes, where the oranges lay trapped in crates.

She hung back just out of Adam's field of vision to watch him. He looked for her, wearing the beret and the long leather coat that made everyone take notice. He'd shop before every tour, buying things she couldn't imagine he would ever need, since he spent most of his time in planes and buses or on the stage. She lived in skinny pants and tiny T-shirts, and when she went to Saratoga in the summer, she packed a couple of bathing suits and wore them anytime she wasn't in the studio or on the stage. She didn't even take a suitcase to Saratoga, just her duffel bag, which she'd bought from the Army surplus store on West Thirtieth Street. But even back at SAB, when the rest of them were going home in jeans and sweats, Adam would suit himself up in something spiffy. Clothes were his defense, and she saw that this afternoon he was well-defended.

She stepped around the corner and into the huge, high-vaulted space of the station, and he seemed to sense that flicker of motion, for he turned and spotted her. As if they were on a stage, he put out his hand, palm up, the gesture unfolding from the elbow. He wanted her to come to him there, wanted her to walk to him, needed to see that she would do this, and so she did, the noise of the station reverberating against her body. When she got close enough, she put her hand in his, and he bent down saying, *I want your mouth,* so she opened her mouth to him and let him kiss her there in the station, let the tongue that had been in all those other mouths course through hers and claim it. He kissed her until he felt that release, the way her head tipped back, her neck bared, vulnerable. And she knew then he was satisfied. No matter what happened today in the studio, she was still his. And when he was finished, he said, "You know I'm sorry." He was talking about this morning. He thought she had called him about this morning. She shook her head. *I'm sorry. I'm the one.* He took her arm then to lead her to the platform, each passageway marked with its track.

They sat close to each other in the nearly empty car—at four o'clock it was too early for the crush of commuters—and when the train began to move away from the platform and through the dark tunnels that led out of Manhattan, Adam opened the paper bag and pulled out an orange. His hands worked the globe of the fruit, his fingers grew wet with spray and stuck with fibers, and she bent her head suddenly to his lap to suck at his hands, the beautiful fingers she couldn't bear to think of working anyone's body but hers. She heard him breathe in sharply above her at the gesture, and when she sat back up and looked at him, he said, "What? What is it?"

She shook her head. She couldn't tell him, couldn't ask him about what she'd heard, didn't want him to know she'd heard it. He hated to be talked about. He was so self-contained, despite what he did with his body at night on the stage or what he might do with it in bedrooms and hotel rooms. She'd come here to ask him about this and now she couldn't ask him.

She would have to write it all down instead, something she hadn't done for a while, since she was sixteen, since her first year in the company, when she had gotten too busy and too tired to do anything but dance and do laundry and sleep. Whatever thoughts she'd had about her father or Adam or Mr. B and the exquisite ballerinas that guarded him, those thoughts had to come and go free of the page. She hadn't even known she'd missed writing, but now, thinking about it, the pleasure of it came back, the black spiral notebooks, the cheap fountain pens. She wrote quickly, without thinking much, not like her dad.

Adam had made his way through all those journals, one by one, until he'd caught up with her, reading an entry or two behind. It was like writing secret letters, a secret history. He would never tell anyone what he read, this she knew, wouldn't even talk to her about it, even when she'd written about him, about that time he'd put his head under her dress at his parents' loft, after a party. He had spread her legs, and she had been wearing a pair of high-heeled shoes that didn't quite fit. When she sat up, so did he. And then, without saying a word, he backed out of the room. She sat there in his bedroom by herself until she could stand and then she went into the bathroom and wiped at herself with toilet paper. When she came out into the loft, he wouldn't look at her; he just stood there talking to Randall. After Adam read this, he shut the book and held it on his lap. He had done that to her only once and he would not do anything like it again for a long time. He would do it to other people, though, over and over, while she waited for him. What if he was still doing it to other people, even now? What if he stopped doing it to her as abruptly as he had the last time?

She would buy a new notebook and write in it everything she was thinking, and Adam could read it and he could decide what to do.

They ate the orange, Adam handing her sections of it, sometimes ripping the fibrous seam from one of them to expose for her the puckered fruit inside; when they finished he held her hand, their sticky fingers interlocked, and she put her head on his shoulder. He took her hair and drew it across his body, tucked it under his other arm so the hair spread across him like a wide, shining sash. He shut his eyes against the lowered sun that slanted through the windows, and yet she wasn't content. Only a few men behind newspapers sat in their car, their jackets laid on the seats beside them. Occasionally, the conductor strolled through to check the tickets. The long, suburban light heated up the train car, and the landscape passed green and white and blue, grass, buildings, sky; all the places she and Adam had never lived rushed past. How many women had he been with? Which boys? She looked up at him, the bulge of his jaw, the full lower lip set against the delicate upper, the ridges that gathered up the slope of skin between his nose and top lip. His nostrils were almost flared, and they trembled with his breath. She could stroke his face if she wanted, run her fingertips along his jaw and up the sheer planes of his face, and he would let her; there was no barrier to this action now, not as there had once been. The intimacy felt unbearable to her. As if aware of her inspection, he turned, opened his eyes, blue glass, translucent, like the best marble in her dad's collection.

He smoothed out the empty orange bag and took a pencil from inside his coat pocket, turned to her and began to sketch. She let him. She didn't turn away. His doodles and drawings of her were scattered in the margins of her journals. He drew the things in her bedroom—her alarm clock, her overflowing bureau drawers, the flowers in her rug, the wigged couples dancing on the fabric of the coverlet—and he drew her, sailing through the sky in her nightgown, cradling a cat that was not a cat but a stuffed doll she had, and once, a picture of her sleeping naked and emaciated in the water-filled bathtub, her hair snarled and stuck to her torso, but she made him erase that. He was talented, had taken art lessons, paid for by Randall, until ballet had subsumed all else. She looked at the wrinkled brown paper he drew on now, but he wasn't drawing her, he was drawing the train car around him, empty of people, empty of her, the rows of windows, the lines of seats, the metal rail backs that rose like nightmarish headrests, the aisle littered with tickets.

They got off at Stamford and stood in the small wooden one-room station to wait for the return train. Adam went to get two coffees from the vending machine, and steam rose from the Styrofoam cups and floated across their faces. They listened to the announcements of arrivals and departures, destinations, originations. Adam looked at his watch. They would have to leave soon, and when they got back to the city they would take a cab together to Lincoln Center, part at the plaza for their separate theaters, their separate dressing rooms, their separate ballets, their separate worlds. He was going on tour this summer and then again in the fall. She couldn't go on like this. She was going to tell him they had to stop what they'd started, that they had to go back to just being friends, if that were possible, if they could put this thing between them to sleep. She was going to say it the very next instant. *Say it,* she willed herself, *say it*. She threw her coffee into the trash, and as she released the cup into the bin he caught her hand.

$\mathcal{B}$ACKSTAGE AT THE theater that night, she put on her costume for *Symphony in C,* the short white tutu with the very low white satin bodice, an extra frill of satin at the V, other panels of it spilling into beautifully folded pleats that lay atop the tulle skirt. Their costumes all looked like elegant lingerie. She had worn this costume for four years, ever since she'd joined the company. They were expected to fit into their costumes year after year. *Symphony in C* was the first ballet she had learned, the first part all the new girls learned. Even though she had a soloist role for *Mozartiana,* she was still in the corps, doing the same corps roles she'd always done, still dancing *Swan Lake,* still dancing Snow, still dancing all the ballets the more promising corps girls had been taken out of. In *Symphony in C,* she wasn't even on until the fourth movement, a supremely humbling movement, in which she'd bound out onto the stage, only to stand motionless in a long row of girls for maybe twenty minutes, backdrop to the more interesting action taking place center stage where the principals and soloists from all four movements cavorted, first one, then two, then all of them. She dreaded those minutes. The one leg and foot she stood upon turned cold, then fell asleep, and then finally, mercifully, went numb. It was as if Balanchine had forgotten them, or worse, held them in so little regard that he thought them good enough only for this. Technically negligible, and yet the poses required enormous strength and discipline to maintain. How had those lumbering, untrained girls back in 1948 done it without wobbling or shuffling? Maybe they hadn't. Or maybe they managed it for the same reason Sandra and her sisters did. Out of love for Balanchine. And the hope of something better.

She laid her pointe shoes on the crest of her tutu and went out to the wings, hands busy in her hair, checking the security of her pins. She had the kind of hair that pins slipped out of easily, and so she was always using hairspray to lacquer it, give the pins something to stick to. She might not have sprayed enough. She stood by the bulletin board to check tomorrow's schedule, or what management hoped tomorrow's schedule would be. The lists were constantly being amended with pencil as the evening wore on and sick calls came in and injuries were accrued. First on the page was the schedule of girls due at the costume shop. She had a fitting at Karinska's tomorrow for her *Mozartiana* costume, a short black tutu with a scalloped bottom and a bodice corseted with black ribbons, trimmed at the top with a strand of white lace. It was the first time she'd had a costume made to her. Her name was still up there in the short list for *Mozartiana*—Ellis, Kumery, Freedman, Fedorova—and she stood there looking at it for way too long, still amazed by the sight. Then she checked the other times and studios. Main at 2 for *Adagio Lamentoso*. And once again for something else, later in the day. Four o'clock. Andersen, Farrell, Ellis, Dunleavy. "Diamonds." She took her hand away from her hair. The rehearsal schedule was a code and embedded in the call for 4 P.M. was some impossible information. She read this list of names again. Two principal dancers, Sandra, the ballet mistress. "Diamonds." There was only one thing this could mean. She was scheduled to understudy the pas de deux from "Diamonds," the last, the most magnificent section of *Jewels*. A major ballerina role. A role Mr. B had made for Suzanne in 1967.

It could happen like this: you could be in the corps de ballet and suddenly find yourself learning a big principal role and then in a weird rush, because of an injury or Mr. B's curiosity, you'd be cast, you'd be on, Balanchine would want to see if you could do it, get in there, take a chance, pull it off. But Balanchine hardly knew her, had hardly looked at her—or not nearly as much as she imagined he would before assigning her a major role. She had watched Suzanne and Kay Mazzo and Allegra Kent dance "Diamonds" a hundred times, but watching was one thing, dancing another. She couldn't do it; she knew she couldn't. It wasn't only the technique she lacked, it was the presence. She didn't know how to be at the center of a stage, how to allow herself to become transformed by that space, how to command it. The principal girls could do that—they seemed to have some secret knowledge. They put on a role and illuminated it. Their personalities lit it up. She was dutiful, she was dull, she was corps de ballet material, circa 1948.

She could feel something pulsing in her throat, and she picked up the pointe shoes perched on her tutu just to hold on to something. The satin fabric was slippery under her sweaty fingers. Why was Adam not here? She hated him for not being here, for having left City Ballet, for leaving her here alone. If Adam were still here, he would run through it all with her—he might even have been cast with her, could have shown her what she needed to do. She fingered the shoes, looked around at the other dancers warming up in the wings, baggies under their tutus, and then at Suzanne, who stood magnificent in her own costume, the white tulle and the bright headdress. At one time, unbelievably enough, Suzanne had been like her, inexperienced and unprepared. That was twenty years ago. Suzanne had told Mr. B then that she knew she was making a big mess of rehearsals and that she really wasn't ready yet for the role he had given her, and he had silenced her with, "Oh, dear, you let me be the judge."

She would have to do the same. She would have to dance and let him be the judge.

Sandra stepped away from the bulletin board and turned toward the stage, which was empty, the lights all set up and ready to go for the first movement. As she gazed into the bright glare, she saw a large figure emerge from the wings on the opposite side of the stage and raise her arms. The figure was gesturing, and at first Sandra thought it was beckoning to her, but then she realized the figure was not turned her way, but toward Mr. B who was already planted in the downstage wing. Sandra squinted, her lids heavy with false lashes.

It was an angel, enormously tall. On her head a gold foil wig rippled in waves as if lifted from a mold, her dress hung sheer as a drapery, and her wings stood ten feet high, sharply scalloped and reaching up to heaven in thinly tapered points. Russian angel. Sandra couldn't breathe. And she was not the only one hushed at the sight—the backstage hubbub had entirely quieted, and it was silent as Mr. B walked onto the stage. He was immediately dwarfed by the size of her. By now, Sandra could make out the girl inside the costume, the costume for *Adagio Lamentoso,* a costume in no way like the one for the little cherubs who charmed the audience in Act II of *The Nutcracker,* with their halos, bell skirts, and butterfly wings. Those were children's costumes, and this angel was a woman, feminine, fearsome, half-real, half-dreamed, like all of Mr. B's heavenly muses, half what they really were, half what he imagined them to be. And what he imagined them to be, they became.

SEVEN

The wives and almost wives stood about his bed that night, shades of themselves at twenty-one, the age at which he had married each of them, even as he had grown older and older. At his left floated Tamara, her ash-blond hair too pale to be real, streaking the air; below her, Alexandra, her face Russian and petulant and superior. Brigitta, the movie star. Maria Tallchief, his first American wife, with the noble head and the strong jaw of an Osage. Tanny, the years having shaved away her wheelchair and returned to her the endless stork legs and her droll wit. Suzi.

George sat up in the bed to find himself wearing a long nightshirt like old Drosselmeyer or Don Quixote, and he threw back the covers, the folds of the gown sucking at his legs like mud. He stepped out of it into the rain that pelted his head and Tamara's, despite her mother's hat. When he took her hand, he saw his own was young again, the flesh bleached smooth. Flowers thrust themselves out of the bedposts and scrolled toward the ceiling as he marched Alexandra in a circuit beneath them.

Brigitta, who wore the fur coat he had bought her in the December of his most desperate wooing, let her breath make icicles as white as her ermine-trimmed hood. The room tilted and he skated on glass to Maria, slid past her on steel blades and Tanny put out her arm, the arm he had not seen her move for thirty years, and he looked into her beautiful face and wept as small powdery flakes of snow blew between them. And then the air grew heavy and lush, thick fronds brushing green up against the windows, and in Suzi's blue eyes he saw his own face reflected: an old man, autumn leaves in his hair, his beard, his nightshirt, and they rustled and crackled as he shuffled back toward his pillow and blanket, the wives waving him sadly on, their faces glowing in the sun and the moon he had given them.

They would all outlive him.

IN THE AFTERNOON, he arrived early for his *Mozartiana* rehearsal, just to stand outside the studio door to watch Suzi show the girl the long diagonal walk that opened the "Diamonds" pas de deux, the walk that he had made twenty years ago to take Suzi from upstage right to center stage. He didn't often have her teach others her roles, had done it in 1969 after she had married, to punish her, to let her know she was not the only one, just as she had shown him he was not the only one. But he wanted her to show this girl. Behind Suzi, the little blonde made the walk as well, moving with great clarity and vulnerability. He watched her, and as he watched, he heard in his mind the single French horn that would sound with her. In the center, the girl met Ib Andersen. The difference in their heights was too much, he would have to fix. The girl moved with the crystalline cool of Elizaveta Gerdt, the wife of his teacher and his favorite ballerina in 1913, at the Maryinsky Theater, when he had been too young to fall in love with a woman, but not too young to fall in love with the idea of a woman. This girl was young, and there was a deep restraint about her, but beneath lay a wide swath of emotion shimmering like the mouth of a great river, and he felt his brain hum and his body grow warm. He had not seen this or her before—perhaps because of the cataracts; with them he could not apprehend the new, could perceive only the shapes of the familiar. He watched her lean on Ib's shoulders and take the long penché arabesque Suzi had made famous, the sweep of her long leg up the numbers of the clock to twelve. Yes. By now he trusted himself. He had seen beneath many dancers, had understood what was great in them before they understood it themselves, and in this girl he saw *Sleeping Beauty*.

It was a ballet he had once wanted to do for Suzi, had offered it like a diamond ring on a velvet cloth to keep her from marrying, but she had married and she had left him and now she was too old. Then he had wanted to do it for Gelsey Kirkland, little Gelsey, for whom he had revived *Firebird*—she was vibrant, tremulous, high-strung, like a bird—but she had flown away across the plaza to dance with Baryshnikov. After *Coppélia,* his conductor had said to him, "Ah, next year, *Sleeping Beauty,*" but it had been next year and next year and next year and still no *Sleeping Beauty*. And now here was this girl at the cusp of womanhood, just as he himself stood on the precipice of death and oblivion. *Sleeping Beauty*'s glittering raiment promised the perfection that lay beyond oblivion. Around this girl's simplicity, her purity, her regality, he would arrange the folds of a sumptuous ballet.

But he would not do the ballet bargain basement. He would

go to the board as he had gone to the board for *Nutcracker,* ten thousand dollars in 1954 just for the tree. "Ballet is tree," he had told them. *Sleeping Beauty* was spectacle. It was fountains and gardens, lake, fairy boat, castle, lords and ladies, coaches, the Carabosse and her attendants, the large black rats, garlands for flower waltz, a thicket of briars, the silken bed upon which the princess sleeps, cobwebs and pillars, spindles and wands, the Prince Désiré, the White Cat, Puss in Boots, Bluebirds, Little Red Riding Hood, the Wolf, the three Ivans together doing their vigorous Russian dance.

*Sleeping Beauty* was a big ballet, fifty thousand rubles in 1890 and all the resources of a company funded by the czar. Here one had to go with one's hat in one's hand to all the rich bankers and burghers, begging for money. And once he had the money, would he have the strength? It had almost been too much for Petipa, the ballet too grand, he was constantly ordering up new music from Tchaikovsky, *I need this for the wedding scene, a galop, a march,* and Tchaikovsky would do, only to have Petipa change his mind, *No, I want a coda, ninety-six measures, after all.* Making a ballet this big was a marathon, a prologue, three acts, apotheosis, but perhaps God and Tchaikovsky would give him the strength. He would say a small prayer to Tchaikovsky up in the top tier of heaven.

IN THE STUDIO working with Victor Castelli that afternoon, he had more energy than the boy, taking him through the syncopated Russian folk steps that made up the "Gigue," the second movement of *Mozartiana.* He bulldozed his way through the phrases, feet landing first on every third beat, like a jig, then on every two, until both he and Victor were dripping with sweat. The dance was a long one, and the folk steps did not come easily to the boy. They did not come easily to any of his American dancers, raised on white bread and shopping malls and television. George stamped and whistled and ran his way through the complicated variation, doing the balkan, the grapevine, stamping and swaggering like a Russian serf, with Victor and the pianist and his rehearsal assistant agape at him, at his sudden vigor. He would pay for it tonight, would be too tired to eat a spoonful of consommé, would fall into bed. But now, he would enjoy. He turned to his reflection in the mirror and smiled. He could still do. He could still do.

THOUGH HE WOULD not get to do everything. Lincoln had always been after him to do something American, something New World. *Birds of America*. Johnny Appleseed. Buffalo Bill. Pocahontas. But the ballet had never interested him. Ideas never had. A good story, maybe. *Orpheus. Apollo*. Music, always. Dance halls, circus acrobatics, leggy Parisienne strippers on the catwalks. Emotion. Women. Ballet was woman. Always his ballets were about that, about man's desire for a woman, his attempt to take possession of her, his efforts flinging him toward her, sometimes missing her, whizzing past her to the wrong side of the sun, the back of her a shadow against the light. Every ballet was a kiss of one sort or another. *Sleeping Beauty*, too, would be a kiss, offered on bended knee, from a young man to a sleeping princess, a hundred and sixteen years old. From an old man to a young girl.

But what kind of kiss? There were so many kisses in *Sleeping Beauty*. He took the elevator to his office. The prince's kiss, yes. But also the fairies' kisses to the babe. The parents' kisses to the forehead of their child. Aurora's kisses to awaken her parents. At the end of the ballet, the palace gates were drawn shut. Behind the scrollwork the audience could see the happy family embracing for perpetuity as the curtain went down.

What did he know of all that? He barely remembered his parents or even himself as a child. By the time he returned to Russia, in 1962, to show off the company he had made here in America, only his brother was still alive, both his parents and his sister dead. Tamara had been killed in a German air raid, his mother had died of old age, his father long before her of gangrene of the leg. He had refused amputation, refused to stump about on one leg. *I? Meliton Balanchivadze?* He would rather die. He looked forward to it. *Death is a beautiful girl who will come and take me in her arms.* George had last seen them all when he was fourteen, when the Revolution had driven them to Tiflis, in the Caucasus Mountains, thousands of miles from St. Petersburg and the Imperial Ballet. Even before that, he had not seen them much. He was at the school, they were at the dacha in Lounati-akki. He remembered the log house with its peaked roof, the pretty windows, the steeple, the raised porch. What else? His bonne, the banya, the steambath too hot for him, the little pig who followed him on walks through the woods, the mushrooms, berries, leaves, twigs, dirt, strawberries, stones, birds. His mother's dress, the one with the pinstriped sleeves, the long, beaded bib that hung down her back topped by a large satin bow. His father's broad face, with the brown beard and the mustache he left unwaxed. Sixty years since he last saw the faces of his mother or father. He kept a framed photograph of his father in his bedroom, saved the few letters he'd had from his mother. In his mother's notes to him from decades ago she wrote,

"Georgik, often I see you in my dreams, but only as a child, never as an adult."

Sitting there in his small wooden chair in his office, the one that was good for his back, he felt the muck of his own loneliness, the muck he'd felt since he was ten and taken as a boarder at the Imperial Ballet school. His parents a three-hour train ride away, he would sit in the deserted reception hall on weekends and play the piano, notes echoing all the way to the chapel where one of the masters sat, supervising the two or three other family-less boys until supper. At night, in bed, he left his world, reading Jules Verne and Sherlock Holmes, stories that came in installments, a dozen kopecks each, great adventure concealed behind the cardboard covers. After the Revolution, the swamp of his loneliness grew and he'd fill it with friends, friends, and lovers. Each year new friends, new dancers, new wives, but the need remained constant. Wives, wives, and more wives, and still he was a lonely man. In *Nutcracker* he had created for himself a family of parents and children, aunts and uncles, *Grossvaters* and *Grossmutters,* but when he took a role, he played Herr Drosselmeyer, the friend of the family, the odd man out, the one who had to buy the affection of the children with the presents he pulled out from under his cloak. He was seventy-seven now. There would be no more marriages, no family for him. For the time left to him, he would be alone. When the board asked him, "Who will succeed you?" he gave them no answer. To the press he would say, "I am Georgian. I will live to be a hundred and ten." Maybe. One hundred years was a long time.

WHAT HAD AURORA dreamed of during those one hundred years she slept? Had she lain beautiful and lonely, as the spiders

spun great cobwebs between the pillars of her castle, as the
bushes grew tall and thick and thorny about the exterior walls,
trapping in their branches the bodies of all the wrong princes,
the suitors who were not the right suitors? Had she shivered as
she heard them approach, sighed when she heard them struggle
in the brambles, turn to bones and dust there among the leaves?

*H*E HIMSELF HAD been, so many times, the wrong prince,
thrashing in the brambles. Forty years ago, he had stood outside
Brigitta's New York apartment for hours, looking up at her window, miserable with desire, night all around him, and though he
had fashioned beautiful dances for her movies and Broadway
shows and though he had painted her dressing room at the theater and had a white ermine coat sewn for her with skins he'd
handpicked, the whole coat wrapped inside a plastic Wool-
worth's raincoat to make the surprise even more delightful, despite all these things he had never been able to possess her. He
had married her and it had been his third marriage, one of his
longest marriages, his most desperate marriage. He had gained
entry and he had kissed the princess, but he could not waken
her, could not make her love him. It would be better had he
died in the bushes outside. One more time he had been that way,
with Suzi, but by then he was old, an old man. When a man was
old, his love for a young woman was everything—pathetic, desperate, ridiculous, essential. He posed precariously on the ledge
of his proposition, while she, assured and all powerful, weighed
his fate. Would she open the window and bring him in? No. He
could not be in that position again. He was too old now, had
been too old with Suzi then, but now he was white-haired, his

body puffy, now a real Malaross, the nickname he had once given himself as a young man. Malaross, the malformed one.

THE KISS OF a lover? No, *Sleeping Beauty* could not be about the kiss of a lover.

YET, sometimes he had been the right suitor, had wooed with success the king's daughter. That would be Tamara, her castle the large St. Petersburg apartment her family did not lose in the Revolution, her father too revered, even by the Bolsheviks, though her father had lost his business, the factory that wove ecclesiastical garments. But his treasures, his museum, remained— the books, the first editions, the sketches by Léon Bakst for *Scheherazade* for Ballets Russes. The king had offered him his greatest treasure, his daughter, once he saw the way things were going between them. They were married in the chapel of the Theater School, she in pale blue crepe, he in tails from the Maryinsky wardrobe, dark eye shadow brushed around his eyes. Yes, with Tamara he had been a successful suitor. And then later, in Paris, with Alexandra, too, though she had cried and cried, had wanted the white dress and the orange blossoms he could not give her, all his papers with Tamara lost in Russia, but Alexandra had come into his bed anyway, had been a wife without a marriage certificate, and later an ex-wife without the divorce papers. Maria had married him also, astonished by his proposal, which had come to her like a bolt from Mount Olympus and to which she had responded obediently, like a handmaiden to a deity. With Tanny he had been forced to say, "I'm a lot older than you. Before you marry me, you should ask your mother." To which she had replied, "I don't have to ask my mother."

For him, there was no mother or father to ask. His parents had not stood at any of his weddings, nor had they seen the faces of any of his brides.

His brides were his dancers, his children his ballets. He had never wanted any other children, had never wanted his dancers to have children. Maria had wanted a baby, but he had not. When they divorced, the headline had read, NO PAPOOSES. It was not until Suzi, until he was losing Suzi, that he proposed to her they have a baby, that she consider what a beautiful, magical child they would make. He had begged her, but by then it was too late, all his proposals too late. If they had had the child, a girl, a daughter, she would be twelve now, almost the age of Aurora, and she would look like Suzi and like him, Russian and American, with his high forehead and her cheekbones, her long legs and his intelligence, her quicksilver movements and his invention, a convergence of both their talents. Blue eyes, probably. Brown hair. And what would this girl be doing now? She would be at the school, of course, across the plaza during the magical decade in which a girl is made into a dancer, and then as she blew out the other end of those ten years toward the stage, how would she move, what qualities would she inhabit? He would love to see. She would have been in his *Nutcracker,* in *Dream,* in *Coppélia,* in all the ballets where he had used children. She would have napped in his office, curled like a kitten in his own chair. They would play four-hands at the piano. For him she would turn the pages. He would feed her Russian food, kasha and meatballs in sour cream, so she would have Russian soul— American body, Russian soul. In his apartment, he would make for her a bedroom of silver and gold, the bedroom of a forties movie star with a canopied bed and a dressing table with ruffled skirt and three-angled mirror. She could sit there and comb out her hair, would have long, shining hair, and she would have a gold brush. She would be the king's daughter and he would give her everything.

He sat in his chair, eyes closed. He had no daughter, but he could make one, as he had made everything else he lacked. He would not be as he had been with Suzi in *Don Quixote*—the poor Don, a fool, a dreamer, a would-be lover. No. This time he would play the king, the Sun King, center of the universe—a father. And his daughter? The little blonde with her delicate ribs, with her legs like scissors, with the nose like Tanny's, hair like Tamara's before she had cut and sold it in Paris, eyes pale blue like Suzi's, this girl with the quick ferocity of motion, this would be his girl. And for her, his daughter, he would open up the treasury and bring out its greatest gem, the greatest ballet.

It would be for this girl as it was for Aurora, born once and then born again.

# The Vision

*In which the prince, lonely and forlorn,*
*is shown by the Lilac Fairy a vision of the princess*

*A*dam hauled his body out of the pool and stood dripping at its edge in the Los Angeles sunshine. The cement beneath his feet was already hot, though it was only eleven in the morning. The rest of the company was doing class inside the cavernous Shrine Auditorium, an ugly white box of a building made no prettier by the domes and minarets of its faux Persian design, but he'd slept late, come out to the hotel pool, a flat body of water beneath a hazy yellow sky swollen with pollution and dense with heat. It was late August, an ugly month in Los Angeles; but inside the Shrine, the theater somehow managed to make a small dark magical world in which American Ballet Theatre had performed a week of *La Bayadère* and a week of *Don Quixote*. Coming out of the Shrine at the end of a matinee was a blinding experience. For half the summer he had been doing this, dancing in dark theaters and windowless rehearsal spaces, and now it was the end of the tour and almost the end of the summer and he was sick of it; he needed the light. At the far end of the pool was a fountain and the sounds of the spraying water disguised the sounds of the free-way nearby. Adam threw himself facedown on the chaise, letting his back get the sun.

He'd taken a couple of Quaaludes and for once wanted not to be aware of his body, not to be aware of how it felt, how it worked, how it affected others, the men and women who moved around him, the company he danced with, the audience who stared at his body, his face, who applauded when he moved. On this chaise, alone by the fountain, the pool silent behind him, maybe his body would quiet, hiss to a stop. The heat and the drugs made him dizzy, and he gripped at the plastic slats of the chaise to stop the spinning.

He missed Sandra, craved her, looking at photos of her was just no longer enough. At night he'd pull out the pictures he brought, ones they'd taken of each other before he left, where they'd propped the camera up on the dining room table and set the timer. She was on his lap in the armchair at the head of the table and they'd put their heads close for a long series of shots. They simply sat, her cheek next to his, and stared at the lens as it clicked and clicked and clicked. The background behind them was miserable—they had left the swinging kitchen door ajar to the mess within, but when he looked at the pictures he didn't look at that. He'd sit on his hotel bed and lay the photos out like playing cards, pick the one to hold as he called her, loving the sound of her voice through the phone, the two of them talking until they were almost asleep.

Before he'd left New York, she did her Tchaikovsky Festival and he had gone each night he could, once leaving the Met right after the opening ballet with his stage makeup still on, street clothes stuck to his perspiring body, just to stand at the back of State Theater and watch her in *Mozartiana*. She had been in the ballet no more than she had always been, good, very good, but that was all. Was it possible to be great in a role that was itself not great? Why else was a dancer with potential always being thrust into the great roles, but to see what she looked like *there,* where she could be properly measured? That the ballet itself was great there was no doubt, though there had been only one performance of it, the first night of the festival, during which Suzanne had dislocated a bone in her foot. And that was that. The ballet had been made for her; Balanchine wanted to see no one else dance it. So Adam had seen Sandra dance her part in the "Menuet" just once, in a costume that made her and the other girls look a bit like barmaids at a funeral, their bodices corseted with crisscrossed ties, black ribbons twisted up in their hair like washerwomen's rags. The dance was full of patterns and tableaus, a dance in and of itself, but also preparation for and introduction to the lavishly emotional pas de deux for Suzanne and Ib that followed it.

For that, even the lighting was altered, Suzanne spotlighted with her usual two DynaBeams that made her glow, giving her extra dimension and impact—as if she needed the help. She already had everything, including the master's eye. Adam had stood at the back of the orchestra that night and, watching Ib partner Suzanne, felt for the first time something of what he was missing by leaving City Ballet. Who could have known that Balanchine would be up to this, would pull himself together to do not only this dance, but ballet after ballet for the festival? If Adam had not run off, he would be the one up there in the Prussian blue velvet vest, the one in the ruffled shirt with the big sleeves, the thick white tights. He would be standing in the center of that bizarre set made of hundreds of plastic tubes that hung from steel trestles chained to the theater's overhead pipes, the Plexiglas lit like an ice palace. Sandra had told him about the days required to assemble that set, the problems with the weight of it, the emergency call to all the theaters in the city for sixty more tons of counterweights to help balance it, the terrible stink of the plastic itself. But from the front it looked like a crystallized snow palace from an Arctic fairy tale. And though Adam had danced with Suzanne and knew the look of her, the smell of her, the feel of her hands and arms, her trunk, her legs, from a distance she looked not at all human, but an element, fluid and fierce, more a ten-foot seraph than the ones in the ballet that closed the festival, *Adagio Lamentoso*.

Adam had never seen Balanchine do anything like that last ballet, that lament, not anything so fantastical, so Russian, so funereal. Angels, monks, and mourners populated the stage, nothing American about any of them, the atmosphere heavy with grief, and yet there was no coffin, no corpse, nor any Shade, not a Wili, not a trace of the standard balletic dead. There was only a boy dressed like a member of a church choir, who blew out the light of a taper to the final notes of the score. And that was enough. It was pure theater, and nobody knew theater like Mr. B. He had spent his life in it. The audience could not move to clap for an endless moment, the ballet had stunned them so. Did Mr. B know something? Was he saying good-bye? Balanchine was old, but somehow Adam always thought he would be there should Adam ever want to return to him.

But then in the center of all this blackness and in direct opposition to it stood the Garland Dance, the odd ballet out, a slice of the party cake that was *Sleeping Beauty*, full of flowers and cavorting young couples and children. What the hell was that? Balanchine had always talked about wanting to do *Sleeping Beauty* and maybe this number was just a preview of things to come, one last gift, to follow this season of death. Perhaps the old man still had some magic in him. Like the magic he'd worked on Sandra.

He had cast her in "Diamonds" for Saratoga, the city where Mr. B tried out girls, away from New York and the press and the subscription audience. It was a place for Mr. B to see. So Adam had helped her, told her how to do her hair, to twist it up higher, to do her eyes with longer, more exaggerated lines, had even worked on the big pas de deux with her at home, talking her through each passage, marking it with her and then dancing it with her in the loft, in her dining room, in between his rehearsals and hers, until he had to leave for his tour. He had the height, the hands, the strength, he had the experience, and he made it all work for her, turned her into a diamond every day. And her fragility, her ultrafemininity, had made him ardent beyond belief. He would have died for her, dancing with her, fell on his knees at the end of the adagio and would have kissed her feet had the choreography called for it. It should have called for it. But it wasn't his ballet to do anymore. And she wasn't his to dance with. He could only watch her. He'd left his tour for a single day in July to fly to Saratoga to see her make her debut, and what he saw there was not a debut, but a transformation.

It was an event, and the audience seemed to understand this, seemed to recognize that what unfolded for them tonight were the arms and legs of Balanchine's newest obsession, the long neck, the beautiful head of Balanchine's newest obsession—the feet slightly overarched, which gave them a particular beauty; the legs slightly hyperextended, which gave her arabesques a gorgeous line—all belonged to this girl, but also to Balanchine, who would now make of them and her what he would. And Adam, who knew every step of this ballet, could not remember a single step of it. She had wiped it clean for him, each moment a surprise—that was how new she made it. And he understood—this was what Balanchine was looking for, was always looking for, someone to come and make his ballets new, someone to make an old ballet vibrant again, throw it out of whack, knock it on its side, squeeze inside it and break it into pieces, and for that person he would then fashion new ballets, new masterpieces. What had happened to Sandra? What had happened to her was she had been turned, pivoted like a piece of cut glass, and what was plain when viewed from one angle suddenly flashed full of light and color at another. But by what means had she been pivoted? By the force of Adam's love—or by the roar of Balanchine's sudden interest? At the last moment of the ballet, when her partner kneeled and kissed her hand in that sudden, tender homage, and when to the final whimsical note of the score, Sandra lifted her head to the audience as if surprised by the kiss, Adam knew she was looking for him.

But when he got to the back of the stage afterward, to the wings, he couldn't reach her. She was with Balanchine, the two of them still on the stage, reviewing a few movements from the pas de deux. She had her hands on her hips, or almost at her hips, on the tulle of the tutu, as she looked up at him. She was that small. Usually Mr. B's dancers made giants of themselves beside him with their long legs and their thick false eyelashes. He made a gesture, she mimicked it, amplifying it when he nodded, only then doing it full out. He held her, one hand in her hand, one hand at her waist to demonstrate some business of the partnering, and Adam knew the section: it was a tough bit. If he were dancing with her, he would have got her through it, and they would look magnificent together—he could see them, had seen them, in the mirrors of the loft, in the dark windows of her apartment—but what he hadn't seen, hadn't known, was that this was coming to her. He stood there in the wings while the two of them danced, Balanchine presenting her and representing her to the front, though the curtain was lowered. And Adam wasn't alone, watching them. Other dancers stood back, stood in the wings to see this. There was something fascinating about it, something tender and courtly and utterly private, the old man, the young girl. When they were finished, Balanchine spoke for a moment, then clasped his hands together and held them to his chest. Benediction? Entreaty? Adam had seen this gesture many times, in rehearsal at a moment when inspiration failed and Balanchine sent a little prayer up to the composer in heaven. *Help.* But this time it meant something different. Consecration. And then Balanchine and Sandra walked off the stage together to the other wing, away from him—Adam should have gone stage right, but he had wanted to avoid Balanchine—and Adam watched their backs until he could no longer see the seam that ran up the center of her costume with all the hooks and eyes and ties. But Balanchine couldn't keep Sandra from him all night.

In the cottage she shared with three other girls, they had been awkward at first with each other, and the girls she roomed with were embarrassed by his presence, he could tell, though whether it was because he was an interloper trampling through the girl cottage, or because of who he was, Adam LaSalle, he couldn't tell. After the girls had gone to bed, Sandra brought a pillow and blanket out to the sofa and they sat there by the open window talking and drinking from the bottle he'd brought, not champagne, but schnapps, something black cherry, which made their mouths sticky and their tongues loose. She wouldn't talk about her father, not even when Adam asked her about him. She talked only of Balanchine. To which Adam only half-listened because he had something to ask her. *Do you still love me?* was what he wanted to ask, but he couldn't, just as he couldn't make love to her there; he didn't like that illicit boyfriend-staying-over feeling, didn't want to be just some goddamn boyfriend, and he was afraid, too, of setting off the reaction she'd had the last time he left her, their last day together before he went off on tour. That morning at the loft, when he'd finally gotten out of bed and unstuck his body from hers, he was already late for JFK. He'd pulled on his jeans, and as he stood staring at his suitcases and his duffel bag, she'd lost control, had become hysterical, something he'd never seen in the five years he'd known her. Her sobbing left her breathless, and there was nothing he could do or say to stop it. Finally, his mother came to the door and, seeing him half-dressed and Sandra half-naked and wailing, left quickly and came back with a pill. But Adam didn't have that pill with him in Saratoga, all he had with him were pills he'd never let her take. So in Saratoga they stayed up talking until dawn, had kissed only when his taxi came crunching quietly up the drive so he could catch his plane back for the matinee in San Francisco. Or maybe that wasn't the reason for it, for his re-straint. She was so shiny that night, pasted over with Balan-chine's silver love, and Adam was afraid of it.

Adam sat up on the chaise, squinting into the sun. That had been the last time he'd seen her—July—and now it was almost the end of August. This had been in some ways the loneliest tour and in other ways the least lonely. Her love for him had taken the edge off his usual misery and desperation, and when he went back to his hotel room at night, he'd smoke some pot or take a Quaalude to make sure that he'd stay in his room and not head for the bar or the lobby and end up in someone's bed. At rehearsal break, after class, in the wings, at his dressing room door, he was often accosted by a girl, a conversation, an offer— coffee, a compliment, a question about tempo or technique, sightseeing—it was all the same thing, invitations to sex, to things that would lead to sex—and he turned them all down. He'd been afraid of what he might do, but when it came down to it, he didn't want any of their voices or faces, their mouths or their cunts. He wanted Sandra, her voice, her face, her mouth, her cunt.

But he hadn't been able to reach her yesterday, the day before that, or today. Or her father. It worried him. She should have been back in New York by now, the Saratoga season was over, yet when he called, the phone just rang and he didn't like it. She should have been home, it was the start of the annual hiatus, which meant lots of sleep, taking class wherever they could (even though they were sick of class, they were more afraid of getting out of shape), and seeing a lot of each other. He was hungry for this, had been waiting for it; this year it would mean more than it ever had, a long stretch of uninterrupted time together. They had been imagining it, talking about it on the phone, and now it was as if she'd disappeared. Where was she? Adam got up off the chaise and walked, flexing his arms and legs. The pool was housed on a deck on the sixteenth floor of the hotel, and with this height came both a glare and a view. He put his hand over his eyes and stared out at the buildings, the mountains in the distance, the hills closer by, the ocean. He was scheduled for three more performances, but what if he walked, just bailed? What could management do to him? He could go back to his room now, book his flight, make a call, be out of here in a few hours, sail across the sky, cut his way through the mystery. What he wanted wasn't here. He'd do it. He'd change his ticket and bolt, arrive unannounced, climb the elevator, ring the bell, break down the door, fight his way along the hallway to her bed, take her. After all, she was meant to be his.

# The Battle

*In which the prince does battle for his love*
*and, with a kiss, breaks the evil spell*

ONE

*S*he lay on the vinyl couch in the hospital lounge. It was late. No one else was there, and the TV, which was always on, had been switched off. She was wearing what she had been wearing since she got home from Saratoga two days ago—a T-shirt cropped too short, basketball warm-up pants, and a pair of pink flip-flops. She'd pulled the rubber band from her hair and wrapped it tight around her wrist, and whenever she had a bad thought she'd pluck the band. She wouldn't go home, even though the nurses told her to. She'd known something was wrong the minute she walked through the apartment door, dragging and kicking at her heavy duffel bag, calling out, "Dad?" The air conditioners were off and the apartment was dark and hot. The first thing she saw after she flipped on the lights was the trash and the old food and the paper, everywhere there were papers, sheets of paper with her father's handwriting, on the dining room table, the chairs, even the floor. And there was more of it in the living room, even in the hallway. She recognized it instantly as a manic writing episode—penciled words even marked up the walls. *Vicksburg, Memphis, my father was a textbook salesman, my mother was an invalid.* Sandra understood her father had begun writing again, but not about the siege of Vicksburg, he had been working on whatever this thing was the whole time she was gone, had not slept, had probably taken to roaming around the apartment in his pajamas and his glasses, his hair mussed, like he did the last time he got sick when he catalogued the hundreds of books he'd collected with her grandmother's money, running through his quarterly allowance in a month and alarming the family when he called Vicksburg for more. And from the look of it, he'd been chain-smoking. She'd stared at the penciled marks on the wall. Why was he writing about his parents? She stood there at the end of the hallway, breathing hard, and then her legs gave out and she was sitting down. She feared she would never find him. But in her room, on her bed, he'd left a note. He had gone to the hospital by himself.

She turned on her back, took the rubber band from her wrist and stretched it between her fingers to let it snap against her skin. The big clock ticked on the wall. The desk with the phone was unmanned. She stood up and paced, listening to the slap, slap, slap of her flip-flops. She was hungry; the cafeteria in the basement wasn't open, but there was a vending machine at the end of the hall. The hospital was cold. She didn't have a sweater. She took a couple of quarters from the coin purse she'd brought from home and bought a coffee, chugged it down standing there, felt her stomach contract from it almost immediately. The worst part of it all was she had wanted to get away from him. This was coming and she hadn't wanted to be there, didn't want to know. She had dreaded walking in from the theater each night to find him smoking in the living room, the double doors pulled shut, or sitting at the dining room table, term papers stacked, untouched, before him. The last time, after her dad had not slept for a week and the living room had become a chamber of cigarette butts, she had called home to Vicksburg. But now she was older, too old to call her aging grandmother, old enough to deal with it herself.

She leaned against the machine for a minute. Her dad was two halls away and she wasn't going to get to see him for another day. Now that she was here, wanting to see him, she couldn't. And the truth was, she was scared to see him. When she was fifteen and visiting her father at the hospital, she had come with her great-aunt, and her father, very pale and chain-smoking, had tried to answer all Patsy's questions while Sandra watched his eyes retreat. They'd sat together in a big room full of couches and tables; one wall was windowed and on the other side of it sat the nurses' station, so there was no privacy. That was in the men's ward. None of the patients wore belts or shoelaces, and Sandra remembered the man who sat in a chair shaking his head and talking to himself, picking at his ravaged face until it bled. Her father saw her looking, said something to Aunt Patsy, and after that Sandra wasn't allowed to visit the hospital again. She had to wait three weeks until her father was released. Her grandmother and Aunt Patsy had wanted her to come back to Vicksburg, but she refused. She had ballet class, she was in D Division, almost in the company, and so Aunt Patsy had been sent north.

At the end of that year she was taken into the corps, making two hundred fifty-four dollars a week, dancing thirteen hours a day.

She threw her Styrofoam cup into the trash bin. Today her father had sent her a note. *I love you. Go home and sleep.* She took the folded paper out of her pocket and held it in her fist. She could see her dull reflection in the vendor glass, but she didn't need to see it to know how she looked. Her hair was dirty, her shirt wrinkled, her pants stained. She was going to have to go home.

$\mathcal{A}$DAM WAS SITTING with his back against the apartment door when she got off the elevator, and he scrambled to his feet when he saw her, saying, "It's all right," because she had begun to hyperventilate at the sight of him. How could he be here? He had another week in Los Angeles. It had been so long since she'd seen him that he had become more an idea than a person, someone she talked to in the dark, a voice. And when she found her own and asked him why he was here, he said, "I left the tour." He put his arms out as if to stop her, and she realized she was backing away from him. "It's okay," he said. "I came home early. I couldn't reach you. I was worried." He was talking rapidly, taking hold of her, his hands checking her as if for broken bones. He brushed at her hair, pulled it back from her face. "What's wrong?" he said. "What's happened?"

"My dad's in the hospital."

"Give me the key," he said. "Let's go inside."

She shook her head. She didn't want him to see the apartment.

"Give me the fucking key. I don't care what the place looks like."

But when they got in there he said right away, "Get your stuff. You're not staying here."

She started to cry. "I shouldn't have left him here. I shouldn't have gone to Saratoga. Look what happened."

Adam took her face in his hands. "This doesn't have anything to do with you. It would have happened whether you were here, not here, not even born. He'll tell you the same thing himself." He let go of her face and looked around. "We'll go to my place."

Which meant they'd go to his parents'. He didn't have a place. She'd have to smile and talk to Frankie and Lucia, to Randall, to Joe, to a hundred visitors. She started to cry again.

"I can't go there," she said. "I can't face your parents. I can't face anybody."

He bit his lip, thought. "Okay. I know someplace else. Get your stuff."

But she wouldn't, she just stood there and cried—now that he was here she could cry—so he had to get her stuff. She could hear him in her closets and drawers. Her room was always a mess, piles of clothes and laundry all over the floor, the big upholstered chair she never sat in heaped with junk, the bed never made. She was only one step away from her father and Adam would see this and she couldn't stop him from seeing this. She sat down in the hallway and looked at the papers on the floor. *My father was a textbook salesman, my mother was an invalid. We lived in Memphis, with the smell of the Mississippi.* Was the same thing written on every page? She couldn't bear to look. She shut her eyes, listening to Adam opening things, shutting things. When he came out he had in his hand a blue leather suitcase, one of a set that once belonged to her mother. He picked up the duffel she'd left in the front hall.

"Let's go."

THE APARTMENT HE took her to was a ground-floor studio on West Tenth Street in Greenwich Village, in a four-story brownstone, in a neighborhood she had never been to before with him. And yet he had a key to the building. The apartment was practically empty. In the big room, a few oversized pieces of antique furniture were set out at intervals, like statues. An enormous four-poster bed. A dresser. An armchair. An armoire. She turned to look at Adam, her face a question; it took him a minute but then he said, "My parents lived here when they were first married. My dad kept it. He uses it—sometimes." He looked away, and she knew that was all she would get out of him.

She was sorry that she'd asked, sorry she'd made him think about it, the thing that used to send him to the Eldorado in the middle of the night. The apartment was Frankie's, kept for that purpose. Sandra had behaved like a baby about the loft and Adam had had to bring her here. When he went around the corner to the little half-kitchen, she looked at the bed. She heard him running water. He came back with a glass in his hand. "Drink this," he said, and she did, not because she wanted it, but as a penance. While she did it, Adam went to the window unit and turned the air on. He seemed to know his way around. "It should cool down in here soon," he said to reassure her, or himself, she wasn't sure whom. Over the grind and whir of the machine, they looked at each other and she could sense him trying to take the measure of her. It was the same look her grandmother turned on her periodically. The time-bomb look. *When will you go off?* She wanted to say something to reassure him, but she couldn't think of anything reassuring, she was too tired, and at last he said, "I'm going to run you a bath."

When it was run, he had to come get her and steer her into it. She took off her clothes, shyly—they hadn't seen each other naked for a while, no matter what they'd said to each other about their bodies on the phone—but he wasn't leaving. He was going to make sure she got in. She did, cautiously, the water was too hot, and only then did he sit down on the closed lid of the toilet. He looked tired, she could see that now. He had come straight from the airport to her apartment and then had sat there, back against the door, waiting for six hours for her to show up. She drew her knees up to her chin and huddled there in the hot water.

"Do you know what it was like for me when I couldn't reach you?" he said.

"I'm sorry," she said. "I wasn't thinking—"

He put up his hand. "I didn't say it for that reason."

She started trembling in the tub, and though she gripped her knees, she couldn't stop it. Adam saw, crouched down by the tub. After a minute, he picked up the soap and began to wash her, what he could reach of her, her back, her arm. He wet her hair, used the bar of soap on it as if it were shampoo. By the time he leaned her back to rinse her, his shirt was sopping, the arm of it stuck to her back, a button on it stinging. He kept a hand under her, as if he were afraid she might not resurface and then when he sat her up again, he offered her the soap so she could wash the rest of her body herself. The last time he'd done this for her had been five years ago, when her dad was last sick. She had smelled of vomit, had soiled her nightgown with it, the bathroom had been dark and humid and the water he'd run in the tub too shallow. He'd stood in the doorway, looking unsure if he should run or stay, and she'd felt in that moment too ugly to cry; later, when he drew her in the bath like skeletal death, her nipples gray and pinched, her mouth slack, she knew he'd thought so too. Did he feel that way about her now, only better able to conceal it?

Abruptly, she took the soap from Adam. "I'm okay. You can go."

He stood up immediately, rinsed his hands in the bathroom sink. He didn't shut the door all the way when he left, and she could see him out there, moving around, flicking past occasionally, and she tried to figure out what he was doing.

When she came out in her towel, he said, "I've got your nightgown laid out," and she saw he had. "Let me—let me help you."

She stood there like a kid while he dried her and pulled the nightgown over her head, got her to stick one arm and then the other into the sleeves. It was a gown she never wore, with a low neck and a low back and tiny sleeves. Why had he picked this one? He did the little buttons up the front, working them one by one up her sternum, concentrating, pulling the material away from her so he wouldn't have to touch her skin, but she felt her nipples go hard anyway, from his hands or from the cold, she wasn't sure which. He lifted her long wet hair out of the nightgown. They were done. She crossed her arms over her chest. The air in the apartment had finally begun to cool and now she was chilled. They stood there looking at each other, and then Adam touched his tongue to his upper lip.

"Look," he said. "I'm going to take a shower, okay? I've been running all day."

She nodded and he went into the bathroom and shut the door.

She went to the window and lifted the blind a little. The street was nighttime quiet. What was her father doing right now? The brownstone sat next to a school, its macadam play yard empty, yellow and red circles and lines painted on the black. She released the blind, let it clatter. Her suitcase was open. Adam had started to put her clothes in the armoire, had unzipped her duffel, but left the dirty laundry from Saratoga in it. He was planning for them to stay here awhile. For as long as her dad was in the hospital. She went in her bare feet over the parquet floors to the kitchen: a few square feet of refrigerator, hot plate, sink. You couldn't cook anything here. You could only warm things up. She opened the refrigerator door. A few bottles of beer. A jar of olives. She was hungry. She hadn't been hungry for days and now she was and she was going to have to tell Adam yet another thing he would have to do for her. She opened the bathroom door slowly, and then stopped partway. Adam was in the shower, his body lathered over with soap, and through the clear shower curtain she could see he was leaning against the shower wall, both hands on the tile, head bowed. The water sluiced down his back, his head, his shoulders, his thighs. He made no sound the whole time she watched nor did he move. She knew why he stood there like that. Eventually, she shut the door. She sat down on the bed, and when Adam finally came out with a towel wrapped around his waist, she couldn't look at him.

"Are you okay?" he asked her.

She nodded.

He put a hand on her wet back. "I think I saw your brush in your duffel," he said, and she let him search for it, bring it to her. "May I?" She nodded and he squatted by her and began to brush, making long careful strokes, the bristles catching on the knots, and there were many of them.

"Are you going to get fired for leaving the tour?" she asked him.

He pivoted to look at her, still on his haunches, his own hair dripping, surprised. She could see his thighs, the place between them where the towel parted. "What are you talking about, Sandra?" Adam said.

"Baryshnikov could fire you. He fired Alexander Godunov."
It had been a scandal, one Russian friend throwing away the
other. *Like a potato peel,* Godunov had told the press.

Adam shook his head. "They're not going to fire me, Sandra.
They need me too much." He gave her his big grin. "Don't
worry. Everything's all right. I swear."

"Because I'm okay here," she said, lifting her chin at him.
"You didn't have to come."

"Right," he said, and he stood up, handed her the brush.
"Okay."

He half-turned away from her, refusing to be provoked, and
she looked at the brush in her lap. The black bristles of it were
tangled with her yellow knotted hair.

"Adam," she said, and he turned back to her. She saw that her
voice was a string, and she could wind him toward her with it.
"I never called home from Saratoga."

Adam came closer, shrugged. "When I go on tour, I don't always call home. I don't want to know what's going on, who my
dad's screwing, if Randall's sick. Sometimes you need to be free
of it, just dance. Do you think you could have done 'Diamonds'
the way you did if you were checking on your dad every ten
minutes?"

"You called me a lot," she told him. "Were you checking
on me?"

"What?"

"Were you checking on me? Is that why you called me so
much?"

"Checking on you? Sandra, I was calling you because I was
missing you. You know that."

She looked down. "Adam," she said, her voice almost a whisper, "do you remember what you did to me in tenth grade?"

He stooped to look into her face, trying to keep up, trying to figure out where she was going. "You know I do," he said.

"My dad went into the hospital after that."

"Sandra," he said. He knew where she was going now. He came and sat beside her on the bed, offered her his hand, made her take his hand, insisted on it, and finally she took it. "Sandra, I'm not fifteen anymore. And I'm not scared of you. Of any of this."

$\mathcal{S}$HE AND HER father sat in the corner of the patients' lounge, which looked just like the visitors' lounge—a TV, groups of sofas and chairs, vinyl easily wiped down—except for the window to the nurses' station. Her father held her hand; with his other he held a cigarette. When she was little, he'd sit like this on the sunporch at night, writing with one hand, holding her hand with his other. Bugs would ping against the long row of windows, driven insane by the lamplight. She associated illness with heat, bugs, summer. The cuffs of his sleeves were unbuttoned and when he raised his cigarette, the sleeve slid up his arm. His skin to the elbow was exposed and pale, and when he saw her looking, he lowered his arm, set his cigarette into the ashtray balanced on the arm of the chair, and buttoned the cuff. The tails of the shirt hung out over his pants. Her father wasn't wearing any socks, nor did he have a belt, and his hair looked suddenly white, all the gold and silver gone from it. Though it was light outside, it was dark in here. The windows were grated and hung with vinyl curtains, floor to ceiling, and hung on metal hooks that scraped across the rod when Sandra had tried to yank them open wider. Because the grating on the windows was dark mesh, little light came in through the shaft that separated this building from the next. The fluorescent ceiling lights made a bald, whitish glare. Maybe that was why her father's hair looked that way. Maybe she looked just as pale to him.

But he wasn't looking at her. Why wasn't he looking at her? He looked just off to the right, beside her, but he was holding her hand and occasionally his fingers would grip hers. She wanted to ask him why he'd written on the walls and all those pages, why he was thinking about his parents and if that was what made him sick, his longing for them, which was something that she understood, something that made her sick, too. But she couldn't ask him because she was afraid that talking about it would make him sicker. And she was afraid, too, that he was angry with her for leaving him and that he would not, as Adam had, excuse it. Adam, right now, would forgive her anything. Because of this and because she was here, now, too late, she was afraid to say a single word, even the word *Dad*. So she kept quiet, and she looked down at her father's hand in hers. She wanted to kiss at his hands, but she did not. They sat together in the gray light until her father finished his cigarette and looked in the pack; he had smoked his last one. He smiled at her, his first smile.

"They've washed these clothes for me. But maybe you could bring me a few of my things the next time."

She hadn't thought of that. She hadn't thought to bring him anything—not clothes, not books, not cigarettes, not papers, not pens, not shoes, not a toothbrush. She hung her head then, put her hands to her face, and cried in shame.

WHEN SHE LEFT Roosevelt Hospital, she stood on Amsterdam Avenue without hailing a cab. She didn't want to go back to the brownstone, though Adam had given her a key, tied it to a ribbon. Without thinking, she turned north toward Lincoln Center. There would be nobody there, maybe some of the staff, but no dancers, all of them having gone home for the layoff to visit their families. She could do a barre, she could practice, she could be alone in a studio, which was like no other place on earth. The stage was that way, too. When she reached the plaza, she ducked through the stage door and the guard buzzed her in. She took the elevator to the dressing room, to her locker, where she had not left very much behind, but she found an old pair of pointe shoes, too soft to do much in, but she wasn't going to do much. She found a rubber band wedged on the floor of the locker and she used this for her hair, and then barelegged in her gym shorts and pointe shoes, she went into one of the empty studios and turned on the lights.

She was halfway through her barre when a head appeared in the window and the door opened. It was Mr. B. He was notorious for turning lights off, wanting to save electricity and unnecessary expenditure. She lowered her leg in its développé. She was embarrassed for him to see her in her gym shorts and camisole and ponytail.

"Oh, it's you," he said. He looked around the empty studio and then back at her. "Why aren't you off visiting your mother?"

She said, "My mother died when I was a baby."

"Ah. For me, also, my mother is forever young. She moved away in 1916, too far away for me to ever see her again. I was fourteen. So I carry her here." He tapped his forehead, between his eyes. He looked at her. "You were too young to remember your mother. So you carry her here." And he patted his heart.

She nodded.

"Your father?"

"He's sick."

He looked at her for a moment.

*Please don't ask me about it,* she prayed, and he didn't.

"You came here. That's good." He sniffed. "Do you want to work?"

## TWO

He was pleased that she had come here, that she had thought to come here. He himself was here every day, it was his place, where he should be, where he belonged, where he called to the muse, and not only on union time. He hated Mondays when his dancers stood idle, when the theater stood dark. He hated, too, the layoff, his dancers scattered, taking classes with other teachers, running off to see if they could learn something new from someone else when he had everything here. It was all here, laid out like a buffet, they could come and take, but instead they looked elsewhere for miracles. But this girl with her dead mother and her sick father had come here.

She wore no makeup, her hair pulled back in a long ponytail, her legs bare, their nakedness revealing the sharp architecture of her muscles, muscles he had helped build. She seemed embarrassed by this, pulling at the waistband of her baggy shorts. He had made up his mind what he would do for her, had already begun studying the massive score. They would start with the Vision scene, the most important section of *Sleeping Beauty,* not only the place where the prince is shown a vision of the sleeping princess, but also the place where the court dances of eighteenth-century France, of Louis XIV, the gavotte, the saraband, the farandole, are shown their successor—classical ballet. The nymphs who surround Aurora, keeping the prince from her, revealing her and then shielding her, did not wear high-heeled slippers and long dresses, but pointe shoes and tutus, standard attire of dancers of the next century. *Sleeping Beauty* was both a ballet about ballet and a tribute to the French court life so worshipped by St. Petersburg of 1890. In the apotheosis, the personnel of Act III positioned themselves about a backdrop painted with the image of Louis XIV dressed as Apollo. The king had once played the Sun God in a court ballet, and so he was depicted, surrounded by fairies with long trains, rays of light, white horses, a chariot. So had Marius Petipa, the Maryinsky's great choreographer who kept, always, one eye on the court, seen the czar.

The ballet had been Petipa's present to Alexander III. In the ballet, no revolutions, no pogroms, no assassinations. The royal family lived. The princess thrived. No, Petipa made no mention in his *Sleeping Beauty* of the mayhem that inevitably follows a period of glory. Like the Brothers Grimm, he had lopped off the last part of Perrault's tale, where the princess, after being wed, gave birth to twins, Morning and Day, only to have the prince's mother give orders for Aurora and her children to be killed and minced and cooked for her supper. Petipa had not used the second part of the story, but the tale hung in the wings, like the Revolution itself, and soon enough glorious Russia devoured its own, the three hundred years' reign of the Romanovs destroyed, Alexander's son and grandchildren murdered, the great palaces turned into offices and museums. But in the ballet, all was secure, the court frolicked at their forest picnic in their high-heeled slippers and their high-heeled boots. And later in that forest the prince is shown a vision of the loveliness of the princess. This vision of Aurora must be so seductive that the prince leaves behind everything he knows to board a boat with the Lilac Fairy as his guide, to sail across a strange lake until he reaches a dark, briar-covered palace, the haunted place that he alone can liberate.

All this he explained to the girl and she listened to him, and when he finished and asked her if she understood, she nodded. New ballet, for spring season. Big event. She nodded again. He shut his eyes for a moment and listened for the score, the cellos, the haunting melody, and when he opened his eyes he saw exactly—the lush foliage of the forest, the prince in his feathered hat and buckled boots, the departure of the hunting party, the appearance of the Lilac Fairy who senses the prince's loneliness, his need to love and be loved. She mimes to him the story of the beautiful sleeping princess and urges him to go to her and with a kiss to break the spell that binds her to sleep. But the prince is skeptical, more modern than the fairy, and he demands proof. Thus the vision.

For this scene at the Maryinsky, the princess wore a sparkling pink tutu, hair up, a crown. He rubbed his fingers against his chin. Perhaps he would do differently. The hair in a long silk cord, like the ponytail the girl wore now, to spin like sugar in the light. She would wear pink, yes. The tutu slightly longer and softer than the one worn in the first act, the one in which Aurora fell, her finger pricked. It was a vision, yes? Everything about the girl would be softened, romanticized for it, as she displayed herself from within the circle of nymphs, stepped beyond their protection periodically to allow the prince to touch her, to dance with her, to imagine the vision real, to create in him the mad desire that would lead him to pursue her through time.

"Next time we'll have Gordon with us," he told her, taking her wrist. "But for now, we'll hum."

W HEN SHE LEFT the studio, he held the door for her and he watched her walk down the hall, her thin back, her empty hands, her bare legs. Usually his girls carried so much with them, their big bags full of warmers and waters and shoes, their bodies camouflaged with an equal amount of gear—sweaters and plastic pants and woolen tights, chiffon skirts. But she had nothing and so he could see her down to the bone, and what he saw there was fear. She felt small, unequal to the challenge he knew she could meet.

He knew her fear, knew the fear of that little girl walking down the hallway, walking toward her destiny. It was a common fear, common to all artists. When Diaghilev revived *Sleeping Beauty* for his Ballets Russes, sinking the company into debt for the lavish but doomed production—after all, he had not the czar's pockets—he hired the ballerina Vera Trefilova to dance Aurora. The night before her debut she sent him a telegram: "If you do not release me from my contract, which requires me to appear in *The Sleeping Beauty* at my age, this very night I will kill myself and you shall be responsible for my death." Diaghilev had laughed, tossed away the telegram. The next night Trefilova performed—magnificently. Diaghilev knew. You had to know within yourself. And if you didn't know, you needed the other who did know. For this girl, he was the other.

As for himself, he had no one. In the early days nobody

thought he was any good. In America, the critics were always carping at him: his work was nonsense, incomprehensible, scarcely worth the labor that was spent on it, decadent; at best, serviceable. He was still, even in the late fifties, getting poor reviews—his *Firebird* for Maria was emaciated, his *Trumpet Concerto* a bomb. Back in Russia, the critic Volynsky had snapped like a terrier at the heels of his first little ballets. Even Diaghilev himself had told George his dances contained false, crude, disappointing moments. All this, that, and the other; he paid them all no mind, would have been destroyed by them if he had. He no longer read reviews, hated written words of all kinds, couldn't stand to read his own mail, had been unable to compose a letter to his mother on the occasion of his father's death. A friend had written it for him.

W H E N  T H E  G I R L  had disappeared around the corner, he took the elevator down to the theater. Whatever empathetic fear he felt vanished with her. Instead there was only the excitement that came to him always at the act of creation, the idea of creation, the dream of what it all could be, which was why he liked to look for youth, for the uncertain potential he could draw out. He didn't like old cheese, smelly cheese. A young dancer was like young cheese, sparkling and sweaty. At home in St. Petersburg, before his father lost all their money and the family had to move to the country, his mother would serve young goat cheese, the block of it so hard they had to break at it with a knife, pour hot water over it. They ate it with pancakes. Old cheese, old dancers. A finished dancer was as dull as a finished ballet, and for him there were few of those. He was always tinkering. Even on the old ballets he liked to tinker—each season they did *Don*

*Quixote,* he dropped this part, added another, changed steps in *Apollo,* and this summer, watching from the wings while Sandra did "Diamonds," he saw the whole movement was boring, only the pas de deux was any good, and he thought to himself, *I should redo.*

The elevator opened and George walked the passages behind the stage, past the dressing rooms, the wings, the storage vaults, the rehearsal spaces, and walked out into the dim space of the stage itself, gold curtain lowered. On the other side of the curtain lay the tiers and boxes and orchestra, their seats plush and red, the dome-shaped lights of gold and crystal dotting the sides of the tiers, props for the house just as there were props backstage, these props out front a promise: sit in this special place, prepare yourself, something magical will unfold. It was a good theater, but not the Maryinsky, with its enormous backstage capacity and expansive stage. On that stage the original production of *Sleeping Beauty* had used real horses decked out in feathers and velvet blankets. Fountains sparkled with real water, the castle was encased in shrubbery of both painted canvas and material cut, painted, and glued to rope. And the costumes! The king wore a waxed mustache and ermine cloak, the courtiers long curled wigs, French-style, big hats with plumes, vestments elaborately appliquéd and paired with striped hosiery. The Lilac Fairy herself appeared in tulle and garlands, wand, and an elaborate pointed hat, half helmet of Athena, half unicorn's horn. From what designer's mind had that concoction sprung? And the wicked fairy, the Carabosse, had a long dark cape. George remembered how Alexander Chekrygin, because the part was played, always, by a man dressed as a woman, had used his cape like a partner, the inanimate the only partner evil could ever have.

The inanimate sprung to life: that was stagecraft. Black magic. Amazing magic. He himself had made plenty of it. In *Prodigal Son* at Ballets Russes they had put the revelers in bald-headed wigs, and from the front their fleshy scalps had looked terrifying; the table they overturned at the close of the act became a boat, the legs of the table now the curved ribs of the ship, the Siren herself the figurehead on the prow, her long scarf held aloft behind her by the many hands of the crew. Wind out of nothing. In his own *Nutcracker,* the tree grew, the Sugar Plum Fairy stepped onto a metal plate and appeared to glide across the stage in arabesque, her gliding made possible by the stagehands who cranked a wire. Marie's bed spun across the stage powered by a little boy who crouched beneath it, and Marie herself, ensconced beside the Nutcracker prince, flew off above the stage in Santa's sleigh, sparklers and firecrackers at its rear. *Sleeping Beauty* would be the apex of such trickery, making what was real in life look real on the stage, making what was magic in Perrault's tale magic on the stage.

How he could do it in Russia, if he were in favor there, but he would have to do it here, on this smaller, less-equipped stage, in America. Because he was here.

And his Aurora was here.

$\mathcal{S}$HE WAS PERFECT—tiny, sharp like a jewel, but fluid, elastic, expansive where he needed her to be. Contained, as if she had secrets, as if whatever was lush within her had not yet tumbled out, not yet been tempted to. This was her promise to the prince—*Whatever is lush within me will be yours*. Her prince. He would have to think, choose her the right suitor, someone different this time, not Peter, not Ib, not any of his Danish boys, his Danish pastries; maybe someone younger, someone just at the cusp of manhood. Could be anyone. How did Lilac Fairy choose? Chance? No. She was the prince's godmother, as well as Aurora's. This he thought he remembered from the story. She chose her own boy. Or did she see in Prince Désiré something special, something lost? Someone in whom need would become a force? He would look at his boys when the company reassembled end of September.

Did this girl already have a suitor from among them? There had been that boy one night at Saratoga waiting cagily in the shadows of the wing, but George had seen him anyway and so had the girl. Her eyes went stage left just for a moment while he was coaching her, but she had not looked there again. Later, he saw them leaving the theater together and he recognized the boy, Adam LaSalle, the one who had come to him a year ago saying, "I want to leave." He wanted to go across the plaza to play the prince. *So go,* he had said. He had showered the boy with everything, every role, the best ballerinas, and the boy took it all, packed it into his bags, and left with it to give it away somewhere else. But he had waited in the shadows of that wing. He wanted one more thing.

He would choose her prince, and it would not be this boy.

He turned from the stage. He himself would play King Florestan XIV. Louis XIV had played the rising sun in his *Le Ballet de la Nuit,* appearing with Aurora, the dawn. So George would accompany his own Aurora. And Aurora's betrothal to Désiré required the king's consent, the kiss itself inconsequential in the face of the will of the king. And the king was the king until he lay on his deathbed. Was a king forever, his legacy alive in his buildings and monuments and institutions, his image paraded and memorialized and aggrandized.

He would go across the street in the heat to the bookstalls, find a book of fairy tales, one that told the story very well, and give it to the girl as a present.

# THREE

When Adam walked off the elevator—goddamn it—his parents were sitting right there at the long dining room table, his dad with his big mug of Coke and his hair tousled, his mom in her robe. At 2 P.M., they looked as if they had just gotten up, which they probably had: they kept theater hours. Adam felt as if he'd lived two lifetimes already this morning dealing with Sandra. They stared at him nonplussed as he shut the grate and sent the elevator down. What he had wanted to do was dart into his bedroom, grab a few things, and get out unnoticed, but that was impossible now. So he braced himself for what he was going to have to listen to. It didn't take long. As he came toward them, his mother said, "What are you doing here? We weren't expecting you until the end of the week!"

"I came back early," Adam said, sitting down at the table, suddenly too tired to stand. "Sandra's dad went into the hospital." Whatever he was expecting this announcement would engender—sympathy, concern, compassion—was not materializing.

Something else was and he could see it in their faces, a sort of incomprehension. He watched them feeling their way toward this new weird thing, and Jesus, were they slow.

"So you left the tour? You walked out?" Lucia asked.

"I didn't walk out," Adam said. "They let me go."

"Adam."

And at the concern in her voice, he just sagged, wanted to put his head down on the table and weep. He hadn't slept well last night, kept waking to check on Sandra, to make sure she was breathing, though breathing wasn't her problem. Last night he had felt exactly twenty years old and beyond overwhelmed, though he'd never let Sandra know it. It was too late for that now. She was his; he had come home for her and he was in charge.

He looked at his mom. "I need to stay in the brownstone for a while, until we've had a chance to clean up Sandra's apartment. Her father trashed the place while she was in Saratoga. Is that all right?" He wouldn't have dared to ask this of his dad, though Frankie sat right there by her.

Lucia looked at Frankie and then back to Adam. "Why don't you two stay here?" she said.

And he wanted to, that was the thing; his mom would be around, just in case, but he had to shake his head. "Sandra—she's got too much going on. She needs some privacy."

"Well, sure, take the brownstone then."

Adam looked quickly across the table to Frankie.

"It doesn't really have a kitchen, you know," his dad said. And by that Adam knew his dad didn't want him to stay there. Which made Adam only more determined to do so. Let him find another place to fuck his girls. "There's only a hot plate."

"I know," Adam said. It was broken. They'd already screwed around with it this morning.

"So you're not rejoining the tour," Frankie said.

Jesus, were they back *there,* again? Adam stood up. "The tour is practically over. There's nothing to rejoin." He was determined to end the conversation before it converged once more into another interrogation. "I've got to get a few things."

He headed across the loft to his room as his parents conferred at the table. About fucking what? His mom was gesturing with one hand and his dad leaned forward, shaking his head. Adam reached his room, shut the door, looked around. His mom had cleaned up while he was away—the bed was made, the covers stretched over it and tucked so tightly there could be no crawling into it, no pulling the blankets over his head, which was what he wanted to do. The surfaces of the bureau and desk had been cleared off, all the junk he'd left disposed of somehow; even the floor looked as if it had been refinished.

What had he come here to get? What did he think he needed? He had clothes enough in the suitcase back at the brownstone. He had come here, he supposed, for something else. His laundry sat in neat piles on the bench at the foot of the bed. His mom had done his wash, opened up the old duffel he'd left behind when he went on tour, the duffel with his amphetamines and his pot and his rubbers, and pulled out all his old dirty clothes. The duffel itself sagged, deflated, on the floor and he knelt down and reached his hands into it—almost empty. Wedged into a crease was the small pouch of drugs. At least he had that. His theater trunk would be arriving back with the company in a few days and he felt a little lost to be separated from his equipment. He'd left without a pair of tights or shoes. He'd go over to the studios when the trunk arrived to get his practice clothes, to face the fallout from management. They had not been pleased about having to replace him on such short notice, and Baryshnikov's assistant had grilled him about the nature of the emergency until Adam stood up and walked out.

Crouching there in his room, he held on to his bag of dope, wondering if he had time for a smoke. He needed something. He sat down heavily on the floor, rolled himself a joint, and took too many hits before he stubbed it out, the taste of it sweet and acrid and harsh at the back of his throat, the feel of it welcome because he knew the calm that would follow. He sat there waiting for it, eventually stretched out on his side by his duffel, almost asleep. But then the door opened and his mother came in to the cloud of smoke and the stink. He couldn't even stand up, he'd smoked so much so fast, could only lie there, heart beating sluggishly, groping for words. "What is it?" was the thing he eventually managed to say. His mom got down on the floor beside him, put her hand to his face just as she used to when he was little and she'd had a fight with his father. She would come into Adam's room, sit on the edge of the bed, put her hand to his face. He'd wake sometimes to find her doing it, just staring down at him, her long hair loose and dark. He was three, four, but even at that age he could tell she'd been crying. He thought then he was the reason. Later he saw differently. Later than that, he saw it differently still.

"Adam," and her voice wafted toward him through the thick air, "doesn't Sandra have anybody else who can help her? A relative?"

This, and what lay behind it, woke Adam like a dart blown into his face, and suddenly he found he could, in fact, sit up. "She and her dad are alone," Adam said. "You know that. All their family is in Mississippi."

"What about a family friend?"

"What's the problem here, Mom?"

"Adam." She shook her head. "I saw what happened to her the day you left for your tour."

"She was crying. It's hard on her when I'm gone. It's hard on me."

"She was hysterical, Adam. She had to be sedated."

He looked down. He knew this. He knew all about this. She put her hand out and covered his.

"I just want you to consider that Sandra might be a lot to take on." She paused. "How many tours do you think you can walk out on because of her? How many rehearsals can you cut? How many times can you call in sick because she's upset you, how many performances can you skip before you've got a reputation for being unreliable?"

He could feel the weight of her hand, the weight of her concern for him, of what she wanted from him, had always wanted from him. And he wanted to give it to her, *had* given it to her, had made himself into Adam LaSalle, burgeoning ballet star. It had been her idea that he leave City Ballet, follow Baryshnikov, become a sort of Baryshnikov himself, because none of the men at City Ballet, she said, were household names, none were big enough stars. So Adam had done it, what she suggested, wanted to do it, wanted to chase this thing she wanted for him. Why couldn't she now want for him this thing *he* wanted, help him to have it? He wanted to grip her hand, shake it off, weep into it all at the same time, but finally he did nothing to it, just let his hand sit beneath it, just sit there.

$\mathcal{B}$UT SHE CAME through for him in the end, packing up a slew of boxes she made his dad bring up from the basement. Into those boxes she had thrown a ridiculous amount of household items, everything from blankets to canned beans, as if he and Sandra would be staying in the brownstone forever instead of a few weeks, and these boxes now skittered and bounced in the back of the truck as his dad barreled down Ninth Avenue. She'd even gotten Frankie to drive it all, and Adam, back to the Village, though Adam didn't want his dad's help and was certain Frankie didn't want to give it. Adam didn't want to be at the brownstone with his father, didn't want to go anywhere near the brownstone with him. The place reeked of failure, and Adam had been superstitious enough not to have wanted to walk through the threshold of it yesterday with Sandra. He wished for the first time in two years that he'd kept his little apartment in Midtown, but he had not, so last night he just tried not to think about where he was, but the place was cursed—already he and Sandra were fighting.

Adam cranked down the window and let in the warm August air. His stomach roiled, queasy. He hadn't eaten this morning. Sandra wasn't hungry, she was never hungry, she didn't care if the hot plate was broken, she was just anxious to get back to the hospital. She'd get coffee, something, there. So fine, they wouldn't eat. He took a cab with her to Roosevelt, went on to Hell's Kitchen. Adam rubbed his hands through his hair, looked at the city going by at such speed, and dared an occasional glance at his father. The two of them weren't talking. Was his dad angry? And with whom—Lucia or Adam? Adam couldn't tell. Frankie stared straight ahead and Adam took note of the terrifying way his father's flesh drew itself into taut wrinkles across his knuckles and how at his elbows the skin hung slack, hung slackly also from the muscles of his upper arms. Adam hadn't seen him close-up in such unforgiving light for a long time. His father was aging, too old at long last for the young girls who slept with him, because it was always young girls, from the beginning it had been that way. The first girl Adam had slept with was a girl his father was going after. At a party in their own loft, Adam had observed the flirtation to which his mother appeared oblivious, watched the girl put her hand teasingly around his father's neck. Adam was almost sixteen then, and by the end of the night and after a series of maneuvers, he was doing the girl, not his father, doing her with this new body of his, this almost adult body of his that had become a powerful tool to distract, to dissuade, to preempt, to seduce, to thwart, to protect. And for a long while, this was so—Adam usurped his father's trolling grounds. But ultimately it hadn't worked, didn't stop his dad, his father went on cheating, and Adam eventually racked up a sickening body count—the triumph, the adrenaline, long gone. Only loneliness drove him on. How could his father keep it up? What drove him? Something he needed and wasn't getting. Something he wanted to get away from. Maybe now it was simply this, the slack skin, the delicate tap of age which didn't tap, but hammered at a dancer. *You're old. Clear the stage.* His dad looked over at him, caught Adam's gaze, misunderstood it.

"I've been working out," he said, "trying to get in shape." He flexed his biceps and then said at Adam's blank look, "For Joe. Rehearsal next week, remember?"

"Yeah, yeah, yeah," Adam said, not that he'd forgotten about it, but to cover his surprise that his dad was actually having to prepare for this. Adam hadn't even thought about taking class, let alone working out. Joe's work was nothing, a technical zero. Adam tried to think of something to say while his dad circled the block looking for an open spot, squinting behind his sunglasses and craning his neck. They circled twice, the cab of the pickup getting hotter and hotter the slower they went until it was a rolling inferno, and finally Frankie said, "I guess I'll just have to double-park." Which was fine with Adam. He didn't want his dad inside. Street was fine.

They made rapid relays, dragging the junk up the steps and dumping it just outside the front door, the two of them sweating and grunting, big veins making chords in Frankie's neck and arms. And when they were done, his dad said, "I'll help you bring the stuff in."

Adam shook his head. "No thanks."

"No thanks?"

"I don't want you—in there."

The two of them faced off for a moment. A taxi rolled by. Then another. The taillights blinked at the back of the truck.

Finally his father said with exaggerated courtesy, "Well, may I come in for a minute and get a drink of water?"

And so Adam had to relent, prop the brownstone door open with a box, fumble with his key to the apartment, which was, all of a sudden, difficult to open. All the while he fumbled he could feel his father staring at his back, could feel his own back stiffening up in response.

And then they were inside, in the dark and cool, and the girls, the specters of the many girls, stirred and rustled and rose up and began to breathe and Adam could feel their breath. His dad went straight to the kitchen and opened exactly the right cupboard for a glass, which he filled from the tap and drank without pause, standing there in the center of the kitchen, and then set down a little too forcefully on the counter. At the sound of it, Adam crossed his arms over his chest. He didn't need to be reminded that this was his father's place. Fuck, no. Adam didn't move, didn't even look away when he said, "Dad, I want your key."

Frankie raised an eyebrow, and then, after a few seconds,

reached into his pants pocket and hauled out a ring of keys, fingered through them, twisted one off and chunked it down on the counter by the glass. It was stupid, Adam knew, to ask for it. Not stupid, ridiculous. His mom had a key, they probably had a spare back at the loft, his dad could get in, anybody could get in, but Adam had made his point. Frankie was out.

After his father left, Adam crossed to the counter, picked up the key, and put it in his pocket, and the girls around him sank away. Once, when Adam was ten and his mom dropped him off a little too early for a visit with his dad, there had been an actual girl here. She rose from the bed when Adam arrived. His dad sent him to the bathroom for a few minutes, and when he came out, the girl was gone. Adam thought his dad had hidden her somewhere, and he kept waiting for her to reappear the whole time they had dinner on a tray table, watched TV, and played a game of cards. When it was time for Adam to go, his dad had said, "We don't need to mention Elise to your mom," and Adam had nodded. He never saw the girl again, but he heard her name in the loft over and over and then he didn't hear it anymore because Randall took him to L.A.

Adam said now, "Fuck, fuck, fuck," just to get rid of her, to get rid of them all, began kicking at the boxes, the long and disordered trail of them, some with flaps that lay open like thighs, others stuck with long skeins of tape like fingers and arms. There was so much stuff. Potato Buds. A king-sized pillow. A plastic bucket. A can opener. Sheets. They had slept on his dad's goddamn sheets last night. Christ. He went to the bed and started pulling at them, wrangled them off the mattress, threw them to the ground. There was so much to be put away, to be used. He wasn't going to bolt. He was going to calm down, stay here, unpack. It wasn't his turn to rant and cry. It was his turn to be strong.

JOE'S REHEARSAL SPACE was a large, odd-shaped penta-gon, a studio with a gray linoleum floor and barres mounted along all five walls, even across the mirrors. In it Adam stood panting, his legs covered in two pairs of warmers and his T-shirt soaked, going over in his mind the dance he'd just learned. He was gifted like that—a quick study—one run-through and he had it. Because his dad's mobility was now so limited, Joe had choreographed a quietly majestic solo for him, which Frankie would perform within the set of that hotel room, the solo full of pulses and contractions that made the most of Frankie's height, authority, and presence without exposing or suggesting any of the arthritic problems that limited his extension or pro-hibited jumping. In contrast, Adam's part in the pas de deux with his father that followed was punched full of action. He and Frankie would make brief contact—clasped hands, a hand on the shoulder—and then Adam would be sent off again in a se-ries of swooping turns, arabesque turns, a wide circle of barrel jumps, basically a testosterone-laden showpiece designed to trump his father, as if Joe were using this dance to humiliate him. Yet Frankie never seemed trumped or humiliated or even humbled. Each time Adam came together with his father in one of the dance's connections or embraces, his father's gaze was im-mediate, generous, and absolutely focused. His dad was a better partner than any of the ballerinas Adam had worked with, whose concern with their pointe shoes or the placement of his hands or their display to the audience had often meant their gazes fixed haphazardly on his forehead or off beyond him at the moments when they faced each other. Frankie looked right at him and his gaze seemed to feed him, and Adam, who had come here expecting the worst, who had come here not really wanting to dance with Frankie at all, began to wish over the course of the afternoon that Joe would do more for them than these intermittent postures.

Randall watched all this intently from his metal folding chair at the front, his back to the mirror, his face registering little, at least from what Adam could see. Despite the heat and the steam Adam and Frankie were generating in the studio, Randall kept on the ratty pullover sweater he always wore when he had the flu, with this green wool cap pulled down to his brows. His face looked suddenly lined, and this panicked Adam. Were all the men in his life suddenly old? Adam shook his head and Randall leaned forward in his chair, chin in his hands, elbows on his knees. It was the four of them together in the room as they had always been—except this time they were making a dance together. And Adam was glad now, for reasons other than Sandra, that he had agreed to do this.

Joe had Frankie and Adam run through it all again, and he was between them the whole time, stepping in to adjust an arm or the angle of a hand, backing out of the way when Adam took off, calling out the counts as if Adam couldn't hear them in the music. What kind of dancers was he used to working with? Joe paused periodically to look at this piece of paper where he'd scribbled the steps, and they'd have to stand there and wait while he did it. Balanchine had it all in his head, made changes on the spot, came up with fifteen different options if something wasn't working, but Joe was rigid, everything had to be done exactly this way, the body had to be made to comply. The muscle tee

Joe wore had gaping armholes that showed off the dark, surprisingly thick hair he had beneath his arms. His hands were strong and sinewy, and each time they grasped at Adam's arms or trunk or thighs, they brought back a memory Adam had forgotten of Joe doing gymnastics with him in the loft when Adam was about five. Joe would lie on his back and bend his knees and Adam would stand on them and balance—then he'd step into Joe's hands and Joe would raise him up so Adam could view the world. They'd practiced a handstand, his hands locked onto Joe's elevated ones, but Adam managed only a rare moment of balance before he took a tumble in one direction or another, Joe's arms always breaking his fall, until Randall finally put a stop to their circus act. Joe was doing that now, with him, with his body, this highly refined instrument the likes of which he didn't often get to use, and he was testing the limits of it.

Sandra came in quietly while they were working and stood there, watching, and Adam felt this amazing relief that she'd shown up—he'd had to work on her about it all morning, wasn't sure still even by the time he left the brownstone if she would get out of bed and get herself over here—she just wanted to lie there and smoke cigarettes and stare at the ceiling. She spent her days at the hospital with her dad and she never wanted Adam to come with her. When she got back to the brownstone in the very late afternoon, she was tired, distracted, wouldn't talk to him, didn't want to eat. She'd smoke and he'd be a dog in a clown suit, trying to entertain her, trying to get her attention, until finally he'd give up. In that goddamn brownstone, there was nothing she found entertaining about him unless he took her to bed. Well, she was out of bed now and she was goddamn well going to be entertained. So Adam pushed himself, even though it was their last time through his solo, just for memory, and he should have been marking, holding back, conserving his strength. But she was watching. She always watched him when he danced.

When he finished, Frankie slapped his back, nodded and grinned at Joe, and Adam took a long drink from his water bottle and went over to Sandra at the barre. He wiped at himself with his towel while she warmed up, not in pointe shoes, but in the heeled jazz shoes Joe had asked her to wear, and they scraped across the floor. While Joe looked over his notes, Adam put his hand out and covered Sandra's hand. She lifted her fingers and gripped at him. He couldn't read the gesture. Was she nervous? He, actually, was nervous for her. He wasn't sure how this would go, if she was up to this, to having a dance made for her which she had to instantly inhabit, at least almost all the way, so the choreographer could assess how it looked. She was used to being rehearsed by repetiteurs and coaches in ballets that had already been created, staged, and codified long ago. The way she executed the steps would not cause them to be altered or redesigned. And Adam wanted this to work, didn't want to ever have to leave her alone again, leave her vulnerable, come back to find her destroyed. With his other hand, he stroked her hair. Joe had asked for her to wear it down, and she looked to Adam even younger than she usually did, something like the way she'd looked when he first met her, fifteen and frightened. He held her hand, her hair. He didn't want her to be frightened.

But when Joe finally brought them out onto the floor, it was Adam who was taken aback by what Joe had conceived for them. The pas de deux had Adam forcefully manipulating Sandra's body, controlling and containing her movements, and then after he had seemingly mastered her, within his arms he allowed what she could and could not do, the dance ending with him holding her hair back in his fist as he bent toward her. She was so tiny his hands entirely enclosed her waist, his fingers almost met across her rib cage, fully engulfed her head when Joe had him take his hands and grasp her temples to turn her forcibly in another direction. Their difference in size meant Adam loomed large over her, colossal, mammoth, hulking. He felt like Othello or Bluebeard or something. Was this how Joe saw him? Periodically, Adam looked over at his dad and Randall, *What the fuck?* But his dad was bent forward, stretching, and Randall's face was impassive. It bothered Adam to be holding Sandra's body this way, and, of course, the more powerful or strident his own movements, the more delicate and hesitant her own. Everything that Joe saw about her—that she was sexually innocent, that she was emotionally fragile, that Adam was running her down like a Mack truck—he put into the piece. Adam was so upset he couldn't even assess how Sandra was dancing. But if Adam was uncomfortable, she didn't seem to be. At each turn, at each interlocking posture, she looked right up at him, and in her cool blue eyes he saw nothing but quiet trust. Did she trust him? He wanted to be worthy of it.

At the end of it, he wouldn't let go of her hand, even while Joe was giving them notes and setting the time to work tomorrow. What did she think of this? he wanted to ask her, but when Joe finished with them and turned to consult with Frankie and Randall, Sandra pulled her hand from his. "I'm late. I need to go visit my dad." They weren't going to get to talk about it. And when he started to say, *Let me come with you,* she shook her head. She was already gone, her mind on her father. He bent to kiss her, and when he straightened he saw Randall, Joe, and Frankie watching them. Why were they looking at him? Was there something wrong with what he was doing? Was there something wrong with this?

So HE HAD to wait until he got a cab for Sandra, climbed into another one with Randall, before he could say, "What the hell was that pas de deux about?" Randall peeled off his wool stocking cap and put his hands into his hair, which was flattened and lacquered with sweat. He didn't answer right away, his face drained, fatigued, but Adam, impatient, didn't care, pressed on. "Is that how Joe sees me? As some kind of overbearing freak?"

"No, no."

"Do you?"

"Adam." Randall leaned back against the seat.

"You don't talk to Joe about me, do you? You don't tell him the stuff I tell you about Sandra?"

"I talk to him about you, but not about Sandra."

"So where's he getting all this?"

"I don't know."

"Oh, come on, Randall. If Joe knows anything about me it's because of you."

And Randall said, "That's a ridiculous statement, Adam. Joe's known you since you were born."

"Well, I'm not what he thinks. I'm not running her life— she's living with me because her dad is sick and she's dancing with me because she's not going anywhere with City Ballet." This last was no longer exactly true, and Randall knew it, turned to him.

"I thought she just danced 'Diamonds.'"

"Once," Adam said, "in Saratoga."

"Well, that's how it all starts," Randall said, "isn't it?"

Adam shook his head. "I don't want her at City Ballet. I want her with me at Ballet Theatre. That's why I'm doing Joe's gig."

"I don't understand."

"I want Baryshnikov to see her. I want him to offer her a contract."

Randall closed his eyes momentarily. "I'm not sure that's a good idea."

"Randall, I can't take care of her from a thousand miles away."

Randall spoke without opening his eyes. "She's not like you, Adam."

"I know she's not like me."

"How well do you think she'd do away from home? How well would she handle all that touring?"

"Her home is a fucking nightmare and on tour she'd be with me."

"Calm down," Randall said, and when Adam sat back, Randall went on. "You're not her cure, Adam."

"Well, what am I, then?" Adam said. "What Joe thinks I am, her . . . her—" He couldn't find the word and Randall interrupted him.

"What makes you think this dance is about you?"

Adam looked at him. "Well, who's it about, then?"

Randall said nothing.

"You and Joe?"

Randall raised an eyebrow.

"He's the domineering freak?"

Randall shook his head.

"What, you're the domineering freak?"

"I've pretty much kept him where I wanted him, haven't I? Kept him there with my money. Still keeping him there."

And suddenly Adam was through, didn't want to hear about it, didn't want to know about it, know who was the freak and who was fucked, just wanted to get out of the cab. Who cared what Joe Alton thought and felt? Randall had made Joe Alton, given him everything he had—Joe should be on his knees and Sandra should be on hers. He leaned forward and put his head in his hands.

Randall reached a hand out and touched Adam. "Maybe I'm wrong," Randall said. "I could be wrong."

$\mathcal{A}$DAM STOPPED OFF at ABT's studios the next day on his way uptown to meet Sandra at the Eldorado. They were going to clean up the place. She didn't want to bring in a service, didn't want anybody to see what her father had done, so he was going there, he was going to mop and scour and run the fucking vacuum for her, but first he wanted to go to ABT, to get some of his stuff from his trunk and his locker—he needed more of his practice clothes, his shoes. That was the pretext for his visit, anyway, but the real purpose of it was to speak to Baryshnikov about the upcoming week at the Joyce. It wasn't going to be easy. He wasn't really in a position to seek favors, that he knew; he'd left Baryshnikov one hour to find a replacement for him his last day in Los Angeles.

The place was deserted, no one at the reception desk, just a cup of coffee on the ledge, studios empty, hallways barren. Adam got his stuff from his trunk and shoved it into the drawstring laundry bag he'd brought with him. He could still see Baryshnikov's assistant, Charles France, twice the size of Baryshnikov, with his big glasses and broad beard and red face. *What do you mean you think something's wrong, can't you call someone and find out before we have to change the whole goddamn schedule,* until

Baryshnikov put up a hand and cut Charles off midsentence: "Someone's sick, something's wrong. Let him go."

Adam went out into the hallway, bag over his shoulder, and went toward the wing where the staff had their offices. He didn't really want to see anybody and he hurried past the opened doors. In the big office, he could see the bulk of Charles, seated at his desk, Baryshnikov standing by him, wearing shorts and clogs, and they were looking over a series of photos mounted on matte board. From the doorway Adam could see they were mocked-up ads—Baryshnikov had licensed his own line of dancewear. Christ, but some dancers could make money for themselves—while everybody else, including his dad, retired broke and had to teach. Charles looked up and saw him, of course Charles would see him, waved him in.

"So our prodigal son returns," he said. "Everything all right now?"

Adam nodded. "Thanks."

"Will you be rejoining us this fall?"

And Adam thought, *Jesus, is leaving three days early throwing everything into question?*

"Of course, Charles, he's joining us, right?" Baryshnikov said, and he dropped the ads, put out a hand, which Adam shook. Misha was shorter than he was, but his presence made up the difference. "I have plans for you, for this fall," he said, and he began to outline them, but Adam couldn't really focus on the plans, the ballets, the premieres, so great was his relief that he hadn't fucked everything up. He stood there nodding, and when Baryshnikov looked at him expectantly, Adam felt he could say, "Look, Misha, there's a girl I want you to see."

"The girl you went home for?"

"Her father was hospitalized."

"Who's the girl?"

"She dances with City Ballet. She's dancing with me at the Joyce next week. Will you come and see her?"

Baryshnikov looked at Charles, and Adam wished, in that moment, he hadn't aggravated Charles so much.

"Please. I need you to see her."

"We have a lot of girls, Adam."

"Not like her. Not like her. I'm serious."

"Do I know her?" Misha asked.

"No. No. She was promoted after you left. She just did 'Diamonds.'" It was ridiculous, he knew, to crow about a role he'd denigrated to Randall just yesterday, and she hadn't exactly been promoted, either, but he was desperate, would say anything, wasn't going to leave until Baryshnikov said yes, didn't know what he was going to say next, but something, he'd think of something, and then Misha turned to Charles, must have made some gesture of acquiescence because Charles said, "Okay, Adam. Leave the tickets."

And by the time Adam got out of the building and hit the street he realized he was sweating so much it was as if he'd done a solo up there.

WHEN HE GOT to Sandra's apartment, he saw the big black trash bags and cleaning supplies spread out on the dining room table. He dropped his laundry bag and called out to her, and he could hear she was back in her father's study. Jesus Christ, the man had even written on the walls, the hallway walls. She was sitting at his desk, sheets of lined paper in her hands, more of them all over the desktop.

"I just started on the papers," she said. "I'm trying to put them in order."

He looked at her face a minute and then said, "Let me just stack them up and you can go through them another time, okay?" She nodded, and he took the sheaf from her hands and struggled to make a neat pile of it. There were hundreds of pages here, but he tried not to look at them. *My father was a textbook salesman, my mother was an invalid.* What was this? Her dad wasn't writing about the Civil War or the siege of Vicksburg. "Have you been reading this?" he asked Sandra. And she said, "Some of it."

Adam looked around the study—the brown walls, the shelves full of old books, a wooden chair with more books piled on it, papers on the carpet that he'd nearly stepped on getting in here. Everything was covered with dust. Her father had sat in this hot little room, remembering. It felt claustrophobic to Adam, and though Sandra had put the air back on, it was going to take this room a long while to cool. Sandra put her head down on the desk, on what little clear space there was, and the window behind her lit up the small fine hairs on her arms.

"Look, Sandra," Adam said. "I don't think you should read any more of this."

Without looking up, she said, "I just want to know."

"The reason's not going to be here." He came around to her side of the desk. "Let's just get the place clean, okay?"

And for a few hours they did that, Adam dragging a garbage sack from room to room, shoving newspapers, cigarette butts, and old food into it, clearing to the kitchen the plates and cups and saucers, the food everywhere—plates stuck on bookshelves, left on the arms of chairs, on the ledge of the piano, in the bedroom, on the bathroom counter. Sandra had pulled together all the laundry and he could hear her back by the little maid's room, running the machines, the dryer making a metallic tumble. He got the vacuum out of the closet and ran it, making a monstrous noise as he drove it through the house, over the oriental carpets that covered much of the floors in each room. He'd never noticed before how overdressed the apartment was, with its tassel-edged fabric lamp shades and its many small tables and sofa pillows and framed photographs that crowded the piano, the bookshelves, and the end tables. The big mahogany furniture, the heavy double drapes in each room, even the brass bed in the maid's room, made the apartment look like the home of a Mississippi matron. Who had done this? Had one of the aunts come up here ten years ago or had the stuff just been shipped directly up from Vicksburg? He'd never thought to ask.

By the time he finished the vacuuming, he was dripping. Housework was as exhausting as dancing. He wrapped the cord around the machine, then surveyed Sandra's room, with the frilled dressing table and the mirror he'd never seen her use, the toile bench and the toile dressing table skirt, the same toile repeated on the bed, curtains, armchair. There was even a lace doily on her bedstand. No food, no cigarettes in here. This was the one room her father hadn't entered.

Adam went over and sat in the armchair, piled high, as usual, with laundry, and that's when he saw the book, on the low shelf of the bedstand. It was an old-fashioned-looking fairy-tale book with an elaborately illustrated cover and a frayed fabric binding. The ribbon that marked the page was a faded pink and the book opened in his hand to the tale "The Sleeping Princess" by Charles Perrault. The title, set in a fancy scrolled type, faced the colorful illustration: the princess on the silken draped bed, her hair in a romantic cascade, the prince bent over her, hat in his hand, the plumed feather grazing the instep of his boot, cobwebs on the pillars about them, and in the elegantly perspected distance of the great hall, a phalanx of sleeping courtiers. Sleeping Beauty. Why did she have this? He flipped to the tale. The prince's mother was an ogress, the prince therefore hid from her his marriage to Aurora and their children, twins, Morning and Day. He pretended to be off hunting in the deep forest for three or four days at a time, coming back to his mother's castle now and then for a night. But eventually she ferreted out his secret and he was forced to murder her to protect his wife and children. In a rage, the ogress had tried to slay them. What kind of grotesque *Sleeping Beauty* story was this? There was supposed to be a sleeping girl, a kiss, a wedding, the end. He flipped back to the front. On the title page an inscription: *For Aurora—George Balanchine*. What the fuck? Adam felt his fingers stiffen around the spine of the book. The large curving G of the signature was matched by the round sides of the *B,* the names trailing off into just a suggestion of their final letters. Adam still had the book in his hands when Sandra came looking for him. She stopped halfway across the room when she saw him sitting there holding it.

"Where did you get this?" Adam asked, and it took her a minute, it took her a whole goddamn minute, before she could make herself say, "Mr. B gave it to me."

"When?"

"Last week."

"Last *week*?" He shut the book. "Sandra—" He changed his mind, got up. "Fine. You want to have secrets, have secrets."

She said nothing, so he was forced to speak again.

"Are you going to tell me what this book is about, or not?"

She lowered her gaze for a moment and he thought, *She's not going to tell me,* but then she said, "I've been going to the theater in the afternoons."

"I thought you've been visiting your dad."

"I was. I am."

"But you've also been going to the theater." No wonder she'd been so quiet, so vacant with him. He'd taken it to be grief, but her opacity was hiding something else, her secrets, her fatigue. She had been rehearsing two ballets at once, morning and afternoon. When was she seeing her dad? Was she even seeing him at all? He looked at her closely. "You've been there today," he said.

She nodded. "I went after the first time I saw my dad. Mr. B was there. We started to work."

"On what? On this?" And he held up the book.

"Yes." She still wouldn't quite meet his eye.

"On *Sleeping Beauty.*"

"Yes."

"What are you telling me, he's doing the ballet *Sleeping Beauty*?" Adam opened the book. "*For Aurora.* He's doing the ballet for you?"

"For spring season," she said.

"When were you planning to tell me? At curtain?"

She shook her head.

"Who else knows about this?" Adam asked.

"Only you," she said.

He was the only one who knew? A three-act ballet was a huge production. Balanchine would already be conferring with his musical director, his designers would be producing sketches and maquettes, the publicity office would be scheming and fund-raising. A ballet like this did not happen in a vacuum. A ballet like this did not happen if it existed only in the mind of

an old man and a young girl. But Mr. B was making promises to
a girl too naïve to see his pockets were empty, nothing there but
lining.

Adam shut the book. "Mr. B's seventy-seven years old, Sandra. He's in and out of the hospital. I don't know what he's
telling you, but whatever it is, it's a fucking fairy tale in itself."

He handed her the book, and she took it from him without a
goddamn word and walked out. Walked out on him. He stood
there and listened for her. How far would she go? To the dining
room? To the entry? Out the door ? No. To the laundry. She
couldn't walk out on him because she still had laundry to do.
And he couldn't walk out on her. He still had to take all the
garbage bags to the back service hall, wait for her to unload the
dishwasher, fold the clothes. And then they would have to go
back to the brownstone together because they were living there.
Together.

He paced the apartment for a while before he ended up helping her fold the big stuff from the dryer, holding the ends of the
sheets to meet the ends she held. They were silent. He watched
her, arms crossed, as she folded her father's clothing into a pile
and put the pile into a small suitcase to take to him at the hospital, and when she did that he could actually feel his heart aching
for her. Okay, he knew why she'd gone to Lincoln Center—for
solace. She hadn't known Mr. B would be there. But once she
knew, she kept it from him. Why? Because there was always
some part of her she held back. He was open to her, but she was
hidden. And it was ridiculous what she had hidden. He couldn't
have her clinging to this notion of some phantom ballet. Balanchine was old, *Sleeping Beauty* an old man's dream; when the
company reconvened in a few weeks he probably wouldn't even
remember what he'd said about it this summer. But what if this

*was* real? She'd never come with him to ABT then. He'd never even see her. That's why she kept quiet about it. She knew if Balanchine liked her enough, he'd dominate her time and her thoughts and her life and soon there'd be nothing left of her for Adam. And she'd allow it.

AFTER HE DROPPED her off at Roosevelt Hospital, Adam stood outside on Amsterdam Avenue. He wanted something—a joint, a 'lude—but he didn't want to go to the brownstone to get it. He looked up Amsterdam Avenue toward Lincoln Center. He felt like a fucking idiot to have believed she was visiting her father every afternoon when she'd really been going to State Theater so that she wouldn't miss her opportunity with Balanchine, to have him alone like that, no other dancers around him to distract him, just her legs and arms and face in front of him, angling successfully for his complete attention. Was she really that manipulative? He hadn't seen that side of her before, only the passive do-with-me-what-you-will attitude with which she'd spent all four years at City Ballet. Well, after all, hadn't he been the one to tell her it was all going to be over for her if something didn't happen for her soon? He started walking up Amsterdam, cut over to Central Park West, crossed the park. He needed to see Randall, even if Randall would say what he said back when Adam was fifteen, *Leave the girl alone.*

Some of the leaves on the trees had already begun to change—and he shoved his hands in his pockets and just moved, just walked, past the carousel, past the ice-skating rink, the gothic milk barn, the bronzed statues of Hans Christian Andersen and Alice in Wonderland, past the sailboat pond to the East Side, to Park Avenue. Another two weeks and it would be Labor

Day, another two after that and he'd be back at ABT's Midtown studios, locked into a two-month rehearsal period before the next tour. A tour he could conceivably be making without Sandra, though that thought was inconceivable to him. So his girlfriend was fragile, cagey, ambitious, a liar. What of this hadn't he known? The last.

He nodded to the doorman at Randall's building and when he got off the elevator the first thing he saw was Eric Gonzalez. The guy was standing outside Randall's door, sleeves of his black T-shirt rolled up to show off his biceps, and when he saw Adam he said to him, "They're not home. I've been buzzing."

And Adam stood there a moment, not sure what to do. He wanted to go in, but he didn't want Eric there. Finally he said, "Well, I've got a key."

"I was supposed to meet Joe here," Eric said. "Maybe he got hung up at the studio."

"Maybe," Adam said. "Come on in."

The place felt big and vacant without Joe and Randall there, and he remembered how it used to feel when he'd come here after school because Randall didn't want him going home to Hell's Kitchen alone. Randall had had a car service pick him up from SAB each afternoon and bring him over. They'd all be off at the studio. Adam would eat everything in sight, ravenous from ballet class, and then throw himself on the old white bed in the old master bedroom, put on the television, wait for Randall. The key in the door would always send him scrambling. It wasn't long before Randall quit the company and started picking Adam up at Lincoln Center himself. He'd stay with him at night while the rest of them were at the theater.

Eric followed him now into the kitchen, and while Adam went right to the fridge, Eric sat on the edge of the table.

"So how come you have a key?" he said.

"Joe and Randall raised me, pretty much. They're my god-parents."

"You're kidding."

"Look, you want something to drink?"

"I'm okay."

Adam found a beer in the refrigerator and unscrewed the cap with his palm, upended the thing in his mouth.

"That's a fantastic dance Joe made for you. What made you decide to come downtown?"

"Randall," Adam said. He put down his beer. "How long have you been dancing with Joe?"

"He saw me in class, asked me if I wanted to sign with him. I jumped on it. I've been in New York a couple of years, going nowhere. I guess you could say my career's been the opposite of yours."

Adam looked at Eric more closely. He was a little older than Adam had first thought, maybe twenty-three, twenty-four, probably desperate by the time Joe saw him. Modern dancers generally had a longer performing life, so it wasn't the end of the world if they got started later. But there were fewer places to work—small ad hoc pickup troupes, low for-performance pay. Joe must have looked pretty good to Eric and he'd do whatever it took to get hired.

"So, you're meeting Joe here?" Adam said, and Eric looked at him for a minute.

"You think I'm sleeping with Joe?"

Adam shrugged.

"I'm not sleeping with him, man, I'm dancing for him. Jesus." Eric got off the table. "Tell Joe I'll come back another time."

Eric started off for the door and Adam's first impulse was to let him go, but then he thought about how Joe might hear about this and what he'd say to Randall, and he thought, *Shit,* and he went out into the living room after the guy.

"Eric, wait." Eric stopped walking and Adam spoke to his back. "You're over here, meeting Joe, and Joe has a history, so I figured, you know, Joe's at it again."

"He asked me over here to help move Randall's bed into the living room," Eric said without turning around. "Randall's having trouble sleeping in a small space. It's making him feel like he's buried."

"What?" Adam said.

Eric turned around. "Randall's been feeling like he's sleeping in a coffin. So I was just going to help Joe move the bed out." He gestured with his hands. "You know, the living room's a bigger space."

Adam had to sit down on the edge of the sofa. Everything he was feeling must have been on his face because Eric said, "Adam, look, I'm sorry, man. I thought you knew about this."

Adam shook his head. He'd been too fucking busy worrying about Sandra to think about anyone else, to know anything about anyone else. Randall in the cab hadn't looked well. He hadn't looked well since Christmas, still ran fevers and endured swollen lymph nodes as if the pneumonia had never fully left him but ran along some subterranean current the doctors couldn't track. He'd had two courses of pentamidine, and he still wasn't well. And now Randall thought he was dying. Adam rubbed his hands through his hair, his spectacularly tousled hair, and to his horror, he found he was crying, which he hadn't done since that time he was ten and his father moved out. He had to get up and pace, coughing and trying to clear his windpipe, which felt about the size of a needle. Eric went into the kitchen and came back with a wad of paper towels, which he handed silently to Adam. Adam pressed the whole bunch of them to his eyes and cheeks. He was embarrassed to be doing this in front of Eric, but he couldn't seem to gather his self-control. A few minutes went by and Eric sat on the edge of the sofa, not looking at him, just waiting, and eventually whatever it was that ravaged at Adam ebbed away, and Adam could say, "Sorry."

Eric raised his hands, *No problem,* and Adam looked out the living room windows.

Eric said, "You want your beer? I'll get it," and he went off to the kitchen, brought the bottle out, and put it into Adam's hand. "What was Randall like when he was well?"

"He was everything," Adam said. "He's still everything."

Eric put a hand on his shoulder, and Adam thought, *Come on, make your move if you're gonna make it, you fuck,* and he was so sad today he'd probably go there with him, sometimes getting off was the only way out of the black mood, but it turned out *he* was the fuck, there was something wrong with him, not Eric, who just looked into his face, hand on his shoulder. And then the door opened and it was Joe coming into the entry, throwing his keys down, standing there in the living room archway, saying, "What are you two up to?"

He CALLED SANDRA hours later at the brownstone and told her he was spending the night with Randall, needed to be with Randall, did she want to come up there, argued with her about coming up there, but she wouldn't, she was so goddamn stubborn, she'd seen her father, didn't want to see anybody now, and he thought, *Sure, she'd jump if Mr. B called.* So fine, let her stay there by herself, let her sit there and smoke and dream about

Mr. B. Adam hung up the phone and took a shower in the bath-room he knew so well, found some of Randall's clothes to put on, and by the time he came out, Randall was already lying in bed, the bed he and Eric had dragged out into the living room and set up by the windows.

"Sorry, Adam," Randall said into the dark. "I'm just too tired to sit up. Come over here."

So Adam went and lay down beside him on the white spread they'd brought out from the white room, the spread Eric had helped him to smooth and straighten, running his hands across the surface and then making two hospital tucks at the bottom corners, laughing when Adam stood staring at his expertise. He'd made the bed feel good, and Randall lay on his back beside Adam, the high ceiling of this living room far above them, pressed even more firmly aloft by the crown moldings, which featured bunches of grapes interspersed with scrolling ribbons and the occasional pineapple. Through the windows the backs, sides, and fronts of other buildings ap-peared cut off at midsection; some poked at the sky, others stopped short. There was still a lot of sky; in this position you could see a lot of sky, even if it was night sky, dark, like the ground bearing down on you.

"Is this better," Adam said, "out here?"

"Better," Randall said. "Yes, better." He raised an arm above his head.

"Why didn't Joe ask me to move the bed? Why did he ask Eric to do it?"

"My idea."

"Well, I was going to see the bed out here eventually."

"Eventually," Randall said.

"And you were going to have to tell me why."

"Eventually." Randall smoked his cigarette slowly. "So what were you and Eric getting into when Joe walked in?"

Adam felt himself flush, was glad that Randall couldn't see his face in the dark. What had Joe said, the fucker? Adam looked over at Randall, who had stubbed out his cigarette into the glass ashtray balanced on his stomach, moved the glass bowl between them. Randall exhaled.

"Adam, you need to be careful."

"Eric was just being a friend. Nothing was going on."

"Adam," Randall said, and there was something in his voice that made Adam shut up, quit trying to defend himself. "Have you ever heard of Kaposi's sarcoma?" Adam shook his head. "It's a cancer." Randall pulled up his pajama top to show Adam a purple nodule on his chest, another on his neck, his upper arm. He'd never seen these lesions before. How long had it been since he'd seen Randall's body, seen Randall changing clothes? "When these tumors attack the lungs," Randall said, "they can kill you. That's what's happening to me." He lowered his shirt, turned to look at Adam. Adam sat up. Randall was dying. It wasn't just that he thought he was dying. He had some kind of cancer. Adam was silent, trying to think it all through, trying to get ready to respond if Randall would ever stop talking. But Randall wasn't finished yet. "Some gay men have pneumonia and they aren't getting well. There's something going on, gay men are dying. Adam, I don't want you out cruising."

"I'm not," Adam said. He wanted to say, *I don't cruise,* which was a fucking lie, wanted to ask something more, what all this meant, how Randall had gotten this, was it from Joe, Joe's fucking around? But he wasn't going to get a chance, because at that moment, Joe came out into the room and spoke into the dark. "Randall, I need you."

Adam turned to look at him, silhouetted in the light from the hallway. Joe's bathrobe, light cotton, blue, was tied around him. He looked thin, and with his hair, which was a slick, glossy black, let out of its perpetual rubber band, he looked young, lost, like a kid.

Randall labored to get out of the bed, saying, "It's okay. I'm here," and Adam watched him shuffle toward Joe, cautious in the dark. Adam was just about to get up and put on a lamp when he saw Randall reach Joe, put an arm around Joe's waist, and the two of them went off around the corner, and Adam knew he wouldn't see Randall again tonight.

Was Joe sick, too? Did he have lesions under his robe? Adam got out of bed, there was no way he could remain in that bed one more second, and went to the big windows that looked out over Park Avenue, balled his fists against the glass. He was losing Randall and he could not lose Randall. For him that would be like spinning in deep space, no tether, rocket ship a speck, then nothing. Adam traced the outline of a dark building, the dark trees that rose up from the avenue. The apartment was silent. He was alone, the state he feared more than any other. Sandra was alone, fifty blocks away, and he was going to go crazy, right here, right now. He needed her. So she kept a secret from him, she was afraid of his rage—he kept secrets from her, too, afraid of, not her rage exactly, but of her revulsion. Maybe for her it was the same. Her dad was sick, she was camping in a strange apartment, Balanchine was someone she couldn't fully trust, she couldn't risk Adam backing away. And he'd found her out and he had. When she found him out, would she? He couldn't risk that happening, couldn't risk losing her, couldn't lose her and Randall both.

He crossed his arms over his chest. He still had these two

weeks, and at the end of them, Baryshnikov was coming to see her. She'd have an offer from ABT before the fall rehearsal period for City Ballet even started, before she could even know for sure what Balanchine wanted from her. Adam pushed back from the window and surveyed the living room, the chandeliers, the mirrors, the sofas, the empty bed. He had to get out of here. He would go down to the street, catch a cab, head back to the brownstone, hold on to her.

## FOUR

On the night they premiered Joe's *X,* Adam stood in his robe in the dressing room he shared with Sandra, his fingers busy in his hair, slicking it up into a spiky mess that made him look at once fierce and decrepit. Or maybe it was the harsh makeup that made him look that way, the black lines all around his eyes from corner to corner that he didn't usually wear, the flat Pan-Cake. He could look downtown because he was downtown, didn't have to look like some balletic dream prince, even if Sandra looked like some fucking princess, couldn't help it, with that spun-sugar hair. Because of all the hair-down Balanchine ballets, he was used to seeing Sandra like this, suited up in some dress that was not really a dress but a facsimile of a dress, a stage dress, her hair falling over the straps of it, her face made up like a cancan girl in a Toulouse-Lautrec poster. It was all he could do to keep his hands off of her. Later. He'd save it for the stage. He was nervous, but she was not—she wasn't dancing for Balanchine. At Lincoln Center she had such stage fright before curtain she couldn't eat or drink, didn't want

Adam even to talk to her if he stopped by the dressing room she shared with all those other girls. He was the one who was about to go on and dance *Apollo,* for Christ's sake. She was just in the corps for *Symphony in C,* but she couldn't talk to him. Fuck, any girl in that room would love to talk to him, but *she* didn't want to.

He put his hands on her shoulders. For two weeks he hadn't asked her where she was going when she finished seeing her father, hadn't argued with her, just sat up and waited for her, didn't know if she was seeing Balanchine or seeing her father or in what proportion. He learned to tell, after a while, which. Elation and despair were not emotions she wore on her gorgeous face like a trowel of makeup, but they were spread there just beneath the skin and suffused it like a blush. He could tell. And either way, he was gentle with her. She had these two poles she traveled between, these two men, three if you counted him. Working with his dad and Randall and Joe, Adam had never felt so flush with family—even his mom and Eric were around, in the studio, meeting them after rehearsal for lunch or dinner—and he had never seen Sandra so alone. Did she wish her father could be here tonight? Her father sat in a room at Roosevelt Hospital and she pretended to everyone he did not. Her weekly calls to her grandmother were performance art—she reported events and conversations that never took place, and Adam was appalled and impressed by Sandra's delivery of it, which was hesitant but not unconfident. But after she had hung up the phone she had to lie on her back and he couldn't talk to her until she recovered. He was allowed to go with her to see her father exactly once, when she felt she needed to go back to the hospital again one night. Allowed to go, but not allowed up, Adam paced the downstairs lobby for the hour it took to satisfy her, and when she came down in tears he wanted to wrap a rain-coat around her or something, throw up a brick wall, throw out his arms to keep whatever it was out, but what he did was take her hand. Yes, of course she wished her father could be here.

He kissed the top of her head. She looked up, met his eyes in the mirror. Her father was still in the hospital; his father sat in a dressing room, mirror pasted up with telegrams, the chairs and ledges full of flowers. The house was sold-out. Yes, some of those seats were filled because of his dad, but not all. Adam knew many of the tickets had been sold because of him. He looked at the clock. Was Baryshnikov out there yet? He looked back at Sandra. She was doing this for him, dancing tonight because he wanted her to, because he was the third pole, the third man she wanted to please. He took his hands from her shoulders and turned to put on his costume. He probably should tell her about Baryshnikov, but there was no point, really, in telling her yet. He had let her take her rehearsals with Balanchine for that ghost ballet of his, but if Baryshnikov made room for her, Adam was going to insist she stop dreaming.

FRANKIE WAS a mountain, that enormous, out there in all the white light, and though Adam caught glimpses of Joe, his mom, even Sandra standing in the wings, he could barely take them in; his dad blotted all that out. Adam stood on the ramp with him, motionless, arm extended, as they awaited the musical cue to move. He'd never been onstage with his father before—Adam had been in the wings watching him, or out front doing the same, or his father sat in the house watching *him,* but it was entirely different being out here together. Frankie had twenty-five years on him—twenty-five years of bulk that gave his body heft and twenty-five years of stage experience that gave him presence. That was where Adam was headed, exciting to see, but also intimidating. Adam wasn't used to this, being upstaged. Forty-five-year-old dancers in ballet companies were corralled into character parts—mothers, kings, doddering old men, stepsisters, witches. Adam didn't dance with them—they cleared the stage when the actual dancing began—and Adam's partners, as well as the members of the corps de ballet that framed him, were almost all in their twenties, with little more stage experience than he had.

Frankie grasped his forearm, which was already slick, and Adam hadn't even started dancing yet; the two of them, barechested, shimmering with sweat, began the long series of snakelike moves that led them down the ramp and onto the stage proper. The windows of the hotel room Frankie had stepped through slid away behind them, the whole set retracted by wires cranked by the stagehands, until they were on an empty stage into which wind and leaves began to blow. Adam locked eyes with Frankie, who was not his father but this masterly creature—his face cut up with lines the Pan-Cake did not mask but seemed to accentuate—who assumed the various postures of a wrestler. And Adam saw immediately and with certainty that Joe had not designed these postures to humiliate his father as he had thought, not at all. Frankie filled these poses like plaster poured into a sculptural shell, and if Adam couldn't take his eyes off him, no one in the audience would be able to do so either. It was an effort to concentrate on what he himself was doing. His father was like a magnet, a force, drawing everything toward him, and Adam felt himself pitched off balance by it, diminished; the feeling terrified him. This was the only place Adam ever felt he had control—the rest of his life was a shambles of broken contracts and open suitcases, of relationships equally broken and temporary—and he was going to be pounded into the ground here. He breathed in deeply, and when Frankie set him free, Adam shot into the frenetic solo Joe had devised for him, and no one was going to be looking anywhere else. He vaulted into the lights and made a scorching circle about the stage—traversing stage right, upstage, stage left, and as he rounded the bend, he saw his father's face and what he wore on it, pride, and the sight of it, like an arrow, nearly dropped Adam from the air.

But he had no time to linger on his father's face, which was suddenly not that of a rival or a fellow, but of a father. Sandra was stepping from the wings in that pink dress with her bare legs. He'd use the steam he'd built up not to blow her over, but to suck her toward him, into this tornado he'd got going. And as soon as she reached him, he caged her in his arms, strung her wrists up above her head, and held them there with one hand, used the other to turn her hips and her knees. Her body, so vibrant beneath his hands, hummed like the warm motor of a bird, just as tremulous and hysterical and temporarily his. To the side of them, Frankie stood watching, erect, still, head slightly bowed, ceding the stage, though not his claim on it, watching Adam, watching what Joe had called *your younger self*. If Adam was Frankie's younger self, Sandra was Lucia's. And Adam understood this dance was not about him and Sandra, or Randall and Joe, but about his parents—his dad's efforts to hold on to his mother, to make her love him, give it all up to him, have the baby that once was Adam, have the baby that he wanted today. Adam grasped Sandra's chin with one hand and thrust the other between her legs, hoisted her into the air he controlled, into the air exploded with light, and at the side of the stage, his father echoed the movement, arms raised, hands flexed. But Frankie's hands were empty. Well, tonight one of them would have his woman. Adam would have her for them both. At the finish of the dance, Adam yanked Sandra's head back by the hair, that long rope of sugary hair, bent his face to hers for the stage kiss, a kiss meant for the audience to imagine, and then, on impulse, he made it real, his tongue in her mouth, *You are mine, here, everywhere,* and the house shook loose.

And when they took their bows, the three of them with their arms linked, Adam was shaking. It was way too much, he wasn't used to this, dancing with all these people he loved. After the first bow, Frankie kept shuffling back to give Adam and Sandra the stage. Adam shook his head, tried to draw his dad forward, but it was not until Sandra left the stage that his dad stepped up, slung his arm around Adam's neck, and stood with him hip to hip, rib to rib. Frankie was breathing fast and hard, but it wasn't from dancing. Too much for him, too? Adam put his arm around his dad's waist and held him. What was the audience applauding—two dancers or father and son? The evening was sick with sentiment and it was steeping them all in it. Finally Adam slipped out from under his dad's grip and went to the wings, left his father out there, center stage. It was, after all, his father's night, his father's last night, let him gather up all he could.

$\mathcal{B}$ACKSTAGE, ADAM HUNG his old blue towel around his neck, a favorite rag, used the unraveling end of it to mop at his face. Already the wings were crowded with dancers from Joe's company, stagehands and musicians, friends of his parents' of two decades who must have bolted back here, and a couple of boys in black who circulated with trays of food and champagne.

Adam grabbed a flute and looked for Sandra—the stage and its environs were getting more crowded by the minute. She was with Frankie, who had his arm around her. He'd found her, but it took Adam forever to get to her. On the way over, he had his back slapped, his ass slapped, his neck grabbed, his face kissed, and by the time he reached her, he felt both manhandled and drunk, the champagne having buzzed right through him. Where was his mom? He saw Joe, Randall on a stool, Eric next to him, and then his mom's hard splinterlike shape as she walked onto the stage—what?—and then toward someone who emerged from the murky black of the draped wings opposite. Baryshnikov. Adam had momentarily forgotten him, but his mom had perceived him, and while Adam watched, she stuck out her hand and Misha took it. Adam hadn't told her Baryshnikov would be here, hadn't told anyone but Randall, and Adam looked sharply across the boards to Randall now. Had he told her? No. It couldn't have been Randall. Whatever energy it took to disclose any kind of information, Randall no longer had. His mom had discovered Baryshnikov on her own. Of course. Adam broke away from his dad and, taking Sandra with him, met Baryshnikov and Lucia halfway across the stage.

"Mom," Adam said right away and his mother understood, said she would get Misha some champagne, and slipped away. And then Adam couldn't think of what to do next, how to get this thing going, while Sandra stood looking from one to the other of them. "You remember Misha," he said finally, and Sandra nodded, put out her hand. Baryshnikov clasped it.

"So this is the little girl who sets Adam on fire."

Sandra looked at Adam.

"I've been telling Misha about you."

Baryshnikov jerked his chin and Adam stepped toward him,

allowed Baryshnikov to steer him away slightly. They stood a few steps from Sandra, their backs to her, but it was not as if she'd vanished and Adam glanced at her now and then as Baryshnikov talked into his ear. They would make her an offer, soloist, not corps de ballet, when was she available. There was more, but Adam, his brain divided between listening to Baryshnikov and looking over at Sandra, couldn't quite crack the codex of Baryshnikov's speech. But Sandra could. She waited there politely at first in her pink dress, arms by her sides, and Adam, who watched her, saw all the expressions that subsequently crossed her face: impatience, suspicion, comprehension, disbelief, and finally the fury that turned her away. He wouldn't even see Baryshnikov now, in his panic. As soon as Adam could, he pumped Baryshnikov's hand, made his own getaway, crossed the stage, pushed through the crowd, so many people, hit the end of the wings, and went through the back corridors to the dressing room. She was in there, packing up if you could call it that, shoving her dance gear into her bag with great big sweeps of her arm, knocking all kinds of stuff to the ground in the process— brushes, hair dryer, a curling iron, a million clips and pins.

"What are you doing?" he said.

"Getting out of here." She threw a shoe into the bag.

"We're going to the Russian Tea Room. My mom's got a reservation for twenty people."

"Invite Baryshnikov. He can have my chair." She chunked a huge cylinder of Aqua Net into the bag.

"Sandra. I know I should have told you Misha was coming, okay? I just—I really wanted him to see you."

"Fine," she said. "He saw me."

"And he loved you."

She shrugged.

"He loved you and he offered you a contract."

"I don't want his contract. I already have a job." She stopped packing for a minute. "Adam, I did this dance for you and your dad. It wasn't an audition."

"I know that, I know that." Christ. He put his hands in his hair. "Look, Sandra. I'm leaving town again in a month and I'm going to be gone a long time. I don't want you here alone."

"I won't be alone. My father's getting out of the hospital, remember?"

"Oh, yeah, that'll be great. Having your dad around is worse than being alone."

"Fuck you." She turned and began zipping up her bag.

He couldn't believe she said that to him. He went over and jerked the bag from her hands. Enough with the packing, the big show. She stepped back, knocked her hip against the ledge of the dressing table, and he wanted to save her from the ledge, wanted to shove her into it. "Fuck me? Everything I do is for you."

"Everything you do is for *you*," she said. "You want me at ABT for *you*. None of this is about me." She was starting to sob, but her eyes were still bright and they were glaring at him.

"This whole fucking thing is about you," Adam said. "The only reason I talked to Misha was because you weren't going anywhere at City Ballet."

"Well, I'm going somewhere now." She pushed at him, trying to push him back, but he wouldn't budge. "Mr. B is doing a ballet for me. Why won't you let me do it?" This last was almost a wail, but still he wasn't budging.

"What ballet? What goddamn ballet? There's not going to be any ballet, Sandra. It's not going to happen."

She put her hands to her face.

Why couldn't she see this was their time, their moment? In

another year, Baryshnikov could move on, Balanchine could be dead, Adam could be injured. Anything could happen—their world was so fluid and so unstable. "Sandra," he said, and he saw her respond to the change in his voice. He drew her hands away from her face, but still she wouldn't look at him. He bent toward her, began to lick at the tears on her cheeks and along her neck. The cross he'd loaned her tonight for luck, Randall's cross, trembled down there in the bodice of her costume. He wanted to suck on it, suck on her tits, all the desire he'd felt in here earlier surging back and giving him a massive hard-on. She let him bite at the bodice of her dress, get down on his knees before her. She leaned into him and he mouthed at her through the material.

"Adam," she said above him. "Adam, come back to City Ballet." He stopped sucking at her, turned his cheek to the satin of the gown. "Mr. B's working again," she said. "He's seventy-seven years old. How many more chances will you have? Please, Adam. Come back."

He breathed in the material of the dress, kept his face pressed to the satin. "I don't know," he said finally. The thought of going back there made him feel suffocated, made him feel like he was giving up the world, going back to an environment even more narrow, more insular, than the one he was in now. He'd been at City Ballet his whole life, ever since he was eight. But maybe he could go back. Wasn't that what he had been thinking about in Saratoga, what he was missing? He'd have to crawl to get there, humble himself, but it might work. Mr. B was proud and difficult, but he needed boys. Though if the old man knew Adam was with Sandra, he'd never have him back. And if Adam did go back, they'd have to hide their relationship and Adam didn't want to hide it, he'd already done that, spent years hiding his feelings for her.

"We could do *Beauty* together," she whispered, her hands in his hair, stroking the back of his neck. Jesus, she was playing him.

Adam shook his head, shook her hands away. "Mr. B's definitely not going to use me with you in *Beauty* or in anything if he gets wind that we're together. He might not even want to use *you* anymore if he knew." He stood up. He'd spent enough time on his knees. "Look, Sandra, ABT's done *Sleeping Beauty* before. They'll do it again. You'll get to do your *Beauty*."

"But it won't be Mr. B's." She spelled the words out like he was an idiot who didn't get it, and her tone enraged him. He had this amazing career, did she think he got it by being an idiot? Did she think he got it by playing the toady for Mr. B?

"Fuck Mr. B. He's a dead man. Forget him." He thought he'd throw something he was so frustrated, actually did throw something, the towel she'd laid over the back of the chair, but that fell without a satisfying thud, so he reached for the bunch of metal hangers on the clothing rack, the crap she still had laid out on the ledge went down with a sweep of his hand, and when none of that was enough, he started kicking her bag, the chair, booted both across the tiny room and into the wall, and in response to this, she picked up a pair of scissors from the dressing table, one of the few things that hadn't made it already into her bag and that he hadn't knocked to the floor, and dragged the open blade quickly across the inside of her forearm, making a series of long bloody slashes before he could even mobilize himself. He was two feet from her and she slashed herself. He couldn't even breathe, he was so shocked. He stood staring at her and she just stared right back at him. Finally he could move and he reached out and grabbed the scissors from her, threw it on the floor, kicked it away, half-afraid she might crawl after it and finish herself off. And then he was reaching for the towel he'd thrown down, for a sweatshirt, Kleenex, anything, something, to stuff at the wounds, which he saw now were not superficial and might need stitches. There was blood everywhere—on the ledge, on the floor, on her costume, on his. She'd started talking at him and she wouldn't stop, every word of it gibberish until finally he said, "Sandra, okay, okay. Just be quiet." He wanted to see what she'd done. He needed her calm. He sat there holding a T-shirt to her arm, and he was shaking, or maybe she was shaking. The whole thing was so weird, part of him wanted to bolt, couldn't believe it had really happened, but when he lifted the T-shirt he could see the slash marks were there and they were deep and they began instantly to well up with blood. It had happened. She had cut herself. He'd pushed her too far, shouldn't have done this, his mom and Randall had tried to tell him, they saw something he didn't see, but he wouldn't listen, thought he knew her better than anyone. He was an idiot.

The door cracked open. It was Lucia, saying, "Come on, you two, the reservation's in ten minutes." The door opened wider and she put her head around it. Adam watched his mom take it all in, the chaos of the room, the upended chair, the blood, the T-shirt Adam pressed to Sandra's arm. "Oh my God," his mother said. "What happened?" But Adam could see it in her face. She knew, she already knew.

y the time she brought her father home, it was a cold September day. The radiators gurgled and popped behind the decorative grilles in the living room. She was quiet, as was he, and she followed her father as he inspected the apartment, looking at everything he hadn't seen since the summer. She was happy to have him home, to be home herself. She hated the brownstone, that dark cell where she deserved to be confined and punished, but now that her dad was released, couldn't she be, too? Her father headed in his naval overcoat straight to the back hallway, let his hand trace along the walls. Did he remember that he had written there, remember the condition in which he had left the entire apartment? He turned the corner and she knew then he was going to his study. She followed him, watched him open the door she'd kept closed for six weeks. There was nothing terrible in the room at all, yet she feared it—the wall of books, the big mahogany desk with the upholstered armchair behind it and the small wooden one in front, the Persian rug they'd brought with them from Vicksburg and had to cut to fit in here.

Her father put on the desk lamp and sat in his chair, coat still on. Behind him, outside the one narrow window, shook the big maple tree, stray leaves already turning red. She leaned against the wall to watch him and the tree. He did not look distressed. He looked unstudied, as if he were here alone, just as he would look if she weren't there. Because that's what she often was to him, invisible. She slid her back down the wall and came to a crouch on the floor of the hallway. Eventually, her father shrugged off his coat, opened the drawer of his desk, found his stash of old Pall Malls, and lit one up. He smoked it, slowly, then used the end of it to light another, all the while staring off, eyes open. When he finished that one, he paused, then looked at her, and she knew he was ready for her, wanted her to come in, to sit down, which she did, on the hardback chair.

"When my mother took to the bed," he told her, "I was twelve years old. I never wanted to do that to you."

"Dad, you haven't."

He shook his head. "There have been times I have, though I didn't want it to be so." He leaned back in the chair, against his dark coat. "I'm certain now my mother felt the same way."

"I thought she had cancer," Sandra said. "She had to be in bed."

"No." He shook his head. "No. She killed herself when I was in high school."

"You never told me this."

"I didn't want you to imagine that I might do the same." He leaned forward over the desk again. "I won't."

"I know that, Dad."

He put out his hand, opened it up for her to take, which she did. He looked down at their clasped hands. "Those cuts on your arm," he said, "are too regular to have come from a broken glass."

Instantly, she pulled her hand away, used the other to cover the scars.

"I wasn't here," he said, "so I can only imagine why you did it."

She couldn't look at him.

"Just as I've spent thirty years imagining why my mother did it." He leaned back in the chair, lit another Pall Mall. "I was sixteen. Would you like to know who found her?"

She put her hands in her lap. No.

"By the time I was nineteen, my father was dead, too. I've known you longer than I knew my mother, my father, my wife. Loved you longer."

She went to him then, put her head to his, turned him around in his chair so they could see, in what was left of the light, the red maple tree outside.

$S$HE WAS SITTING on her bed in her nightgown, smoking, when she heard the key turn in the front door, and she knew it was Adam. She had meant to call him to tell him she wanted to stay with her father tonight, but she had put it off because she was afraid Adam would argue with her. Before it was possible, Adam was in her bedroom, having stalked her to the most likely hole, and he was pulling off his gloves, his black wool beret, shaking out his hair, saying, "It's midnight. You were supposed to have been home two hours ago. I've been calling."

"I unplugged the phone," she said. "I didn't want to talk to my grandmother. She's called twice already."

"So, what?" He gestured at her, her nightgown. "You weren't going to let me know that you were staying here? I was worried about you."

He was always worried about her now. Since the night she'd cut herself he worried about her, watched her. She'd be sitting on the bed or standing in the bathroom and she'd feel the flick of his gaze which he'd retract the instant she turned to meet it. There was no question of her leaving City Ballet anymore, just as there had been no question but that she needed twenty-eight stitches in her arm and could not go to the Russian Tea Room with Joe and Randall and Frankie and their friends. "I'm sorry," she said, and she stubbed out her cigarette in a jar lid. "I'm sorry. I'm sorry. I would have thought to call sometime soon." It wasn't a good answer.

He stood there flapping his gloves. "Okay. Fine. We'll stay here." He threw his gloves and cap down on the bed, started unbuttoning his coat.

She shifted on the bed. She didn't want Adam to stay here tonight. If he stayed here, he would want something from her, and whatever she had she wanted to reserve for her dad. Adam had had her all summer, had asked for more of her than he should have. She watched him take off his shirt, throw it onto the toile chair. She crossed her arms. He wasn't staying here.

"So, how is he?" Adam asked.

"Adam," she said, and he looked at her because of the way that she said it, "I've been thinking I should move back here for a while."

"You mean, by yourself, without me?" She saw the way he lowered his arms.

"Just for a few months," she said.

"What? I'm supposed to bring a little suitcase over to your

place? And then you're going to come over to my place sometimes with your toothbrush?"

"It's just for a little while."

"And then what?" he said.

She shrugged. "I haven't thought about it."

"Well, I have." Adam came toward her, sat on the edge of the
bed, reached for her hand. Reluctantly, she gave it to him. "After Christmas I start getting my money from Randall," and
when she looked at him uncomprehendingly, he said, "My trust-
fund money. It's more than I make each year from dancing. I
want to buy us a place to live. Sandra, we won't need your dad's
apartment or the brownstone or your grandmother's checks or
your four hundred dollars a week from City Ballet. I can take
care of us. Will you come live with me then?"

Why did he always do this, why was he always one step ahead
of her and then turning around to drag her forward? She was
being a shit and he was loving her, and she didn't know why he
did. He hadn't shaved today, and his whiskers were lit up red,
blond, and silvery white in the lamplight from her bedstand.
The tiny hairs closest to his lips made a blond ring like a small,
misplaced halo. She leaned forward and licked at the whiskers, at
his lips, which were soft, at his chin, which was not, and then he
caught at her with his teeth: he wanted her to answer him. She
took her face away. She couldn't leave her father. He had come
out of the hospital for her, and she couldn't leave him. Look
what had happened the last time she had. She looked down at
her hand in Adam's, their two hands resting on the bedspread,
and then, while she watched, Adam withdrew his hand from
hers, straightened up. She hadn't even realized he'd been leaning
toward her.

"Sandra, we're not going to be able to make this work between us if I'm away half the year and when I come back we're living apart."

"I can ask my dad if you can stay here."

"I'm going to sleep in the little maid's room again? You're going to set me up off the kitchen?" He got up from the bed. "That's not what I want, Sandra. That's not anything like what I want. Maybe that's what you want. You and your dad burn so cool, you don't need anybody, but I'm not built that way, Sandra, you know that."

"Adam, please."

"Please what? Please stop living with you? Stop loving you? I can't go backward like that, Sandra. Goddamn, I don't know how you can."

"Adam. Adam." She got out of bed and began picking up his shirt, his hat, his gloves, his coat. "My dad's sleeping. We'll talk about it tomorrow." She brought the clothes around to him and pressed them into his hands.

"What's this?" He looked down at the clothes. "You want me to go home?"

"Just for tonight." She was going to have to plead. She prepared herself to plead.

And for a minute he didn't move at all and she went still, too. Was he going to throw something? He looked at her, then down at the clothes in his hands, and then he was looking only at her. "No fucking way, Sandra."


IN THE MORNING at Karinska's, the light poured down from the windows, so narrow and set so high that Sandra felt as if she were standing in a chapel. She shifted from one foot to the other while the dressmaker pinned on her the Aurora costume for Act I. Adam had made her doubt that this dream would come to life, but the costume she stood in was proof of its reality. It had gone, at least, this far. In this dress, Aurora, on the occasion of her twentieth birthday, dances for her parents—the barren parents who had at last had this one cherished child— and for her four suitors, though she chooses none of the princes, not Charmant, Chéri, Fortuné, nor Fleur-de-pois, letting the rose each one gives her drop to the ground at the end of her dance. All the steps were sprightly, quick, light, young movements, with quick changes of direction, small jumps, punctuated by a series of turns in which the leg was raised into développé, as if the princess were testing the very air, piercing at the boundaries that contained her in childhood. She was ready to spring out, to be noticed, to be plucked, and her costume reflected that: it looked like a flower, pink, the tulle skirt short and with many layers that opened like the petals of a rose in which her body sat like the stem.

She fingered the bodice of the costume, which was trimmed with silver rickrack, as were the straps. The seamstress tightened the long seams of the bodice with pins. No dummy of her body stood in the row along the wall, although the women had taken her measurements. The pins pricked through the satin fabric and the cotton backing, a sewing machine made a run down a length of cloth, two older women chatted in Russian or Hungarian or Romanian—all the women in the costume shop came from Eastern Europe—as they threaded the sequined sparkles onto the frames of a series of crowns. So many crowns. It was the first day of autumn, the first day the company reconvened after the break, her father's first day back at Columbia. He would be getting dressed for work now, smoking as he stood at the kitchen sink, drinking his black coffee.

And then Mr. B was in the doorway, the brass handle of an umbrella looped over one arm. He raised his chin at her in greeting, and she ducked her head, a little embarrassed to be seen in her princess finery, as if she'd been caught doing something she wasn't supposed to, grasping after something she wasn't allowed to want. But Mr. B came toward her, stroking his chin, and then conferred with the seamstress about the silver rickrack that trimmed her straps and bodice. "Too much," he said. "Only on straps." The woman nodded, took the seam ripper to a spot, but Mr. B raised his hand. Later. He wanted to see the costume for the Vision scene. She was to have one costume for this act, another for the Vision scene in Act II, and a third for the Wedding in Act III. Very expensive. The seamstress had told her this. She nodded, put down the ripper on the long table covered with appliances and notions, the tools of the dressmaker's trade.

Sandra went obediently behind the screen and the woman helped her out of her tutu, sucking in her breath and tsking when she saw the places where Adam had sucked so hard, which Sandra had contrived to conceal from her before, turning her back to step into the costume. She had the same red bruises on her neck, but those she had covered with makeup. The seamstress took the tutu away. Sandra flushed and bent her head, crossed her arms over her chest, stood there behind the screen in her thin tights. On the other side of the screen, Mr. B also waited, while the seamstress went to find the costume. He didn't move; his attention was completely focused on the thing he wanted and would wait for. Sandra put her arms down, then with one hand touched lightly between her legs. She had bathed, but when she stepped into the first costume, she had felt Adam's semen leak from her. She had frozen, midmovement, to try to hold it in, but it had seeped from her, anyway, soiling both her tights and the costume, though she had not been found out. The seamstress had not looked down into the body of the dress.

The dressmaker came back with the costume for the Vision scene, and this too was pink, so the audience would recognize Aurora, with some of the same silver trim on the fitted bodice, but the skirt had been altered. Fewer, longer layers of silk tulle fell softly to midcalf. Her legs would be seen through this translucent shimmer. The woman hooked her up in the back. Sandra looked down. The neckline fell in a sharp V, not the rounded neckline Mr. B generally preferred. A skin-colored gauzy fabric stretched across the V; at a distance this would not look like fabric, but like jewel-studded flesh. The straps on this costume were thin, almost invisible. She was meant to embody a languorous sexuality that a man would crawl across space and time to possess. Much of the Vision scene had to do with the prince's mounting desire, the prince chasing, momentarily possessing, and then reseeking Aurora until he told the Lilac Fairy he had seen enough, he had to have the girl. The vision of Aurora then vanished and in her place appeared the fairy lake with the boat that would guide the prince toward the princess he must awaken.

What man would make this journey for a little girl? A man would do this only for a lover. In some versions of the tale, the prince knows the girl, in others he is a stranger, but when he encounters her slumbering in a wood or in a castle, her limbs soft and her hair tumbling, he rapes her, his desire his imperative. A kiss was not enough. Sandra felt her face flush as the seamstress tugged at the bodice to draw the neckline lower. The very thing Mr. B wanted her to project was the sexuality that this morning so shamed her. Sandra knew without being told that this would be a hair-down section of the ballet, and she reached up to release her barrette before the seamstress could even whisper, "No crown for this costume." When she had fanned Sandra's hair across her shoulders, she took Sandra's elbow to bring her out from behind the screen to present her to Mr. B, drawing out for him this vision from behind the screen, this woman's body only just hidden behind the costume, waiting to be awakened.

Mr. B was pleased. He gestured to the seamstress and spoke something to her in Russian, and the woman went away and came back with an elaborate costume and wig—a collar broad like a petticoat, a cloak, the fur trim a mock ermine, buckled shoes—a court outfit, not the costume for the prince who would have to dance, but one for a character who had merely to make an entrance and lead a processional, play some mime. This, Sandra understood, when Mr. B held the pieces of the costume to his body, was to be Mr. B's costume. Mr. B was going to dance this ballet with her, would play the King, her father. He rarely took a role on stage—Drosselmeyer in *Nutcracker*, the Don in *Don Quixote*, but that was all long ago. Now he had trouble negotiating the breadth of Lincoln Plaza, had to use an umbrella as a cane. The dancers could rarely persuade him to take a bow at curtain, and yet he was prepared to don this elaborate, heavy French court costume to take her hand and lead her about the stage in one of the ballet's many famous entrées. It was too much and she began to cry the tears she had pressed back before, the dressmaker rushing forward to cup her hands under Sandra's chin before she could stain the bodice of the gown.

The seamstress hustled her behind the screen to strip her of the dress before she could do it any damage, and Sandra put on the T-shirt and the jeans she had worn to walk over here, smoothed her hair with her hands, and came around the screen. Mr. B was bent over one of the long tables, inspecting a series of sketches; the three Romanian ladies had put down their bead-work and were standing by him, gesturing. From the way they used their hands, Sandra guessed they were discussing head-dresses, then trains. Mr. B heard her approach and looked up. She loved his face, the regal nose, the severity of expression when his upper lip closed to cover his overbite, the way his face exploded into warmth when he smiled. She came up to them all at the table and the women parted so she could stand next to Mr. B. The sketches were laid out all over the table; others waited in a pile. There were designs for the clothes of the king and queen, lords and ladies, pages and sentries, for the six fairies, the Carabosse, the nymphs, for the villagers. There were more for the peasantry and the lords and ladies and friends of the prince in Act II, the wedding guests of Act III, Puss in Boots, Red Riding Hood, Cinderella, Bluebeard, the various concoc-tions of Perrault. It went on and on, hundreds of sketches for hundreds of costumes, none of them yet constructed except for his and hers, and with the costumes went a hundred different dances, ensemble work, entrées, tableaus, small group work, so-los, pas de deux for Mr. B to invent, to teach, to adapt. He had not yet begun any of this. She watched his hands move over the sketches, make gestures as he spoke in Russian. His hands were soft and graceful, the palms plump, the fingers tapered, the tip of one of them lost in a gardening accident. Whatever had left him so enervated was now gone. The lush foliage and strong sun, the thick perfume of summer, had animated his pulse, drove him now into fall and winter with a purpose. She was essential to that purpose.

$\mathcal{S}$HE CALLED ADAM at the brownstone that evening, to tell him about the costume, about Mr. B's costume, about all the sketches, but she got no answer. She tried him over and over, every hour. The last time she let the phone ring twenty times, and then she hung up and went into the dining room where her father had laid his lesson plans out on the table. She knew now that Adam had vanished on her, disappeared on purpose. She was not going to be able to reach him. And she knew why. It was because this morning, at dawn, she woke Adam and begged him to go back to the brownstone so he wouldn't be here when her father got up. Adam hadn't been happy about it, but he did it. She had given him everything, so he couldn't refuse her. He had gotten dressed, found his clothes, his coat, his gloves. By the time he pulled on his hat, his face was dark and drawn. She had watched him through the peephole while he waited for the elevator outside. She hated herself for what she was doing to him, wanted him to refuse to leave or to insist that she come with him, and yet if he turned and tried to open the door she knew she wouldn't let him in.

She sat at the table and bit at her nails. Methodically, her father turned the pages of a book. She watched him for a few minutes, then went into the kitchen and made a pot of coffee. When it was ready, she brought a cup to him. He looked up, smiled absently, and when he went back to work, she sat in a chair at the other end of the dining room table and watched him. She was here, she had sent Adam away so she could be here like this for her dad, who eventually looked up from his notes and papers quizzically. "Don't you have anything to do?" No, she did not have anything to do. She had been prepared to return to the life she had before Adam. But that was not going to be so simple. Adam had been here, and it could never be as if he had not, and it appeared her father did not need her supervision. Not tonight, anyway.

By the time she got down to West Tenth Street, she was almost afraid to get out of the cab. It was late, and the ground-floor window of the brownstone showed no light. Adam might not even be home. He could be anywhere, anywhere in this city. But she had the key on its pink ribbon and she had sent the cab away. She would wait for Adam, the way he had waited for her at the door of the Eldorado.

Inside, the apartment was dark and quiet, the parquet floors clouded with dust. From the streetlight coming in, she could see the sheets and the big down comforter heaped like the shape of a man in the bed, but when she moved close and touched it, she saw it was only cloth. She sat down. Adam's coat and clothes were on the floor by the side of the bed, on the leather arm-chair, as if he had just been here. She picked up his shirt and lay back, put it up over her chest, wrapped the arms of it around her neck. Already the place felt foreign to her, as it had that first night he'd brought her here. Where was he? She kissed at the fabric of the shirt. And then the bathroom door opened and Adam was standing there and she sat up with a start. He was wet, his skin and his hair wet, he must have been taking a shower but she had heard no water running and the bathroom behind him was dark. He stood there looking at her, his lips almost blue in his pale face in the pale streetlight. He wore only his Jockeys, as if he'd been getting dressed or undressed and then had gotten stalled. She could see, even in this light, the thick veins in his arms and hands and thighs.

"What are you doing here, Sandra?" he said, and there was something wrong with his voice.

She said, "I've been calling you. Why didn't you answer the phone?"

"I pulled the damn thing out of the wall. I know everything

you're going to say." He went around to the other side of the bed
and that's when she smelled him and realized he hadn't been in the
shower at all, he'd been sick, was perspiring, he'd been using, had
locked himself in this apartment and been using all day, and she
knew—he'd been using because of her. He'd not only used, he
was letting her see it, though usually he tried to hide it from her,
never talked about it with her. He was pulling on his jeans. "Do
you have any idea what it felt like to be sent packing this morning—after what we did?" and she had to look down. He turned
his head to look at her. "I'd never have sent you out like that,
never, I don't care if my dad had been in the bin a thousand years."

She knew he wouldn't have.

He leaned over the bed, leaning on his fists to put his face to
hers. "And the ridiculous thing is—I can't live without you, but
you can live without me."

How could he even think this? He had taken over her life so
completely, she didn't even feel that she owned it anymore.

"I'm going to throw up," Adam said. "My heart's beating too
fast," and he got off the bed and went into the bathroom and
shut the door.

She went to his pants on the chair and then to his coat, put
her hands in the pockets, searched the lining for any inner pockets. What had he taken, what drugs? Where were they? She sat
there, hunched up by the big leather coat, thinking, her hands
cooled by the satin lining, her brain shaking like a rattle. She
crouched there for a minute or two longer, and then went to his
duffel. From it, she pulled bottles and baggies—Quaaludes,
weed, cocaine. Had he carried this stuff around on tour with
him, through airports? Or had he bought the drugs here, since
he'd gotten back to New York? She read the labels on the bottles. Dexedrine. *Take one every eight hours as needed.* Valium. *Take*

*as needed*. Benzedrine. She knew Adam used when he was miserable, and he must have been miserable while he was away. She knew he used, she just didn't know how often, how much. There were dancers who used drugs in every company—a few dancers at ABT everybody knew used too much cocaine—even Mr. B was known to offer a dancer a vitamin on occasion that was not a vitamin. But Adam was not stocked for an occasion. She heard him retching in the bathroom, he needed her, and she got up and opened the bathroom door.

Adam was sitting on the toilet with the lid down, his elbows on his knees.

"Did you throw up?" she asked him.

He shook his head. "Nothing left to throw up."

She poured him some water into the plastic bathroom cup, made him sip at it. "What did you take?"

"Did some lines. Took some Valium." He raised his face to look at her. "I always use when I'm on tour."

"You're not on tour now," she whispered.

"No, but I'm thinking about going on tour," he said, "thinking about what it's going to be like. Not what I wanted it to be, that's for sure." He put his face in his hands.

She bent down and touched his knees, his ankles, her face at his face, but he wouldn't look at her directly. She put her face down to his feet, felt the strong bones in them shift against her face, rubbed her lips against them.

"Sandra, don't do that."

"Why not?" she said without moving.

"Because I'm too sad and too fucking angry with you to have you kissing my feet."

She sat up. "Do you want me to give up everything? Because I will, Adam, if you make me."

He shut his eyes. "Sandra, I don't think there's one goddamn thing you'd give up for me. I've already asked." He turned his head and she saw the small muscles working in his jaw. "So I've decided on something," he said finally. "I'm giving you up."

## SIX

He paused by the door of the main rehearsal hall, the stagelike space that matched foot for foot the proportions of the New York State Theater, and watched a rehearsal of *Nutcracker*. It was *Nutcracker* season again, his twenty-seventh, and the girls skated across the floor, making the short sharp turns of snowflakes in descent. Rows and rows of girls, the youngest girls, newest to the company and new to his eye. Snowflakes in the great forest, very Russian, gateway to the Land of the Sweets, the great box of candies Marie and the Nutcracker prince find themselves in. How else to get there, from one world to another, except in a great white blur, like a dream from which no one, at the end of the ballet, wakes.

Christmas was for parents and children; without one or the other he had for years dreaded the morning, but when he was small, he had loved the holiday. St. Petersburg was all dark on the eve of it, the city all dark, all of Russia dark, waiting for the Christ child to be born. The tree branches doubled their size with snow; the snow lay thick on the lowered wings of the angels that encircled the basilica of St. Isaac, on the ornamentation of the steeples, on the arms of the cross. His family went to St. Vladimir's, mother, auntie, George, Tamara, Andrei, the children in velvet and bows and formal collars, as he had dressed the children in his *Nutcracker*. At the apex of the service, the congregation snuffed out their candles. In the darkness, the choir sang out *Gloria,* the sound a shock, Christ is born. At home, the scent of pine mixed with the scent of wax candles. The gold paper angels and stars wore the reflections of the flames, as did the long strips of tinsel, the round bodies of the ornamental glass pears. Christmas was tree, party, and now, in this country, *Nutcracker*.

He had made the ballet in 1954 for Maria Tallchief and Tanaquil LeClercq after he had exchanged one wife for the other, and in his guilt he had given Maria the main role of the Sugar Plum Fairy and in his passion he had created a new role for Tanny, the Dewdrop lighting among the flowers. Ballet was woman, but it did not have to be one woman. His was the only *Nutcracker* with two ballerinas. He could make what he wanted, make of a woman what he wanted. Tanny was nothing to him at first, a little girl at the school, her tutus starched, her headbands glued with flowers. He had scolded her for dancing with the affected manner of an old-fashioned ballerina at a music hall; then she had to be reprimanded for talking too much in class and for mimicking her teachers. She had mettle. And temperament. When she joined the company, she had cried because her *Four Temperaments* costume—a hip-length blue wig with a unicorn horn centered in the nest of it, wings that covered her arms all the way down past her fingers—made her feel trapped. He had had to take the scissors and make a slit for her middle finger to come through. Yes, that was what he had done for her, for all his girls, brought them up and then brought them out.

Maria, too, had been nothing and he had made her his first big American ballerina—up until that time, he had used mostly foreign-born dancers, Tamara Toumanova, Alicia Alonso, but for Maria he made *Firebird* and *Orpheus* and *Symphony in C,* so she was born—fierce, fast, exotic, with her black hair and her formidable technique. Yes. He made ballets and he made ballerinas, and he was going to do both again.

He had felt the stir in the studio this morning when he led Sandra into company class. Without a word, he had placed her at the barre by Suzanne, then turned to demonstrate the first set of tendus. He had made his announcement. He had intended the gesture to have weight, had deliberately not prepared the girl for it. She had come, late, down the hallway, dragging her army bag, her hair held up in a clip, and he had waited for her at the studio door, observed the change in her face when she saw him waiting, when she understood he was waiting for her. He had raised his hand: she was not to run. He was scrutinized, always, by his dancers. By now he had grown used to it, and that audience, his truest audience, first audience to his every creation, his every passion, had watched him yesterday escort to the barre the last girl on whom he would have energy to expend. She was, he knew, an unexpected choice. Not a new girl fresh from the school, but one new to his eye; not tall like Suzi, but small, like a cat; not fifteen, sixteen, seventeen, but twenty. In other ways not so unexpected, and those who knew to look would see in her the ghosts of dancers that came before her.

But his attention, he knew, came at a cost. The other girls had drawn back from her. And this girl had already stood back from the others, even before this; now this privacy spread out before her like a carpet, spread behind her like a train. Between rehearsals he saw her sitting alone with her coffee or Coke in the lounge, saw her each afternoon on the telephone in the hall-way—whom was she calling? the boy? her father?—alone, whispering, pleading, her head bent, face turned toward the wall, as if she wished she could crawl into it, as if she were being left behind. She had what he had: no one. After class, she left the studio alone. He watched her shoulder her heavy bag, the weight of it making her list to the side. She was too tiny for it, but he loved the sight of her with it—the sweep of her neck with that hair, so thin and so fine, twisted up away from the delicate column of bones, the shift in her hips, the long legs, her feet in those pointe shoes with the extra long, elegant vamps. The bag, U.S. Army green, drab, absurd, he liked. What it spoke of was a certain lack of vanity, lack of interest in this life, which he shared. Their real life was lived in the theater.

He would have to watch out for her himself.

He turned from the studio door, made his way down the hall, looking into each studio as he passed. In this one, a girl practiced the sensuous languor of Coffee; in the next, a mass of girls arranged themselves like petals of a flower blown this way and that; in another, four girls danced the delicate pointe work of Marzipan, which sent the ruffled skirts of their costumes shaking, big fabric truffles trembling against the top layer of tulle; behind them, big hoops in their hands, waited the boys and girls for the next variation—Candy Canes. In the next studio, the couples doing the Spanish-flavored Hot Chocolate rehearsed. All around him, dance by dance, Act II was being readied; and this afternoon, when the children finished at schools all over the city, they would converge here at Lincoln Center, the girls with ribbons in their hair, to rehearse Act I, the big party scene, Christmas with the family. He reached the end of the hall and looked into the small studio there.

Sandra and Ib Andersen, the partner he had picked for her, were working through the *Nutcracker* grand pas de deux, had gotten there early, before him, to do this. The pas de deux had been made for Maria's strength and aplomb. This girl brought to it something else—not bravura strength, but the strength of an icicle or a tear—clear, gleaming, and sharp—its strength all the more poignant for its temporality, its fragility. She had a head for crowns, this girl, and he carried one in his hands now for her to rehearse in—a prop as essential as the short rehearsal tutu she already wore. He watched through the window. Her dancing became flushed with a warmth, a vibrancy that tempered the ice. She sensed him. He was there, and she knew it.

HER APARTMENT WAS in the Eldorado, a tall, white brick building with a canopy that extended to the street, narrow iron windows one pushed open, like the windows in the old 1930s apartments George had lived in in Hollywood. Of this prewar building George fully approved. He rose, in the mirrored elevator, with his wine and his flowers wrapped in paper, not cellophane. He had often felt anachronistic when he visited the boxlike apartments of his various ballerinas wearing his cravat and bearing his Old World gifts, but here he did not, not in the lobby, not in the gilded elevator, not in the private entry hall, not as he was ushered into the apartment by Sandra and her father, who had, she told him, suggested that George be invited for the evening.

The father was younger than George had expected, but with the manners of an older man, offering George his arm to escort him into the big living room that overlooked the park. The father's face bore deep furrows, deeper than a man his age should have, and his blond hair was sifted through with silver. The girl had told him her father had been hospitalized at Roosevelt, that he had been there two months, part of that time unable to receive visitors. Then, later, he had wanted no visitors but her. Sequestered the father might have been, but at the moment, he lived with his daughter in an apartment of bourgeois splendor, the decoration of which reminded George of the apartment his family had occupied in St. Petersburg, the twelve-room flat they owned for five years after his father had won the lottery and before he'd spent all the money, recklessly, investing foolishly, kopecks falling through his fingers, until finally his family trekked like refugees off to Finland. His father was an artist, not a businessman. What had brought this family their riches? This apartment displayed all the Old World comforts—many books and objets d'art, velvet sofas hemmed with silk fringe, gilded lamps fitted with fabric, not paper, shades from which hung colored glass beads or bright tassels, upholstered chairs with clawed feet, a small multitude of tables, doubled drapes held back from the windows with gold braids. Who had furnished this place? Clearly such an action was beyond both the girl and her father. What family did she come from, this girl with her blond hair and her army duffel bag?

He sat in a large chair, the father on another beside him, chatting gently of this and that, the weather, mild for October, and then the girl came in with a tray of three glasses filled with hot tea, the glasses themselves set into gold holders, old-style, cubes of sugar on a small plate. George sniffed his approval. She brought out a platter of cakes and cookies, and all these things at the wave of the father's hand were placed on the big tufted leather ottoman that served as the coffee table. It was just the three of them, not a foursome. The boy who had come to watch her in Saratoga, Adam LaSalle, was not there. And that boy's absence did not surprise him.

Earlier today, he had watched Sandra with that boy from the window of one of the studios above Lincoln Plaza, watched the girl in her ponytail stand by the fountain and talk with him, the boy he had given all his best ballerinas to partner, the one he had allowed to dance in all his ballets, the boy who had packed up all that knowledge in his suitcase and carried it across the plaza to the Met, where he was, George understood, plying it with great success. The boy had stood with his back ramrod straight; he would not put down his bag even when the girl had put down hers and begun to gesticulate with her arms. She raised a hand to his face, which he blocked, shook off. He was shaking his head, too, and then he turned with his bag and began to stride across the plaza toward Broadway. George watched as the girl stood there for a moment, and then she turned toward the theater, disappeared within. And so she missed what George saw: the boy stopped for a moment, turned as if to go back to her, and then, seeing her gone, continued on.

George sat propped on the sofa, two pillows under an elbow keeping his dizziness at bay, and he saw the girl was anxious. Was it about this, the boy? All night she was up and down, pouring tea, collecting plates, turning the pages of her father's music when he sat at the piano to play for them. While he played, George looked closely at his face, and in his exhausted eyes George saw sorrow, pain, and something else, defeat. The father was not fully well, and the arms of illness were not the arms of death, a beautiful girl, but the limbs of a terrifying hag. This the daughter sensed; this, the source of her anxiety. It was not about a boy. She saw her father slipping away, though she did not know why, whether from hunger, boredom, or thirst, and so she sought to put a stopper to each. But none of those things was the cause, and George saw he would bleed away regardless. She would be alone soon, a daughter without a father. George put down his glass.

He would make for her a room of silver and gold, and when her father disappeared, she could come and live with him.

To amuse, he played at the piano also, after the father, a little Vernon Duke, a little Gershwin. He played from memory, with the girl at his right and her father to the left. He could hear their pleasure, and at certain passages, the father tried his voice. He knew words here and there, had a surprisingly sweet tone, the words tinted with the round and graceful sound of the Deep South. It was funny: the girl had no such sound to her own voice, it was flat and plain, the voice of anywhere. And then even Sandra played, "Für Elise" and "Ode to Joy," the Beethoven pieces of a beginner.

At the end of the evening, she came down with him to fetch him a cab, the doorman not good enough. The man stood behind them in his uniform, but the girl sent him back into the lobby. She would wait with George. The night was clear, the park a shadowy forest held at bay only by the strip of tar and concrete before them. Traffic was light. They stood, waiting for the streetlight a block away to change, to bring the torrent of taxis and cars down their way. She crossed her arms over her chest, she had not worn a coat, and she was small. Yes. He would have the front bedroom cleared out and painted, and a bedroom suite delivered, the furniture not dark like the furniture in her house, but white, Swedish-style, like the furniture in his family's old dacha, like the sunlit reaches of northern Finland, long days, long seasons of sun. He would ask Karinska about the fabrics— maybe yellow, maybe blue. Pink. Yes. Drapes of pink silk so pale as to be almost colorless, held back from the silk sheers beneath by fabric roses as big as cabbages, a white bed, its four posts like birch limbs, dressed from top to bottom in white, gold, and pink, a tufted chair pulled to the mirrored dressing table. It would be ready when the time came.

And when it was time for her to marry, her suitors could visit her, could pay her court, and when she had chosen a husband, then he, too, could live there. Why not? George himself had lived for some time with Tamara's family on Grafsky Alley, the two of them sandwiched into Tamara's girlhood bedroom, until her mother had made that impossible, with her bacchanals and infidelities that so troubled Tamara. If not for that, they could have lived in the family's apartment indefinitely, in that place protected by her father's standing and reputation from the travails of the Revolution. Perhaps if he and Tamara had stayed there, in the embrace of her family, in the embrace of Russia and the Maryinsky, they would have weathered their lives better, perhaps become one of the solid theatrical families that populated the theater they grew up in—husbands and wives dancers, their children also dancers, like Marius Petipa and his daughter Marie, like Pavel Gerdt and his daughter Elizaveta. Such families were legion! Revolution had disrupted the natural order of things, had scattered the young dancers to the winds, to Diaghilev, to Europe, erased the old patterns.

Well, he had remade Russian ballet here, made a school and a theater that generations of families could thrive in—already had! The Neary sisters and the Duell brothers, Jacques d'Amboise and his son Christopher. There would be more, undoubtedly, and why should this girl and her beloved and their child not be a part of this? The husband, if not a dancer, would wait for them at home while they were busy at the theater, busy himself with the child until she herself were old enough to be brought to the school. George had not been a father, had not had a child with any of his wives, but now, he was still alive and therefore it was not too late to become *père* and *grandpère,* one kingdom at the theater, another at home.

## SEVEN

On the stage of the Palais Garnier he was resplendent, nothing in *Le Corsaire* beyond him, suited up in his custom-made costume, one of several his mother had encouraged him to have tailored back in New York for this series of European gigs. He would make more money in these six weeks than he would make the rest of the year at ABT. Covent Garden. La Scala. Le Palais Garnier. Deutsche Oper. His engagement book looked like Nureyev's, though Nureyev had been booked years in advance in the major cities of the world and Adam was now just at the beginning of all this. But his mother was right: he could not make an international name for himself buried in New York. ABT had to be a base, as the stars of the sixties and seventies had used it. From the balcony of the Metropolitan Opera House, he and his mother had watched Natalia Makarova and Ivan Nagy, Carla Fracci and Erik Bruhn, Rudolf Nureyev and Margot Fonteyn perform as guest artists, Lucia whispering, *That could be you,* and now it was he, though it was not, on this side of the curtain, all it had looked to be from the front. It was his first night dancing in Paris, and in the blank dressing room they had given him, he had laid out a few lines. He was jet-lagged and he'd had only a day of rehearsal with the French ballerina he danced with tonight, but that was not really the reason he was using. The travel and the loneliness were disorienting; to sleep on the planes and in the hotels he used tranquilizers; in the morning, amphetamines; before performance, a line or two or another Dexedrine.

Which was why tonight his heart was pumping double-time as he traversed the stage with the barrel turns and twisting leaps, the all-out bravura of the show-stopping *Corsaire* pas de deux, a number concocted from the various bits and pieces of all the male character solo work from the longer ballet, the pas de deux a bag of tricks and acrobatics, one-armed lifts that tested the strength and derring-do of both man and woman. He could see the dancers of the Paris Opéra standing in the wings as he made a big circle about the stage, some in costumes from the previous ballet, some from the one to come. Adam was an event, an object of interest, envy, irritation, admiration, their attitudes about him another thing he didn't want to think about, a distraction. What did it matter? A few more nights and he'd be out of here anyway. They could hate him, love him, it didn't matter, all that mattered was this moment out here on the stage, in a life distinct from his own life, the only door out of it and he wanted to be out of it.

At the wave of applause, he was in the wings and his French girl was out on the stage. He had sixty seconds to blot himself delicately with a towel and then he was back out there with her, a little vertiginous from the exertion—the gilded boxes and tiers of the red interior of the Garnier swinging dizzily, the exit lights leaking long streaks of color in the air when he turned, the girl herself a blur of costume in his hands, the glass of her tiara braying in his face as he handled her. It was all disorienting. He hoisted her above him—she was light like Sandra, this was good—and as he ran with her about the stage as if she were a sail or a cape, he saw the awed expressions on the faces of the dancers in the wings change to apprehension and then horror. He had run around the stage with her perhaps one too many times; the music had rushed ahead of them into the next bars, they should be following those, doing the next sequence of steps, but he was lost, and so he kept running, his partner stiffening and tipping above him, the dancers in the wings starting to shout at him, *Arrêtez, arrêtez,* some of them with hands over their mouths. He managed, finally, to bring her down, a black blot obscuring the hot yellow stage lights, almost stumbling over her as she thrust herself in front of him, more ready than he was to pick up the cast of the dance where it should be. He flailed behind her for a few seconds before he realized where she was, where they were, and then it was over, he was lying on the floor at her feet, his back arched, one arm up in the air.

The curtain came down and hit the boards with a heavy swish and the French girl had bared her teeth at him, "You fucking bastard," the only English he'd heard her speak in two days. The curtain went up and her lips stretched into a smile; she took his hand, though she would touch only her fingertips to it, and moved downstage with him to take a bow. And the bows went on and on, each drop of the curtain marked by an explosion in French; each cranking up of the curtain, the pasted smile, the curtsey. At the last of it, while the stage was being wet down, he tried to apologize to her, but his tongue was too thick, too twisted, too slow, too slurred to wrap itself around English, let alone French. She stared at him a moment as he made some sounds, then turned on her heel and made for the wings, tutu waddling its behind at him, and he had to laugh. He went to the wings, got his towel, walked toward his dressing room, down the yellow and red halls, all around him the dancers pulling away, cutting their eyes away. Nureyev, the new artistic director of the Opéra and himself currently detested by the rank and file, stared at him curiously, knowingly. Adam shut the door, shut them all out. He shucked off his fifteen-hundred-dollar tunic, his twenty-dollar tights, his forty-dollar dance belt, his fifty-dollar leather ballet slippers and got into the shower where there was nothing but the water pulsing down, the feel of it and the sound of it enveloping him. He ignored the faint knocks on his dressing room door, *Monsieur LaSalle, un moment s'il vous plaît,* turned the shower on harder, opened his mouth to sing, though what came out sounded like bellowing, and so he bellowed. *Go away.*

WHEN HE LEFT the theater, he stopped at the big newsstand to buy a pack of the Gauloises Frenchmen smoked in the bars and cafés and bus stops, drawing on them with such slow satisfaction he figured their effect had to be something like weed. But they were just cigarettes, shot full of tar and nicotine, disappointing and tasty. He smoked one on the walk to his hotel; by now his tongue and his brain had sorted themselves out. This was not the first time he'd fucked up in the past couple of weeks, though it was the most public. At La Scala, he had slept through a rehearsal, waking only when one of the *régisseurs* rang his hotel room to inquire about him. And he'd been hardly able to speak intelligibly, blaming his confusion on jet lag when he'd taken one too many pills, the effect of which was to lay him low into sleep for twenty hours. He'd never yet gotten lost on the stage as he had tonight, his brain tucked into some weird warp like that. He sat down on a sidewalk bench and hunched over his cigarette. It was early November and cold. Behind him the chairs of a café were tilted against the bare tables. Inside, behind the glass, a few people sat at the dark bar. He'd been in too many bars the past weeks, having too many drinks. In London, he'd gone out into the alley behind one of those bars and allowed a boy he'd just met to kneel before him and give him some expert head, the boy's mouth taking all of him in, the boy's fingers inserted deep into his ass, and it was nothing like, a different planet from, a tentative blow job given by an inexperienced girl. It was the first time Adam had been with anyone but Sandra for almost a year, and since that moment, there had been many others like it.

But now he was in Paris, alone. His hotel, the George V, waited. It was dangerous to do what he was doing, which was to sit by himself with a cigarette, unmoving, undrugged, because he knew he was going to think about Sandra, which was forbidden. He was afraid he'd lose it if he thought of her, and so he'd refused himself the pleasure, not that it was pleasurable, not at all. But now in the dark, in the street, until he finished this cigarette, he would permit himself to think of her, to think of the way she'd bent over his feet their last night together, the way she'd wailed, *Why can't you wait for me, the way I waited for you?* And even as he was walking her down the hall to the apartment door, he thought, *What is she talking about, when had she ever had to wait for him?* At the front door, he'd had to unwrap her legs from around him, peel them off like tape, unstick her from his body, get the apartment door open and hold her from him, the whole time feeling as if he'd peeled off one of his own limbs. She didn't get it: they had to move forward or everything would just disintegrate. He'd waited too long already not to go forward.

But that was not the last time. She would call him or he would call her, and each time the conversation was the same and it could go on for hours until one of them finally hung up or fell asleep, phone dropping from their hands. Sometimes he just didn't pick up, let the phone ring and ring, pulled the plug, but even in the silence he could still feel the insistence of her. *I can't work, I can't concentrate, I can't sleep,* she'd say to him, and he'd say, *Do you think I can?* But still she wouldn't say what he wanted her to say, couldn't say it, that she would put him first. And so he took pills, smoked dope, showed up to rehearsal a few times so fucked up, management had to speak to him, but what could they say—he danced like a demon, plowing through the roles he'd be doing when they started touring in December. Only inside the steps, inside a thorough sweat, inside the center of a reeling room did he find any relief. He hated being alone at the brownstone, the two months they'd spent together in the place hung there like a weeping ghost despite the drugs, despite the television. He'd bought the thing at an appliance store on Broadway and turned it on the minute he walked in; none of it could blow back the monsters.

Sometimes in his desperation he'd go see his parents, but now his father was always talking about *his boys* at Juilliard, *his boys,* he always said that, *I have this boy* or *one of my boys,* and there was only so much of that Adam could stand to hear. His mother never missed a minute to talk about his agent, his career, and finally just to shut her up, he said, *Fine, let him book me, I'll go.* ABT was only rehearsing; he'd skip that, rejoin the company in time for *Nutcracker.* You need to get away, she told him, but he knew what she wanted him to get away from. He wanted to go, wanted to get away, couldn't stand this city anymore. The only thing about it he *could* stand was Randall, but if he went by Randall's at night, he might find him asleep in his bed in the big room, green wool cap pulled low over his forehead and ears; he was always cold, couldn't regulate his body temperature. The place was an oven—in fifteen minutes Adam would be soaked, couldn't breathe, Joe and Eric at the big Biedermeier dining table playing solitaire in their undershirts, neither of them talking; there was just the sound of Randall's strident breathing and the slap and slide of the cards on the polished table. The place was too quiet, and in the chair by the bed, looking at the evaporated Randall, Adam felt sadness boil in his gut, and by the time he got back to the brownstone he'd call Sandra and they'd go through the whole damn thing yet again, with her begging him to come over and him telling her it just wasn't going to be like that between them anymore. He was glad to go to Europe, glad to go away, but he couldn't leave without saying good-bye to her.

He knew her schedule, went up to Lincoln Center early enough to catch her as she arrived for company class. He knew he was going to see her, but still he wasn't prepared for it, for the sight of her out on the plaza. She ripped right through him. It was one thing to avoid her in theory, another thing to do it in the flesh. She looked thinner than he remembered, if that were possible, her chest making a prominent cage over her heart. *I can't keep food down,* she told him when he asked, and when he said, *Sandra,* helplessly, she said, *I'm not doing it on purpose, everything's just making me sick. Look,* he said, *I'm going tomorrow, I'll be in Europe for six weeks,* and he didn't even get to the part he'd planned to say, about how the break would be good for them, because she reached out to hit him, and he reacted instinctively, his arm going up to block her, and she started weeping, long tears running down her chin like the tears she'd wept the last time he went on tour. When he reached out to wipe at them, his palm to her cheek, she knocked his hand away and began to shout, *Why did you do this to me? Why did you ever do this to me?* He got halfway across the cacophony of Columbus and Broadway before he said, *Fuck this,* it wasn't worth it, he'd just take from her whatever she could give, turned to go back, but she was already gone, on to the next thing, couldn't even wait the fifteen seconds for him; his heart was a jackhammer and she was already gone.

He got up again and walked, this time toward the Seine, over the Pont Alexandre III, leaned against a stone wall, looked toward the Hôtel des Invalides. The city was incredibly lavish, the Opéra beautiful beyond belief, with its great stone facade, its columns and balconies and pediments on its gold dome, a statue of Apollo holding aloft his lyre. The square white boxes of Lincoln Center were, by contrast, some junior, kid-sized versions of a theater, scraped clean because no child could imagine such decorations as these. The place intimidated him, as did Nureyev's Quai Voltaire apartment, where Adam had been invited to dinner, the apartment overly lavish, overheated, and overstuffed with the trophies of Nureyev's long career—antiques, rugs, silver, paintings, fabric, objets, all of which Nureyev showed Adam as he walked with him through the rooms. The man had danced in every opera house and theater in the world, his career spanned decades, and now he lived here, alone, in this dark apartment, attended by an entourage of fawning boys and paid assistants. The press had called Adam an American Nureyev, but he was no Nureyev, didn't want to be a Nureyev, didn't have the man's stamina, didn't have his ability to live such a solitary life.

Adam was tired already—tired of traveling, tired at the thought of the cities ahead.

The cocaine high was now gone and Adam knew enough to recognize he was hurtling down the dark trough that followed. He needed to grab on to something—a glass of wine, a joint, a pill, anything before he hit the craggy bottom. Maybe others could tolerate this relentless sense of alienation, the continuous loneliness, but not him. He couldn't even live alone in New York; hotel rooms in strange cities were truly beyond him. The George V was ridiculous, and he dreaded returning to it. He'd have been better off in some youth hostel with a shared bedroom, more the style his mother traveled in anyway when she toured the college auditoriums of America. He knelt and riffled through his bag, but there was nothing of use in there. Everything he'd scored here in Paris, he'd left at the hotel except for the slim packet of coke, now flushed down the toilet at the Opéra in some paranoid conviction that his dressing room might be searched while he was onstage. If he wanted something, he'd have to go back to the George V.

IT WAS LATE afternoon, dark, when he woke in his satin bed, chandelier pressing down on him from the ceiling, the message light blinking on the phone, and at first he thought it was the middle of the night. But it was the wrong kind of light, the wrong kind of quiet, a late afternoon lull, not a premorning stillness. He sat up. Fuck! He was fucked, fucked, fucked, had missed the day's rehearsal, needed to be at the theater by six o'clock for makeup. He didn't want to know who had called, didn't have any explanations for anybody. He picked up the phone and ordered a meal, went into the bathroom to inspect his waxen face; his lips were cracked and chafed, and his nostrils and his eyes burned. His jaw looked overlong, his chin too jutting, too narrow, covered with stubble. He needed to bathe, he needed to shave; he still reeked from last night, as did his clothes, his hair, everything. He switched off the bathroom light, stripped and climbed into the elevated marble tub before it had been filled, let the water run until he was almost submerged. His whole body ached, almost floated, and he tipped his head back, skull on the ledge. At some point he had this thought: *What if I just don't show up at the theater?* And that thought became a conviction.

What would happen? There would be phone calls to the room, a phone call to his agent, more phone calls, perhaps a visit from the hotel staff. The blinking phone light indicated there had been calls already. He lay there in the tub in the darkening bathroom in a state of excited panic, the tank watch on his wrist making a green glow-in-the-dark sweep of the minutes. He would go, he wouldn't go, he still had time, he would have to leave now, until finally it was too late to try, past six, he was beyond doing his makeup, warming up, management would have called in a replacement, there would be a fine, some penalty to pay, some consequences to face, if only Nureyev's fury. What if some lackey of his from the Opéra came here, to the hotel, demanded a key, demanded that the door be opened, the room searched, drugs impounded, dancer arrested? This thought, and the bath water, which had grown cold and grimy, roused him, and he sloshed out of the deep and dried himself, tripped about the hotel room pulling on clothes, a scarf, a coat, his boots, gathering up all his pills and packets and shoving them into his bag. When he left the room, he saw the meal he had ordered sitting on a cart outside the door, and he stood in the hallway a moment, lifted the metal warming lids to stuff some of the food in his mouth: a roll, a leg of chicken, a boiled potato. The hallway, long, empty, carpeted in blue and gold fleurs-de-lis, lay before him like a treadmill, ready to trip him up. He took the stairs down from the fifth floor and, once out on the street, found himself inexplicably walking toward the Opéra.

Buses and taxis and cars on the Place d'Opéra dropped people off at the long stone steps of the theater, and streetlights lit the facade bronze and gold. All was as usual. The audience would arrive, the dancers perform, the announcement made as the houselights went to half—*Mesdames et messieurs, le rôle de Solor ce soir*—what did he care? He was free. He didn't have to do it. He felt giddy. He felt like a criminal. He would go get something to drink, something more to eat, like a normal person for whom curtain time meant nothing, eight o'clock an hour like any other hour. He headed for the Café de la Paix, just at the corner, and took an outdoor table though it was cold, the umbrella above him too high, its circumference more a parasol than a serious London umbrella, to offer much protection. He turned up the collar of his coat, wrapped the scarf around his neck again and again, flipped the end of it back over his shoulder, saw a girl at another table watching him. He looked down, then back at her, then away. If he looked at her again, she'd get up and come to his table. He had been fucking only boys in Europe, as if that, somehow, made him less unfaithful. Less unfaithful to whom—the girl he had broken up with?

How many weeks until Christmas, how many more weeks until he was back in New York? He counted them off on his fingers under the table, then shoved his hands into his pockets. It was impossible to imagine, really, what it would be like not to have to dance anymore. When Baryshnikov had fired Godunov,

Adam's first thought had been, *I wish that were me.* Sitting here, free of everybody—his parents, Randall and Joe, Balanchine, Baryshnikov, even Sandra—he felt he wouldn't ever need to dance again now that he'd stopped for a moment, just got off the train. On those commutes out to the suburbs of New York and Connecticut, he had never thought to do that.

That's how he felt sitting there in the café, like he'd gotten off the train. He checked his watch. The big red curtain was already up, the front panel of it hiked to one side like a woman's skirt. The stage—its wings, its machinery, its backstage space—took up so much of the theater's square footage that the house sat no more people than State Theater did at home, despite the size of the building, its palatial hallways and foyers. All of it would be dark now and empty, everyone's focus on the lit stage. People had paid money to see him, to watch him stretch his legs, jump, pose, toss his hair. But he wasn't there. He was here, drinking a few glasses of wine, waiting for his next meal, getting ready to pick up a girl, like any other man tonight in Paris.

$\mathcal{H}$E ENDED UP telling Nureyev he'd had food poisoning, was too sick, too feverish even to call the theater, Adam not quite ready to trash everything on an evening's whim. He managed to finish his second week at the Opéra, plowing through his pharmaceuticals to do so, making calls home or to Randall, but Randall's pulseless, weak voice upset him. One night in a moment of absolute bowelless, bottomless weakness, he'd called Sandra, but no one answered, though he let it ring and ring. It was late enough at night in New York that she should have been back from the theater, late enough in the autumn that winter season should have started, with the long round of *Nutcrackers* that required her presence. She would be dancing what the principal girls always danced: Sugar Plum or Dewdrop, one role had a cavalier, the other danced alone among her flowers. How would Balanchine want to see her? Probably both ways. Every way. Adam had put down the phone softly and when he left Paris he decided to leave off thinking about home, about anything, anyone. He had to stop thinking of her, had to stop. Wasn't that the point of a separation anyway, relief? To show her what it was like to be without him? To see himself what it was like to be without her?

It was when he got to Berlin that he remembered Randall had come here once long ago, to Berlin and then to Cologne, to get away from Joe. Punishment. Relief. Both. Randall couldn't stand to see Joe desiring Eli Strauss, with his long, gaunt face and his tall, thin, planklike body that he drove like a machine through the pieces Joe created for him. Randall was still healthy then, he was only thirty-six, and he could walk, so he walked out of there, walked across the Pacific Ocean and across Europe to Germany, where he hunkered down and waited in these same gray oppressive cities, his mood growing darker, like the cathedrals, the rivers, the mountains. He didn't have long to wait. A month. It was a full month before Joe flew to Cologne, renounced Eli. Adam had been in Europe almost a month and a half and Sandra was not going to fly over here, was not going to renounce anyone. How could she renounce her father? And as for Balanchine, she was under the spell of the greatest sorcerer.

So in Berlin he stopped calling everybody.

The Deutsche Oper was his last stop, the opera house a raised cement-colored box with a wall of windows that looked out at a city he barely saw. He had no time to walk the streets, which was good. He would just get into trouble if he walked the streets. He took class with the company, rehearsed afternoons, ate at the theater canteen, performed, walked the mile back to the Hotel Savoy on Fasanenstrasse with his coat collar turned up, cap pulled low. He took no one to his room, turned down the offers of the boys and girls at the stage door. He didn't want anything warm. He didn't want any sensation. Once at the hotel, he'd sit in the street-level bar, the Times Bar, for an hour, the gleaming dark honey parquet floor rolling out beneath him, the wooden chairs around the bar, the big leather chairs around the small tables places of refuge. The tall windows took in the whole street; some buildings still wore their brick facades and the bare trees stood like black scarecrows. He'd have a few beers, speak to no one, then go upstairs to his very plain room with its brown 1950s hotel room furniture and drop onto the bed. He'd fall asleep sometimes in his clothes, wake to find the bedspread still smoothed and tucked beneath him. The German audience was very correct and very polite and he took his ovations nobly, though he felt absolutely dead inside. He barely recognized the person who fulfilled the contract in Berlin.

And then in this bleakness, Sandra called him, her voice a little crazy, he could hear that right away. She must have phoned Randall, tracked him down. He sat up in bed. Sandra was in Vicksburg, she'd taken her father to Vicksburg, but that wasn't why she was calling. She was pregnant, she said. He felt himself starting to shake, dead man coming alive.

"Adam. Adam?"

"I'm here." He stood up, the bedclothes dropping from him.

"I bought a test at the drugstore and I just took it."

"Where are you?"

"In the bathroom."

"You dragged your grandmother's rotary phone into the bathroom? I thought you said the thing's an anchor."

She started to laugh and he could hear it when she segued into tears, which he interrupted.

"Sandra, I'm flying back to New York tomorrow. I'll just go on to Vicksburg from there. I'm finished in Europe. Tonight's my last night."

"You're coming here?"

"Yes. Yes. I'm coming there. Don't worry. Everything will be all right."

"You've never been here."

"I know," he said. He'd never been to Vicksburg. She'd always gone there without him. They had separate lives, spent holidays apart, with their own families. Not anymore. "Give me the address," he said.

When they hung up the phone, he started pacing, opened the curtains, and stood, naked, at the fourth-floor window, looking out at the street. He put his fist against the casement. He knew just when they'd made the baby, that last night at her house when he'd refused to be sent packing. She would be almost three months along, and the thought of it, that she'd been carrying his child all this time he'd walked out on her, made him feel like punching through the glass. But he was also happy, there was no denying it, and triumphant, there was that, too. He had claimed her in a way that no father, no sorcerer could. He turned from the window. She could dance in a hundred Balanchine ballets now for all he cared, sit at a thousand sickbeds.

That night, he tore down the house.

## ACT III

## The Wedding

*In which the prince and Aurora marry,*
*and the court celebrates the occasion*

ONE

hen the Russian Orthodox marry, the priest holds crowns over the couple's heads," her grandmother said.

"Would have been forty-eight for me this past spring," her great-aunt Patsy said.

"With H.T. it would've been—"

"Forty-seven, baby."

Her grandmother exhaled smoke. The bedroom was full of it: both her grandmother and Aunt Patsy were addicted to tobacco. Sandra's job was to man the rococo silver cigarette lighter. When they needed it, she'd get off the bed and crouch by one of their chairs, thumb the lighter's silver handle until the reluctant flame flared up. The silk upholstery of the chairs used to be pink, was now grayish, boudoir chairs with four upholsterer's buttons punched down into the cushions in a decorative way. The tray table, where they'd been playing cards until an hour ago, was now the ashtray. The two of them tamped their butts directly onto it because the big silver urn, the kind you'd find in a hotel lobby, was too full of butts already. It was Sunday, early December, almost eight o'clock, and her grandmother and Aunt Patsy had now begun enumerating the properties left to them through widowhood: china, silver, crystal glasses, pieces of cherry and mahogany furniture, pianos, oriental carpets, Turkish carpets, ivory bric-a-brac, apartment buildings, the taxi company, land.

Sandra lit a cigarette, holding the big lighter to her own mouth with two hands. She was anxious about being here, anxious about her father, anxious about being away from the company, about getting out of shape, about missing a week of *Nutcracker,* about Adam, about not getting her period, something she never thought about at all, but now she thought about it every other minute. That and her breasts, which had turned into breasts that seemed to grow larger every day. She was sure she would no longer fit into the bodice of the Sugar Plum Fairy costume she'd been measured for almost eight weeks ago. It had barely fit her before she left, and she had to somehow wear it again a few days from now when she flew back to New York.

It was last week, while she sat in the kitchen, brooding, that her father had come in and said to her, "Sandra. I think I need to go home." And when she looked at him funny, he'd added, "To Vicksburg." He had stopped teaching his classes a while ago, he told her, had resigned his position, and she hadn't known any of this because she was back at the theater thirteen hours a day. She couldn't blame not knowing on Adam, on being distracted by Adam, because Adam wasn't even there. So she had agreed: she would take her father home. But she'd gone first to Mr. B, to ask his permission, and Mr. B didn't seem at all surprised, just told her to take good care of her father and then come back. But it wasn't quick. They had to take the train because her father'd gone phobic. They booked a sleeper and the trip took two days and a night, and that night strapped into the bunk above him she wondered, *What is he thinking, thinking, thinking,* the steady roll of the cars on the track putting her half to sleep until she didn't care anymore, just looked out the dark window at the land going by. When they got off the train, one of the big yellow Checker cabs from her grandfather's taxi company was parked at the station to meet them.

The details had already been worked out, though not entirely to her grandmother's satisfaction. She had wanted Sandra to stay in Vicksburg, too, but her father was adamant that she return, and finally her grandmother had agreed that only her father would stay, would work on his book in the basement, in her grandfather's old office; her grandmother would pay the mortgage in New York, her father would remain the perpetually adopted son, *my father was a textbook salesman, my mother was an invalid.* Grandmother had had the maids clean up the basement, set out for her father an ancient Corona typewriter and a ream of paper, and when Sandra had gone down there with him to inspect it all, he had swept his hand over the old metal desk and said, "My new study." In his voice, no irony. He had already begun to write and it was exactly what she saw back in New York. He was not going to write about the siege of Vicksburg.

The noise downstairs rose up through the ceiling, and they could all three hear the baby-wail of one of the children. The whole family had nothing to do on a Sunday but visit. And every afternoon *somebody* came by—usually Sandra's aunt, Adele, her grandmother's good daughter, the one who stayed at home and married a nice boy and had her own daughters, both older than Sandra, both with children of their own. Adele or her girls came by during the week; on Sundays after church, everyone came, even the men. And when they all weren't there, the family pictures all over the house reminded Grandmother of them. Snapshots of the mother Sandra did not remember and whose face she had memorized were everywhere, clipped into gilded frames or set in mod acrylic cubes that showed faces from all sides. A ridiculously large painted photograph of Sandra hung above Grandmother's headboard. Someone had dressed Sandra in an antique baby smock; she looked both minute and Victorian, and she hung in the place of honor because she was the favorite grandchild: she was all the family had left of her mother—except for her father.

A car pulled up at the front of the house, and when Sandra got up to see who it was, she knew what her grandmother would say, "Your mother used to hang out this window, call to her boyfriends," because that's what she always said. But it wasn't anybody's boyfriend out there today, it was her Uncle Isaac, dressed in his black Sunday suit, pockets bulging with the communion bread he brought home for the housebound. And that wasn't all he brought home for the family. Out front were parked a Buick, a brown Seville, an Eldorado, all American cars from Uncle Isaac's lot. The brown Seville was her Uncle Isaac's, the others gifts to the other uncles and children. Her Uncle Isaac had brought by a car for her father the other day, a classic fifties car, finned and white, with a red interior, the knobs of the radio big, round, metallic, and glistening. Because her dad had left the Mercedes in New York. For her. Even though she didn't know how to drive.

Where was her father now? In the basement? Out walking? She had to get out of this room, couldn't breathe, but it was rude to get up and leave her grandmother and Patsy without a reason. She needed an excuse, so she made her excuse the need to empty the big ashstand. She dragged it into the hall, the thing as heavy as she was, the bowl of it filled with the dead weight of sand. She paused in the upstairs hall. She was staying in her old bedroom, all the white furniture brought up from the basement and returned to their former places when Sandra and her father had moved to New York. Her father had the big back bedroom, his old room, the room he'd once shared with her mother, who had bought a suite of mod furniture for it, the style ludicrous and incongruent with the rest of the house—gold papered headboard, black-and-white zebra spread, white cubes of Formica bedside tables and bureaus. No one had moved that stuff to the basement. Sandra dragged the urn past the bedrooms and into the tiled bath, locked the door. She picked the butts out of the urn and threw them in the toilet, where they unraveled, softly. And then, because this was what she had really come in here to do, she lifted her shirt to examine her breasts in the bathroom mirror. She wanted to show them to someone, but the only person she could show them to was Adam and he wasn't here.

She didn't want to think about Adam, had spent the past months trying not to think about him, trying not to think about the night he gave her up, had had to carry her out the door and put her in a cab. She'd gotten sick almost immediately, started throwing up, losing energy, and though she'd call him at home and at the studio, call him from the pay phones at the theater be-tween rehearsals, leave messages for him with the receptionists, he wouldn't take her calls. And then, on the rare occasion he did, usually late at night, it was almost worse—his voice husky, low, hoarse, pained, resistant, the two of them talking until the conversation ran down, until she fell asleep, exhausted, the phone in her hand, having made him say finally, *I love you, I still love you,* which he said over and over again, what good was it, while she cried until she just went out like a light, flat on the floor beside her bed. Her sorrow blew everywhere and she could never leave it behind. Even when she rehearsed the regal, grand pas de deux of the Sugar Plum Fairy and her cavalier, all she could hear in the music were tears. She didn't know why— the dance took place in the Land of the Sweets, was supposed to be the sweetest of all the confections, and yet in the undersweep, the cymbals that marked the grandest lifts, there was the sound that spelled out *This you cannot have.* Whom did Tchaikovsky love but could not have?

Then she saw Adam out on Lincoln Plaza by the fountain, waiting to tell her he was going to Europe, would be gone for six weeks, and she just wanted to hit him. He put up an arm to block her first blow, and his face was so sad it startled her, it was as sad as hers, and it grew even sadder when she started wailing, *Why did you do this to me, why did you ever do this to me?* When he turned his back and walked down the steps of the plaza to the street, she went into the theater and thought, *I'm going to kill myself,* and ever since then she thought of that every day. If it got too hard, she'd tell herself, she'd just swallow a bottle of her father's pills. She took Valium, a few from every vial he had left, that and a few other tranquilizers, kept them in a plastic aspirin bottle in the bottom of her duffel bag. They were there with her, wherever she went, they were under the bed down the hall right now, and she felt better knowing that any time she wanted to she could take them and end it.

Sandra lowered her shirt, opened the bathroom door. The thing she'd bought at the drugstore last night, had made her father wait in the new white car while she bought, was inside its bag beneath her bed, shoved inside her duffel next to the pills. In the morning, while everyone slept, she would pee on the stick. She wasn't going to think about it now. She couldn't remember exactly the last time she had her period, she hardly ever got it, maybe sometime before Saratoga, before "Diamonds." That was May or early June. Six months ago. She couldn't calculate. As she stood there in the hall trying to figure out weeks on her fingers, she saw her dad come up from the basement, climb the stairs, walk past her without seeing her, and enter his black-and-white bedroom. She was free to stand there and watch him as he studied a picture of her mother on the bureau, white as ice.

IN THE MORNING, when the house was quiet, her grandmother and her father asleep, Sandra locked herself in the upstairs bathroom, crouched on the tile, and took the box out of the brown sack. She held the thing in her hands and stared at the tub, its clawed feet, the green porcelain light plate, the dark grout around the octagonal tiles that made a dizzying pattern of the floor. On a rack in the shower hung some of her underwear, which Grandmother's maids washed by hand in the sink for her and then hung, as if she were a princess.

She fingered the box, drew it toward her. If she was pregnant, she was three months along, maybe more, which meant by April she'd be huge, ridiculous, not Aurora, not anything. She turned on her back and felt under her shirt at her breasts. This wasn't her body. Her stomach was no longer flat, her clothes just a little tight, her jeans hard to button. Maybe she was just maturing into more of a woman's shape, the way Adam's body had changed over the past few years into a man's. Maybe it was just her turn. And if it wasn't, if she were pregnant, what would Adam do? She didn't even know where he was, hadn't talked to him since he left the country, wasn't sure if he still loved her, if he'd grown tired of it, exhausted by it, couldn't imagine him not loving her, he had loved her for so long, since that day in class when she read that essay about her father. But she had been a little girl then, fifteen, living with her father, and now she was twenty, and she had treated Adam badly—that's what he discovered she'd do with his love once he gave it to her. And what would he do when he discovered she was pregnant? He might be angry with her, frightened, trapped just as he'd gotten away. Maybe not. Maybe he would love her more.

But he had never said he wanted a baby. He was a dancer and dancers didn't have families, and if they did, it didn't work, somebody had to stop dancing. In Adam's family, that had been Randall. In her family? It would be she. She would be the one unable to dance, not for a while, not the same way. Mr. B wouldn't want her anymore, he'd be furious with her, she'd have to leave the company, stay home with the baby while Adam went off on tour for months at a time. She couldn't take care of the baby by herself in New York; she'd have to come live in Vicksburg with her father and grandmother. It would be 1961 all over again, and she'd be living the life her parents had failed at. If she were pregnant, she would take the Valium. She'd never call Adam. He'd never know. Mr. B would never know. She would always be his perfect Aurora, the one who would have been perfect, the one he could imagine, always, in his mind's eye, moving through the steps he'd created and the ones he had yet to create, the ones that still slept within him. She got up and went to her room, box with the pregnancy test still in her hand, knelt by the bed and pulled her duffel out from underneath it, groped in the dark until she had the bottle of aspirin. She held the box and the bottle. She would do one and then the other.

$B$UT THAT WASN'T what happened. She did the one and then she called Randall, who had Adam's itinerary and gave her Adam's number in Berlin. She could tell by Randall's voice, cautious, slow, that he was worried about her calling Adam. She had grown hysterical in the bathroom by herself, and by the time she got the international operator, she could barely speak all the numbers into the handset. Adam's voice went soft the minute he recognized hers. He'd said, "Yes?" when he'd first picked up, sounded harsh and foreign, and she felt, in that moment, how far he was from her, but then he said her name. *Sandra*. He kept saying her name, it took him a while to understand what she was telling him, because he couldn't make sense of it, because she couldn't say it right, and when they hung up she took all the stuff—the Valium, the box, the stick she'd peed on, the wrapper it came in, the instructions, took it and shoved it all into the duffel, shoved the duffel under her bed, lay down on the narrow mattress, the icy blue tulle of the bedspread stiff as grass around her.

$S$HE WAS UPSTAIRS in her grandmother's room playing cards on the chrysanthemum tray table, the afternoon already split from its light, the two of them playing in the electric blue of the muted TV, her father downstairs in the basement, in his makeshift office, the retinue of female relatives in the kitchen putting together a dinner plate to bring up to Grandmother, when Sandra saw the Checker cab, one of her grandfather's own fleet, pull up to the house and Adam climb from it. She stood up so quickly she pitched over the tray table, and the cards shot into her grandmother's lap. But she didn't lean out the window and call to him, she ran out of the room and down the stairs and out the front door onto the drive. Before she could even reach him, he was holding out an arm, saying, "Wait, wait," his eyes beyond her. When she turned she saw why: her relatives had crowded around the front door, the one she'd flung open in her now ridiculous rush to greet him, and he did not want to misstep, to offend them.

He then spent the entire evening charming her grandmother, her great-aunt Patsy, her grandmother's other sister, Bessie, Aunt Adele, Adele's daughters, even, when he came by to collect Adele and Bessie, her Uncle Isaac. Her father had sat in the living room with them, too, smoking quietly, looking at Sandra now and then, watching the show. Did he know why Adam had come? Did he guess that she had gotten into the same trouble as her mother? He knew. And he did not like Adam here, she could tell, did not like that he was now back in Sandra's life. She hadn't known her father felt this way about him. He had never said anything about Adam and she had never asked. He had allowed Adam into their life, and that was enough.

Adam did not look tired, though he told them all how he had slept erratically on the plane, had spread out on some seats in the terminal at JFK while waiting for the flight to Mississippi. He described London and Paris and Milan and Berlin to them, even pulled out from his Louis Vuitton garment bags the costumes he had had tailored, allowed her various female relatives to put their hands all over the thousands of dollars of velvet and brocade and sequins, stopped short only of putting the costumes on and modeling them. He looked at her from time to time, and she thought, *What are you doing?* It wasn't like Adam to be this warm, this gregarious. Usually he held himself aloof, and because his beauty and his talent were so intimidating, others kept their distance, too. This deliberate effort to engage, to seduce, was usually something Adam reserved for her or for the stage, for the audience sitting in the dark, but today her grandmother's living room was the stage, her female relatives the audience, and Adam was wooing them.

He was wooing *them* because he wanted *her*.

He had come here to claim her, to take his place beside her in the family. He had not come here just to comfort her or to talk. She held her breath. Wasn't this why she had called him? He was going to ask permission for her, but he was not asking it of her father. Adam had never tried to charm her father, had even seemed, actually, to contrive to avoid him. Maybe it was that Adam instinctively understood the locus of power lay here, with her grandmother. What would her grandmother allow? Adam was leaning forward to talk to her grandmother now, and Sandra sat on the sofa beside her great-aunt Patsy and watched the performance, which also included extremely circumspect behavior toward her. He barely looked her way. Yet she did not feel invisible, just the opposite—too visible, too desirable, and so he had to pretend indifference the only way he could, by pretending she wasn't there. She watched his hands, his mouth, and when he turned in her direction once, he stopped talking, faltered, forgot what he was saying. The two of them stared at each other and she felt him touch her, run one finger down her throat to her sternum, though he did not, and then her grandmother asked him a question and he turned away.

And, finally, when all the company had said their hundred good-byes over and over in that way her family had of never being able to take their leave, and Sandra thought at last they'd be alone—no. Her grandmother made Adam lock up, man of the house, gave him the responsibility of shooting home all the tiny dead bolts and chains of all the doors, front, side, back. Sandra waited upstairs for him in her grandmother's room, and she could hear him below struggling with some of the locks. A little something was wrong with everything in the house—doors stuck in their jambs, the lace curtains over the sink were yellowing, the linoleum rippled like the sea from stove to dining alcove, drawers had to be jiggled along their tracks. The garden was an overgrown nightmare of sticker bushes and vines.

Upstairs, her grandmother used the delay to bring out some filmy piece of cloth from her bottom dresser drawer; the cloth turned itself into a negligee, circa 1962, empire waist, ribbons at the seam, sheer off-the-shoulder cap sleeves bunched into buttercups with elasticized bands. And though Sandra protested, her grandmother forced her to put the thing on. Her grandmother's cigarette ashes batted around them as they twisted, getting one of her arms and then the other into the ridiculous nylon cape that draped the gown. Grandmother tied the ribbons, yanked at the sleeves, pulling them down off Sandra's shoulders, completely intent; when she was satisfied, her grandmother made her look in the dresser mirror.

"Now, you know what this is for?" she said. "You won't wear it until then?"

The gown was a translucent green, the flesh of her body interrupted by the bang of a puckered, frilled bra.

"Where did you get this?" Sandra asked her.

"I've been saving it. We'll show it to Adam when he gets up here."

"I don't think that's a good idea," Sandra said. She could see straight through the thing.

"Why not?"

"Adam's tired."

"So? This will wake him up."

Sandra sat down on Grandmother's bed. What was she doing now with her iron will? The rhinestones glued to the corners of her glasses glittered at Sandra, sloppy triangles, as she assessed her barely covered granddaughter. And approved. Now there was nothing to do but wait, so they waited. This was going to be terrible, embarrassing, ridiculous, and there was no way out. When they heard Adam come up the stairs, her grandmother called out to him, and he turned their way toward the bedroom, uncertain, he had never been up here before, didn't know the way, but her grandmother was going to show him the way. He saw Sandra before her grandmother announced, sotto voce, "Adam, look at Sandra," and to her, "Show yourself, baby."

There was nothing for it then, so Sandra got up and paraded, material raucous as she moved. The gown furled lengthwise around the columns of her legs; the cape blew backward from her shoulders. Her hair looped around, Kewpie doll–style. The slick nylon was not a shield, not a screen, but an X-ray to the points of female anatomy—breasts, pubis—the gown riotous, as tacky as sequins and feathers, and gaudily sexy. She could barely look at Adam, but he was looking at her, and, unbelievably enough, he was not laughing. His eyes were going to the places her grandmother wanted them to go, had known they would go. He had not fooled anyone downstairs.

"It's for her wedding night," her grandmother said finally. She put a new cigarette in her mouth.

"Grandmother!" Sandra said, but her grandmother plowed right through Sandra's protest as if it weren't happening.

"Why don't you two go on over to the courthouse tomorrow?"

And Sandra, nonplussed, stopped parading, put her arms across her chest and said, "No."

"Why not?"

Sandra stared at her with narrowed eyes and her grandmother stared right back.

"Why not?" her grandmother said again.

"Because we're going back to New York in a few days," Sandra said. "We don't have any time."

"The ceremony's ten minutes." Her grandmother turned to look at Adam, questioningly, cigarette held up by two fingers. "You can have your church wedding later, right, Adam?"

"Yes," Adam said. "We could do that."

Amazed, Sandra turned to look at him.

And behind her, Sandra heard her grandmother click her false teeth together, satisfied.


$\mathcal{A}$LONE AT LAST, in the narrow guest room, where Adam's bags had been deposited—and where he was to remain, Sandra now understood, until they had made that journey to the courthouse—Adam closed the door partway and turned to her. "I can see right through that top. I was standing there looking at your tits with your grandmother watching me. Does she dress you up like this for all your boyfriends?"

"I don't know," Sandra said. "You're the only boyfriend I've ever had."

Adam touched his tongue to his upper lip. "Boyfriend. I don't want to be your boyfriend anymore, Sandra. I don't think I ever wanted to be your boyfriend. I think I've wanted to marry you since I was fifteen. So you have to tell me now—what do you want?" He came toward her, gathered the neckline of the gown together with his fingers, pulled gently at the negligee as if to test it, then with one motion peeled it down to her waist.

"Jesus Christ," he said when he saw her breasts, and he knelt before her, put the backs of his hands and then his palms to them and she leaned into his hands, saying his name, *Adam, Adam, Adam,* and he said, *I'm here.* He bent his head and pressed his cheek to her stomach and put his arms around her, rubbed his skin, his whiskers against her belly. He was thinking about the baby, not about her. She wanted him to think about her. She put her fingers into his hair, into his mouth for him to suck at, which he did, softly, and then she got down onto her knees beside him, frantic to unbutton his jeans, her mouth at the steel teeth of the zipper. Above her, Adam said, "Sandra, what's gotten into you?" She could hear the amazement in his voice, and at that, she had to sit back and laugh. "I don't know," she said. "I don't know." He looked at her speculatively, and suddenly she was embarrassed. She had ripped the metal button right off the waistband of his jeans. He was shaking his head. "Look, let's wait a minute here. I want to talk to you." He stood up and led her to her bed, made her sit at the edge of it, then walked back to the other side of the room, as if he needed to keep that much space between them. He shut the door all the way, and she pulled the bodice of the gown back up over her breasts, lifted her chin. He watched the gesture.

"No. It's not that," Adam said. "I want it. I've had a fucking hard-on since I saw you in the driveway. But I've got to talk to you about something. I'm going to leave ABT. I'm not going on any more tours."

She gripped at her gown. "Why—"

"I don't know. Everything that's happened these past couple

of years—it's just not worth it, what I get from it. It just doesn't seem like anything to me, just ego." He paused. "I can't do it anymore. It's making me—sick."

She looked at Adam, at his face, which she couldn't read. When he spoke next, she realized he couldn't read hers either.

"Is that okay with you?" he asked. And she saw in him something she didn't often see—uncertainty.

She knew she should protest. It wasn't a good idea. He was a brilliant dancer about to walk away from a brilliant career. But she didn't care. She wanted him to. She wanted him with her. What she finally said had nothing to do with what he'd asked. "I'm just so tired," she whispered. "All the time."

"You're pregnant," Adam said. "You're going to be tired."

"What am I going to tell Mr. B?"

"Look, Sandra, this is life. And Mr. B's had a long life. He's seen a lot. He'll work around this."

"What about *Sleeping Beauty*?"

"You'll be dancing again by the summer. I'll stay home with the baby."

He was serious. There was something different about him, as if something harsh had been rubbed across his face once or twice, and she could see now that he was tired, that perhaps Europe had been difficult, that paying court to her family had been an effort, that he was not finished here yet, that he still had her to tackle. He was watching her carefully from across the room.

"Are you going to marry me?" he said. "Tomorrow? At that courthouse?"

She nodded.

"Swear on it," he said. "Swear on it or there will be no screwing in this bedroom tonight."

She nodded again, and he said, "Swear."

"I swear."

"You're sure?"

"Yes."

"It's not just because you want this, is it?" he said, gesturing at his torn pants.

She almost laughed, shook her head instead.

He came toward her then.

"Adam," she said, before he got all the way there. "You can't leave me again. You can't leave me."

"I won't. I won't leave you." He was at her side, looking right into her face.

"Swear on it."

"I'll never leave you. I won't ever leave you." He looked at her, *Is that enough?* and when she nodded yes, he said, "Okay, then." He put his hands over her hands, pulled them away from her chest so the nightgown fell away.

## TWO

She came to him with a gold band on her finger, the ring a sliver so thin as to be almost invisible, but a ring is a ring; no matter the size, it bore the weight of the same oversized promise. He should know—he had given enough rings in his lifetime. She had arrived, unannounced, a knock on his office door. He had been sitting there thinking, in fact, about the Rose Adagio, which Aurora performs in Act I with her four suitors, the boys flamboyant in their buckled boots and capes and feathered hats. The adagio is all about balance, the balance and precision available only to those who are not in love. Aurora is able to maintain her balance on a single pointe en attitude precisely because she does not love any of the four suitors who offer her, hopefully, each in turn, their hands. But she will be toppled in the wedding pas de deux, absolutely upended, both feet pointing up to the catwalk, head almost brushing the stage, his own exaggerated version of the fish dives Petipa made famous in Act III. Yes. Petipa had recognized the manner in which love blew the beloved to a different dimension, one unfamiliar, where footing was uncertain, love's intent splendorous, its reality somewhat less so, perilous even. And so, in this dimension, he found the girl when he opened his door.

He recognized it at once; she was pale, uncertain, her features strained, dressed in a cashmere coat and a fur hat he had never seen before, and which, he understood, before their conversation ended, her husband had bought for her. She removed the coat, but not the hat, and it perched there like a black cat, voodooed with diamond stickpins above her light hair, so light it had come to look like snow flavored by the thinnest honey. She had knelt by him to deliver her news: she had married in Mississippi, she was pregnant. She had, perhaps, one more month to dance before she became an absurdity. And then she wept. He wanted to know the husband's name, and when he heard it, he rose from the chair, unsteady, sparks shooting at the periphery of his vision, zigzags like lightning bolts, neon blue, red, yellow. He could not find his balance, reaching, as he staggered, for furniture that was not there, the chairs, the tables, the piano gliding away from him, until he found himself, finally, facedown on the carpet, and he saw, instead of the wool fibers, water, endless water, the Atlantic he'd crossed in 1933. He saw bits of her: her feet in black boots cut so narrow and pointed they looked like the boots of the wife of a medieval *burghermeister,* she was now a wife, her hands, the hand with the golden ring, the ends of her hair, and finally her face, porcelain, with the high forehead and the elaborate nose, a face made to conquer the stage, the hat a lush black mink, a second set of hair, the hair of Snow White, ebony, not that of Aurora, who was fair. The face beneath the hair of ebony and the hair of corn silk was terrified, skimming along the ocean beside him, her breath blowing white and black against the white and black. And when they hit the shore, the water turned a thin blue, pale as a layer of tulle over sand, and he found the strength then to sit up.

She had chosen the wrong boy, the wrong suitor, the wrong father for the child, but it was now too late to fix. She had done it in secret, away from him, without his advice, and who could know better than he? Far from New York, in a small city at the bottom of the country, a civil ceremony in a courthouse, as he himself had done on too many occasions, no one to watch out for him, no one to control him, to guide him, to say, *Not this girl*. No. Love had taken him from himself and walked him into this romance and that, poked his nose into one hurricane after another, rain and wind and black skies, tree limbs and roofs torn from their trunks and flung into the air where they mixed with the debris, sand, pebbles, leaves, dirt. He was a pebble himself, a man without family. He drew the details out of her—the stone columns, the portico of the courthouse, the suit she wore, the family present, the pen she held to sign her name to the document, *Sandra Ellis LaSalle*. And when she had told him all that he could bear to hear, he allowed her to help him back to his wooden chair. Her blue eyes, lined he saw in black paint—she had prepared herself for this visit—met his. He looked away. And then he said to her something he would later regret, the kind of remark he had made in anger or in the face of offense again and again throughout his life, and he saw her receive it as a blow. *Go. You're a thief.*

He sat up in his office for hours after she had gone, the pages of orchestration for *Sleeping Beauty* a rebuke on the music stand beside him. She had betrayed him. A line of fairies in his life, so he thought, yet each revealed herself to be a Carabosse. Each time, each time a girl stepped up to him, he expected to have bestowed upon him a gift, a blessing, and received instead a curse. Without this girl, her trunk, her limbs, her feet, her hands, her neck, her shoulders, her face, there could be no *Sleeping Beauty,* no pleasure in doing it. And after she had the baby, she would want to stay home, and he, her husband, would be the one to go off and dance, roam the world in his tights, while her talent languished in the nursery. There would be no *Sleeping Beauty*. He would fold up the sketches and the maquette and the pieces of costume already executed and bury them in the storage tomb deep beneath the stage.

## THREE

*A*dam stooped to look at himself in her dressing table mirror, checking that the studs were secured in all the right buttonholes running the face of his tuxedo shirt. Sandra was in the bath, she'd been in there too long, he was going to have to pound on the door in a few minutes and get her out. He'd got all the studs right, straightened up, ran his hands through his hair, his hands, his left hand with the ring on it; even when he looked at it, he couldn't believe it: he was wearing a wedding band. The reversal of fortune had been so sudden, so sweet, he couldn't draw a connecting line between the man he was in Europe and the man he was here, now, in New York City, putting on a tuxedo for the wedding party his parents were hosting for them tonight at the loft. He was sweating inside his shirt and he hadn't yet put on the cummerbund or the jacket, which were laid out on the bed, Sandra's bed, beside the dress he'd bought her, one of the many things he'd bought her. He'd blown a wad of cash on her in Vicksburg, his fee for the whole two weeks in Berlin, wanting to show her family that he could afford her. Not that he needed to. Her grandmother had sent them back to New York with a check the size of the continental United States. Her grandmother was not relinquishing control over her yet.

But she was his. He had married her and they had spent their wedding night together in her old bedroom in Vicksburg in the same narrow bed. In her new body, this body with the breasts and the sloping belly, she was not a girl or his girlfriend or his ex-girlfriend or his best friend, but his wife, an unbelievable fact, and they whispered to each other *husband, wife,* those words a powerful erotic incantation. He had been prepared to be gentle with her, a little afraid of this body that carried within it another body, but she didn't want him gentle. Her sudden carnality had, in fact, unnerved him some—was this, his body, the only thing she loved about him, after all? But she was his wife and she wanted his dick, so with her grandmother in the room on one side of them and her father in the other, Adam had fucked her again and again, until he was drenched with sweat and she was raw and he felt somehow purified, as if he'd both reclaimed her and poured everything that was soiled and shameful about him into her where it was released. Why did she have this effect on him? Always, she had it. He decided then he would not tell her about what had happened in Europe. He had wanted to tell her, that was the thing, wanted to confess it, to tell her not only about Europe, but about everything he'd done, everybody he'd been with, that was what you were supposed to do when you married, tell each other everything about yourselves, no secrets, but how could he tell her about the beds he'd been in, the drugs he'd used, the way he'd almost gone delinquent on his contract in Paris? She wouldn't want to hear that, to know that. She was twenty and pregnant and she just wanted to know that he had come for her, that he would make it all right, and that's what he was going to do, he was going to make it all, all right.

The day they got back to New York, he moved his stuff out of the brownstone and brought it here to her dad's, where he stood dressing in Sandra's room tonight, their room now. This room was, he realized, the master bedroom, though he'd never thought of it as such because it was Sandra's. But her father, he now saw, had assigned himself the smaller middle bedroom almost as if he knew his time here was temporary. The place seemed as vacant of him as it had once seemed full. What remained was a stillness like a dream, the apartment seemingly untouched, her dad's bed made up with just a coverlet, the tops of the dressers bare, the closet empty. Adam had always been a little intimidated by her father, by his education—in Adam's family no one but Randall had gone to college—unnerved by his illness, uncomfortable about his own relationship with Sandra. "What does your dad say to you about me?" Adam had asked Sandra once, and Adam was not surprised when Sandra told him, "Nothing." Her father had been here, now he was gone, and his abdication left a hush, and Adam did not know how big or how wide this hush was for Sandra.

Adam went into the enormous kitchen and opened the freezer for the bottle of vodka her father always had stashed there. The Stolichnaya lay on its side and Adam drew it out, poured a shot, and standing there by the counter, downed it. Everybody would be at the loft tonight. He had called Randall from Vicksburg and then his parents, and Randall had sounded so good, so strong after he heard the news, that Adam could take anything, even his mother, whose dismayed congratulations was almost a curse. He wanted to tell her it was going to be all right, he knew what he was doing, but she had seen Sandra with her arm cut up to the elbow, had gone with them to the emergency room and watched Sandra shaking. *I know what I'm doing,* he wanted to say, but he didn't say it, it wouldn't have convinced her. The next day, Frankie called down there to find out when they were coming back to New York; he and Lucia wanted to host a party in their honor. Adam wasn't sure what to make of it. Ever since he'd danced with his father, there had been this cautious rapprochement between them. Was this party his mom's idea? His dad's?

He put down his glass. He didn't know what kind of mood Sandra was cooking up back there in the tub. Today she had gone to see Mr. B to tell him what she'd done, even though Adam didn't want her to. The party was tonight and the old man didn't need to know everything right away, like God. She could talk to him next week, when she rejoined the company, but she couldn't wait. He'd gone with her and stood out on Lincoln Plaza—she wouldn't even let him come into the building—and it seemed to him she was up there forever, the sky getting darker and darker as he paced by the fountain, by the glass doors of the theaters he no longer danced in. And when she finally came down, he didn't like the look on her face. He was just thinking about going back there to the bathroom when he heard her step out into the dining room. The dress he'd bought her was a black lace V-necked shift, narrow, sleeveless, the simplest thing he could find in that Vicksburg ladies shop, and the sight of her in it made his heart do a funny Stoli-soaked beat. She was so goddamn beautiful, but usually she stored that beauty, pulled it out only for the stage. And she didn't look like a girl anymore, she really didn't, and for him, that transformation was the most amazing of all. He put down his shot glass and took a step toward her, and in that moment he could not have stood it if he did not possess her. The old man had lived his life, had had more than his share of wives, more than enough women who had given up their lives to him, to his genius. This one girl he would have to share—or else let her go.

 By midnight, everybody was there who was going to be there. The orchids and lilies heaped on every table had begun to open and emit their heavy scent. The loft did not, for once, look grossly underfurnished or underpopulated, but perfectly suited to the occasion, even beautiful. Sandra kept her hand in his the whole night as they walked between the white-draped tables to accept the congratulations of so many people she did not know—his parents' friends, Randall and Joe, Randall leaning on a goddamn cane, old dancers from Martha Graham's company and Paul Taylor's, former and current dancers from Joe's, set designers and costumers and musicians, even some of his dad's students from Juilliard, a few dancers from ABT his mother must have invited, something Adam didn't want—he wasn't really comfortable with anyone from the company, had even fucked a couple of those girls during one of his desperate tours a year or so ago, and now here they were at his wedding party. Christ. That was his mother, always angling, always campaigning. He hadn't told his parents yet that he was planning to break his contract with ABT. When he called home he hadn't said anything about Sandra being pregnant, either, just that they were married.

It was two weeks until Christmas, and his parents had had the caterer string the place with colored lights. Baskets of oranges and lemons flanked the buffet and the bar. A three-piece band played swing music, and he and Sandra danced, bits and pieces of the steps they'd learned years ago in SAB's ballroom dance class until they found themselves dancing whole sections of waltz and tango and swing without even knowing how. He could feel her spirit lighten as they moved, which was not what happened to him when he danced: his spirit grew coiled and dense and blew out of him with the force of steam from an engine. But she grew purer and lighter when she moved, grains of sugar spun into fibers. Tonight he was focused on nothing but her and the soft lacy fabric of her thin black dress beneath his hands, the long pale hair that she had somehow curled at the bottom, her feet in their slim high heels. Still, he caught the edge of the whispers, *Balanchine,* saw the second, sideways looks she was given, the looks he'd been on the receiving end of for years, ever since he made his debut in *Apollo.* What had been happening for her these past few months while he was gone? Well, whatever it was, fuck it. She wasn't Balanchine's princess tonight, she was his, and when the music changed he took her into a series of quick turns and back bends, pitching her low over one arm, at one point drawing her across the floor at this angle, the ball of her foot in its high-heeled shoe making a slow hiss. He might be a soon-to-be ex–American Ballet Theatre dancer, but he still knew how to dance.

When the band took its next break he went to the elaborate bar to get two glasses of something, the bottles with their steel beaks lined up row after row, the glasses balanced like pyramids—shot glasses, wineglasses, martini glasses, brandy glasses, cocktail glasses—and by them a great mound of cashews and candied fruits, and around him the flowers, the lights, the tables, the band, the waiters with their great silver platters. There was no way, Adam realized suddenly, standing there with his drinks, that his parents were behind the planning and execution of this. It had to have been Randall. Of course his parents hadn't done this. He put the drinks down.

Adam looked around for Randall, spotted him, finally, seated with Joe on a red velvet banquette the caterers must have trucked in, cane propped before him. Randall's tux, Adam saw, was too big for him, and his face was fatigued. Randall was not, tonight, wearing his cap, and the hair Adam had imagined it covered was gone, buzzed away, a short shelf of gray bristles all that remained. Why? Why had Randall done that? He looked, at a distance, just like the man Joe had left him for ten years ago: gaunt, bald, exhausted, but still interesting, always interesting. And while Adam watched him, Randall dropped the glass he was holding. He couldn't even hold on to a goddamn glass, and when Joe bent to pick it up, Adam saw his face crack, and for a minute Adam thought Joe was going to split in two, fall apart right there in front of him, and then it was gone, Joe's face reconstituted, features smooth, composed. Adam turned to find himself face-to-face with his dad, who had seen everything and who gave Adam a slow, sad smile. "It took us two hours to get him into that tux," Frankie said. Adam clutched at his father's forearm and he could not let go. Frankie put a hand over the one Adam had stuck to him. "We're going to have a big Christmas this year," Frankie said, nodding at Randall, and Adam understood. Big Christmas. Last Christmas.

"I'll be around," he told his dad. "I'll be here. I'm leaving ABT."

"Leaving?" Frankie said. "What are you going to do? More Europe?"

"No. I'm just going to be around." He looked at his father's face, checking to see if it were safe to say this. He took a breath. "Sandra's going to have a baby. In May."

"You're kidding," Frankie said, and he turned to fully face Adam, who wasn't prepared for it when his father suddenly grabbed him, put two hands to his neck and pulled him in for a kiss. "Adam, that's wonderful," and Adam nodded, relieved. His father wasn't angry. He was happy. Frankie let go of him then to turn and graze the party, and Adam knew he was looking for Sandra. They both saw her at the same time. "Give Randall something to live for," his father said, without looking away from her. "And you."

Adam turned back to his dad. What did Frankie know about him? Adam liked to think of himself as a cloud, impossible to grasp, a shape-shifter, but apparently he was neither of those things. Frankie was still studying Sandra, and Adam, watching him, saw his expression change, his eyes narrow. Adam looked quickly across the dance floor to where his mom stood talking earnestly to Sandra. The two of them turned and retreated to the galley kitchen, which rose like a stainless steel castle in the center of the loft. What were they talking about? What did his father think they were talking about? Adam strained after them, but the steel shell eclipsed them, and one of the girls on the dance floor, mistaking his gaze, winked at him. Adam looked away, but it was too late, she was coming toward him, asking if the groom wanted to dance. Adam shook his head, could feel beside him his dad's amusement. Adam couldn't quite remember if this was one of the girls he'd been with last year or not, but her presence was acutely embarrassing to him, even after she had walked away, shrugging. He didn't want his dad thinking that he was in any way like him. But when he finally braved a glance around, Adam saw his dad wasn't looking at him anymore.

He was looking at Randall, who was struggling to stand up from the banquette to greet Sam, a composer who'd worked with Joe and Randall for years. Randall moved slowly—why was he trying to move at all? When had this happened? At the time Adam took off for Europe, Randall had just begun spending more time in bed than out of it. But he could still walk when Adam left for London, had not yet begun this tumble down the stairs, missing steps along the way, heading straight for the landing, boom, debilitation. When Adam called him from Vicksburg, he had talked about what they'd do together when Adam got home as if he were still capable of doing it. It didn't seem possible that that voice had emanated from this body, and Adam looked at his father to say, *How can this be?*

Adam moved toward Randall, Joe, and Sam, and though he stood there with them, one hand on Randall's back, nodding as the three of them talked, he heard nothing in his distress. He should have gone to see Randall right away, this week, seen him at home first, not here. And then he felt Randall reach around him with his free arm and hold him close. Randall didn't turn to him, didn't stop talking to Sam or Joe, but Adam knew he was in and of the moment, in and of any moment, the most important thing in the world to Randall, and with that knowledge came something akin to peace, the first real peace Adam had felt in months. He rested his head on Randall's shoulder—Randall still had his height, the one thing he hadn't yet lost—and though the shoulder was bony, it was still broad. Randall's fingers gripped his upper arm and when the grip grew stronger, Adam was a little slow to understand that Randall was signaling him— he needed help, he needed to sit down, and Adam used the arm he'd stationed at Randall's back as a support, shifted some of Randall's weight onto the side of his own body, his own hip and thigh, the way he would support his ballerinas in the delicate walking movements of *Romeo and Juliet* where the girl moved seemingly weightlessly. This he could do for Randall. And when Sam and Joe had drifted off, Adam was able to ease Randall back down to the banquette, all the skills he'd ever learned in partnering put to the test. Randall's back was wet; Adam could feel dampness through the tux, and when Randall said, "Good surprise?" for a moment Adam thought he was talking about this, his own disintegration, but no, Randall was gesturing at the room, the tables, the candles, the people, and Adam nodded. "Good surprise."

"There's more," Randall said, and Adam smiled, but he could feel one part of his mouth ripping down, wrong direction. Randall took his hand, rubbed his thumb over Adam's wedding band. "Amazing." Adam was just about to answer him when he saw his mother and Sandra emerge from the steel wall of the kitchen, and he didn't like it, the look on Sandra's face. What had his mother been saying to her in there? Sandra's face had never looked strained like that, frozen like that, in Mississippi, but they were one week in New York and already the frozen look was there. Adam rose from the banquette, almost an involuntary motion, and though Randall still had hold of his hand, was gripping it, in fact, to keep him here, he broke free and crossed the floor to meet Sandra, the music the band was playing suddenly not swing or jazz or salsa, but a weakened Tchaikovsky. He had just reached her side when his father began to speak in a voice meant to be heard over the crowd, and though Adam took Sandra's hand and bent his head to ask her, *What's going on?* his father's voice rode all over the question, flat-

tened it. Only when Sandra turned her head Frankie's way did
Adam realize his father was toasting them, offering his best
wishes for the happiness of the new couple, calling on everyone
to raise a glass to their prince and princess. The waiters brought
around trays of champagne and as the guests said, "Here, here,"
the music, the Tchaikovsky, grew louder, amplified electroni-
cally by the track being played on Frankie's big reel-to-reel
down at the far end of the loft.

And from that direction there appeared a fantastic creature—
bulbous-headed, furred, an enormous gray cat walking on two
legs, no, not walking, dancing, dressed in the clothes of the
French court and elaborate red boots; behind him, carried on a
palanquin, lay his consort, White Cat, the girl who had earlier
asked Adam to dance, on her head a wig of white curly fur and
pointed ears, the insides tinted pink. So this was why these
dancers from ABT had been invited—entertainment. The girl
made as if to lick and clean herself as Puss in Boots chased the
fish he carried on a pole before him. Adam held Sandra's hand
as the next characters stepped out of the darkness and into the
circle the guests had now, laughing, backed up to make for
them. Within two seconds this crowd had gotten the joke;
which of them didn't know *Sleeping Beauty,* Act III, the linchpin
of classical ballet? Into the circle next stepped Little Red Riding
Hood, basket over one arm, red hood of her red cape drawn up
over her golden wig, breasts spilling out of her white peasant
blouse; circling about her the fantastically costumed wolf, with a
long nose and a black rubber snout, white ceramic fangs, did a
few do-si-dos before he grabbed up the girl and made off with
her over his shoulder, her legs kicking a protest in their
bloomers. Where had they gotten all these getups? From ABT's
wardrobe? Next out in quick succession were the fleshy pie

faces of Bluebeard and his wife, the former flashing a scimitar, and then Goldilocks and a brown bear, Cinderella and her prince, who stooped to place upon her foot a glass slipper. The guests who had been calling out, *Who is she? Oh, it's Goldilocks, Oh, it's Cinderella,* were now clapping, but the spectacle was not yet done—after Prince Fortuné and Cinderella came out one last couple, Désiré and Aurora, in silver, white, and ermine, and two pages also so dressed trailed the princess to hold her train. As they crossed Adam and Sandra they bowed slightly, then passed them by with a sweep of ermine, and Adam watched Sandra look pensively after them.

Wasn't that unbelievable, just unbelievable?" Adam asked of Sandra in the taxi going uptown. It was the best of the many presents Randall had given him over the years. The suit of armor, the window boxes, the artwork, all of these were static things, but this dance tableau at the party had been alive, magically unfolding, staged and performed just for him, as if he truly were a prince, and Sandra a princess. When the mock prince and princess had bowed to them, Adam understood for a moment what it was to be a king the players entertained. Everyone in his little world was a player strutting upon a stage for the fancy of the king, players even when playing princes. And the biggest figures were still no more than that; even Mr. B grumbled about having to go hat in hand to all the rich bankers and dentists for the money to stage his ballets. In America, their pockets; in Russia, the pockets of the czar. They were all beggars, hoping to please for their suppers. It was pleasant, tonight, to have laid the supper, to be the one who must be pleased.

He reached for Sandra's gloved hand. Gently, he rolled the

glove back from her wrist and stroked with his finger the soft skin above her pulse. Up front, on the other side of the partition, the driver listened to reggae music. Adam said Sandra's name, asked her again hadn't the evening been great. The roots of her hair were so pale she had to have been bleaching again, her nervous habit. She did this every time her father got sick, went white blond, as if she could vanish. What did she want to vanish from now? She turned her face to his, and now he could see it, now he couldn't, as the streetlights flicked by, flicked by, flicked by, now light, now dark, now light, now dark.

## FOUR

*J*ust before she left for Vicksburg, Sandra had been moved from the big dressing room she shared with seven other girls to this smaller one shared with just one other, a veteran principal dancer of whom she had seen little yet, this being *Nutcracker* season. Her own promotion to principal dancer was not yet official, but the move to this dressing room signaled perhaps it was to come. Her face, made flat by the Pan-Cake, looked appalling in the mirror, like one of the bald-headed revelers in *Prodigal Son,* until she used the dark powder to contour it, the pink powder to bring her cheekbones forward. Before Adam took her to the theater tonight, he had made her a big shake with milk, bananas, strawberries, and yogurt, but she was afraid by the time she got out on stage the energy the shake had given her would be gone. The Sugar Plum Fairy's big solo and pas de deux came close to the end of the ballet, at almost ten, which had become for her like Cinderella's midnight. By midperformance she sometimes felt herself folding up inside like a lawn chair, ready to be put away. She had no reserves; the baby she could not yet feel had taken them, and she was helpless out there in her starched tutu and cumbrous crown, ridiculously dependent on her partner to hold her up, to keep her pasted together until that last big curtain-ringing pose. Adam savored her reviews, but she did not read them. Reviews did not matter to anyone in the company. There was only one review that counted. And Sandra knew that Mr. B knew it was all already too much for her. But she could not bear to leave. And despite what he had said to her, *Go,* he had not barred her from the theater. He still cast her, and so she still danced several nights a week, either Sugar Plum or Dewdrop, *Nutcracker* the only ballet the company performed the five weeks between Thanksgiving and New Year's. And when the run was over and she went on leave, the mouth of the theater would close for her, the way back lost. Mr. B would forget her, as he had forgotten others, those dancers he no longer wanted to cast or even to see, dancers he would look away from in the halls as he had looked away from her in his office.

She pushed herself back from the ledge before the mirror where her makeup and sponges and tissues were strewn, and put on her thin cotton theater bathrobe over her bra and tights, stuck her feet into a pair of old ballet slippers with the heels so mashed the things had become mules. She was not on until the second act, and the curtain had already gone up on the first. She liked to watch it. She was almost too late to see little Marie asleep before the wide pink wall with the big white doors to the living room. When Franz wakes her and they bend to peek through the keyhole, the scrim is lit suddenly from behind to allow a magical glimpse of what the children saw: their parents putting the final touches on the tree. The guests arrive in their cloaks and the little boys play leapfrog, pressing their noses to the scrim, which eventually rolls up to allow them access to the sparkling lit tree and the wrapped presents. Inside the living room, the backdrop suggests tall windows with curtains, open doorways leading to other rooms, pictures and furniture against the walls. The children dance in long lines and walk beneath the arch made by the arms of the adults. The maid shows in more friends, more relatives, the men all in dress coats, the women in lace and satin-trimmed dresses, little bits of lace and ribbon pinned to their heads.

Sandra watched the spectacle from the wings and she knew suddenly what it was: it was Adam's big Christmas, the one he had been talking so much about, the one they were going to celebrate this year at Randall and Joe's with a big tree and sugared fruit topiaries. The wedding party in the loft had been a spectacle, too, just like this, even down to the dancing dolls Drosselmeyer brought out to perform—the stiff-legged soldier, the pretty girl with a hair bow and her cavalier. The only thing the big party at the loft had lacked, as would Randall and Joe's Christmas, was children, but she was the walking correction of this. She held her fingers to the thin lapel of her robe and watched with little Marie as the lightning flashed and the thunder boomed and the owl on top of the clock hooted and the fat-bottomed mice orchestrated by Drosselmeyer spun through the room. The children in the audience oohed and aahed and shrieked, and when the tree began to grow, rising up an impossible height to Tchaikovsky's horns and violins and cymbals, the tinsel of both tree and music shimmering like water, like ice, like crystal, the audience hummed with appreciative sound.

She went back to her dressing room where her dresser stood ready to help her. She wore two costumes in the second act—the first, a long pink romantic tutu; the second, an ivory satin with a short skirt frilled and fluted at the edges for the pas de deux. The costume was excessively pretty, with pink satin piping and small fabric roses running up and down the straps and the V of the bodice, and the dresser had to pull tight on the hooks at the back of it. By the time the woman had encased her in the costume, Sandra was almost weeping with panic. She wasn't going to be able to move. She couldn't go on. She heard the applause and then the roar and chaos that meant intermission had begun. She put a towel over her shoulders and hoisted her big-buy size of Aqua Net into the air and sent a fire-fighting burst of spray over her hair, her neat French twist, even over her crown where the teeth of it scraped her scalp. She put the can down, pulled the towel off and stood, hands on hips, to survey herself in the mirror while the dresser tugged on the fabric and slapped Sandra's hands away.

Sandra stepped back, went out the door and down the halls toward the wings, went out onto the stage to test the feel of it. The thick curtain muffled the sound of the audience; on her side of it, the stagehands raised and lowered the sets—bringing down the backdrop of laced doilies and frosted meringues, rolling out the tiered dais, the candied throne upon which Marie and her Nutcracker prince would sit, four tall candy canes arching about them, to eat sweets and creams and view the fun. The poles looked like candy, as did the backdrop and the participants—the whole of Act II was candied and pastried—the Land of the Sweets, stuffed with peppermint sticks and chocolates and coffees and marzipan, flowers and dewdrops and truffles. She bounced on the balls of her feet, tested out a relevé, an arabesque, a pirou-ette. The downstage wing was empty. Mr. B had gone some-where to check on something. The company dancers had begun to joke that when Mr. B was really gone they would put a life-sized cardboard figure of him in his usual spot to watch over them. No one could really imagine dancing without him.

She had found her composure by the time the curtain went up. The lights were bright in the Land of the Sweets—already she felt herself perspiring. Though she was not dancing yet, she was center stage, the queen of the land, and with her wand she animated all the candy players. She tried to remember what Adam had coached her to do, that she must be suffused with presence every second she was on the stage, even when she stood at the side of it and the others danced. Adam never wanted to be ignored, not for a second, and though that was all that she wanted, she would fail if it happened. A lead dancer must be fascinating. The audience doesn't care if she's tired or ill or out of favor or pregnant. Her variation she danced while surrounded by the little-girl angels from the school, their faces as bright as their gold cloaks and full of awe as they watched her make the sugar crystal movements. She was a sugared plum, a pudding topper, something silly, whimsical, yet made very special here. At her bow she did again what Adam had taught her—to lift her eyes to the balcony, to sweep her gaze from left to right. *Look for me,* he had said. *I could be anywhere.* The audience wanted to be sought and they would applaud to draw her to them. She did not have to dance again until all the others—the Candy Canes, Hot Chocolate, Coffee, Marzipan, Tea—performed their variations.

In the sanctuary of her dressing room, she fanned herself with her hands, tried to lift the crown slightly from her head. Last year, she had been Snow, with a headpiece the size of a chef's hat, rising high in all its gilt and rhinestone splendor. She wouldn't have the strength to hold her head up in that thing now. She sat down on the chair, mashing her tutu, risking her dresser's wrath. She'd stand up before the woman got here with her short tutu for the pas de deux. The worst was yet to come. The adagio was devilishly difficult, made for Maria Tallchief with her amazing technique, and Sandra had never felt so ill-equipped for the battle.

And when it was time for the pas de deux, the music evolved into something rich and grand and strange, something more than beautiful, something too beautiful for her. Violins and harps and piano and horns echoed and played off one another, making a big musical braid, and Sandra and her partner stepped into the weave of it. Their interlocking arms and poses culminated in a series of lifts of all kinds and from all types of preparations. Ib carried her through it, his sweet face worried for her, his arms reluctant to let her go even for the second it took to switch positions. At the end of the adagio, as Ib tossed her high into the final fish dive, one plucked from the famous series of such dives danced in the wedding adagio of *Sleeping Beauty,* she saw that Mr. B stood once again in the wings. He had come to watch her. He was not looking away. But all she could think was, *Thank God it's almost over.*

When Ib led her center stage for her bow before the big coda with all the characters from the second act, she looked again for Mr. B. He was there in the wing, in his blue double-breasted jacket with the gold buttons, head large and domed. His fist gripped the curtain for balance, but still his feet shuffled as the fabric above teetered and swayed. Mr. B was ill, there was something wrong not just with his heart or his eyes, but with his brain. And she knew. He didn't have time to wait for her to have her baby, to recover, to return. By next Christmas he would be too sick to stand, to think, to make real the dream he held now, ready to lose. *Thief*. The world was not going to get its *Sleeping Beauty* because of her.

$\mathcal{S}$HE WOKE BEFORE Adam, as she had every day for the past two weeks since they'd come back to New York. It was not yet light. It was never light: December had such short days. Adam could never sleep well in complete darkness, had for years plugged in a string of old Christmas lights his mother had hung in his room. Maybe it was because Adam slept so far from his parents at the other end of the loft that he needed something to beat back the dark. Here, they slept with the hall light on. Their baby would sleep next door, in her father's room. Adam had already said so. To him the baby was as real as if it had already been born; to her it was not yet that substantive, not yet anything. But Adam had bought a crib, which would be delivered today, had begun to move her father's furniture to the basement storage, had begun to dream a room for his child, had even asked her grandmother back in Vicksburg if she still had the christening gown Sandra wore in the big poster-sized photo above Grandmother's bed. She did and she brought it out, yellowed, set the maids to slowly bleaching it with lemon juice in the upstairs bathroom sink. Sandra and Adam had told no one about the baby, but it was understood by all her family that there would be a baby. They were married. By the time they left for New York, the baby dress was white and ironed and wrapped in tissue paper. Mr. B had expected she would return from Vicksburg a ballerina; instead, she had returned a wife, and pregnant. Wasn't that what fairy tales were all about, the shock and tumble of thwarted expectations? The rose becomes a spindle, a grandmother is a wolf, a pack of boys turns into donkeys.

Sandra turned on her side to gaze at Adam. He slept, always, facing her, his hand on the sheet beside her, his beautiful face open to her inspection, so open to her all the time now it frightened her. Nothing made him sad anymore, not Randall, not his parents, not the ugliness when he broke his contract with ABT just before their West Coast tour began. She wasn't exactly sure what he did when she left for the theater in the morning. He didn't want to take class anywhere, said he'd do a barre at home, but she didn't believe it. His theater trunk and costumes and dance gear sat untouched in the little maid's room off the kitchen. She suspected he spent the day shopping for the baby, shopping for Christmas. She was afraid of how much he'd been buying, what he might want to buy next. Adam turned twenty-one in January, and with his money from Randall she was sure he would want to buy an apartment for them and would want her grandmother to sell this place.

She got out of bed quietly and went out into the hall, pausing first, as she always did, at the door of her father's room to inspect what remained of it. Each day it was a little different, another piece of his belongings extracted. Adam had commented to her last week how vacant of her dad the apartment felt now, and she had looked at him, nonplussed. Her father had had so much presence that it seemed to her he had left some of it behind, impossible to carry it all away in a single trip. When she came in the front door, she thought sometimes she could see him sitting at the piano, a glimpse of his hair, pale as a river gull, the tone of a low C on the keyboard. Sometimes she heard a sigh and rustle from his room, the sound of an insomniac turning in bed. It was her lullaby, once, and she had listened for it, the click of the lamp, the scrape of a chair, the sighing and rustling. When she called him in Vicksburg, she felt she could never ask him what she wanted to ask, afraid to hear that he was unhappy, that he wanted to come back, equally afraid to hear he was happy, that he didn't want to come back. She could never ask him what he thought of her marriage either—she was sure he disapproved of it, though he had stood witness to it, as had her grandmother in her purple satin dress and matching jacket, the first time she'd left the house in years. Sandra breathed in his bedroom: it no longer smelled like him. His bed was gone. Adam must have had it moved to the basement. Two Mother Goose lamps preened, unplugged, on a new white bureau.

Her stomach lurched and she went to the kitchen to see what she could eat that wouldn't come back up. She often threw up and she knew that partly because of this she did not have strength. She peeled back the foil lid to a cup of yogurt, spooned some into her mouth. The minute the cold glop hit her stomach, her body rebelled, and she barely made it into the little bathroom off the back hall. Yesterday morning she'd thrown up her vitamins, and by the time she made it to class her stomach still had not settled. She felt Mr. B watching her, but it was not the same way he had watched her before, not with speculative excitement, a possessive knowledge, but with a sober cautiousness, a resentment. She was a vessel now for another creation, and she felt herself consumed by it as Mr. B watched, as she struggled to prove to him the lie that she was just the same.

She flushed the toilet, went into the maid's room. She had to lie down. She held on to the brass bedpost, pressed her cheek to its coolness, looked at the zippered garment bags Adam had hung on the foot rail. The room was too cold; the radiator had been shut off. She reached out an arm and pulled on the long zipper of one of the bags, then another, one after the other, and fingered the beautiful sequined and velvet tunic of a prince, a second tunic just like it but made of black and silver instead of maroon and gold, the white ruffled shirt and brown suede vest of a peasant, the golden pantaloons and jeweled suspenders of a slave boy, a raisin-colored cape, heeled boots, a feathered cap— all the props and costumery necessary to play the heroes of classical ballet.

Baryshnikov had been infuriated with him for breaking his contract at the last minute, after all the scheduling for the fall and winter rehearsals and performances had been clocked out. His mother had told her that night of the party that Adam's career was really gathering steam, that his reviews had been tremendous, *Don't let him do anything to slow it down,* by which Sandra supposed she meant their marriage. And when Sandra had lowered her eyes, his mother said, *What?* and then Lucia knew, knew right then without being told, about the baby and the look on her face had frightened Sandra—it was the face of the Black Queen in the mirror when she was told Snow White was the fairest of them all, of the witch in Hansel and Gretel opening the hot oven door, the stepmother in Cinderella locking up the girl as the prince arrived with the slipper, the hag who bartered for a baby in Rapunzel. Why were there so many ogresses in fairy tales ready to do harm to young women and children? Sandra had left the kitchen, shaken by Lucia's face, fearful of what it meant for the future Adam envisioned for them.

He hadn't told his parents yet about ABT, Sandra was sure, which could only mean he expected the news would displease them, displease Lucia. And why shouldn't it? Adam was a fabulous dancer with all these fabulous costumes sealed in garment bags in a maid's room on Central Park West. They didn't belong here; he didn't belong here. In his theater trunk sat cases of makeup and Pan-Cake, spray bottles of Aqua Net, and dance belts and ballet shoes—white and black—dance boots, brown and black—and a big plastic bag of tights, each pair rolled meticulously. Every last bit of it unused. In his dance bag she found the humbler items, the sweatpants and warmers and T-shirts, deodorant and cologne, Altoids, a pair of obviously favorite white canvas shoes sewn with double elastic crisscrossing bands. She sat on the floor, held the white shoes in her hands. She sat there a long time, the room slowly going gray with light.

Eventually, she put the shoes back, and when she did she felt the taut inner pocket of the duffel. His hiding place for the baggies and vials of his drugs, as much a necessity for Adam, she supposed, as the costumes, the makeup, the shoes. Wedged beneath the coke and the Quaaludes lay something else, something that crunched like foil. A strip of Trojans. She pulled it out. There were more. Package after package of condoms was stuffed deep in the pocket of the bag. He had taken these with him to Europe, too, along with the shoes and the costumes. Her stomach began to turn inside out again, and she leaned forward, but nothing came up this time. All fall, while she was here pregnant, he was there, with these, screwing his way across the continent. He probably took women to the brownstone before that, just like his father. They were going to have a marriage just like his parents'. And she was going to suffer just like Lucia. She sat back on her heels in the cold room. He had stashed the Trojans here, a secret. He did not want her to know what he had done, did not want her to think about what he might do. It was such a secret that he could not even use one of them with her. He had used these rubbers with everybody else, but he had never used one with her. Why hadn't he? Because. Because why? Because he didn't want to? Because he didn't think she'd want to? Because he didn't think she could get pregnant? Because. There was only one because. She was pregnant because he wanted her to be. He wanted to ensure she'd be his.

But standing in front of the Eldorado a week later, she felt less certain. The morning was cold and it had begun to snow, just white dust, early in the winter for New York. She wore the camel hair coat Adam had bought her and the black heeled boots Adam had bought her, and in the cold she felt like a tiny leaf, yellow and blowing. She pushed her hair inside the collar of her coat, the ponytail a long serpent. She suddenly wanted to talk to Adam about what she was doing, knew she should talk to Adam, but Lucia had said on the phone this morning, *Talk to Adam if you want, but he'll* make you keep the baby, and Lucia was right, that was exactly what would happen. Adam would never let her do this, but she had to do this; she could not have a baby now. She would make it up to him, they could have another baby later, when Mr. B was too ill to work anymore. The frailty, the dizziness, the noise in his head—she was convinced now that Mr. B was dying. He had told her he believed he had two years to live, but she didn't think he had that long. She would make it up to Adam. In a year they could have another baby. Her coat had no buttons and the wind kept fingering it open, lifting up her dress. Above, the canvas canopy flapped. Behind her the doorman had given up asking her to wait inside and had gone by himself to the comfort behind the glazed front doors. What would Adam say, what would her father say, what would anybody say about this? She would tell no one; the baby was lost, like a child in a fairy tale, sent away to be lost in a dark forest, to starve, to be devoured by wild animals. She had to do it. Where was Lucia? And then behind her, Sandra heard a cab pull up to the curb. She turned and now the wind held her back. The door to the cab swung open, the door to an oven, the lid of a cauldron, *Come in, my child.* The air was filled with confectioner's sugar, the wind making it sift and swirl.

## FIVE

*A*t first he couldn't breathe, air punched out of him, shopping bags scattered to the floor about him as if he had actually been punched, and then he pushed past his mother in the dining room to the back bedroom where Sandra lay, her face looking like a wax facsimile of itself, and when he saw her he knew it was true. He sat down for a minute on the stool at her dressing table and she watched him, her face a scramble of misery, fear, regret, sorrow, and he saw nothing there he could rail against. He put his hands to his face and sobbed, the violence of it making him feel as if he might vomit, and when he looked up, he saw silent tears running down her pale, dead face, along her neck and into her colorless hair. He remained at the dressing table stool, he could not go to her. Eventually his mother came to the door of the bedroom and looked in. At her appearance, Sandra closed her eyes and turned her head away and Adam rose, his mother retreating as he advanced until the two of them were back in the dining room where they had started.

In his rage and despair he couldn't speak, and into the silence his mother began to disgorge words, none of which he could comprehend, none of which he could take in. Why was she still here? Her great deed had been done, there was nothing left for her to steal or ruin, she had taken from him everything, almost everything, he didn't want to hear what she had to say, and he turned his back to her and began methodically to punch the dining room wall, left hand, right, left, right, until the plaster started to split and a small crater appeared and his mother's voice was silenced. The pictures thundered against the wall, crackled in their heavy frames, bouncing on their wires, threatening to tumble from them. The skin broke open over his knuckles and he could feel the bones creamed by the dense material of the wall, and when his mother attempted to pull him away, he let out his first sound and shoved her from him with a force that knocked her into the table, the thick chairs colliding heavily against each other, the noise bringing Sandra down the back hall to the doorway of the dining room. He stopped what he was doing when he saw her. She stood there in her white night-gown, hair in her face, and Adam watched her look from him to his mother in a sprawl on the carpet and then back to him. His fists bled, his chest heaved, his insides churned, but still the sight of her kept him from what he surely would have done next. He couldn't look at his mother, stood there looking at Sandra, at her face and her imploring eyes. He couldn't stay here, if he stayed he'd kill his mother, so he kicked back through the debris he'd left scattered in the entry, back through the front door, which he had opened, so unexpectedly, into this hell.

And then he was outside, on Central Park West, and it was cold. He crossed his arms over the coat he had never taken off and started walking south, his legs eating up the blocks, moving,

moving, to foil his brain. Why had she gone to his mother, why hadn't she come to him, why had she gone to her? It made no sense, the two of them were not even close. Whatever state Sandra was in he could have talked her out of. He knew how she thought, how she panicked, how fear limited her vision. Living with her father she'd learned to shut down the scopes, to see nothing ahead, nothing much of what was around her because it was all, so much of the time, bad. She could only see what it was like now, this minute, not six months from now. And so in that state she had had the baby hacked out of her and now she was emptied of it and empty.

He had to pause, thinking of exactly what she had done, had to put his hand against the brick side of a building, head lowered. They should have stayed in Vicksburg until after the baby, then come back to New York. It wasn't good for her to dance here, try to keep up with everybody else as if being pregnant were like having a head cold, something you could dance through. He could see the way her mood had shifted after their return. He had almost rescued her, marrying her. But back in New York, none of it was good: the apartment without her father, the disappointment of Balanchine, the struggle with her changing body. Adam went to the theater every night she danced, and afterward, when he met her at the stage door, he saw in her face and body the depletion she felt.

On the nights she didn't dance, it was better. They'd sit up in bed and play double solitaire and he'd make forays to the kitchen to bring her what he thought she could eat. Sometimes they'd sit in their pajamas at the piano bench and she'd play for him, the gold clock with the flying angels on it ticking away like a metronome. Or he'd read to her, let her fall asleep on the big sofa, and then he would sit there guarding her, her hair shimmering, her face peaceful. When they made love, it was sweeter than it had ever been because there was nothing desperate in it, because they owned each other. After, she'd hold him and stroke his hair, the whiskers around his mouth, pet him in ways she hadn't before, as if she really believed now he belonged to her. Some nights she'd sleep curled up, her arms flung around his torso. Or she'd want him naked so she could sleep with her breasts pressed to his back, her thighs tucked up behind his. He'd follow her instructions. He'd do whatever she wanted. The nightmare of Europe had fallen away from him. All his thoughts were of now; he'd worry later about his dancing, his career. He could pick it all up again whenever he wanted to, but she seemed somehow not quite able to believe that, her own experience at City Ballet too much beyond her control to believe, really, that any dancer could own his fate. It was his fault, he'd brushed away all Sandra's concerns about it, even when she'd shared some of his mother's hysteria about his broken contract at ABT. Like it mattered. But maybe he'd been too sanguine about it, should have reassured her more, made some concrete plans so she wouldn't listen when his mother opened her meddling mouth to say things like, *Make sure you don't ruin Adam's career,* right in the middle of their wedding party. Fuck.

He shoved himself away from the building and kept walking. His hands were aching terribly now. Under the next street lamp he paused to examine them: they were bloodied, swelling, not his hands at all. He could not make the fingers work, only his thumbs. He shoved his hands into the deep pockets of his overcoat and walked. He passed one big squat box of an apartment house after another, the numbers sliding downward from 900 as he strode the city blocks, the park massed to his left, all the brambles and thorns and shrubbery sky-high, no stars to light it, pocked by street lamps. He thought about walking all the way down to the brownstone, but by the Sixties he was tired and his legs were weak and he turned to cut through the park. He'd go to Randall's. He took the familiar route across the park, the one he'd trekked a thousand times between Lincoln Center and Randall's, but tonight everything seemed menacing and strange—the trees, the pathway, the barn, the statues, the pond. The trees shook and whispered as he passed, the path seemed to disappear before him and then wend its way in unexpected directions, the barn looked like a mausoleum, the statues gargoyles, the pond a circle of dark ice. What if he threw himself in there, let the heavy fabric of his coat become saturated enough to hold him just below the surface, the tips of his shoes scraping the shallow bottom? It wouldn't be as bad to drown in shallow water as it would in deep. In that still water, he'd be carried nowhere, just float, waterlogged, until the sun came up and chopped this wretched night from this wretched day.

RANDALL WAS SITTING in the living room by the long row of windows when Adam came in. Randall raised his hand in greeting, and for a moment, Adam stood in the entry looking across the room to this man he loved, this man who had elected to love and protect him. Randall's expression was inquiring and Adam understood from it that he must look deranged. He tried to smooth his features as he hung up his coat, stalling, but the effort was ridiculous. When had he ever been able to conceal anything from Randall? He put out his hand to Adam in a silent *What is it?* And Adam heard the sob in his own voice. "Sandra got rid of the baby this morning." Randall's face went grave and he put out his other hand and when Adam went to him, Randall pulled Adam into his arms, which held him with greater strength than Adam expected. "Mom took her," Adam said. "Sandra would never have figured it all out without her help."

Randall held on to him and Adam realized now he was shaking. Randall called to the kitchen, "Joe, I need vodka and an ice pack." And when Joe came to the kitchen doorway, Adam could feel Randall gesturing above him, sign language, and Joe retreated to the kitchen, came back with two big wads of ice tied up in towels and a shot of Stolichnaya, which he handed to Adam.

Adam sat back on his heels and downed the drink while Joe and Randall exchanged glances at the condition of his hands.

"You're going to have to go to the hospital, Adam," Joe said. "I'll take you."

Adam wiped at his mouth with his shirt sleeve. "Not now," he said. He sat down on the floor, put his hands on the carpet, and Joe set the ice on top of them like two money bags from a bank robbery. Joe brought him another shot and held it to his mouth, and this time Adam sipped at it.

"Who's with Sandra?" Joe asked.

"Mom."

"You're sure?" Randall said.

"She was there when I left."

"Okay. Because Sandra shouldn't be alone."

Adam raised his head to stare at Randall.

"She shouldn't be alone, Adam."

"Mom was with her."

Randall nodded.

WHEN JOE AND ADAM got back from Lenox Hill Hospital, Adam's hands were bandaged into two white boxing gloves. He had broken the second, third, and fourth metacarpals in both hands and crushed most of his knuckles, Joe reported cheerily to Randall. Eric was there, sitting beside him, the two of them eating. Eric brought Adam a bowl of stew. Adam struggled with the spoon for a while before he realized, unbelievably, that he wasn't going to be able to feed himself. Eric edged closer to Adam, and without a word, picked up the spoon and began to feed him. Adam was too hungry and too exhausted to have any pride left. He could feel the rough whiskers all over his face, his hair falling lank and greasy along his forehead each time he bent to meet the spoon. None of them spoke. The morphine they'd given Adam at the hospital had wiped his brain clean of thought, and all he registered was the food, the next spoonful of it coming at him. He wanted to eat and then sleep, the food settling his stomach, knocking him out. When his bowl was empty, he leaned back on the banquette and shut his eyes, and Eric and Joe took all the dishes to the kitchen where Adam heard them running water, opening and shutting drawers, laughing softly as something hit the floor. Adam listened to them, the sounds comforting, lulling him into a half-sleep, and he opened his eyes only when they came back into the room to get Randall ready for bed.

Joe carried a basin and a washrag, and Eric held a towel and pajamas. Joe washed Randall's face, neck, and hands, handed Randall his toothbrush, held the basin into which he spat. And then they began the process of getting Randall out of his clothes. Whenever there was something more intimate to do, Joe did it and Eric stood back. Randall had to put his arms around the shoulders of both Joe and Eric in order for them to remove his trousers and hike up, inch by inch, the soft sweats he slept in. By the time it was over, Randall's face showed his exhaustion. He couldn't lift his feet, so they knelt and slid his socks over them. That was why Randall was sitting in the same chair when Adam and Joe came back from the hospital. He couldn't move at all by himself. And that was why Eric was here when they got back. Randall couldn't be left by himself, either. Soon they would have to get a night nurse. The two men half-carried, half-walked Randall to the bed by the windows. Randall had not looked at Adam once.

And then it was his turn. At first Adam protested, tried to wave them away, but when at Joe's command he tried to undo the buttons of his shirt and immediately found it impossible, he acquiesced soon enough, allowing Joe and Eric to help him off with his clothes, put him in something of Joe's to sleep in. At each turn his big mitts would get in the way, bashing someone or clobbering at the clothes. Finally Adam simply held his hands above his head like  the boxer he was and let Eric and Joe do what they needed to, however embarrassing. He reeked, could smell on himself the anxiety and terror of the long day, but he didn't feel he could ask for a bath or endure the indignities that would produce. He needed Sandra, and at the thought of her his body convulsed. Joe and Eric paused, and Joe studied his face, which Adam was sure was contorted with grief. When they were done, Adam shuffled over to Randall's bed, climbed over his body to lie under the window. Joe and Eric gathered up all the discarded clothing and towels and rags and the basin, and, after going around to switch off all the lights, the two of them disappeared down the long hallway to the bedrooms. Did Eric sleep here now, too?

Adam lay in the darkness beside Randall and listened for sounds, but there were few—running water, the flushing of a toilet, the click of a door, the slow in and out of Randall's respiration, the occasional honk or screech of car brakes below on Park Avenue. He wasn't sure if Randall was still awake. Adam moved his hand slowly across the coverlet toward Randall, until he clonked Randall's hip with his plaster mitt. "I'm not sleeping," Randall said, and put out his hand to hold Adam's wrist just above his cast, his fingers making a gentle circle, and at Randall's touch, Adam vanished, asleep.

*H*E WOKE FIRST in the morning, light coming in on his face from between the slats of the wood blinds, his hands aching fiercely, and he rolled on his side, brought his hands up to his chest. He could see from here what he hadn't noticed last night, the Christmas tree in its stand in the corner of the dining room, the scent strong, the fir fresh. It had been strung with lights, but not yet decorated. Usually the tree stood right here, where the bed was now, before the windows, the lights of it visible to passersby on the street below, the first thing you saw when you walked into the apartment. Last night he hadn't looked left or right, just straight, beeline to Randall. God. There would still be Christmas. Time hadn't stopped. The sun hadn't woken Randall yet, and Adam lay quietly while Randall slept, which wasn't much longer. Still, he had time in that juncture to think of Sandra, her face last night in the bed, in the doorway of the dining room, her body pruned and empty, his mother, his hands, his stumbling explanation of his hands at the emergency room, some bogus story about trying to cram a table through a doorway that proved too narrow. What was Sandra thinking this morning? Was she awake yet? Was she in pain? He hadn't even talked to her, hadn't even asked. He rolled over again onto his back and the movement roused Randall, who opened his eyes and said, "So. Another day." He gestured to Adam, who saw the bottled water on the end table and clumsily grasped it between his casts, brought it to Randall. He drank from it slowly, nodded his thanks. And then Randall lay back and Adam sat up against the windows.

"Does Eric live here now?" Adam asked.

"He stays over in the white room sometimes." Randall shut his eyes. "Without him I think Joe would go out of his mind."

Adam nodded, though Randall couldn't see it.

"When I went off to Yale, I thought I'd never come back to New York. Big surprise."

"Are you sorry you did?"

Randall opened his eyes. "And have missed out on you? Never." Randall smiled slowly. "Worth it."

Adam looked down, swallowed.

"Yale was beautiful, a whole new world. I met O'Connor, studied art, walked out into a place where nobody had heard of a plié and nobody cared. Before I went there, I was thin. I came out of there fat, ready for Joe, ready for Joe Alton Dancers, ready for all my mother's fucking money, ready for your parents and for Eli and for Europe, for Eric and for you and for this." He gestured at himself.

Adam felt himself starting to lose it again, but Randall shook his head. At the same time they both heard the sounds of someone coming down the hall. There would be *good mornings*, a few questions, coffee, food. Another day. Adam rubbed at his face with the tips of his fingers, with his wrists. He couldn't face it, wouldn't face it, wanted to bury himself under these covers in this living room and wish it all away. *Adam*. Randall was talking to him.

"You have to go see her today."

Adam shook his head. "No."

"I'll have Joe call over there and tell Lucia to go home, that you're coming back."

Adam said nothing, kept his wrists to his face.

"Adam. I don't know why she did it, but I can tell you this: her purpose was not to hurt you."

"I know what her purpose was."

"And what's yours?"

Adam lowered his arms to his lap. His head and his hands were aching.

It turned out to be Eric in the hallway, Eric who came into the room, asking Randall, "Do you want breakfast first, or a bath?"

IT WAS AFTERNOON before Adam could make himself go over to the Eldorado. He'd gotten himself cleaned up, a painstaking procedure involving Baggies and rubberbands, flying soap, and, finally, Joe to scrub every inch of him as Adam stood in the bath nearly crying with frustration and humiliation. Joe had remarked, "I did this about a million times when you were a kid," which sent Adam off again, and Joe went silent, put an arm around him along with the towel, held him for a minute. Adam allowed it, wanted it.

His stomach was going crazy on the elevator up to Sandra's. He didn't think he could manage the key and so he rang the doorbell a few times, waited, ended up knocking on the door with one of his casts, a clumsy sound. Nothing. He called her name and waited. She wasn't coming. Somehow he managed to drag his keys from the pocket of the jeans Eric had laundered. His wedding band came out with the keys and fell to the tiled floor with a *ping,* rolled in a crazed spiral that sent Adam chasing it across the entry and under the marble table with the fake flower arrangement. He managed to scoop the ring onto his forefinger and fork it into his pocket. Then, holding the key between the fingers of both hands, he inserted it into the lock and turned it, fumbled the door open.

The apartment was terribly quiet, empty-feeling, and he clunked through it, wondering for a minute if Sandra had gone back to his parents'. The crater he'd punched into the dining room wall remained, though the plaster and paint fragments had been swept up, the pictures straightened. As he walked down the back hallway he began to call Sandra's name. He didn't want to scare her.

He found her on the floor of her bedroom, almost to her bathroom, and at first he didn't understand. A small pool of vomit stationed on the carpet by her face said she'd been sick, and he knelt by her, said her name before he realized she was unconscious, breathing shallowly. His own breathing came fast and hard. Jesus. His stomach tightened in panic. He knew nothing about the procedure she went through, the complications. He ran his clumsy plaster clubs down her arm and the side of her body. Her nightgown was hiked up and he could see the thick pad she wore between her legs was stained with blood. Maybe she was getting up to get another pad, maybe she was hemorrhaging, maybe she was nauseated, heading for the bathroom. He turned his head to look at the open door of the bathroom and he saw on the floor a plastic Baggie. Two. A vial on the ledge of the sink. He knew what they contained—his Quaaludes, his Valium, the pills he'd taken to Europe with him, the ones he'd kept hidden in his ballet bag stashed in the maid's room off the kitchen. How had she found them? If she'd taken them all she'd have taken something like forty pills and the sound that rose about him in the bathroom was the noise of his own despair.

Getting her off the floor was stupid and unnecessary, but he had to do it, shoveling his casts under her until he could lift her in his arms and stagger to the bed, where he held her while he struggled with the phone, tried again and again to hit the right buttons with his floundering, retarded fingers, and then it was another terrible struggle to find his voice, the operator saying over and over, *Calm down, sir.* And then there was nothing to do but wait, Sandra in his arms, her nightgown damp, her limbs flaccid, head lolling back no matter how many times he shrugged up his shoulder to lift it, and finally he simply lowered his head to hers, to hold his cheek to her cool one. *Sandra.*

## SIX

She woke to find Adam sitting in a chair by her hospital bed. His eyes were closed and she used that time to look around the blank room. Nothing she wore was her own, nor was anything she looked at. There was nothing to remind her of herself or of Christmas—no poinsettias, no artificial tree hung with colored balls. The ward was quiet, it must be night, the occasional door down the hall opening and closing. She didn't know how long she had slept, what time it was exactly, early evening or late—or even what day it was. Adam looked as if he hadn't slept for a while, except for his hands, which slumbered inside two bulky casts. She studied them for a moment, then remembered the way he had squared off against the dining room wall. Adam was here. What did that mean? His hair was wet and combed, so he hadn't been here long, though he had already fallen asleep beside her. She was the girl in the bathtub, the girl with the sick father, the girl in a hospital gown, but still he was here.

She didn't know how she could have done what she did, but

that morning, after Lucia had been sent away by Joe's phone call, Adam was supposed to come right over, but then Adam was nowhere, nowhere, Sandra was sure he wasn't coming, he was leaving her again as he had done when she was fifteen, last February, this fall, and she found herself thinking, *Goddamn it, I'm gonna kill myself,* and she went into the maid's room, knelt down and reached into his bag for the pills, chewed some of them quickly, the paste of them so bitter in her mouth she almost gagged, took the rest of them back to her own bathroom to swallow down with water. Adam's face had been an agony when she saw it briefly in the emergency room after the stomach pump but before they took her upstairs. She understood later what this meant—that he had come to the apartment after all, that he had found her.

She made a sound, and immediately Adam opened his eyes, got down off the chair and knelt by the bed, propped his casts up on the blanket so he could reach for her hand. His fingertips stuck out from the plaster and gauze. Rubble. Their fingertips touched. She stroked at his fingers with her own, traced over the bumpy surface of the casts. She put her fingers to his face, to his wet hair, the back of his neck, and he kept his head low. The moon filled the room now, brighter than the light in the hallway. Eventually, she lifted her hand from Adam, and he looked up.

"You've been here a few days."

She nodded.

"They're moving you to another ward tomorrow."

She said nothing.

"Your dad's flying out," he said, and at her dismay, "I didn't know whether I should call him. But it didn't seem right for him not to know."

"I don't want to see anybody, Adam." Her throat hurt to speak and Adam watched her for a minute.

"I know," he said, finally. "You can tell him that."

She looked down, not wanting to ask what she wanted to ask, but he divined it.

"I told Mr. B you lost the baby and there were complications. You'd be in the hospital awhile."

She felt a rush of gratitude. Adam could have said anything, had the right to have said anything, could have disgraced her; instead, he protected her. What would Mr. B say if he knew the truth? He would be horrified. Suicide was a sin. Abortion? Mr. B loved children, always used them in his ballets, worked with them with such obvious affection. He would never be able to fathom her act. *Why did you do such a thing, dear?* She couldn't bear for him to know any of it, couldn't bear for her father to know it, for Adam to know it. If only she hadn't gone to Lucia, if only she had done it on her own, a complete secret, which she could then forget, let drain from her, gone, tell Adam it had been an accident, the baby had spilled from her. To this boy who had had so much grief at home, she had brought more grief, more grief that had to be hidden.

She put her hands to her face and kept them there, but she had no tears. The abortion, the pills, the stomach pump had left her with no relief. Adam was watching her again. "Mr. B asked me to give you this." So he had not called Mr. B, he had gone to see him. Adam pulled a chain from his pocket and put it next to her on the bed. The chain was strung with a small medallion. *Saint George. Pray for us.* It was Mr. B's name-day saint. Had Mr. B taken this from around his own neck? She closed her hand around the medal.

"And *I* brought you this," Adam said. He held up a small suitcase she had not seen, that he had carried in and set by the side of the bed while she slept. He swung the suitcase up to her. "Open it," he said. She did. The suitcase was full of her clothes, and at the bottom of it, he had put something else. Her fingers felt at it—a hard shape like a box—but when she drew it out, she found it was not a box but a book, the fairy-tale book Mr. B had bought her in the late summer, which now seemed so long ago.

She discovered she had tears left after all, and she began to cry because Adam had known the book would comfort her. He watched her with his own sad face, and then he pulled her pink plastic comb from her suitcase and began to comb her hair, the tips of his fingers and thumbs clamped deliberately at the comb's spine, but still his grip was wobbly, the spindly teeth tearing through the length of her hair. And all the while he did this, she wept, until finally he dropped the comb and began kissing her hair, trying to grab hold of it with his fingers, and then he gave that up and simply kissed at the cloth of her hospital gown. She turned her body, turned into his kisses, which were now at her forehead, her cheeks, her ears, her neck, and then finally her mouth. There was something sickening about their kisses, but they could not stop. Adam sucked at her lips, her tongue, her eyelids, the lobes of her ears, his hands clubbing her, both of them breathing hard, and then he began to groan, pressed against her in his clothes, pressed against her hospital gown. She lay back and held him close to her, let him thrust his pelvis against the big bulky Kotex she wore between her legs— the bleeding would never stop—and when he came, he made a strangled sound she knew she would remember the rest of her life. He lay on top of her for a while after; she could feel him crying. She held him until his breathing slowed, and when he struggled to stand, she helped him. She put her arms around his waist and pressed her face to the buttons of his shirt.

"Sandra," he said, above her. "I've moved in with Randall and Joe. If you need me, you can call me there."

"Moved in with them?" She looked up at him.

He nodded.

"For how long?"

"I can't stay in your apartment. It makes me sick to be there, I can't sleep. I just pace. The other night I just paced around till dawn. I thought I should stay there so it would seem like we were still together, but I can't do it."

"Seem like?"

"Sandra," he began, and then Adam's face collapsed. She watched it happen.

She knew then she could never tell him, never. There had been two babies, not one. She had been carrying twins.

$By$ THE TIME she allowed her dad to visit, she had been moved. It was Christmas Eve and she met him in the lounge with the vinyl couches and the Christmas tinsel, the lounge he had sat in, the lounge she had once sat in with him. When her father had been hospitalized, it had been terrible for her to have to wait to see him, but she understood now for him those days had been a necessary nothingness, with no one to please or dismay or hurt or anger. He had not wanted her even to wait in the lounge, and now she understood that, too. He was not prepared for her, just as she was not prepared for him. She had never felt so flat, as if the inside part of her that carried all her secrets and emotions had gotten up and walked away, walked out of here and left this tent of skin and bones behind. And the tent had shrunk. She had dropped a size in a week and had to roll the waistbands of her pants to keep them up. No belts. But her father took no apparent notice of any of this. She sat by him, her hands dangling between her legs, the two of them sharing a cigarette. Nowhere else in the hospital was smoking allowed; but here in this ward, the psych ward, the prohibition was eased. She had always believed if she stopped dancing she would end up here, but she had gotten that only partially right, had gotten a lot of things only partially right. Her father wasn't talking, and she didn't have to. He knew what it felt like to be where she was. But once again she couldn't begin to imagine how it felt for him to be where *he* was, visiting a daughter he had surely never wanted to see here. She hung her head, and while he smoked, she picked at the waistband of her pants and at the rubber strap of her flip-flops. Then she took the cigarette from him and inhaled. He had brought her no presents, and she was grateful.

Christmas music played from the radio at the nurses' station. At the end of the third song, she said, "What did Adam tell you?"

Her dad said, "Enough."

She lowered her head. "Adam—"

"Adam's in a lot of pain." He passed her the cigarette. "And so are you." He watched her draw on it. She held on to it, did not pass it back.

"He's moved in with Randall."

"For now. This won't be the end of it."

She looked up at him wryly.

"You're alive," he said. "So, it's not the end of it." He leaned over, took the cigarette from her. "Not a day goes by when I don't think about what would have happened if your mother hadn't wrecked that car. Some days I have one ending for the story, other days, another." She watched him inhale. "I would have liked to know." He offered her the cigarette, and when she took it, he leaned forward and took her head in his hands. "I would like to know the ending to your story. Or at least the middle. So you'll have to stay."

She looked into his eyes.

"Otherwise," he said, "my story is no story at all."

He leaned back and they listened again to the Christmas music, to song after song after song about the Savior on high, snow, family, holy nights, bells, Santa, reindeer, chimneys, mangers, Bethlehem, stars. She would be released in six days. She could go with her father back to Vicksburg, he said, stay at her grandmother's for a while. Her grandmother was well. She could sit in the front bedroom all day with her, empty her ashtrays, play bridge, eat red beans and rice. She would rather stay here in this ward, this nowhere place, than go there. Maybe if Adam came with her—but Adam wouldn't come with her. He'd never come with her and he'd never trust her again. He had once trusted no one but her and Randall, now only Randall. No, she couldn't go to Vicksburg with her dad. But going back to the Eldorado, to State Theater, to Mr. B seemed equally impossible. She had no strength for any of it. There was nowhere to go. She would have to stay here forever. She had smoked the cigarette down to the filter without noticing until the cigarette refused to draw, dropped the butt to the floor, and her father bent and picked it up.

"Take my pack," he said. "I'll bring you more tomorrow."

$\mathcal{S}$HE SAT UP alone that night in her room, looking out at Amsterdam Avenue, flipping her makeshift ashtray, a jar lid, in her hand. What kind of tree did Adam have at Randall's? She had not asked. He had called her just before dinner. They hadn't had much to say. His hands had stopped hurting. He had something to eat last night for the first time in a while. Randall was too weak to eat. They were going to get him a feeding tube. Nothing about his parents. He wasn't seeing them, hadn't seen them since that day he took her to the emergency room. His dad would come by tomorrow, for Christmas. His mom would not. She had moved out of the loft, moved in with a friend for now, down in Chinatown, at the bottom of the city. Sandra listened to this silently, afraid to ask why, afraid to know if it had anything to do with what had happened to her, knowing it did. She told him her news. She'd be home next week, at New Year's. Her dad would stay with her for a while. They didn't talk about what she'd done. It lay there between them like an abyss and they could barely talk across it, barely see each other. She knew she had ruined things. There was nothing left.

She put her head against the cold glass of the window. Where would she be next Christmas? She could feel the year laid out like a plank before her, so many days in it. Would she still be married to Adam? Would he ever come back to her? Would she be able to return to Mr. B? If so, only because he didn't know what she'd done. He would think this curse had tumbled to her from the heavens, not that she had sought it, had pulled it down from the skies onto herself. No princess did that. Trouble rained down unfairly upon them and they were forced to wait in their locked towers, in their transformed bodies, in their glass coffins for rescue, for a prince to break the enchantment. Even Aurora was not responsible for her great hundred years' sleep, nor for what happened to her during it. Her father had shown her an early version of the *Sleeping Beauty* tale, a fourteenth-century French fable in which the princess Zellandine pricks her finger on a spindle and the prince who finds her sleeping, Troylus—

her beloved, but not yet her lover—takes her virginity, impregnates her. But still she does not wake. She does not wake until the child of that union is born and suckles at her finger, thinking it his mother's breast, and the spindle is at last drawn out. She wakes to the blood, the child, and still she marries Troylus. And what was their marriage like? The tale doesn't tell.

Sandra pulled back from the window, crossed her arms over her shrunken breasts. Aurora's story was full of rape and sleep and fire and ogresses and vipers until Perrault and the Brothers Grimm sorted it out, supplied it with fairies and kisses and weddings. She could jump from the window, she could step in front of a taxi, she could swallow the pills still hidden in her duffel at home, about which no one knew. Or she could live with her grief to spare Adam any more of it. Spare her grandmother. Spare Mr. B. Spare her father who had stayed alive for her. Give them all a different story.

## SEVEN

*A*dam slept now on a couch in the living room at Randall's, his sheet and blanket rolled by day and stuffed behind one of the cushions. There were plenty of bedrooms to pick from, but he didn't want a bedroom. This was temporary. He wanted it to be temporary. He wasn't sure what future was possible, he only knew he couldn't go home to the loft, couldn't stand the brownstone, and he couldn't go back to the Eldorado, though Sandra had been released from the hospital two months ago and was living there now in the big apartment, alone. He knew she slept alone, lived alone, and her loneliness was palpable to him even at this distance of thirty blocks with a park between them. These past weeks he had lived among his family, such as it was, but she had served these weeks like a sentence. He had essentially abandoned her, and he felt the vast landscape of his neglect; yet, he couldn't make himself return to her. He was too mixed up, everything in his mind crazy, and every time something of hers turned up in the stuff he'd grabbed and packed in his flight, he saw it as a rebuke: a blond hairpin, one of her thin ribbed T-shirts he'd mistaken for his own, her tiny, spiky hand-writing on the edge of an old envelope. Each morning when he woke bewildered on the couch, he swore this would be the day he would go back to her, finish what needed to be finished between them, whatever that was, and that's what he was afraid of. Was she still his wife? But the end of each day found him here, on Park Avenue, sometimes still in the clothes he'd slept in. While she was in the hospital everything between them was on hold. He couldn't live with her there, so it didn't matter where he lived, didn't matter if he'd moved out, away from the big furniture, the tasseled lamps, the men and women doing the minuet on the toile. But now she was back and her father was gone and Adam knew he should be with her, but he couldn't do it.

She was waiting for him to make a move; from the start it had been like that between them, she waited and he advanced, but now he just wasn't sure what it meant to advance. Did they continue their marriage? How could he kiss her, how could he hold her, everything she had once meant to him—safety, comfort, be-lief—she no longer meant. How could he make love to her now, knowing she had drawn his baby out that passage between her legs, its head collapsed like an empty balloon? She couldn't love him, couldn't love him the way he loved her and have made that choice. To think of it made him ill, made him want to take his hands, newly freed from their casts and strangely wrinkled, and beat them against the wall again, against the cushions of the couch, against his body, against hers, against his mother, whom he had refused to see since that day.

But mostly he just felt exhausted, spent, as weak as Randall who no longer got out of the bed. Their small world blew around him here in the living room, day and night, whether Randall slept or woke. He now had an IV taped to a vein on the back of his hand and a feeding tube taped to his trunk, and there was a nurse who came three times a day, wearing a mask and plastic gloves. Randall had wanted Adam to wear a mask, too, but Adam refused. If he hadn't gotten what Randall had by now, it wasn't that contagious. When Adam moved out, Joe said, they would get a night nurse, but for now Adam could hear what Randall needed, went to the side of his bed once or twice a night to check on him. Though Randall's body looked decrepit, his voice was still strong and round. If Adam weren't sitting there beside him to see it, he'd never have known Randall was sick, and when Randall spoke, he spoke, unbelievably enough, of the future, of the house he and Joe would take for the summer in the Hamptons, of the fall season Joe was planning, of the two new dancers Joe was adding to the roster. Frankie had begun to help Joe run the company, and in the evenings he'd stop by and the two of them would sit at the dining room table and talk softly of their plans. They wanted a big, full-length ballet for the fall and a maquette had been made up for it.

On one of those nights, his dad had taken Adam aside in the kitchen to tell him that his mother had moved out for good and that he was filing for divorce. Then he folded Adam into an unexpected bear hug. Pressed up against him by the refrigerator, his face in his dad's neck, Adam had whispered, *Why,* and Frankie had answered softly, heavily, *Your mother doesn't like real life.* And Adam understood. She had not wanted him and she had not wanted another baby with his father and she had not wanted Adam to have one, she'd gotten Sandra to do what she'd wanted to do twenty years ago to him, and that had been it for his dad, too many babies his mother had not wanted. The end of his parents' marriage had nothing to do with Adam and everything to do with him, and he had let his father hold him in the kitchen because he too was a man with a wife who did not like real life. Then they went back out into the living room and sat by Randall, and Adam looked at the low table by his bed with the oxygen mask, the pill bottles, the books Adam read to him, the maquette, the toys for the kitten.

Randall had told Joe months ago that when things got really bad he'd want a kitten, and the other night he had said, as Adam, Eric, and Joe were sitting around the bed watching some made-for-TV movie, "Joe, maybe it's time for that kitten." Adam, who hadn't known anything about it, had sat there speechless while Joe began to cry, no, not cry, sob, hands over face but too lost to get up and go to some other room. Randall was the only one not horrified; Adam and Eric looked away. And the next day there was a kitten, this kitten, quick and orange, who batted at the piece of red yarn Adam now shook in its face, then dragged along the sheets of Randall's bed. Randall, without opening his eyes, smiled at the sounds, woke perhaps because of them or the small pressure of the kitten's paws against his body. So Randall was awake; lately it had grown harder to tell. Maybe this afternoon he would stay awake for the magic hour, which was what Adam always thought of the time between dusk and curtain. Adam had not danced in a theater since he got back from Europe, but he didn't miss it. All he felt was relief: no Pan-Cake, no resin, no adrenaline, no tulle or velvet, no baton rising in the pit, no houselights going down, no applause to suck up to, to suck on, no impossible feat of assembling himself on the stage like a performing monkey. His dad and Joe had asked him to dance for them next season, but Adam didn't want to.

For the first time since he was ten, he had empty days where nothing was expected of him or his body, and he had lost whatever the energy was that drove him on. He had lost weight, too, was thinner than when he had been dancing. He had been afraid that he would fall apart left to his own devices, without Sandra, without the rigorous schedule that had until now governed his life, that he'd start swallowing drugs and fucking indiscriminately, as he had in Europe, but that had not happened. He was content to sleep on the couch, to read to Randall, to open the door to the parade of visitors that began each day after lunch and continued until late afternoon. Some of them wore masks. Some of them sat farther away from Randall than others. But they came, old friends from college, friends of Randall's parents, dancers from NYCB from the fifties who had known Randall before he went off with Joe, gallery owners and artists. Yesterday, John O'Connor flew in from Los Angeles for a visit. He looked something like what Adam remembered. He had gone with Randall to visit John in 1971, the summer his parents' fighting had driven his dad to move out. They'd stayed at John's house in the Hollywood Hills, and all Adam could remember was swimming every day in the backyard pool, the perimeter of it bricked and covered with leaves and flower petals. Randall and John sat on ornate metal chairs pulled to the water's edge, the better to watch him. Adam held his breath underwater, scared them both he stayed under so long in the blue, his body soaking up the color of the pool that was painted the color of the California sky. Now John, wearing canvas shoes, a loose Oxford shirt, and sporting a stubby gray ponytail, sat beside the bed and assiduously ignored the wheelchair. The two men talked quietly, intimately, and Adam understood suddenly that these two men had had more than a friendship, that it had lasted for years, and that Joe had endured it.

Adam lifted the kitten onto his lap. It was so young. That must have been why Randall wanted it: this animal couldn't be any further from death. As it yawned, it made a small yip. It used its tiny claws to climb to Adam's chest, where it tried to curl up to sleep. Adam slid down in his chair so it could, was still in that position a half-hour later when his dad came through the front door. Adam put a finger to his mouth, and Frankie nodded, came quietly into the room, drew up an armchair beside Adam's. His dad put out one of the big hands so like Adam's own and stroked the kitten, which remained motionless on Adam's chest, and his dad laughed silently. Since Lucia had moved out, Frankie had begun seeing a young girl from Juilliard, one of his students, a girl with long red hair. Adam had seen her once, down in the lobby of Randall's building. His dad never brought her up here, but he could have: for the first time the sight of one of these girls did not fill Adam with desperation.

Lucia was gone, banished to a sublet on the Lower East Side, to a bastille at 2 Confucius Plaza, a massive complex, brick buildings, a concrete courtyard into which a pitcher of winter wind poured, a wrought-iron fence. It was the abode of a witch—black, barren, surrounded by spikes. Adam had taken the train down to Chinatown last month to stand outside her gate. He didn't want to see his mother. He didn't want to talk to her. He just wanted to know where she hid. On the subway uptown, Adam had put his head in his hands, wishing he could reel back time to the first day he made love to Sandra, go back to that Connecticut motel when he should have used a goddamn rubber or pulled out, to the spring when he should have gotten her on the pill, and all that had happened between them since would have happened another way. The pregnancy, even as far as it had gone, had altered her body, the instrument she had honed, thought she owned. For a dancer the transformation was a theft. Robbed of her body now, robbed of what else later? But would she have married him if she weren't pregnant? Would she have? Yes. Yes. She would have. He could have persuaded her. Maybe.

And now they were married and now everything was a mess. He'd never been in a mess with a girl before, never even had a girlfriend before. He'd never understood why Randall didn't just leave Joe once and for all, why his mother didn't just end it with his dad, but he was starting to understand it all now. The way Joe and Randall's story ended was they stayed together. His parents? Different ending. Unexpected. Surely soon enough he and Sandra would decide how their own story would end.

Adam let his head rest along the back of the chair, now that his dad was here to watch Randall. He had found he could fall asleep so quickly, just shut his eyes and he went to the same place as Randall, as if sleep were a plain and all Adam had to do was close his eyes to join Randall stretched out there. He was out and then not out, his father's voice rousing him, asking again quietly if he'd reconsider dancing for Joe. Adam raised an eyebrow without opening his eyes. Why was he asking this again? Adam had said no just the night before. Adam opened one eye; Frankie was looking at him, waiting, as if it were really possible that Adam might change his mind. Not only possible, probable. And why not? Wasn't dancing what Adam did for a living, wasn't this what he'd been doing since he was ten? Adam cleared his throat, mouth full of excuses and declinations, but before he had a chance to say anything, Randall spoke.

"I hear Balanchine isn't well. He was too sick to do much this season. If Adam does anything, he should go back to City Ballet for the *Götterdämmerung*." Randall turned his head, and Adam looked at him, trying to fight the nausea rattling its way up from his stomach. Did Randall think it was time for Adam to get out, get on with it? Adam sat up, the kitten scrambling, as panicked as he was, but Randall didn't move, his eyes on Adam. "But I suspect," he said, "that Adam doesn't want to dance anymore at all."

undreds of people, impossible to see for certain if she was here, perhaps in the back.

She had returned to him in February, too thin, which he didn't like, her hair so pale it was barely yellow, her finger still with the wedding band, her husband nowhere in sight. She was quiet, everything about her muted, and he did not have her dance, he wanted her to regain her strength. He would ask, later, how it had been, but however it had been, it could be no other way. God had decided. The child was not meant to be. Any woman could be a mother, but not every woman could be a ballerina. And this girl was meant to be a ballerina, a great one. He would see to it. There would be no *Sleeping Beauty* this spring, but he would do something for her for the Stravinsky Celebration in June. It would close the spring season, celebrate Stravinsky's centennial, it would not be like the grand Stravinsky Festival of 1972, but a reminder: a great man would have been one hundred. Stravinsky's body was gone, but when his music played, he was here, still here. One got old and left this world, but beyond this world lay another, where all this decayed material went to rest, and reversed. In that world you were born dead, got younger, died at birth. And it was all going on at once, at the same time! Everything at once, over and over. Death was not an end, but a beginning of something else, which led again to the other, and it was happening all around, all around them, though with the apparatus God had given them they could barely sense it, barely grasp it. But he felt something, knew something. *Eye hath not seen, nor ear heard the things which God hath prepared.* The world was larger than it seemed, denser. Otherwise, where from this world of shoe leather and bricks and overcoats and salt sprung music and dance?

From God, a great God, the Father, and each Easter His Son was reborn. Easter waited all year, the way the lily, Victoria Regina, waited for a hundred years to open, to spread its waxy petals in fabulous display, to be admired. What did Victoria Regina smell like, like an ordinary lily, sweet and astringent? Or like a woman, like yeast, leg open in développé à la seconde? Female or flower? Both were stunning, mysterious, fertile. The church overflowed tonight with lilies and with women, worshippers who stood shoulder to shoulder, candles in hand, waiting for the entrance of the priests shortly before midnight. At home, more candles, at the windows, on the table by the bottles of Roederer Cristal, the czar's favorite, and by the platters of *pashka*, red-dyed eggs, iced *kulitch* that rose like fruited towers a foot high, store-bought this year only because he was too ill, too tired; his dancers had begged him, *Don't bake,* so he hadn't baked, but nothing from the bakeries met his standards. With all this, George would fete his favorite dancers and his old Russian friends at midnight after the service as he did every year. Russian Easter arrived always within a week or two of spring season, a herald, trumpets and cymbals, good omen. The tall windows along the side of the sanctuary showed the outside to be black, cold, and full of rain, wind rolling down the street, taking with it leaves and petals. He raised his chin, craned his neck to survey the crowd. He did not see her.

The doors to the side of the iconostasis pitched open and in strode the priests, choir behind them, for the processional. *Blessed is our God now and forever and to the ages of the ages.* The priests' vestments made of them golden idols, brocaded and embroidered and festooned with Russian crosses, on their heads miters, tall and flat, or domed and bejeweled. The priests bore candles and icons, lanterns and banners, crucifixes and incense, and this profusion of color and beauty was followed by sound, the clear high intonations of the choir. The church—for him, first theater. As a boy alone in his room, his favorite game had been to play bishop conducting High Mass. For hours so could he amuse himself. The congregation organized itself now to follow the priests. In St. Petersburg, at St. Vladimir's, the processional circled the church itself, leaving the cathedral empty, empty as Christ's tomb. The priest played the disciple who came to pay homage only to discover the Lord was not there— He had been resurrected. But here in New York, it was impossible to walk around a church cemented to a city block and pressed so tightly to other buildings. Instead, they walked the perimeter of the church courtyard. Tonight, the chilly wind and slanting rain made even that impossible. So the procession shuffled along beneath the covered balcony and down the stone staircases at each end of it.

The wrought-iron lamps blinked and grew vague in the driving rain. George felt himself slip and Karin steady him. The iron gates to the street made a rattle and clang; the large gold cross on the roof glistened with wet. He supported his candle with one hand, to support his body he groped with the other at the red brick wall beside him, at the coat belt of the person in front, at the elbow of one to his side, afraid to fall, carried along by the press of the crowd. As he turned, he saw Sandra at the top of the stair. A fur collar trimmed her coat, a scarf partially covered her hair; she had left at home her Russian hat. She saw him, ventured a small smile. That was good. When he turned his attention back to his taper, he saw the flame had gone out. Karin touched her candle to George's, and the black wick bulged yellow, only to dwindle and vanish a few paces later. He turned at the bottom of the stairs with his dead candle and proceeded back up them again. This time an old babushka—his own age!—wearing spectacles with lenses thick as shot glasses and frames that looked as if they'd belonged to her late husband, relit him. George looked about. All around him the lit tapers flickered, his own had been the only finger of dark, had become this without a sound, a hiss, a whisper, a warning. The rain, tumbled by the wind, fell sideways now. The cold had made its way inside his coat and stabbed at his bad lung; the bottoms of his trousers were damp, as were his suede shoes. Up the steps he trudged, seeing only the backs of the winter coats in front of him, the back of Karin's hat, her belt, her heels, and before he reached the top, his candle had gone out again. And once again it was relit.

He had been afraid many times in his life since the Revolution—around him had flocked many disasters—but he had always skirted them, making his ballets, too busy to look up, to let disaster find him. But tonight calamity was cleverer than he and it came to him to roost, settled on his chest, and there was no ignoring the great feathered weight of it. It was hard to move with the bird clawing at his coat, and his heart strained beneath it, beating against it, his breath making a small nest he stepped heavily through, breathe, step, breathe, step. He was careful to hold the candle, wax warm under his fingers, away from his mouth and nose. The back of his neck was wet, his shirt inside his coat also wet. He reached the passage along the side of the sanctuary, saw himself reflected in each of the tall windows as he passed, small man, old man, felt even before he saw in one of them that the candle he carried before him was once more dead. This time, he said, "Leave it. It's not supposed to be lit," and he saw in the window the black crow sitting on the wax stalk. The priest at the head of the processional drew open the heavy church door and peered within. The sweet air of the sanctuary rushed outward at them like the breath of God, and the priest proclaimed, *"Kristos voskrese!"* and all around George the congregants answered him, *"Voistinu, voskrese!"*

Christ is risen. He is risen indeed.


*W*HEN DID YOUR symptoms first present?

When. When. A few years ago he became unsteady sometimes on his feet.

The dizziness?

Yes. The dizziness. He was afraid of falling, always. Tottery. Something was wrong with his brain. He could pirouette to the right only when standing on the right foot. If he tried to turn from the left foot, he lost balance immediately.

And the cardiac problems.

Yes. The angina. The triple bypass.

And what else?

The factory operating in his head. The constant cacophony.

If he played a single note on the piano, the noise was unbearable. And when the factory shut down, still his ears roared.

Vision?

Fuzzy. Cataracts. Glaucoma. He couldn't see his dancers, couldn't read, watch TV.

The balance. Back to the balance. When did you first have this difficulty exactly? Describe.

He sat awkwardly on the big examination table, blue paper robe tied about him with a white plastic string, his hands a long distance away at the ends of his arms and covered with liver spots. He had become puffy and ugly, his ankles down below swollen, his hair white, all white, worn a bit longer now in the back to compensate for the dome in front. What did he think of him, this doctor? When he went to Alfredo's, the maître d' called him Maestro, seated him at a big corner table. Here at this table in this paper gown, he was just an old man with an illness no one could diagnose. He had been to this specialist and that, had endured one test after another, and still his symptoms were a mystery—it was not Alzheimer's, it was not brain tumor, not a blood clot, it was not this, not that, but a tangle, a skein to be sorted out, laundry for someone else to iron, and yet still he was here, a wrinkled old man who had to carry on.

The centennial for Stravinsky, fifty-five ballets to Stravinsky's music—a mountain of ballets—and yet he could not do. His health was unpredictable. Some days he woke confused and weak and could not work; others he rose from the chair time and again to demonstrate what he wanted. Three new ballets: *Elégie, Tango, Variations for Orchestra,* two of them old ballets he would redo, all three of them small, but still he'd been forced to use dancers he knew well—Karin, Suzanne, Jacques, Jacques's son Christopher—his family. With them, he could move just a finger and they knew what he wanted, shift and they knew what it meant, incline his head and they leaped or turned. He wanted to do something for Sandra, his little blonde, but to work with someone new required a strength he did not possess. She needed to be coached, to be shown, each step demonstrated, explained, refined. It was not defect on her part, just the reality of making a young dancer into a ballerina. This he had done over and over, more than once in each decade, and he knew the process well—time-consuming, exhausting, exhilarating, addictive. For that he needed to be well. And he was not well. His press conference for the centennial had been staged in his office, where he sat on the sofa, propped up securely with pillows, answering forcefully questions he was not sure had been asked. Perhaps he could fool the press in his suit and his silk cravat, but he could not fool himself, and increasingly, he could not fool his dancers, his assistants, the board. They had begun to press him, to ask him to appoint a successor, to plan. They suggested Peter Martins or Jerry Robbins, but it would have to be Peter. Peter knew what a ballerina needed. Peter was the future, unless for himself he could find a cure.

He was only seventy-eight. Petipa had lived into his nineties, had retired, unwillingly, at eighty-four, a bureaucrat with a pension, but there was no real replacing him, not ever. Russian ballet was great because of Petipa, Petipa and the Romanovs. Petipa's genius had reached its peak in his last decade of work, the 1890s—*Sleeping Beauty, Nutcracker, Swan Lake*—boom, boom, boom, one major work after another. For him, no such bang—instead, a whimper. The other day, when he had looked, impromptu, for a studio to coach Suzi in, there had been nothing, no nook, no cranny available, and he had ended up working with her in the orchestra's rehearsal room, amidst the clatter of music stands and the treachery of the waxed floor. His office, which had once been large, had shrunk over the years as the company ate up more and more space, and it seemed now his role in it also had shrunk. The company could practically run itself, a machine on automatic, and he as its once operator needed only now and then to adjust a crank. He was almost a figurehead, a piece of carved wood, an appendage, functionless. But without it, the sailors on the ship would not sail.

He looked into the face of this doctor, this American face, this doctor with the American name. Perhaps he should go to Europe, to Switzerland, to one of the clinics there, something near Mont Blanc, perhaps the very sanitarium where he had been cured, sixty years ago, of tuberculosis. He could sit alone on the verandah again, wrapped in blankets, look out at the pine trees, the snow, the mountain. But while he was there, Serge Lifar had stolen the directorship of the Paris Opéra right out from under him. It wasn't good to disappear. When you were gone, you were forgotten.

LAST NIGHT OF the spring season, the season so long it wasn't even spring anymore, but summer, July 2, hot, very hot, no longer just warm, last ballet of the last night. He stood in the wings to watch his boys in their white and gold brocade tunics, in their blue velvet tunics with the great feathered scallops of gold brocade and white, his girls in their corresponding tutus of white and gold or blue and white and gold, the small headdresses in their hair. This all he had made—this ballet, these dancers, this theater with its great gold curtains, the fringe at the bottom of it three feet high, this audience who came to see. There was no ballet in America when he arrived here by boat in

1933, no czar here with his treasury, no court with its need for opulent productions to satisfy an appetite for entertainment, for diversion. That wealth and those needs created great theaters in Russia and drew from all across Europe great talent, which converged on St. Petersburg to make great art, to bring ballet to full flower, her beauty as fresh one hundred years later as it was the day she was presented to court. And he had brought her to America, then brought the audience to her, lured them to her, and now look at them with the *brava*s and the whistles and the flowers they wrapped in cellophane and thick ribbons, weighted so they could hurtle through the air, circumnavigate the orchestra pit, and land at the feet of his dancers.

The applause, thunderous, louder than the factory in his head, churned also with voices calling for him, and he saw his dancers turn to him at his spot in the first wing, downstage right, and begin also to clap. He shook his head, made a small gesture with his hand, *no, no,* but still the noise would not stop. He felt his assistant take his elbow, lead him forward, and he stepped carefully, sliding one foot in its brown suede shoe, then the other, until they had reached the place where the curtain parted. A stagehand drew one of the great curtains back, his assistant steadied him at the other, but still that was not quite enough. George had to grip with his right hand the folds of curtain that hung at his side, use all his will to stare into the great red theater with the round lights mounted like crystal eyes all around the boxes and balconies, to stare into the shouts and applause, the audience rising to its feet to honor this old man in his striped cravat and double-breasted blazer, Maestro. They knew: Death was coming. His death would end the century, ballet's greatest century. They were there to witness the last of it, and it would soon be over.

He turned back to see his dancers, their faces, their love for him. He saw off to one side his little blonde in her costume of white and gold, her hair like spun sugar. What he had promised her she waited for patiently. He had promised. He had promised. He was Ba. He was Lan. He was Chi. He had written it, the acrostic of his name when he was a schoolboy.

*Fate smiles on me.*
*I am Ba.*
*My destiny in life is fixed.*
*I am Lan.*
*I see the keys to success.*
*I am Chi.*
*I will not turn back now.*
*I am Vad.*
*In spite of storm or tempest.*
*I am Ze.*

He would rest over the summer. Perhaps in the fall.

## NINE

In November, Mr. B went into the hospital and each Monday, early, Sandra visited him there, her heels clicking down the long hall past the nurses' station to his corner room on the top floor, a good room for someone who was going to be in the hospital a long time, which was not what Mr. B had expected, not what any of them had expected. He had been admitted for tests and observation after a fall in his apartment that had fractured four ribs and his left wrist. He had balked at first—he wanted to go to Europe, to the clinic where he had been cured of tuberculosis, to the Zurich clinics where he had gone in his search for rejuvenation, to become as youthful as his dancers. But eventually his objections ceased, and he had stayed here at Roosevelt, two blocks from the theater, near them all.

He could no longer sit, was not always lucid, unable anymore to call the telephone backstage to check on the performances. When Mr. B could still see, he had read or watched westerns on television; now he listened for hours to the radio, to WQXR, a classical station. Russian poured from his mouth; old friends turned into strangers. But still they came to see him, his old friends, and his girls, the most beautiful girls the hospital staff had ever seen, in their heeled boots and leather jackets, their wrists strung with bracelets, their beautiful long hair adorned with clips and jeweled barrettes. He could tell them apart by the sounds of their steps in the hall. *Karin, Suzanne, Merrill.* He would call out their names as they approached. Sandra came early to avoid the others, but she could not always do so. One morning she arrived to see Karin in a chair by Mr. B's bed, stroking his hair and crooning a lullaby to him in German. On other days she found him in the company of the famous dancers he had worked with over the decades—Tallchief, Danilova, Baryshnikov, who brought him delicacies from a Georgian restaurant in Brooklyn, Nureyev, kneeling by the bed, crying silent tears, Geva, Zorina; the famous critics—Dickie Buckle, Martin Bernheimer, Edwin Denby, Robert Garis; his old Russian friends. The men brought their conversation. The women dressed to please him. Maria Tallchief wore Yves Saint Laurent. But lately he had grown too ill for visitors, too ill for the birthday party thrown last week in his room, for the *kotletki,* the wine, the champagne. The party was for his closest friends; she had not been invited.

At his doorway she paused. He was sleeping, arms thrown back above his head, perfect fifth position port de bras against the pillow, breathing deeply, chest rising and falling beneath the bedclothes. He told her once he still saw pretty people doing pretty things. What things, what people? She wished she could know. She came and sat in the chair by his bed. Someone had brought him a box of paper whites and it waited quietly with its green stalks and a few tiny white blossoms on the table. By his bedside he kept the big book his staff had brought him, the first copy off the press of the catalogue of his complete works, every dance he'd ever made, which Mr. B called the "bible." Not a bible, but his worldly goods. He had little else—an apartment, a condo in Southampton, a Mercedes, two Rolexes, a small bank account. His dances were his riches. By his bed he also kept a book of photographs of his girls, of which she was one, the girls from the company he had made dances for, wanted to make dances for, wanted to make legends. Winter season had started several weeks ago. By that time she had gained enough weight and he had convinced her to color her hair a dark gold, *So, dear, you will not look like bald head on the stage,* and he had begun to let her dance again. When he saw she seemed to thrive on it, like a cheetah fed red meat, he cast her more and more often. But he had seen her in nothing, had missed the opening week of performances, would miss all the rest of the weeks as well. He had promised her she would dance in *A Midsummer Night's Dream* the Titania he had made for Melissa Hayden and in the *Bugaku* he had made for Allegra Kent and the role in *Jewels* he had made for Suzanne Farrell and the one in *Ballo della Regina* he made for Merrill Ashley and the *Davidsbündlertänze* he'd made for Karin von Aroldingen. He had wanted to give her the roles he had made for his other dancers, the only gifts he could give her now. But he had not been able to do all the casting for winter and spring before he had gone into the hospital.

She knew she should hurry, but instead she stretched her hand across the sheet and over the thin hospital blanket. Mr. B did not stir, his fingers moving slightly as if he were playing the piano. They had sedated him, as they had sedated her. Mr. B had not asked much about her time in this hospital, and she had volunteered nothing. For her the hospital had been a pocket of relief, the stage now for her another one, a place set off from the rest of the world, the rest of her life.

She had little else. She had seen Adam once, before he left for school. Randall had made some calls, could, like Mr. B, pull himself together for an occasion, and had gotten Adam admitted to Yale; and so Adam had come to see her in late August to say good-bye. His father was taking him up to New Haven. His casts were off, but one of his fingers hadn't healed right and was still taped to a metal splint. He was thinner, nine months of not dancing had made him thinner, and he had let his hair grow long, longer than he had worn it for the stage. They stood in the dining room, too awkward with each other to advance any farther into the apartment. The apartment, so vacant, so empty, seemed to vibrate around them, and she started to see black spots. He pulled a chair out for her when he saw she was losing her balance, then sat beside her. "I don't want to divorce," he'd said, "unless you do." She shook her head. He looked down. "I just can't let go of it yet." He put his hand out to hers, moved it across the polished surface of the table, and she saw despite what he said, he no longer wore his wedding ring. "It's here," he said. He touched his chest, and when she shook her head, *I don't understand,* he drew a necklace from under his shirt, showed her how he'd strung the ring on a chain next to Randall's cross. She wore her ring, still, on her finger, which he'd looked for, she saw him look.

When he stood to leave, they kissed good-bye, the softest kiss. "Want to take a train ride?" he joked, but she knew: he didn't want her on that train, though she could see it, entirely, the seats, the windows, the conductor, hear the names of the Connecticut towns: Greenwich, Stamford, Darien, Westport, Fairfield, Bridgeport, New Haven. She put her head down on Mr. B's bed. *A Midsummer Night's Dream, Bugaku, Jewels, Ballo della Regina, Davidsbündlertänze.* There would be no *Sleeping Beauty,* either, for which she had given up her husband and children. What would they have looked like? What of Adam's beauty would they have worn? What pleasure would they have given Adam, the family that loved him, her father who had no other family but for her? She made no noise as she lay there half on the bed. There was only the sound of her breathing and Mr. B's, the scrape of his fingers as they moved against the pillowcase.

*H*e stirred in the bed, hands working about his face, the pillow, as if he could pluck at the briars that imprisoned him.

The ballet was done at last, all done, all here, impossible to condense, to adapt, as he had long thought he would—the Prologue with the fairies, genies, and young girls bearing gifts to the newborn Aurora, the rats accompanying the Carabosse to the christening, the beauteous fairy of the lilac. The entrées of the first act, of the lords and ladies, of king and queen, even the Rose Adagio, in which Aurora rejects the suits of the four princes, Chéri, Charmant, Fortuné, and Fleur-de-pois—done. Aurora's finger pricked by the spindle, her gentle stagger, the kingdom put to sleep. Done. Act II, the prince's hunting party—pairs of duchesses, baronesses, countesses, marquises, and eight huntresses, the dances of the court and a game of blindman's bluff. The Vision, where Aurora and her nymphs tempt the prince, and the prince makes his journey, his feverish quest across the lake and through the briars into the castle where he renders the kiss, engenders the promised awakening. Finished. The final act. The wedding, with the royal retinue, the procession of the fairy tales—Red Riding Hood and the Wolf, the Bluebird and Princess Florina, Puss in Boots and the White Cat, Cinderella and Fortuné, Goldilocks, Tom Thumb—the fairies of the minerals with their offerings to the couple of diamonds, gold, silver, and sapphire. The grand pas de deux with the exaggerated lifts. All there, all the steps, all the players, all in his mind, and he unfurled the pageantry of the ballet for himself by the hour. At the end of the ballet, the great wrought-iron gates of the castle would close around the court, encircling the kingdom, keeping its treasures within. As the ballet would remain. Within. Behind these gates, these walls, these thickets.

He turned on his side, knees tucked to his stomach, back curved. There were other dreams within him, and he could not always smother them: skeletal horses, teeth bared; the great Mongolian steppes, cavernous, freezing, vacant; the faces of the drowned and starved and shot. He reached through the brush for something stronger than the ballet, the small icon he kept at his bedside, drew it back toward him. He closed the icon in his fist. In paradise, people walked about in robes of purple and gold and God was an old man with a long white beard. *Must believe.* St. Nicholas, pray for us. St. George, pray for us. St. Andrew, pray for us. St. Vladimir, pray for us. The icon warmed in his palm. Skies blue and scarlet. Golden nimbuses of the halos. Thrones on high.

# Apotheosis

*A tableau, in which Louis XIV, dressed as Apollo,*
*is paid homage by the characters of the ballet*

*A*dam sat at his desk, which was shoved up against the window of the dorm room, air coming off the glass so cold it felt like glass itself. He hated the steam heat, the knocking radiators, would rather wear gloves and a sweatshirt and shiver in his ice palace. Along with the gloves and the sweats, he wore on his feet a pair of mukluks, on his neck the cross Randall had given him, on his head the green wool cap that Randall had worn to the end, until the night he had pulled the feeding tube from his side, ripping an artery, saying, "Enough," and bled silently, painlessly, to death, saturating the sheets, the mattress, the carpet, the clothes Joe wore as he held him and said good-bye. Randall had left Adam almost everything—buildings, bank accounts, bonds, art. Adam bunched his fists to his chin and leaned on them, the pages of the book crumpling underneath his elbows. It was late, 3 A.M., the dorm around him silent, bodies on the beds and chairs and carpets fallen where they were, highlighters and books and girlfriends in hand, asleep. He didn't belong here, everything about him built for some other purpose, some other life, some other place. There were so many days when he wanted to pack it in, give up, take the train home to New York, flip open the latch of his fucking theater trunk. But he hadn't done it. Home was a drained lake, everything broken branches, fissures, and cobwebs, nothing to go back to, better to stay here, behind these thick walls banked with snow and ice. He turned out the light, leaned forward on the desk, let his body crush the book, the papers, let the pens roll and rattle beneath him, let his cross and his wedding band curl up on the tangled chain inside his shirt. He shut his eyes, dreaming, breath skimming across the lake, the forest. He was here. If she wanted, she could come find him.

$\mathcal{M}$R. B WAS GONE, State Theater full of roses and lilacs, lilies and mourners.

Sandra stood behind the great gold curtain. Off in the wings and behind her upstage, the other dancers for the first ballet tonight, *Divertimento No. 15,* were quietly warming up, no banter, no clowning, everything in their world changed. Mr. B had died this morning, early, 4 A.M., alone, on the day the church celebrated the Feast of the Resurrection of Lazarus, which the bishop had said was a good day to die. Mr. B had prepared for death, but they had not prepared, could not prepare for a world without him.

There were five principal girls and three boys in this ballet, and by some silent consensus they came and stood by her in their places even before the call to do so, before the houselights slowly dimmed to half. And then Lincoln Kirstein, black suit, round-shouldered, jaw heavy with grief, stepped out from the first wing and crossed the proscenium, his footfalls louder than the chirps and twangs made by the musicians, who, when they saw him, silenced their instruments. The audience out front grew as quiet as the orchestra in the pit, the dancers behind the curtain. For a minute, there was nothing. Someone, one of the boys in the ballet, reached for Sandra's hand. And then, finally, Mr. Kirstein spoke. "I don't have to tell you," he said, "that tonight Mr. B is with Mozart and Tchaikovsky and Stravinsky." There was more, but she wouldn't hear it in her effort not to ruin the beautiful artifice of her face, which Mr. B would never see again, as she would never again see his—one more face she had lost, one more face to attend her dreams.

And then Mr. Kirstein was gone and the music began to saturate everything—the dancers, the stage, the wings, the house— and when the curtain went up, it swept the audience toward them, pushed them into the dance, into the horns, into the violins, into the music Mozart had made and Balanchine had embodied. He had conceived the steps almost thirty years ago for a different generation of dancers—for Tanaquil LeClercq and Pat Wilde and Diana Adams and Melissa Hayden and Allegra Kent—but the steps now belonged wholly to this generation, to the dancers on the stage right here, right now, would belong just as wholly to the dancers of the generations to follow. The variation for each of the women almost overlapped one another, they came so swiftly, Sandra no sooner finished dancing than another girl took her place, one divertissement following another, like a pulse, a pulse that could not be stilled.

HE LAY BENEATH a blanket of gardenias, a cross propped in his hands; a second, the one that had belonged to Doubrovska, his Siren of long ago, stuffed into his breast pocket.

The coffin was simple, wood; of this he approved. He wore a suit, the lapel pinned with the President's Medal of Freedom and the rosette of the French Legion of Honor. Too fancy. Around his forehead was wrapped the traditional Russian blue and white ribbon, linen, printed with a prayer. The small church held a thousand people, each one of them holding a candle, and the air was suffused with the smell of the burning tapers, flowers, and incense. Shuffling by him, weeping, touching his hands, kneeling, kissing the ribbon over his forehead, leaving behind a flower, were wives, friends, dancers, musicians, costumers, critics, supporters, his audience. This was the last of the three funeral masses, the last of his moments among the comfort of the living before being abandoned to the ground. The coffin was open, but at the end of the service before he was borne out of the cathedral, it was closed against their faces, against the faces of the icons, the priests, the pallbearers, the angels, and the mourners blew their candles out. In the dark he felt himself hoisted high, lifted to the shoulders of the pallbearers, and carried out the doors of the church to the top of the long flight of stairs. The church bell tolled, the small choir chanted.

The procession stalled for a moment as the pallbearers stumbled, and his body shifted inside the box. And with that small movement, his spirit stirred and broke free. Above the rooftops of the city he soared, over the tall sedate buildings of the Upper East Side, down the long grand row of museums, across the wide reservoir, past the large music halls and the theaters great and small, Juilliard, the Met, State Theater in quick succession; in all three theaters this week his ballets would be performed—his *Valse Fantasie* and *Western Symphony* and *Symphonie Concertante* and *Divertimento No. 15* and *Concerto Barocco* and *Symphony in C* and *Ballo della Regina*; and down in the theater district, still another of his ballets, the Broadway revival of *On Your Toes,* which he had made in 1936, shortly after arriving in this city. He held on to his cross. And then he was rising toward Battery Park, past the magisterial bridges, the Williamsburg Bridge, the Manhattan Bridge, the Brooklyn Bridge, and out over the water, over the East River, higher now, the air thinning out, white mist all around him, wind pulling at his clothes, at his collar, at his pockets, at the laces of his shoes. Still he went higher, no longer a man, but a cloud, carried across the great ocean on the currents that traveled always west to east, drove him now back over the water he had crossed so long ago, drove him over the great countries of Europe he had once left behind, the great opera houses of Europe he had forsaken—the roof of this one he knew and this one and this, too, and then the current turned northward to take him up along the leg of the Baltic Sea to the gulf, to the white Italianate buildings that sprang from its marshes centuries ago at the behest of Peter the Great. St. Petersburg. He was returned. And here at last the winds died, and he was allowed to drift slowly through the funnel of time where he sank, eventually, into the body of the boy who stood on the boards of the Maryinsky Theater, 1914. The ballet was almost over, the characters from it—Aurora, Désiré, the King and Queen, the Lilac Fairy, lords and ladies, Puss in Boots, Bluebeard, the seven brothers of Hop o' My Thumb—were already arrayed about the painted backdrop that at its center held the image of Apollo, rays of light shooting from his immortal person. Georgi, too, was there, in his cupid costume from the last act, posed with the others, one leg back, hands on his hips, and as the great curtain came down, he reached through its shadow toward the backdrop, raised his finger to the finger of the god.

In the writing of *The Sleeping Beauty,* I relied on numerous sources to create an accurate portrait of the dance world of the early 1980s and of Balanchine, his life and his world.

In May 1981, George Balanchine began work on *Mozartiana,* his last major choreographic endeavor, for the Tchaikovsky Festival in June of that year. Descriptions of his creation of this masterwork and descriptions of his rehearsals for other Festival ballets, such as *Adagio Lamentoso* and the Garland Waltz from *Sleeping Beauty,* were drawn from fact, as are the details of Balanchine's life. His clothing, the decor in his apartment, his feelings about his ex-wives, his childhood memories, his philosophizing, his religiosity, his illness and debilitation, his hospital stay, the programs danced in the theater the day he died, his funeral are all documented in various biographies and memoirs. And yet, despite the employment of all these particulars, the Balanchine character created here is, ultimately, a product of my imagination.

Beyond the inventions of Balanchine's thoughts and conversations and the fictional details applied to real events, where the novel departs dramatically from the recorded facts is in my creation of a pocket of good health for Balanchine in the summer and fall of 1981, and in my creation of a last muse for Balanchine. Sandra Ellis is a fictional character. While it is true that Balanchine was inspired by a few young dancers in his last years—among them Darci Kistler, at sixteen one of the youngest principal dancers in the company's history, and Maria Calegari, of whom Balanchine said while hospitalized during his final illness, "This is my next ballerina"—the character of Sandra is not meant to be read as either of these women or indeed as any female dancer in the company at that time or previous. And while Balanchine had long entertained the idea of doing the ballet *Sleeping Beauty,* the impulse to do so stirred over the years by various dancers, among them Suzanne Farrell, Gelsey Kirkland, and Darci Kistler, he did not choreograph the ballet for his own company, save for the Garland Dance from Act I, which he produced for the 1981 Tchaikovsky Festival. What Balanchine might have done with *Sleeping Beauty* had he lived is a subject for speculation, based on his remarks about the ballet and the bits and pieces of it choreographed for various companies over six decades.

The other dance personalities, dressers, makeup artists, assistants mentioned in the book, while real, are portrayed fictitiously here—and Rudolf Nureyev, who did not assume the directorship of the Paris Opéra until 1983, is placed there in the novel two years earlier for dramatic effect. Alexander Godunov was fired from ABT in June 1982; in this novel this occurs in 1981, also for dramatic purposes.

For a picture of Balanchine's life as a whole, Bernard Taper's extraordinary book *Balanchine: A Biography* was a wonderful source; also helpful were Richard Buckle's *George Balanchine, Ballet Master;* Francis Mason's *I Remember Balanchine;* Lynn

Garafola and Eric Foner's *Dance for a City*; and Robert Garis's *Following Balanchine*. Two recently published biographies, Terry Teachout's *All in the Dances: A Brief Life of George Balanchine* and Robert Gottlieb's *George Balanchine: The Ballet Maker,* were also useful. The memoirs of his wives were invaluable: first wife Tamara Geva's *Split Seconds* and his second "unofficial" wife Alexandra Danilova's book, *Choura: The Memoirs of Alexandra Danilova,* covered both the Russian ballet world before and after the Revolution, including their experiences (and Balanchine's) with Diaghilev and his Ballets Russes. Balanchine's fourth wife, Maria Tallchief's memoir *America's Prima Ballerina*; Holly Brubach's interview with fifth wife Tanaquil LeClercq, "Muse Interrupted," in *The New York Times*; and the memoirs of his last love and great muse Suzanne Farrell's *Holding On to the Air* helped provide a personal and professional picture of Balanchine in America. In addition, the anthology *Portrait of Mr. B,* edited by Lincoln Kirstein, was also helpful, in particular Jonathan Cott's "Two Talks with George Balanchine," as was Charles M. Joseph's *Stravinsky and Balanchine: A Journey of Invention.*

The various memoirs of his dancers—Merrill Ashley's *Dancing for Balanchine*; Allegra Kent's *Once a Dancer*; Gelsey Kirkland's *Dancing on My Grave*; and Edward Villella's *Prodigal Son*—were also essential. Greg Lawrence's portrait of Balanchine in his book *Dance with Demons: The Life of Jerome Robbins* was informative, as were the more pedagogical books: Suki Shorer's *Balanchine Technique*, Balanchine and Mason's *101 Stories of the Great Ballets,* and the first edition of *Balanchine's Complete Stories of the Great Ballets,* with its marvelous essays by Balanchine and interviews with him.

In creating the day-to-day activities and thoughts of Balanchine during his last years, Robert Maiorano and Valerie Brooks's *Balanchine's Mozartiana: The Making of a Masterpiece* and Solomon

Volkov's *Balanchine's Tchaikovsky* were especially useful, as well as W. McNeil Lowry's *New Yorker* article "Conversations with Balanchine" that appeared in a September 1983 issue. I relied also on Arlene Croce's books—*Sight Lines; Going to the Dance;* and *Writing in the Dark, Dancing in The New Yorker*—which describe several decades of performances of New York City Ballet, as well as those that took place in the last years of Balanchine's life and the week of his death. The *New York Times* dance reviews by Anna Kisselgoff, too numerous to mention, were also invaluable to me.

In drawing a picture of the School of American Ballet, I used Jennifer Dunning's *But First a School,* Joan Brady's *The Unmaking of a Dancer,* Toni Bentley's *Winter Season,* and Christopher d'Amboise's *Leap Year,* along with Gelsey Kirkland's memoir, all of which detail the school itself, the teachers, and the atmosphere there. For a sense of American Ballet Theatre in the early 1980s, I relied upon John Fraser's *Private View: Inside Baryshnikov's American Ballet Theatre;* Clive Barnes's *Inside American Ballet Theatre;* Elizabeth Kayes's *American Ballet Theatre: A Twenty-five Year Retrospective;* the Kirkland memoir; and my own experience taking class at the company school. The books *Striking a Balance* by Barbara Newman; *The Private World of Ballet* by John Gruen; and *Thirty Years of Lincoln Kirstein's New York City Ballet* by Lincoln Kirstein were also important sources.

My conversations with Elizabeth Allen, a student at the School of American Ballet (1974–1982) and a publicist for New York City Ballet from 1990 to 1992, also helped me to depict the school, the atmosphere of the company, and Balanchine's attitudes and health in his last years, as well as to understand the tremendous preparation for Peter Martins's *Sleeping Beauty,* staged in 1991. My interviews with principal dancers Jennie Somogyi and Alexandra Ansanelli of New York City Ballet for an unrelated magazine article gave me a sense of the lives and routines and struggles of dancers currently in the company, as well as a sense of what it was like to be a newly promoted ballerina. Conversations with Tommy Flagg of Terpsichore Management, who handles dancers from both Ballet Theatre and New York City Ballet, were also helpful. I drew also on my own experiences as a trainee for Harkness Ballet in New York City in the midseventies in creating the picture of a dancer's life.

In understanding the ballet *Sleeping Beauty,* and Russian ballet of the nineteenth century, I am indebted to Roland John Wiley's *A Century of Russian Ballet,* to Boris Kochno's *Diaghilev and the Ballets Russes,* and to Arlene Croce's article on *Sleeping Beauty* published in the *The New Yorker* in May 1991. Tim Scholl's book *From Petipa to Balanchine,* with its wonderful chapter on the history of the ballet *Sleeping Beauty,* was an important resource, as well as his *Sleeping Beauty: A Legend in Progress,* which contains photos of the original 1890 production of the ballet. I'm grateful also to Professor Scholl for sharing with me his sources, unpublished papers, and playbills in which Balanchine spoke of his intentions for the ballet. I'm grateful, as well, to Laura Jacobs, dance critic for *The New Criterion,* for her e-mailed anecdotes about Balanchine and his dancers, as well as for her article in *New York* magazine, "A Tangle of Roots," which explores the various productions of *Sleeping Beauty.* A big thank-you to Mindy Aloff, columnist for *The DanceView Times,* consultant to The Balanchine Foundation, and professor at Barnard College for her insights into Balanchine and for the extensive list of sources she suggested to aid me in my research. I'd like also to thank Karin von Aroldingen of The Balanchine Foundation and Peter Martins, Ballet Master in Chief of New York City Ballet, for their correspondence with me regarding this project, as well as Balanchine biographers Rober Gottlieb and Bernard Taper for reading my novel in manuscript and offering their comments and suggestions. My thanks also to Toni Bentley, author of *Costumes by Karinska*, for her e-mail clarifying the dates Karinska first worked with Balanchine in Europe and in America.

At the New York Public Library for the Performing Arts, I was able to view some bits of extant choreography Balanchine had created for *Sleeping Beauty* through the years—the film of a dress rehearsal in which Balanchine supervised his company in a run-through of the Garland Waltz at State Theater just before the Tchaikovsky Festival in 1981; a snippet of the wedding adagio done for ABT in 1949. Balanchine did other bits and pieces here and there—the Bluebird and fairy variations as well as Aurora's solo in 1949 for ABT, a wedding-scene pas de trois in 1927 for Diaghilev, a pas de deux in 1945 for Frederick Franklin and Alexandra Danilova, which she recalls in a radio interview and rues the fact that none of them could remember it when they wanted to revive it a few years later. Films of the Kirov Ballet's *Sleeping Beauty* with various casts were also helpful in understanding the scope of the ballet. For my descriptions of other ballets danced by both American Ballet Theatre and New York City Ballet, I drew on my attendance at live performances of both companies. The Balanchine Library films available from Nonesuch Dance Collection gave me the opportunity to study a still wider range of Balanchine's work.

In understanding the fairy tale itself, I am indebted to Jack Zipes's *The Great Fairy Tale Tradition* and *The Brothers Grimm: From Enchanted Forests to the Modern World*. For information on the Civil War and the Siege of Vicksburg, I relied on Shelby Foote's *The Civil War: Fredericksburg to Meridian*.

And finally, my gratitude to my editor, Julie Grau; her assistant, Alex Morris; and my agent, Sandra Dijkstra. To my husband, Todd, and my children, Madeleine and Aaron, my thanks for your love, patience, and support.

**Adrienne Sharp** is the author of the short-story collection *White Swan, Black Swan*. She studied ballet from the age of seven and trained with the prestigious Harkness Ballet in New York City. She received an M.A. from Johns Hopkins University and was awarded a fellowship in fiction at the University of Virginia. She lives in Los Angeles.